Sway
THE AMPED SERIES: BOOK TWO
M.J. Woods

Sway
The Amped Series: Book Two

Cover design by M.J. Woods Books
Cover photo licensed by Adobe Stock
www.mjwoodsbooks.com

Published by Dog Ear Publishing
4011 Vincennes Road
Indianapolis, IN 46268
www.dogearpublishing.net

dog ear PUBLISHING

ISBN: 978-1-4575-5597-8

This book is a work of fiction. Places, events, and situations in this book are purely fictional and any resemblance to actual persons, living or dead, is coincidental.

This book is printed on acid free paper.
Printed in the United States of America

for everyone that has taken the leap with me

thank you

Acknowledgements

This page is the most difficult to write. I hoped I'd be able to finish one book someday, and here I am thanking people as I reach the finish line of a second. It's been a long and tiring race.

Somewhere in the middle of my trek to the end of *Sway*, the office building I worked in for twenty-two years burned to the ground. This was the building my family's law firm occupied for forty years. After a tragic event like this, when loss of precious life results and your own little snowglobe world is turned upside down, your perspective changes. You also learn quickly that you have a choice. Stay still, hanging upside down with your knickers around your head and likely drown in that little globe, or right yourself as best you can and just keep going.

Along the way, I've also been tripped up by two tiny, adorable children. I've stopped racing altogether in favor of the local coffee shop (or a karaoke bar). Finally arriving at the end, I realize I haven't actually left my house and I'm breaking a finish line tape covered with cat hair (or is it fur?) and dog drool. It's possible only critics are waiting to greet me when I cross that line.

But dammit, *I got here*. So, thank you...

...to my editor Cheryl Meany, for your hard work and for loving the continuation of this story. Thanks for sticking with me when I decided to procrastinate and you became the busiest lady I know.

...to my first readers, for your ongoing enthusiasm and encouragement. I sincerely appreciate each one of you and your unique insight.

...to my Aunt Sue, for all of your time, attention and encouragement in finalizing my manuscripts. Your advice has been truly invaluable.

...to my parents, my parents-in-law, sister-in-law and my children for your love and support. I love you more than coffee.

...to my BFF Jill, for always being there no matter what. I love you, sister.

...to my husband, just...*thank you*. You're the best partner a girl could ask for, especially when writing wins the arm-wrestling match for my attention. An extra kudos for the cover design of this book, which you helped create when I foolishly thought it could only exist in my head.

...to anyone spending their precious waking hours actually reading this book, especially if you don't know me. I never thought I'd see the day.

~M.J. Woods

1

Aidan

June 1, 2016
Wednesday Evening

I know I'm lost in a nightmare, but I can't find my way out. As hard as I fight and as fast as I run, the darkness engulfs me that much faster.

I'm running after Alexis, chasing her as she heads into shadows. I almost reach her when I'm pulled from behind by something painful, something stronger than me.

I feel a hand brush my face. My eyes snap open and fear that I wasn't dreaming floods me. Her gorgeous blue eyes look back at me, bringing me back to the present.

But her expression is unfamiliar, full of emotion. I've never noticed her look at me this way. It's not plain concern. It's deeper. I look away for a moment, instinct causing me to avoid the rawness of her gaze.

Something else is apparent when I look back at her.

She is extremely tired.

After the few days of emotional upheaval she endured with her sister in Arizona, and traveling, and the way I took her on the plane – her exhaustion is warranted. We've just pulled up to her home in Mirror Lake, where she insisted she needs to be.

But she is here with me now, as she's been since we left the airport.

I stay still, letting relief sink in.

Alexis is here, safe and mine.

I relish her warmth around me, her body steady across my lap. Just the smell of her settles me. I pull her into my chest, resting my head on hers.

Having her closer causes a switch to flip and my fears scatter.

Despite the overwhelming flood of emotion, I want her to stay.

I need her to stay.

"Don't go." *Please don't go.*

"It's okay," she says, pulling away to look at me. "I will see you tomorrow."

I shake myself alert when she denies me.

Tomorrow is soon enough.

I left Dimitri with a lead to follow in California, and I won't address it if she comes back to the loft with me. The only thing I'd want to do is get lost in her.

I check my watch.

Nine p.m.

In an hour, I need to catch Dimitri by phone before he heads from one business to the next.

I let Alexis out and kiss her goodbye. The weather is downright dreary, the chilled air matching my mood. She invites me in but I decline.

Byron backs out of the driveway, leaving Alexis standing alone in a cold drizzle. A dense fog removes her from my sight too soon. Everything in my being is telling me this is wrong, that I shouldn't be leaving her.

But I'm doing this for her, giving in to her stubborn will when she insists she tend to her obligations.

And in the meantime, I'll deal with my own.

I need to focus my attention on the Irelands. Removing them from my existence is the only way to fold Alexis into my life without harm coming to her.

There will be time to explain all of this to her tomorrow.

For now, I just have to keep going.

At ten o'clock I'm in my home office at the loft, showered and dressed down in pajama bottoms. Dimitri is talking through the speakerphone of my landline, giving me the information he's gathered today while I've been traveling.

"So, Armstrong isn't lying?"

"No, man." He exhales a drag of cigarette smoke. "He's one hundred percent accurate. It didn't take a lot of digging to uncover that much. I haven't even delved into the punk's phone contacts yet to see where that leads."

"This is from your connections in Cali?"

"Yeah, I've still got a few. Not one of them would be reliable in the light of day but, as far as intel they're legit."

"That's good news."

"In a way. But I'm not sure how – or if – we can directly connect Ireland to distribution. Everyone knows it's him, but no one would be willing to expose him. They know his rep as well as we do."

Dimitri had spent the last twelve hours looking into Shane Armstrong's claims about John Ireland. In California, Armstrong had caught me off guard with his accusations before attempting to throw his right hook. I'd left Curtis to tend to him after I'd knocked him out cold.

Though I'm surprised by Armstrong's claims, they are believable. The task will be proving them. Between Ireland's discretion and deep connections, it wouldn't be easy.

"We have Armstrong," I say. "We might be able to use him."

"After the way you left him?" Dimitri scoffs. "Curtis tells me he was not a happy surfer when he woke up."

"He'll cooperate."

"Maybe. But if Ireland offers him more than you do, he'll flip sides. I'd bet the house on it. The dude's an asshole by reputation. And he isn't reliable to begin with. If he's ever your key witness, you're fucked."

This much is true. The thought pisses me off so much that I remain silent as Dimitri goes on.

"This could be a shit storm of epic proportions. I think you need to reconsider going after Ireland. Let him take himself down. Let's get creative about distancing you from him instead of provoking him."

"I'll think about it." I'd likely think about nothing else.

"I'd say that's a good call."

"How's Nikki?"

"A little concerned that I've been locked in my office at the dealership all day, but otherwise she's great." I can hear his smile on the other end of the line.

"I can't believe you're engaged."

"You mean you can't believe I found someone to put up with my shit for all eternity."

"Yeah," I laugh. "I guess so."

Nikki is an emerging artist in L.A. with a passion for dark art and Harley motorcycles.

She must also have a thing for Greek men with tattoo shops because she agreed to marry my departed brother's closest friend, for better or worse. She is originally from Brooklyn, but Dimitri told me she'd made L.A. her home ten years ago.

"I'm a reformed man," he says. "You should try it."

I'd met Nikki once a couple years ago. I'd been catching up with Dimitri about how his business was doing, and she'd wandered into his shop asking about a tattoo. We talked the other night over a couple of beers and he reminded me that, ironically, I'd been there when they first met.

As Dimitri tells it, their relationship grew from that day. They had their share of struggles, he said. But he'd come to realize she was a catch – one he decided he couldn't live without.

My thoughts immediately go to Alexis. I had seen the change in Dimitri in the first five minutes I'd spent with him in California. He'd passed up flirtations from a female bartender without a second thought. In the past, he'd easily bed her within the hour.

He was in deep with Nikki which in itself was not unsettling.

Realizing I may be in a similar situation is a potential problem.

Alexis is becoming more important to me with each passing minute. If I hadn't been pre-occupied with the Irelands while in California, Dimitri would have noticed a similar about-face from me.

All because of Alexis.

This could prove to be detrimental to all of us, given the hurdle we were struggling to clear. I push the thought aside and tell my friend congratulations again on his engagement.

"And when does the deal close on the new dealership location?" I ask.

"Boss says next week. As soon as the Vegas location is secured, we can close on my purchase of this location."

"You must be pumped."

"I'm grateful is what I am. Never would have imagined I'd own two successful businesses."

"You deserve every success, man. You've earned it."

"We both know this deal would be a year away if you hadn't stepped in while you were out here. Fuck, man." Street noise in the background cuts out, and I hear the door chime at the tattoo parlor as he enters. "You're the reason I'm alive at all."

I don't acknowledge the emotion that builds hearing his words. There's no value in agreeing with him out loud.

No part of me wants to dredge up old wounds.

He lets my silence be my answer.

"Listen, I gotta jet. I'll call if I think of anything we can use, but I still say backing off is the best approach. If Ireland's left to his own devices, he may fuck it up on his own."

"I don't see that as likely."

"Why not? Stella is safe now, out of his hair. Maybe he'll let his guard down. He's going to be in a bind to replace her."

"Maybe. But I can't wait for him to get in his own way. I need him out of the picture and soon."

"Let's just weigh our options. Try coming at it another way. We have to consider every angle."

"I'll think about it," I say again. He may have a point, but I'm not ready to admit it.

"At least let me run some scenarios before you decide."

"I can give you until Sunday."

I have enough on my plate between now and then.

I have to talk to Alexis about this whole mess before the press begins spewing celebrity gossip, then get to Manhattan over the weekend to secure my program for the gala. My attorney needs to be on board with the Myers deal. Between finalizing the event by this coming week and the approvals pushing forward for the Center, my plate is full.

"Look into those leads from Armstrong's phone," I remind him.

"I will."

"Thanks, Dimitri."

"You know it. Anything for you, bro."

At midnight, I'm in bed but restless. I've had no resolution to the Irelands, no revelations or epiphanies about how to cut the head off the snake.

I miss Alexis to the point of aching, which is becoming the norm. I consider going to her but decide against it. Charlie is there. We've been apart less than twelve hours, but I know I want to reunite with her in private.

I pull my phone off the bedside table and text her. I'm caught between hope she'll respond and hope that she's sound asleep, knowing how much she needed the rest. She doesn't reply.

I finally drift off, waking up pissed when the alarm goes off at four-thirty. I'm not rested at all. I turn off the alarm and allow myself to get a couple more hours of rest.

My sleep is dreamless and I wake at seven-thirty to go about my usual routine, putting in a few miles through the city streets. I stop for a coffee at Starbucks before I go back to the loft to shower. By nine, I'm dressed casually in jeans and a t-shirt and looking for something to eat when Lionel calls my cell.

"Morning, Lionel."

"Good morning."

He doesn't say more. This is not a good sign with him. He never wants to be the bearer of terrible news, always hesitating before he delivers any. It's his truest tell.

"What the fuck is going on, Lionel?" I ask flatly.

"I take it you haven't seen *The Tattler's* online report."

"They released early?"

"Yes, sir."

"Goddammit. Does anyone do what I ask anymore?"

"We've contacted Miss Simms but she isn't answering."

"Of course she isn't. In her boss's eyes she's cracked the story of the week. She's probably on vacation in Santa Barbara by now."

"I can't control it now, sir. It's out there."

"I know, Lionel. It's fine."

There's only one person I need to reach before the news spreads like wildfire. She's the only person that would be hurt without knowing the real story behind the breaking story.

"I'll be in touch if I have anything more."

"I'll be available." I disconnect, pacing the kitchen.

If I can reach Alexis before she hears about it, everything will be fine. The story is only breaking early by a matter of hours here on the East Coast. I'd asked that it come out for the evening news cycle, but clearly Rebecca Simms had defied my instructions outright and leaked it for the early news in California.

I could have this misstep cost her the rest of her pathetic career.

Right now, that isn't important to me.

Before I can dial Alexis, Byron calls from his line downstairs in the office.

"Yeah," I answer. "Please have something good to tell me."

"Not as such, sir. Channel Eight is calling. They want a comment about *The Tattler* leak."

Fucking great.

"Tell them we decline to comment."

"I did, sir. A crew is setting up for a live shot outside the building now."

Now I swear out loud.

"Is it that slow of a news day?"

"Anything to do with you is news here."

"Make it go away, Byron."

"I'll do my best. I didn't want to alienate anyone without your approval."

He has a point. I am trying to get this city on my side. The last thing I want is to drive a wedge between myself and the local press.

"Melanie Adams is outside," he says. "They plan to air the video, even if you decline to comment."

"Then let them." The only thing left to do is break the news to Alexis before she can hear about it from television or from someone other than me. "I'm not giving any interviews or comments."

"I'll convey the message, sir."

I hang up, my adrenaline spiking.

Let them spin it any way they want. It doesn't matter as long as I can get to Alexis.

I check the time. Nine-thirty. She must be at her office by now. That would give me time to get downstairs to mine. I'd take the chance she wasn't receiving live news reports on her phone.

I make my way to the elevator at a fast clip. I dial Alexis but my phone has no signal in the ancient lift. By the time I have signal enough to call out, I'm moving through the cubicles on the second floor, ignoring the morning greetings from my staff. I look down at the street below.

The camera crew is set up despite the rain, with gray skies and wet pavement as their backdrop. Presumably Melanie Adams is the reporter standing under an over-size blue umbrella as the cameraman signals he's rolling.

Fuck.

I slam the door to my private office and remote the television on, turning to Channel Eight. *The Tattler* video is on screen as Melanie's unmistakable voice provides commentary.

I dial Alexis again, but she doesn't pick up.

Maybe she's with a client at her office. I dial her work line and her receptionist answers.

"Greene Law Office. May I help you?" She sounds like a teenager.

"Ms. Greene, please."

"I'm sorry, she's been delayed this morning. I expect her soon. May I take a message?"

"No, thank you."

I disconnect, urgency spreading through me.

Where the hell is she?

By ten-thirty, the excitement of the live report outside is long gone and the story is out there. I called Alexis five times, but she won't answer. I don't recognize the urgency in my own voice as I leave her a voicemail on the second call, then again on the fifth.

I have no idea how to move forward without knowing if she's heard the news. If she hasn't, I don't want to open my mouth about it before we are standing face-to-face. If she has, she's avoiding me on purpose.

I'll have to allow her to do just that until I can give her no choice but to hear me out. That would be the only way with her. She'd be too stubborn to reason with until I could convey the facts.

And I know she won't let me do that without a fight.

I decide to distract myself for an hour and let it play out. I don't have much control at this point, and acting on anger would not be a valuable use of my time. I page Samira and she arrives with her tablet, awaiting instructions.

We go over the gala prep, decide on invites, and discuss Allen Richardson. Alexis already informed him we no longer needed him, but I ask Samira to be sure the message is conveyed by our office directly to him.

Thirty minutes later, we've gone over the rest of the morning's business and I've dismissed Samira. I buzz Byron.

"Sir?"

"Can you tell me where Alexis is?"

He's quiet a moment. "At her office, sir."

"Thank you. That's all for now."

I decide a text might be the best way to get her attention. It would give her an out, a way to respond without being confrontational. I'm confident I can determine what she knows by her reply.

If that doesn't work, I'll go to her and put myself in front of the firing squad.

Why haven't you called me back? I need to talk to you.

Now.

No response.

I wait only a few moments then send another, changing my tactic.

IF YOU DON'T CALL ME
I'LL BE AT YOUR OFFICE IN
TEN MINUTES.

She replies within a minute.

Finally.

But her reply is too polite. There is no caring behind her words, no mention of the news, no tone of fury for me.

She knows.

And she doesn't want to face me.

We exchange a few more messages, but try as I might to insist we talk, she claims she's suddenly too busy. She's headed somewhere with Charlie now. She's going out of town to see Ben's family this weekend. She'll call me when she returns.

Like hell.

I grab my car keys from the office and let Byron know I'm headed out with the Corvette. If I don't find Alexis at her office, I'll drive around until I track her down.

By the time I've parked the car a few blocks away from my office and crossed the street to hers, she's gone. I lay on the charm with her skinny blonde secretary (whom I pegged correctly on the phone – she's not yet twenty) and learn Alexis is having lunch with Charlie at the pub across the street.

Damn. Had Stella not called, I'd have caught her in time.

Stella has also seen the news report. She gushed for five solid minutes about the resulting attention she was getting at The Meadows Rehab Center.

I made it clear the media was spinning the story as they saw it, but it didn't matter. Stella would soak up the attention from the misguided souls that surrounded her. I put it out of my mind as quickly as our call ended.

Let her believe whatever she wanted.

It's Alexis I'm concerned about.

I make my way across the street. Before I enter the pub, I'm allowed full view of her sitting at a booth across from someone. Her back is to me, but I know it's her. I know her from behind as well as I know my own reflection.

The person across from her interests me more than she does. The man she's with is unmistakably not Charlie. He's white and older than me, probably in his mid-forties. He's dressed in a decent suit and blue tie but his professional appearance does not match his demeanor.

He's leaning over the table as he talks, intently focused on her. He reaches a hand across the table towards hers.

My expression tightens, eyes going wide as I try to get a better look and figure out who the fuck this guy is. I can't help the clench of fists at my sides as I move a step closer to the window, ignoring the people that hustle by me on their lunch hour.

Before I can take in further detail the man gets out of the booth, leaving the restaurant from a side exit. The door dumps out into the street that intersects with Harrison, away from the main entrance. I head in that direction, watching him look around in a paranoid fashion as he hurriedly jumps in his vehicle. He pulls away before I can get a closer look at him or get the plate number of his grey sedan.

I go back to the front of the building, looking through the window again. She's still sitting there, her back to me. This time Charlie is with her, and they're chatting away as he sits in the same seat I'd seen the stranger in just a moment ago. She hands Charlie her phone and he watches the screen intently for longer than a minute.

I'm starting to wonder if I imagined the stranger across from her.

Maybe it wasn't a stranger. Maybe it was a colleague she bumped into.

But the way the man was speaking to her was too intense for a casual conversation. It didn't look like a chance meeting. Whatever he was saying had purpose, had weight.

I breathe myself into control, then wait an extra beat before making my way through the front door of the pub. The hostess starts to ask me if I need a table, but I put a hand up before she can speak. I have my eyes on my goal.

My look is forceful enough. The woman doesn't try to dissuade me as I move past her.

I'm done letting anything get in my way.

2

Alexis

Charlie and I are sitting in a booth at the pub across the street from my office. At his insistence that we need more than a salad but less than a shot of liquor to get through the afternoon, we've ordered burgers and fries. Billy Joel's "Big Shot" is being piped through the bar at a low volume while I fidget in the uncomfortable wooden booth. I'm trying to find the courage to tell my friend about the news report.

I escaped before Aidan could show up at the office, and he hasn't bothered contacting me again. My reaction is somewhere between relief and nagging disappointment.

"This song is about Mick Jagger's wife," Charlie says. "Did you know that?"

"I thought that was a rumor."

"Nope," he says. "Fact. Howard Stern interview. 2010."

I smile at him as our lunch arrives. He loves getting one over on me in music trivia. Charlie digs in while I pick at my fries. I haven't had an appetite all day.

Before I can get a word out about why I've asked him here, Charlie's attention switches from his plate to the bar. He's eyeing a handsome guy sitting on a stool a few feet away from us.

"Charlie, I'm going to need your full attention if you want me to spill my guts."

"That guy over there is cute," he says, "and he keeps looking over at you, Lex. Do you know him?"

I give the guy an inconspicuous once over as I sip my water. He's under six foot, lean and healthy but not necessarily built. He's dressed in a suit and tie, but he looks wired and on edge. He's nursing a shot of something which seems unusual in the middle of a Thursday.

"Nope, never seen him before in my life." Before I can go on denying I know who the man is, he's tossed back the rest of his drink and is coming towards us. Charlie gives me a nudge under the table with his foot as the guy saunters up to us.

"Hi," my friend interjects before the guy can open his mouth. "Can we help you?" He sends his charming smile at the mystery man.

"You must be Charlie."

"I must be," Charlie says, "and you are?"

The guy turns to me. "And you're Alexis Greene?" His voice sounds familiar, but I can't place it.

"I am," I say. "I don't believe we've met."

"Whitmore," he says. "Mark Whitmore."

Oh fuck.

I don't know what the hell the attorney for Renewable Energy is doing here but it can't be an accident that he is standing in front of me right now.

"Mr. Whitmore," I say. I extend my hand to shake his. "What can we do for you? I didn't realize you were in town."

"Can I get a moment with you, Alexis? In private?"

"I can take a hint," Charlie says. "I'll just use the restroom." He excuses himself from the table. Once out of Whitmore's sight, he throws me a cautionary look. I acknowledge, nodding in his direction as he points to the spot he's standing in and mouths "I'll be right here".

Charlie powered through the rest of his lunch when he returned to the table. My plate is still half full. My hurt and embarrassment over Aidan were enough to chase away my appetite earlier but with Whitmore's unexpected intrusion, I regret eating anything at all. What he said to me left a lingering knot in my stomach.

Charlie has asked, but for his own safety I haven't given him any straight answers about what Whitmore was doing here. He doesn't need to know. When he reluctantly accepts my assurance that everything is fine, I'm able to revert to my original reason for asking him here.

I tell him about the news report, cueing it up on my phone and handing it over so he can watch it. He's shaking his head as he hands the phone back to me.

"Lex. She was in the hospital. This doesn't mean he was fucking her."

"I know," I say with a sigh. "It isn't even that."

Well, kind of it is.

What if they did? What if he couldn't resist being with an old 'friend' that needed him and hours later he was with me on the plane? I push my plate away, now unable to even look at the remains of my food.

"The point is he didn't share this with me. When I asked him about what had him so tense, so exhausted, he said it was business. It wasn't business. It was his fucking girlfriend."

"Former girlfriend," he insists.

"Whatever. I can't believe you're defending him."

"I'm not defending him, Lex. I just don't want to see you screw up a chance at happiness because of this. I can't see him doing this to you, taking up with his ex after the time you've spent together. It doesn't add up."

"If I can't trust him..." I trail off. I shake my head, dismissing Charlie's words before I end up shedding more tears. "If it was nothing, why didn't he just tell me he saw her?"

"Let's think about this. As far as you know for certain, he was in her company for all of five minutes. Don't you want to give him the benefit of the doubt? Get the rest of the story?"

My senses are unexpectedly assaulted from behind before I can answer. I close my eyes, heart pounding, muscles tense as I inhale his scent.

"I was going to ask the same thing," Aidan says at my back.

"Well, on that note," Charlie says, "I'll just be heading back to the office." He sets a bill on the table.

"I'm buying," I insist. "I already told you."

"I know. This is for Aidan to buy himself a shot. He's going to need it." He winks at us and leaves before I can say anything more.

Aidan takes the seat across from me and I turn my attention away, eyeing the television screen above the bar. My arms are crossed over my chest, intuitively protecting myself. I can't even look at him.

"Alexis, please."

I don't acknowledge him.

"Look at me." There's a sternness to his voice that gives me shivers.

Reluctantly, I give in to return his gaze.

"It's not what you think."

How did I know he was going to lead off with that?

"Really?" I start in indignation. "Since you have no idea what I think, perhaps we should start with that. What did you assume I'd think when I found out you were in California with her?"

He turns his head as he sighs, rubbing the back of his neck.

"I don't want to do this here."

"Yeah, well. You came to me," I spout. "I didn't ask you to."

"You wouldn't call or see me. I had to improvise."

"By sneaking up on me in a bar? You're getting really good at that," I throw at him. "I didn't want to see you, Aidan. I thought you could take a hint."

My words don't have any effect on the anger that underlies his expression. He has something else on his mind, something more than the news report. After a few deeper-than-usual breaths, he speaks again.

"Who was sitting here with you ten minutes ago?"

"Why does that matter? You're off seeing your girlfriend in California without telling me, and you're going to give me shit for talking to someone?" I can't even believe him. He must have seen me with Whitmore and that's what he's mad about?

He's got no right.

"Tell me who it was," he says. "Someone you know? A colleague?"

"This is killing you, isn't it? You can't stand not knowing who I was talking to." I've seen his controlling tendencies in action but this is just…

Damn. The intensity burning in his eyes is almost frightening.

"Alexis," he insists, "tell me now."

I lean forward, keeping my stern voice as soft as I can manage. "How about you fuck off? I do not have to answer to you." I straighten my posture against the hard wood behind me, assessing his reaction.

He is not wounded as I thought he might be.

His expression is closer to irate.

"I'm not doing this here." He says it with a venom I've not seen from him before. He throws more bills on top of Charlie's ten, abandons his seat and grabs me by the arm, pulling me out of the booth. He doesn't hurt me, but it's definitely not a friendly grip.

Out of sheer hope to evade embarrassment I say nothing, letting him keep his hold on me as we make our way to the street. I want to shout at him but don't have the guts to make a scene. We're in the middle of a city sidewalk dodging the lunch rush. When he lets me go, all I can do is stand there fuming.

The rain gave way to sun and clouds an hour ago and the air is warm again. I'm wearing a sleeveless pink top that buttons down the center, tucked into my black skirt. Looking down at my elbow where he'd held onto me, I notice my skin now matches the color of my shirt.

I look up at him, watching him pace back and forth in a single step, running his hands through his hair. He doesn't look at me as he speaks.

"Just come with me. Please."

"I don't see the point. You went to her and you didn't tell me. I don't care why you were with her. You don't owe me any explanations. Can we just drop it so I can go back to my life? I'm not cut out for this shit. I just want…"

Before I can say another word, he charges me, picks me up off my feet, and throws me over his left shoulder. Thank God my wallet has my phone in it, secured by a loop around my wrist. My skirt is held tight by his arm wrapped around my legs, keeping me from baring all to the public.

Even so, I'm mortified.

I object as discreetly as I can, but a few people on the street take notice of this impressive demonstration. One guy whistles loudly from another direction in appreciation, mistaking Aidan's anger for chivalry. No one stops him though. This is not the strangest thing people witness in the streets of Stanton on any given day.

"Aidan, what the hell!" I'm shouting now, not caring who's watching. "Put me down!"

I'm carried to a Corvette parked at the curb two storefronts north. It's an older model. The marina blue two-door convertible is in pristine condition and the top is closed.

Aidan's left arm secures me over his shoulder while he pulls a key from his pocket and unlocks the passenger door. He's less winded than I am when he sets me upright and opens the door.

"Get in." His voice is as stern as it was in the restaurant.

"No." I'm insistent, ignoring a nagging feeling in my gut that tells me to hear him out.

"Alexis if you don't, I will *put* you in."

I have no doubt he could do it, but my body language demonstrates my defiance clearly as I straighten my clothing. I refuse to let him commandeer me.

Then I get a look at his face.

Ho-lee shit.

I resolve that I'm not going to win this one and get in the car.

He climbs into the driver's seat and I realize this is the first time he hasn't had someone driving us around. Behind the wheel, he is in charge and in control. He grabs mirrored aviator shades from the dash and puts them on.

Goddamn my dwindling willpower. He's sexier than I've ever seen him.

"Do you have any clients this afternoon?"

"No."

"Good. Buckle up," he orders as he does the same.

He starts up the car, which is loud enough to drown out any thought. He moves expertly around the various potholes, shifting in and out of gear like a professional racecar driver as we go through the downtown traffic lights. In minutes, we're on the highway heading south at eighty miles an hour towards Mirror Lake.

I speak up over the noise of the engine. "Where are we going?"

"Somewhere private."

I lean over into his space a bit, trying to assess his intentions. He's staring at the road, not paying me any attention as he radiates his gruff demeanor. I don't know what right he has to be mad but it's obvious he still is.

"I think you should slow down." Traffic is light this particular Thursday afternoon, but it wouldn't be odd to pass a State Trooper. "If you get a ticket, I'm not going to fix it for you."

Even though I could.

"They have to catch me first." He turns to me revealing a sarcastic smile, then increases speed as we blow by the exit for Mirror Lake.

"If you're going to keep me against my will, at least tell me where the fuck we're going."

He says nothing as we exit the highway in Raeford a few miles south of my house. This is the only exit that leads to Falcon Lake traveling west on the county highway.

Raeford is an even smaller town than mine. One traffic light, one gas station, no stores or restaurants. Fields and cows outnumber homes and people. There's nothing in the way of amenities until Falcon Lake which is ten miles away.

At least now he's slowed down.

He motors down the main road, probably heading for one of his lakefront properties. After several miles, he makes a right down a side road that travels around the lake. We meander along the twists and turns past several small, older cottages dotting the shoreline to our right, one on top of another.

About two miles in, the shoreline moves out further, taken over by a large lawn. The car slows enough for me to take in details of a boathouse on the shore next to a few dock slips.

He makes a left at the driveway of the property, across the street from the impressive waterfront. We climb the steep gravel driveway and I'm fearful for this remarkable car. I cringe as it plods along the rocks and dirt, hoping it isn't damaged by the stones pinging up from below.

I was apprehensive being in his presence when we left the city, but he seems to have relaxed since we got off the main road. I roll my window down seeking fresh air. It's hazy and humid, the sun peeking through cloud cover.

We pull up in front of a colossal log cabin. The logs are gorgeous in their own right, but the whole place is breathtaking. The car stops at the base of a wide staircase that leads to a wraparound porch. We're parked at the side of the house in front of a large detached garage.

Aidan shuts off the engine and drops his hands to his lap, staring ahead.

"What are we doing here?" I ask.

"I needed to get out of the city."

"And what gave you the impression I wanted to come with you?"

He doesn't answer, still looking ahead. Finally, after what seems like forever, he speaks.

"Who was sitting in the restaurant with you?"

I sigh in frustration. I don't want to tell him, to give him the satisfaction of knowing that yes, I probably need to share this information with him. When I'd insisted on the rooftop of his loft that he keep me on his project, I'd promised to tell him the minute anything like this happened.

Reluctantly, I answer.

"It was Mark Whitmore."

He whips his head to look at me. "Renewable Energy's attorney?"

"Former attorney, apparently."

"They let him go?"

"I'm not exactly sure."

"Did he call you? Set up a meeting?"

"No, he just showed up at the pub. Charlie and I were eating lunch and he asked if he could have a moment of my time. I guess he'd gone to the office and Claudia told him where to find me. Charlie excused himself so we could talk privately."

"And? What did he want?"

I can't answer at first. The lump in my throat is too big.

"*Alexis*," he says, glaring.

"He wanted to warn me."

He throws me a look. "Warn you how? Did he threaten you?" I can see the fury building in him at the thought.

"No, no. Nothing like that," I assure him. "He just wanted me to be careful."

"I need you to tell me exactly what he said."

"He said he no longer works for R.E.E. or his old firm. He's moving to Florida with his wife and kids. I guess he's admitted to practice in Florida as well as Pennsylvania."

"He came all the way up here to tell you this? It would have been in the opposite direction of his destination."

"He's flying out from Stanton Airport to head to Orlando. His family is already down there. He's moved his whole family away from Pennsylvania, Aidan. Someone doesn't just up and do that – uproot their kids to move hundreds of miles away – unless there's reason to, right?"

He ignores my question. "Did his firm pat him on the head and send him off with a severance package? Or is he running from R.E.E.? He seemed to be looking over his shoulder when he drove away."

"He didn't tell me if he'd been fired from the firm or what happened with R.E.E. but I got the impression he didn't have much choice in the matter."

"What was his warning to you?"

"That I should watch my back. That R.E.E. has resources and they're not done fighting for Myers' land. He said things could get…"

"Ugly?" He says it before I can get the next word out of my mouth.

"Dangerous. He used the word dangerous. He told me to distance myself as much as possible."

"From the Myers' sale?"

"Yes," I hesitate, "and from you."

He gets out of the car in a hurry without responding. I stay put just to be stubborn, watching from my window as he climbs the steps to my right with keys in hand. He unlocks the door and disappears inside. I'm tempted to stay here and sulk, to wait him out until he decides to come out and take me back to Stanton.

On the other hand, as pretty as this car is, it isn't comfortable. The interior is pristine but it's also hot and sticky. Even with the window down, the air is stuffy with fumes.

I get out and go after him. He's left the door to the house ajar and I stop and admire the massive work of art, an intricate tree carved into a stunning slab of wood. Rustic knots are sanded smooth, and the shiny surface matches the polished hickory floors underfoot as I enter the immense house. I have no idea where Aidan has gone to. I run my hands along the door in appreciation before closing it gently behind me.

To the right of the foyer is a grey fieldstone fireplace tall enough to stand in. There are few furnishings and what is scattered about is protected, draped in white fabric.

I can hear Aidan talking on his phone from some distant place in the house. He's using an urgent tone, probably giving Byron instructions about the information I've just shared with him. I hear him say goodbye from somewhere to my right.

"In here," he calls, his voice reaching me in an echo from the direction of the fireplace. I leave the foyer for the sound and find him in the kitchen. He's standing at a bank of windows, looking out at the lake below. The water is some ways away but worth a pause to behold.

I stand shoulder to shoulder with him, unable to take my eyes off the view.

"It isn't what you think," he says again.

And we're back to discussing Stella.

Great.

My insides ache.

"Well, you dragged me all the way out here," I say. "Enlighten me."

3

Aidan

I turn to her, looking her over. She's exasperated and fatigued - but still stunning enough to make me short of breath. All I want to do is hold her, to make every doubt she's feeling go away. But her body language is guarded now that I've brought up Stella. There's no other way around it.

I have to talk my way through this.

"I take it you saw the news report this morning," I start.

"Yeah. It's been the highlight of my day." She doesn't turn her attention away from the view.

"I'm sorry you had to learn about it this way," I say. "When I said I had business in California, I meant it. That's all it was to me."

"Seeing your girlfriend is just business?"

"Alexis," I scold, "don't be childish. You know what she is – or rather, isn't – to me."

"No, I know what you've told me. But I don't know anything, really. Once I stopped to think about it, I realized all I've known since we met is what you've fed me."

"Bullshit," I say, deepening my tone. "I've never been anything but honest with you."

"Except for this," she qualifies. She finally looks at me, anger in her eyes. "You specifically failed to mention you were going to California to be with Stella."

"It wasn't to be with her. I saw her for all of a few hours."

"Why don't you just tell me what's going on?"

"I can't," I say. "Legally. I can't legally tell you anything."

"Oh Jesus, that's rich." She rolls her eyes, heaving a sigh of impatience.

"Let me finish." *God, she's so stubborn.* "I shouldn't tell you anything. But I'm going to anyway."

"I don't expect you to ignore your legally binding obligations for me." Any hint of sarcasm has left her. "You should know that about me, Aidan. If you have an understanding with her, especially if it's in writing, I respect it. What I want is for you to leave me out of it altogether."

I look at her in disbelief, involuntarily wincing.

That fucking hurt.

"Leave you out of it how?"

"Just let me go back to what I was before I knew you. I was doing just fine. I don't need this." She looks pained as the words leave her lips and I'm instantly relieved.

Either she's lying to me or she's lying to herself.

"I don't believe you."

She turns away, looking to the afternoon sky and the lake below, arms crossed under her chest. She inhales, closing her eyes as a tear betrays her words and trails down her cheek.

I move around to stand in front of her, raising my hand to her face. She rests her head there, her eyes still closed. She doesn't resist the comfort I offer and I pull her into my chest, my chin resting on top of her head.

"Just let me explain, baby. I can't stand to see you hurting because of me." My chest tightens at the thought she might walk out of my life as quickly as she came into it. I already know I wouldn't want to survive that.

She lets me hold her, eventually signaling with a quiet nod that she wants me to go on.

"I went to California because her father insisted and because there was no other way to get her out of trouble. The last thing I wanted to do was leave you, especially with your sister's husband being lost. But with Stella's father in my way, this project could be dead in the water."

She leans back, looking up at me in confusion.

"I don't understand. What does her father have to do with the Center?"

"He's an investor, a board member. But as you can imagine, his daughter is more important to him than my ambitions here in New York."

"So what, you're not allowed free will? You and Stella can't mutually decide not to be in each other's lives?"

"I wish it was that simple." She says nothing, her expression urging me to go on. "He isn't concerned for her because he cares about her. He treats her more like a pawn than a daughter. He doesn't want to deal with her bullshit or worry about her causing him problems, causing defamation to their family name."

"She'd do that?"

"She would, and she's already started to."

"Why?"

It's a simple question. Though I could go on for an hour to answer it, I stick to the point.

"She didn't want our relationship to end, Alexis. And neither did he, simply because it kept him from having to deal with her."

"But it did end?"

"Yes. I told you that. And it didn't end well. She's been acting out since we parted ways. Partying, blowing money. She's made some terrible business decisions. When he found out about her latest escapade, he wanted to have her committed."

"Literally? Like to an institution?"

"Yes."

"Was that medically necessary?"

"No. She's always been a brat and when she doesn't get her way, hell hath no fury. But she's not mentally unstable."

"Okay, so what, you had to keep him from committing her?"

I release her and sit at the kitchen table, gesturing for her to sit too.

"I did. She is not mentally unstable, but she's recently developed a taste for cocaine. I had to help her before it became a habit."

"Jesus, Aidan." She reaches out across the table to lay her hands over mine. "Why didn't you just tell me?"

"Because technically he could sue me into destitution for repeating any of this."

She blinks fast, eyes wide. "I…I don't even know what to say."

"She was admitted to the hospital last week and her father kept it out of the media. But he didn't want her released until I came out there. In fact he wanted me to stay in California, but I refused."

"What is it to him?"

"He wants me to babysit her, essentially. If it got out that she was struggling with something that could be construed as an addiction, no matter how new of an issue it might be…" I pause. "If the press gets a hold of that, shit will hit the proverbial fan."

"And her father will pull his investment here," she finishes.

"Yes, or worse."

"What a fucking bastard," she spouts with distaste. "With the influence you have, you can't put a stop to his reign over you? Do you really need his backing for this?"

"No. And I'm working on a way out. But there's more."

She shakes her head as if that's unfathomable.

"If word about Stella gets out, he will publicly say that I'm to blame for his daughter's drug use."

"That's ridiculous," she scoffs. "No one would believe you could have steered her in that direction."

I look down at our joined hands. I didn't want to tell her this way. I return her gaze to see her expression conveying an eagerness for me to go on.

"I have a past, Alexis. I wasn't always on the path you see me on now. I can assure you, if word about that history ever gets out, which her father has threatened to make happen, it won't be that unbelievable."

She looks floored. She didn't anticipate this.

"There are situations he's helped me with in the past, things very few people know. The details are not relevant. Let's just say it isn't to my advantage to have John Ireland oppose me in any way – publicly or otherwise." I pause before I say more, suddenly fatigued.

"But you have influence with the media," she pushes. "Can't you keep them at bay until Stella gets help? My interview with Melanie didn't even make the news. I know you had something to do with that."

"Yes, but that's here. Nationally, it's different. John Ireland has connections and they are as deep as mine. He has his ways of knowing things, of having one up on me. But I'm working on it."

"How does her father know so much about you? He doesn't seem like the type you'd openly share with."

"John Ireland has been an acquaintance of my dad's since I was a kid."

"Doesn't your father object to this blackmail?"

"He doesn't know." I look at her emphatically. "And he won't know. I can handle it."

She shakes her head in disbelief. "Is Stella's father the one that threw a punch at you while you were out there?"

I absentmindedly rub my face. I thought it looked much better today.

"No. All you need to know is that was a random event. One that won't be repeated. I don't make a habit of surrounding myself with violence."

"I'm wondering if you don't bring it on yourself," she mutters. She looks away. "You have quite a temper."

"I've been known to. I won't deny that. But I also know how to control it. And I don't choose violence to resolve anything."

If she only knew what I've been through.

"Look, I was angry when I dragged you here, but it wasn't you I was angry with. It was the situation. I knew something was going on. I saw the way Whitmore was talking to you. Add to that the Stella mess, and yeah, I was pissed."

"I get it, okay?" She looks at me intently. "I can understand that. But the toxicity of this, of Ireland wanting to lash out just because his daughter is an irresponsible train wreck that can't handle a break up?" She shakes her head again. "Like I said. Ridiculous."

"I know it seems that way on the surface. To a degree, you're right. But the situation goes deeper than this. I'm learning the whole thing is..." I trail off, recalling the claims Shane Armstrong made about Ireland's recent illegal activities. "It's more fucked up than even I knew."

She looks at me, again thrown off by everything she's learning. I can't blame her in the slightest.

"I'm handling it." I reach over and lift her chin so her eyes meet mine. "I promise you I will take care of this. Right now, the Irelands don't know you exist. It's better if it stays that way."

"For how long?"

"Until I can be sure they aren't a threat."

She casts her gaze down at our hands. She doesn't like this news. "So how did the video of the two of you get out?"

"The reporter I spoke to released it earlier than I requested, but I'd set it up to come out later today. I leaked it."

She just looks at me, again not understanding my actions.

"I did it so people would know she was ill and that I was stepping in to take care of her, which is essentially what happened. I knew there would be assumptions made that we were back together but that couldn't be helped. No matter how much control I have over what is reported, I will never control how people perceive it or how the media spins it."

She looks pained. The thought of people believing I'm back with Stella obviously makes her uneasy, probably more than it does me. I'm used to ignoring the opinion of the media. She is not.

"I'm sorry it has to be this way, that I didn't tell you. But I had my reasons. Some out of legal obligation, but more importantly to protect you."

"I don't need protecting." Her usual strong will emerges, a fire lit in her eyes.

"There will be people that want to hurt you just to get to me. If you are going to be in my life, you do need protecting."

Her eyes go wide again.

We've never discussed this, her being in my life on any long-term basis. This may be a revelation to her, but not for me. I don't want to be away from her. I'd been painfully aware of the fact since she'd gone to Arizona.

But if I want her in my life, she needs to be aware of the chaos that comes with being in my orbit. She may be independent under normal circumstances, but she'll have to give in on this and let me do what I must to keep her safe.

In the alternative, it's possible she'll run far and run fast knowing all this. The thought slays me in a way I can't come to grips with.

"I intended to tell you all of this last night," I go on, "but you didn't stay. Then you wouldn't answer my calls this morning."

"I'm sorry," she says. Her shoulders drop in obvious regret. "I should have listened to your voicemails. I should have given you a chance."

"Then your favorite reporter showed up outside my building this morning asking for an interview," I add with sarcasm.

"Melanie," she says. "Persistent bitch, isn't she?"

"I refused to comment. Byron dealt with it."

"I'm sure she was disappointed that you wouldn't see her." Her smile indicates her satisfaction at that. "So where is Stella now?"

"In a treatment program. I delivered her there myself Tuesday night. She'll be there for four weeks. The doctors are confident she's gone in soon enough to prevent a full-blown addiction. She will have strict requirements after that, of course. But the plan is for her to be well enough to accompany her father to the gala here in July."

She rolls her eyes in contempt. "I don't want these people anywhere near me, Aidan. I especially don't want them coming here."

"I don't expect you to be comfortable with it. I may be able to keep it from happening this way but I need you to be prepared for the possibility."

"You can't tell me that you actually need her father's money to pull off the Center."

"No, you're right. I don't."

"Then what is it that he has over you? Why does he have to be involved in your life at all?"

"I used his help to uncover the intentions of R.E.E. Without him – especially without his connections here in New York – I never would have confirmed they were just a shell company for Waterman Oil and Gas. I suspected it myself, knew in my gut they were after Myers' land for drilling. But I had to use Ireland to confirm. I still don't have proof that would legally hold. But I learned enough. I had to be sure before I acted on my ambitions, to know what I was getting myself into."

"Okay, so you used him. But now it's over. You've taken care of Stella. You've got the Myers land all but locked up, and R.E.E. will be out of the picture. Can't you just cut ties?"

"That's the question mark right now. I have to weigh the consequences. John Ireland is a powerful man. If removing myself from Stella's life results in his daughter becoming an erratic mess that's now his problem, I don't know what he'll do. He doesn't want her to become his cross to bear."

"So, if she remains your problem and not his, he'll leave you alone?"

"Essentially, yes. I want them both out of my life, but it's going to take some doing to make that happen. I need you to trust that I'm doing everything I can to reach that goal."

She doesn't say anything.

"I'll always be upfront with you. But I also have to protect you and the project." I move into her vision, willing her to look at me. Her eyes are so blue. I'm lost in them, wishing they were not so full of concern. "Alexis, right now you and the Center are my only priorities."

Her eyes light up at my confession.

The words are not meaningless to me, but they are all I can offer her now, hoping they're enough. When she says nothing, I get up from the table and move to where she sits. I kneel next to her, our eyes even.

"I'm not presenting you with an easy situation. I know this," I say. "This is something you should put thought into, whether you even want to see me anymore. I just..." I lower my voice to a whisper. "I'd like a chance to make your choice easier."

I hope she can't sense my anxiety in this moment.

She could easily walk away. Remove herself from all of this.

That would be the logical thing to do. The safest thing for her.

But that would mean I lose her.

"Don't answer now," I insist. "Let's just...I didn't even think this out. I just grabbed you up and drove off. I've been wrapped up in this mess for awhile, and I've had enough. I just need a break." I stand up, gesturing to the front room. "Look around. I haven't even had a chance to spend time here yet. The utilities were turned on last week but Byron's only been in here a few times to outfit the place with bare necessities."

"Well we're here now," she says as she looks around. "This place is unreal."

"It is. See?" I say playfully. "Sometimes it doesn't suck to be with me."

She smiles and it wrenches me.

I can't lose her.

"I'm just thrown by all this," she says. "First you flip everything upside down in my world. Then my sister needs me and my mother reappears, and now this. What would you do?"

I nod, running my hands up and down her arms. "I know, baby. I don't know what I'd do if things were reversed. But right now I know what I want to do to you."

She raises a brow at me.

"Have you forgiven me?"

She exhales in exasperation. I know she has, but I need to hear her admit it.

"I don't know what to make of all this. It's so much to take in. I understand the reason you didn't tell me about California," she says, "but I want to know more. About you. About your past. About what the hell I'm getting into here."

"You will," I promise, "but right now I want to take our minds off of all of this. I don't want to think about anything."

I pull her out of her chair and take her over, kissing her rough and eager. She doesn't object, instead meeting my greed with her own. I'm rock hard, aching for her in seconds. I turn her towards the kitchen island and she stretches her arms out, hands gripping the granite in front of her. I move her hair away, my lips assaulting the nape of her neck.

"Tell me you forgive me." My hand moves around to her waist, untucking her shirt from her skirt.

"Yes," she whispers. "Yes, I forgive you."

I stand behind her, using both hands to pull her blouse off over her head in a hurry then toss it on the table behind us. I kick off my shoes and send them sailing across the floor and she follows my lead, kicking off her flats. Her hands rest back on the counter, waiting in a panting heat. I take her skirt down, leaving her standing exposed in a bra and thong.

She starts to turn around but I lean forward into her backside keeping her firmly in place.

"I want you from behind." My jeans hit the floor in a thud, but not before I pull a condom from my back pocket.

"Seriously?" she asks. "Am I that predictable?"

"It's a necessity with you around," I breathe. "I can't resist you. At the sight of you I want you, baby."

She tips her head back, moaning. I tear the foil open and wrap myself. I slip her thong off, then test her from behind with my fingers, aroused even more to find her wet.

"You're always ready for me, Alexis. *Mi piace come bagnato sei.*"

"English," she says with heavy breath. "Tell me what you said."

"I love how wet you are," I repeat for her understanding. I can feel her already fighting a climax as my fingers work her over, her clit throbbing in agreement.

"Inside me. *Please*," she begs. "*Now*."

I comply before she expects it, thrusting into her just as I'd once promised, without hesitation, without fear of breaking her. I'm at her fast and hard, cradling her hips in my hands as I drive into her.

She moans louder as I reach around her front, massaging her clit in a circling rhythm. She leans forward, breathing hard and pushing back to meet my aggressive momentum. I watch her grip the granite in front of her, holding tighter as I feel my skin slick with sweat.

"*Yes*," she manages. "Don't stop, Aidan."

"Come for me baby," I urge. "I need to feel you come."

She does as I ask on cue, unraveling around me. Her legs become unsteady as she pulses and quivers from the inside out.

"That's my beautiful girl," I whisper, leaning over her. "*Ecco la mia bella ragazza.*"

She pants, trying to catch her breath as I pull out. I haven't come yet, but she turns around to see me taking the condom off, tossing it aside.

"I loathe these things," I say.

She just shrugs and I can't help but wonder if she's ever known another way. She grabs my jeans and folds them up, laying them at my feet. She kneels on her makeshift cushion, taking me into her mouth before I can say anything. She's watching me, looking into my eyes as she works me in slow rhythm.

Holy fuck.

My head drops back as I groan in acceptance of her technique. Her hands rise to grip the base of me, fondling as she takes all of me.

"Alexis…oh God… holy *shit*…"

I can feel myself build, already on the verge of release. Somehow this simple act has never felt so good. She lets me fill her up, sucking as I slide down the back of her throat. She's licking me as my body settles, my hands laced through her hair, cradling her head.

"I can't believe you just did that," I manage. "That was… holy hell…"

"What?" she asks. "It was what?"

"The best," I say, trying to get my words out, "best I've ever had."

She sits back, resting on her heels, head down in submission. I tilt her chin up with a finger. "Did you mean to do that?"

She nods modestly.

"My God, Alexis. That was…like I said. You're very good at that."

She smiles in response and I pull her to her feet, wrapping her in my arms.

"Let's see if the water's up and going." I toss her over my shoulder and she howls in protest as I carry her to the master suite on the first floor.

"I wish you would warn me when you do that," she says when I deposit her in the middle of the bed.

I head for the bathroom and start the shower, letting the spray spit and sputter as air fights its way through the water lines. I rifle through the cupboard and find toothpaste and a packaged toothbrush, appreciating that Byron knew enough to stock the bathrooms in case of guests.

I exit the bathroom and toss the toothbrush at her. "Think you might want this?"

She snatches it in midair, still seated on the bed.

"Smart ass." She jumps down and follows me.

As I'm pulling towels from the cabinet, she's at the sink rinsing me out of her mouth, preparing a toothbrush. I watch her slowly drag the bristles across her tongue.

I'm mesmerized with her, unable to peel my eyes away. She looks back at my reflection, watching me as I watch her. The way she drags the brush is intentionally suggestive and I ache for her mouth to be on me again, more quickly than I imagined possible.

I step closer to her, still watching her in the mirror as I remove her bra. I cup her with both hands from behind, feeling her shiver as I move her hair away from her neck. I lick behind her ear, down her shoulders, nipping at her collarbone. She drops her toothbrush on the counter and I lead her into the shower.

Like my bathroom at the loft, the shower is roomy and spray jets line the walls. I leave them off and let the rain showerhead above spill down on us as we stand embracing beneath it. Water beads up on the porcelain tiled walls that surround us.

I raise a hand to the base of her neck, pulling her in to kiss her as heatedly as I did when I first saw her yesterday on the plane.

"You are amazing, Alexis. I've never felt this before," I admit in a whisper. "I can't get enough of you." She bites her bottom lip, as though she's holding back. "Say what you're thinking."

"I don't have much to compare it to."

"Then don't compare."

"I don't want to be away from you," she finally admits. "Then when I'm with you, I can't resist you. If you wanted to have sex in the middle of the street, I'd have no choice but to comply."

"You're into voyeurism, hmm? That could be interesting."

"No," she laughs. "I just mean I wouldn't be able to defend myself if you wanted to. I've never felt this way either."

I pull her closer, her chest gliding over mine. She sways back and forth, rubbing herself over me as her nipples harden into pebbles.

"Stop," I say sternly. "Or I'll fuck you again right here."

And I have no more condoms.

She looks up at me, grinning in defiance. "Really?"

"Don't think about teasing me," I insist. "You will lose."

She moves back and forth again, letting her chest caress me, bringing my nipples to attention too.

"I mean it," I warn.

"Are you…" she hesitates. "Are you clean?"

"Disease free. Addiction free," I say. "But I am not sterile."

"I'm on the pill," she asserts. "And I've never had this before," she says, letting a hand move down to stroke my now throbbing erection.

I crush my lips on hers.

God, I want her.

"Not in here," I insist. "Let's get out."

Just as I did at the end of our first shower together I towel her dry, then myself, and we head for the bedroom.

"Hold on," I say. "I'll be right back."

4

Alexis

Aidan leaves the bedroom, and I remove my towel to wrap my hair up. I pull the drape off the enormous sleigh bed, then go to the closet in search of sheets for the gorgeous piece of furniture. The headboard is made of dark wood, the thin slats accented with nail head trim. I find a set of white sheets (no doubt expensive because holy hell are they soft) and have time to put on the bottom sheet and climb up before he comes back. I take in my surroundings while I wait.

There are hickory floors in here too but a huge rug is placed underneath the bed to soften the space. Another bank of windows is to my left. The drapes are drawn closed, making the room dim and hiding whatever view lies outside.

Aidan returns moments later still wrapped in a towel and carrying a bottle of water, a glass with ice, and his phone. His chiseled frame is perfection. I'll never be able to look at that body without aching for him.

He sets everything on the bedside table, then gestures for me to come to him as he stands at the bed. He kisses me, reigniting what we started in the shower. My lungs feel empty of air when he stops.

A mischievous grin graces his lips. "You want the real feel, baby?" His eyes are lit up, dancing in anticipation. Then he's kissing me behind the ear, moving down my neck. His lips are so soft, making their way down to my navel while his hands roam me in worship.

"Mm-hmm," I finally manage. I'm head back, eyes closed, unable to form full words.

"I'm warning you right now," he says as he comes back up to look me in the eyes. "You'll never want to go back."

"That good, huh?"

"You have no idea." He picks up his phone and taps away, setting it back on the nightstand as music fills the air.

"I take it your magic music genie was as necessary as turning on the lights?"

"You know it," he says with a grin.

I smile at his song choice. Jason Mraz's "I Won't Give Up" surrounds us at high volume. I'm still kneeling in front of him on the bed, facing him.

As he stands there it's impossible to ignore the new way he's looking at me, his steel blue eyes revealing adoration. My body is radiating with chills without him laying a finger on me, my breasts lifting, my nipples intensely tightened.

My head rests in the palm of his left hand as he looks down at me, pushing hair away from my face.

"Listen," he says. "This song reminds me so much of you. Of us." His gaze is penetrating, intense. I close my eyes to avoid the overpowering emotion. "I heard it in the most ridiculous place this morning, and I've heard it a thousand times before. But the lyrics…" he takes a breath. "The minute I heard it today, when I really listened – I wanted to play it for you that very second."

"Where?" I ask softly. "Where did you hear it?"

"I can't tell you that," he says. "You'll laugh." He's suddenly bashful, a version of himself I've yet to see. It's yanking my heart right out of my chest.

"Tell me." I close my eyes again, hoping it will help him reveal his source. "I promise not to laugh."

I hear him heave a sigh and feel his gaze on me. "Standing in line at Starbucks," he says. He waits a beat. "Lame, right?"

I open one eye and, though I promised not to, I can't help let go a soft laugh. "Not lame," I say. "Maybe a little cheesy."

"Cheesy isn't what I was going for."

"Sometimes I like cheesy."

And I'm more than liking this song.

I'd never really paid attention to the lyrics myself, but right now I'm in awe at the words I'm hearing as the song goes on, knowing that he's meant them for us. Words about my soul, that he won't give up on *us*.

That he's giving me love.

Love?

Did I really hear that right?

The music stirs me, making the overpowering sensation he always causes come on stronger than ever before. Just being this near to him, the lyrics...

I can hear his towel hit the floor as my eyes stay closed, just listening all the way through until the song ends.

"Play it again," I whisper, "please."

He kisses me sweetly, teasing my lips with his. "It's on repeat." He eases me back to the center of bed, climbing up after me. I'm flat on my back as he removes the towel from my head to reveal damp hair underneath while straddling me, just like the first time we were together.

He moves down to kiss me with more heat, the song rising in a perfectly timed upsurge as he enters me, and I'm completely taken over.

The feeling of just him – skin on skin – is better than I'd ever imagined. I already know he's right, that I'll never want him the old way, with something between us, something preventing this feeling of him inside me.

The song surrounds us as he moves gently in and out. He's palms down on the bed, weight resting there as he watches me relish every movement. My hands are all over him, roaming his taught muscles, enjoying every sensation from sight to sound, touch to taste.

He is consuming every single part of me in this one slowed-down moment in time.

"Alexis, do you feel this? I can't even..." his voice hitches as he tries to get words out, but they fail him as he drops his head, lowering himself down to me.

"I've never felt anything like this, anything better." I press my hands into his chest, feeling his heart beating. "Stay still for a minute."

I wrap my legs around him, savoring the feel of our bodies entwined, how deep he is this way, completely bared to me.

"Careful, baby. I'm close," he whispers. "You feel so good."

"Not yet," I plead. "I don't want to lose this feeling, Aidan." My breath is short, my voice strained. "Please stay."

He lifts up, setting his gaze on my eyes. My back arches and he comes down to tease my nipple with his tongue, then swallow me up with his entire mouth. I unwrap my legs, leaving them opened to him, letting him move freely as he starts to thrust faster. His mouth moves to my neck, moaning as he licks all the way up to my ear.

"Questo bisogno così tanta, Alexis. Ti senti incredibile."

I don't know what he's uttering, but my mind has caught up with the way he's overwhelming my body. My fingertips dig into the flesh of his back, moans escaping me as I climax around him.

This peak of satisfaction was unknown to me before this moment. It comes over me in waves, not letting up. My mouth is parted, lips dried out from exhaling. My body quivers involuntarily from my toes all the way up.

"That is the best feeling in the world." He's kissing my lips, my throat, my breasts. "You're okay?"

I close my eyes and quickly nod.

He starts moving again, picking up speed. His last push comes a moment later as he explodes into me, uttering more Italian and weakening me beyond reason. *"Non rinunciare a me, baby. Non voglio perderti."*

The sensation is other worldly, feeling him fill me up as he melts my ear with his words. It's the same rush as always, the same high, but intensified tenfold. This feeling of being filled up is new to me, and doing it with him…

I can't stop tears from releasing this time as the stupor of bliss overtakes me.

He shudders, allowing his release to let go of its hold over him, then leans up to read me.

"Baby," he says in obvious concern. "You sure you're okay?"

Again I nod, hoping he'll know what I'm feeling without having to express it in words. There's no way I could. He's kissing me, wiping tears away, waiting for me to respond.

"I'm good," I manage, sucking in fast breaths.

Holy shit. What I am is out of air.

I smile at him, trying to ease his worry. He slowly withdraws, and my reaction at his absence deepens my emotional fall. Again I feel like I'm letting something go that I never want be without, something I'd been missing out on for so long.

He gets up and goes to the bedside table, pouring water into the glass of ice.

"Can you sit up? I think you need this."

I nod, pushing myself up to sitting, leaning against the headboard. He grabs a pillow off a nearby chair and props it up behind me, then hands me the water. As I come down from my high, I feel a gushing between my legs.

He goes to the closet, pulling a soft green blanket off the shelf and laying it over me. He sits next to me, taking the water and swallowing some himself before putting it back on the table.

"Better?"

"Yes," I say. "Thank you."

He smiles devilishly at me as he leaves me one more time, grabbing another pillow and placing it next to mine as he quietly urges me to lay down.

I fix the pillow under my head and lay on my side, facing away from him. It's easier to ignore the sensation of how soaked I am this way, with my legs relaxed but tight together. He slides down next to me, covering us both up and spooning me from behind.

"Sleep baby," he says softly.

"Mm-hmm," I moan in tired acceptance as he kisses my neck, his hand caressing my hair, then sliding over my arm, massaging my shoulder. I welcome rest, complying with his need to forget the outside world. In this cocoon it's just us, nothing else. I'm beyond content.

"Tell me what you said," I whisper lazily.

"When?"

"The last thing…Italian," I manage. I'm drifting in and out, the rhythm of his heartbeat lulling me into sleep.

He doesn't answer me right away and, for a moment, I think he's fallen asleep.

"I said don't give up on me, baby."

I'm drifting into dreams of him easily, unsure whether it's in my subconscious or in reality that I hear the last thing he whispers.

I don't want to lose you.

I wake up alone, naked and still covered with the blanket. The curtains in front of me are opened now, revealing that daylight is expiring.

What the hell time is it?

"Hey you." I feel the bed dip as Aidan climbs on, snuggling up behind me.

"Hey yourself," I say. "What time is it?"

"Close to eight," he says.

"Holy shit! Eight at night?" I can't believe I've slept that long. It couldn't have been past two in the afternoon when we got here. "I need to get up."

"Take your time. There's no hurry." My urgency eases as he rubs my naked back.

"Do you ever sleep?" I ask, still lazing on my side staring out the window to the encroaching darkness.

"I did," he says, "for a couple hours." I turn to him for a minute, assessing. He still looks tired.

"I need to get up," I insist. "I should get in touch with Charlie. And the dog. Oh, shit."

"Relax," he says, rolling me over to look at him. "I've taken care of it."

"What did you do? I can't…you can't keep taking over like this. It's my responsibility."

"Babe," he interrupts. "I called Charlie already. He knows we're fine. He let Byron in the house to pick up Huck. He's tied up on the porch."

Apparently – and as usual – he's way ahead of me.

"I've got dinner about ready. You wanna grab a shower?"

"You cooked?" I don't hide my disbelief.

"Umm, no," he laughs, "but I did light the grill. And Byron delivered us anything else we'd need for the night."

I sigh in relief, giving in to being taken care of. I'm too wiped out to fight it.

"I guess I'll grab a shower then. Did he happen to bring any clothes for me?"

"Yes. In the closet," he says. "He packed a bag for you. Come out to the kitchen when you're ready." He kisses me tenderly, until his hands start to roam over me, pushing back the blanket. His tongue takes over my mouth and he nips at my bottom lip.

"Oh, hell no," I say in protest. "Down, boy. I need a shower, and I'm starving."

"Mmm," he responds, kissing my neck, and I'm tingling from where his lips leave off, a buzz thrumming all the way to the tips of my extremities. "You taste fine to me," he says, "and I'm hungry, too."

"Aidan, no… wait…"

He removes his shirt, kneeling next to me in his jeans.

Dammit. I can't resist the sight of him shirtless.

He tosses the blanket off me completely, leaving it on the other side of the bed. My nipples harden as I'm left chilled and he steals a chance to close his mouth onto one, then the other. He favors neither, going back and forth to tease me until I'm moaning in acceptance.

He gets off the bed, moving to stand next to it while facing me, the windows at his back.

"Turn around," he instructs. "Lay this way."

I do as he asks, staying on my back parallel to the footboard of the bed.

He grabs me behind the knees, spreading me wide and pulling me to the edge of the bed.

"Wait, I should get a shower first," I say, my breathing rushed. My ears are overcome with heat from a crazy combination of modesty and excitement.

"No, baby. This is how I want you. Be still."

I try to relax, but cover my face with my hands as he stands at the side of the bed between my legs.

"Not a chance," he says, leaning into me. Gently he removes my hands from my eyes. "Here, this is better." He places each of my hands on my breasts, then covers my hands with his own, encouraging me to play and explore beneath him. As I find my own rhythm and close my eyes, he lets go and climbs over me to reach for the pillows. He lays one beneath my head and tosses the other one to the floor.

"You look amazing. I could come just watching you." My eyes peek open, waiting for him to get his jeans off. When he doesn't, I move to sit up and do it for him but he eases me back, returning my hands to my chest. "No baby, this is all you. Lay back and relax."

I do as I'm told, knowing with him objecting will only prolong the inevitable.

"Take a deep breath," he says. "Close your eyes."

Again I do as I'm bid, settling back into arousal. Once he's satisfied with my resumed position, he disappears, kneeling on the floor. I'm expecting to feel his mouth on me next, but instead he rests his hands on my inner thighs, massaging me.

My legs relax involuntarily, falling away as a finger enters me, another gently working me. A moan leaves me and I feel my nipples extend to capacity, breasts full and taught as I grip them.

"*Bellissima,*" he says. "*Non vedo l'ora di assaggiarti.*"

Before I can ask him to repeat in English his mouth is on me, his tongue diving inside me, still working me with one hand. My breathing comes shorter and faster as he laps me up. He switches up his tactics to move his mouth north while his fingers are moving faster, driving hard.

"Yes," he murmurs into my right thigh, then bites me softly. "You're almost there. Let go."

He comes back with the same unyielding method and I'm coming violently, swearing to God and calling out his name. I feel something release I've never felt before, my insides soaking as my head goes fuzzy with stars.

I'm suddenly hypersensitive to his touch, wishing he would stop, the feeling too intense. Finally, he allows me relief as his mouth abandons me.

"Holy shit, baby," he says, rising up to lean into me. "I need to be inside you. Are you ready?"

I nod as he discards his jeans, again revealing a lack of underwear. I'm full on smiling, loving the sight, but not sure how I can handle him once more.

"I promise this will be quick," he reassures me.

He tugs behind my knees again, this time pulling me towards his erection. He grabs the pillow from the floor and places it under my hips. He speaks up when I give a questioning glance.

"Trust me."

He lays his hands on my hips, pulling me to meet him as he slides into me, gently at first. I'm soaking, numb from my release and ready for him to do as he pleases. He increases his pace, watching my reaction to every movement. This position is new to me, and I'm in disbelief at how good it feels this way.

He drives faster, his release imminent. I lean up, wrapping my legs around him as best I can, caressing his chest, thumbing over his nipples. I tease him with my tongue, then suck until he can't hold back.

"Alexis," he moans. "*Fuck.*"

He explodes deep inside me, several bursts one after another, until the pulsing stops and I collapse back on the bed. He's still standing as he leaves the depths of me, then falls on his back next to me. He says nothing, breathing hard.

"Shock and awe as always, Mr. Pierce." I laugh, unable to hide my shit eating grin.

"Did you know you could squirt?" he asks. I have no idea what he means.

"Umm, no?"

He laughs at my innocence. "So much for you to learn, baby," he says, rolling over to hover above me. "But, right now, let's get a shower. And I need to feed you."

"Great plan, Mr. Pierce."

Aidan showered quickly and left me to dress, insisting if he didn't he would have to have me again. When I exit the bedroom to head for the kitchen, I can smell something grilling. The appetizing scent pours in through an open window.

I'm thankful for Byron's thoughtfulness. Everything I needed – from underwear to clothing to a full-size toothbrush – was packed for me from the things I had at the loft. I'm in flip flops, capris and a teal tank top, searching out my dog and my Aidan.

I find them on the porch together, relaxing on an impressive wooden swing. Aidan has allowed the dog's head to rest in his lap while he is engrossed in his tablet. Huck barely looks up as I approach.

"Looks like you two are cozy."

He turns his attention to me. "You look beautiful in that color."

"You don't look too bad yourself."

He's in a fresh pair of jeans and one of his tight white t-shirts that pulls taut over his pecs and compliments his tan biceps. He pulls off the look better than any Hollywood celebrity, leaving me aroused just looking at him.

I'm also stirred with emotion seeing him comfortable with my dog.

"What can I do to help? I'm ravenous."

"It's all set," he says. "I just turned off the grill. Chicken and shrimp on skewers. Sound good?"

"Oh, hell yeah." He laughs at my enthusiasm. "Did Byron happen to bring any wine?"

"He did. Let's go in." He gestures to Huck. "You think he'll be all right out here?"

"We better bring him in. Without his fence, I don't trust him not to roam."

I head back through the porch door to the kitchen, the dog following. I rifle through the refrigerator, which is gigantic and vastly empty save the things Byron must have delivered for us. I find the wine and a salad that looks almost too beautiful to eat along with a bottle of vinaigrette.

Aidan comes in with a foil covered plate. "There's pasta in the warming drawer. In the oven," he says.

I search for a potholder and pull the pasta dish out as he gets out plates and silverware. I'm reminded of the moment in my kitchen when he kissed me for the first time, and I can't help but break out in a full grin. It was just shy of a week ago, but so much has transpired since that moment.

"Penny for your thoughts," he says.

"A penny?" I tease. "Please. You can afford more than that."

He laughs in genuine amusement. "Depends on what I'm paying for," he fires back.

"I was just recalling when we put dinner together in my kitchen."

"Ah. You mean when I kissed you for the first time?"

My cheeks flush as I nod.

"You're right," he says. "That is worth far more than a penny."

He comes over to where I stand at the kitchen island which is twice the size of mine. It seats eight comfortably. He kisses me gently, teasingly, a hand at the back of my neck.

"That kiss was," he begins, "no," he corrects, looking at the ceiling, then retraining his gaze on me. "That kiss *is,* and forever will be, the most unforgettable I've ever experienced."

"*Meh,*" I shrug. "It was okay."

"Okay?" he says, feigning argument. "Just *okay*?"

"I mean it was good and all. But it wasn't like a ten or anything."

"I call bullshit." He pulls me to him, a hand on my cheek, tugging my hair just as he did that night. He takes over my lips with the same greed and I'm left just as breathless, just as wowed as I'd been the first time.

"Well?" he asks quietly, his head resting on mine.

"Okay," I manage, "that was pretty good."

My legs feel like they're made of liquid.

"Yeah," he says. "Pretty good, my ass."

"I'm so hungry, I can't even think about your ass right now. Unless that's on the menu." I grab his backside, pulling him closer.

"You should stop now," he says, "unless you plan on eating cold food."

5

Alexis

We're huddled on the porch swing together at ten o'clock. My legs are outstretched at my side as Aidan pushes us, his feet dragging on the plank floor. There's only darkness in the distance and the porch is dim, lit with only soft lights from above. The stars are prominent in the night sky and it's cooled back to the low seventies.

Huck had a brief trot to the yard to do his nightly business and is sound asleep on the floor nearby.

"I can't believe how calm he is," I comment. "Usually he'd be more alert in new surroundings."

"Byron might have had something to do with that."

"Really?" I say with skepticism. "How so?"

"He walked Huck a few miles before they came out here. Worked with him a little bit."

"Trying to train him?"

He nods.

"I can't believe the two of them," I say smiling. "Have you seen them together?"

"I've not," he says, "until tonight when he dropped him off. Byron is amazing with animals."

"And gardening. And being your go-to for everything. How'd you ever find him?"

"I could tell you but I'd have to kill you."

"Very funny," I spout. "Does that mean he's part of your past?"

"In a way."

"You're not sharing," I say. "You know everything about me, Aidan. When is it your turn?"

"I don't know everything about you. I know it's unfair that I knew some things before I met you, but I'm not used to discussing my private life with anyone. Not in depth anyway."

"I'm not either. But I am willing to go there for you." His eyes show remorse and he pulls me in tighter, his right arm wrapping me up. I can tell he doesn't want to displease me, but he's not ready to show his cards either. "I don't want to force anything out of you, but I'd be dishonest if I said my curiosity wasn't growing by the minute."

"I have to go to New York tomorrow," he starts. "I'm leaving early. We have the rest of tonight together, and then I'll be in the city until Tuesday. I don't want to broach this subject with such little time to have you hear me out."

"What's in New York?"

"My lawyer, for one. If we're expecting Myers to accept tomorrow, I need to meet with Bill Hoffman. And I have other business with him."

I'm not sure if I should, but I ask anyway.

"About John Ireland?"

He nods. "There are other things I need to do for the gala too. And fires to put out about the Center. Remember I told you Richardson had a conflict?"

"Yes." I'm so glad he's no longer in the picture. I didn't have a good feeling about him at our first meeting at the Sheridan, and he'd been no help at all.

"His brother is a real estate agent downstate. His office is near one of Renewable Energy's affiliates." He knows he has my full attention as he goes on. "R.E.E. promised Richardson's brother the listings for the lots, the ones for the housing tract they intended to build."

"Holy shit. All of them?"

He nods.

"It would have been their land to list as they desired though. So I guess that's not unheard of." I consider the fact a minute. "But on vacant lots, those commissions wouldn't have amounted to much."

"It wasn't for the bare land before any builds. The listings he was guaranteed were for single family residential homes, once houses were built. We're talking thirty properties at three hundred thousand a piece."

"That means..." I trail off.

"It means Richardson's brother is out a good amount of money if he's losing those listings. And he isn't affiliated with any umbrella agency. He's a private broker."

"So any commissions would have gone directly to him," I conclude. "At least half of each transaction, depending on whether a buyer had their own agent." I'm thankful for the courses I took when I got my real estate license, back when I wasn't sure I would finish law school and follow my father's path. Selling real estate had been my fallback plan, but it has proven useful in my practice and to make connections in the community.

"We're talking hundreds of thousands, even if he wasn't the only broker on all the homes."

"My God. What is he doing about it? Do you think Richardson was going to leak information to his brother?"

"It's possible, but he was never privy to anything that wasn't already public knowledge. His brother may not even be an issue, but that's just it. I don't know for certain. I have an eye on it, but the bigger concern is R.E.E. They're going to go after that land somehow. And with Whitmore confronting you today..." He doesn't finish the thought.

"I'm not concerned about them offering more and you shouldn't be either. I'd never let Myers sell to them or to any affiliate of theirs. And I know him. He wouldn't want to."

"Money can change things, Alexis. Especially the kind of money they'd add to the pot to secure the land. It can change people."

"Not Myers."

"I'm inclined to agree with you, but I have to stay a step ahead of them, of what they intend to do to keep themselves in the game. If it isn't through Myers, they may go through me, stop me through some other channel. Or…"

He hesitates. I can tell he's withholding.

"Or what?"

"Or through you."

"I don't know, Aidan. I doubt that."

"You promised to trust me," he says, sitting up. His posture has changed. He's rigid and governing. "I'm reminding you now of the agreement we made at the loft. If I uncover anything dangerous, I'm removing you from all of this."

"I can handle myself." I'm assertive, but inside my resolve is wavering. I can't imagine the lengths this company might go to but instinct tells me it's far-reaching, well beyond what is visible on the surface.

"Not the point." His tone is adamant. "My decisions on this subject will be law. Do you understand?"

I force myself not to gulp at his intensity. This topic is clearly his way or no way. As much as I want to fight him, I can't ignore the obvious fact that he's more experienced with this than I am. I nod in agreement.

"Good," he says, relaxing back onto the cushions of the swing. "Are you going to see Ben's family this weekend?"

Oh.

My heart sinks. I forgot that I was not completely honest with him about this.

"No. I was supposed to, but I already canceled. It was just too much this weekend."

"Let me take you. Next weekend."

"No, Aidan." I consider my words, not wanting to seem ungrateful. "It's nice of you to offer but I'm not ready for that. It would be too weird."

"I don't have to be with you to visit them. We can go up and stay at my family's place. Is Ben's family still on the St. Lawrence? Just over the border from New York?"

He knows where they live?

I should not be surprised, recalling his extensive 'research'.

"Yes, that's where they live."

"That's not far from our place at all. We'll go up and stay for the weekend. You can go and visit them while we're there."

I look at him with my head tilted, considering.

"Alone. You can go visit them alone."

"Okay," I resign. "I guess that would be all right."

"We can leave Friday night. We may need to stay out of the area anyway, if things blow up with R.E.E."

"How long have you had a place up there?"

"My parents have had our spot on the river for years, before Thad..." He stops, then starts again. "We used to vacation there when we were kids for a few weeks every summer, even through our college years. My dad would fly us from California to a private airport near the border, then we'd drive the rest of the way."

The Thousand Islands area is one of the most beautiful places I've ever been, though I haven't traveled far. The elite own homes up and down the St. Lawrence River, even if they use them as little as one week out of the summer. When I met Ben and started visiting his hometown, I often admired those places as we'd pass them by boat. The gorgeous homes often left me feeling sad though. Many sat empty for months or even years. It seemed such a waste that no one enjoyed them during our short season of good weather.

Knowing his family probably fit into this category of absentee owners, I withhold my opinion.

"I love it up there."

"I always did too."

"So your dad flies?' I ask. "That's so cool."

"He does. It's his biggest passion, after my mother."

"I didn't think you were back east much until you came to Yale."

"We'd be in Canada for those few weeks every summer, without fail. But no, we never came here. I think our place up there was a way for my mother to come back without having to revisit her past here in Lake County. She always loved the beauty of this area," he says, "but she just couldn't come here. It was a way to come home without coming home, if that makes sense."

I look up at him. I want to ask how it was for her when they lived here, ask what his family experienced to cause all the pain that comes out in his voice. Instead I just nod. "It makes complete sense. And you stopped going up there after you lost your brother?"

"Yeah." He looks at me with a solemn expression, then pulls me closer. "So you'll let Ben's family know?"

"I can text his sister tomorrow. I don't usually bring Huck with me when I travel up there. I'll have to talk to Charlie. Or maybe I'll kennel him."

"Charlie just got done being the beast's caretaker. Would you consider letting Byron take him?"

"I don't know, maybe. Do you think he would?"

"I think he'd love it."

"Okay," I resolve. "But don't think I've forgotten the topic we started on."

"I haven't." He rubs my back as he swings us gently back and forth. His tone is serious.

I look up at him. "When you're able to talk to me, you will. I know it's your past but I want you to feel you can talk to me about it. It's part of who you are. I want to know everything."

He closes his eyes, his head falling back in unrest.

"What is it?"

"I don't want to ruin our time together."

I can sense he dreads this topic.

"Are you afraid if you tell me about your past my opinion of you will change?"

"Perhaps."

"Well..." I pause.

What could be that bad?

Maybe I don't want to know after all.

"I can't promise you that, but I can tell you as of this moment I can't think of anything that would change what I'm feeling for you."

He isn't convinced. I can tell by the way he's shutting down.

"For God's sake when we arrived here, I was fuming with jealousy that you were with your ex-girlfriend. I'm still here now. And I slept with you." I look at him pointedly. "Twice."

He smiles in amusement before a concerned expression returns. "I'm sorry for how the thing with Stella played out. It wasn't my intention for you to be hurt." He looks into my eyes, deepening the severity of his words. "That's the last thing I wanted. The last thing I would ever want."

"I see that, but you have to realize holding back with me about anything is hurtful. You've trusted me from day one, Aidan. Don't stop now."

"I haven't," he says. "But I don't want to delve into it tonight. I just want to be with you, shut everything else out." He pulls my legs over into his lap, taking me into the now comfortable position wrapped up in his arms, his head resting over mine. "Being with you is intense enough, Alexis. It's such an escape for me," he whispers. He rubs my bare arm, leaving me wanting more of his touch.

If he's not ready, he's not ready.

We sit in silence for a while, rocking with a warm breeze blowing around us. I'm growing more tired by the minute. After a glass of wine and the day we've had, I'm beyond sleepy, even with a nap.

"We should probably get to bed. We're both exhausted," he says. I sigh in agreement. "I'll have to drop you off tomorrow on my way to the city, so we need to be out of here at six."

"Ugh," I groan.

I get off the swing and head in, calling Huck to join us. I feel funny having him in these plush surroundings, afraid he's going to break something or make a mess.

"What should I do with him? I don't want him to hurt anything."

"Will he sleep on the floor?"

"Probably not. I wish I had his kennel with me."

Aidan gestures to a couch in the living room. "How about there?" he asks. "It's leather, and it's covered up anyway. He won't hurt it."

I urge the dog to climb up and he does, turning around a few times before he collapses in fatigue. I love up his head and plant a smooch on him, following Aidan to the bedroom. Before we make it to the door, I can hear Huck snoring.

"I guess he's comfortable," I laugh.

"Good," he says. "I'm right behind him."

I brush my teeth as Aidan is busy making the bed with fresh linens. I love that he just does these things. Even with enough money to buy a small country, he never seems too full of himself to do something as simple as make a bed.

He joins me at the vanity, unpacking his travel bag. "Bed's all set."

"Good. I'm about to crash hard."

"Check my luggage in the closet," he says. "I got you something."

"What is it?"

"Something to wear. Go look," he grins. He bends down to rinse his mouth and I'm gone in a flash, wondering what he has decided to present me with now. I pull out a *Zora's Closet* bag from his small suitcase and find a silk negligee inside.

Of course.

I pull it out, thumbing over the spaghetti straps and eyeing the modestly cut v-neck. It's an elegant but simple slip style. The color is a jewel-toned purple, the bottom hem trimmed in black lace. I undress and throw it on, realizing it's very short, falling above mid-thigh. I have my back to the closet door as Aidan comes in behind me.

I can feel his eyes on my backside, which would be made visible if I lifted my arms. "Turn around." His tone is firm but laced with admiration.

I lift my hair and settle it back down around my shoulders as I turn to him.

"You look amazing. This," he says, tugging at the hem of his gift, "this is what you should be wearing to bed. If you wear anything."

I smile, flattered at his attention. He takes off his shirt and comes to me, and I pause to admire him. I trace my index finger down his sternum, pausing at his tattoo to trace the outline as I've done more than once.

"What does this mean?"

He reprimands me with a look. "Not tonight. We agreed," he says. "And you need to stop being so unaware of your looks. You are sinfully beautiful, baby. Don't you know that?"

"I've never been told that."

He shakes his head in disbelief. "Such a pity." He undresses the rest of himself then takes my hand. "Come to bed."

I follow quietly, half hoping he'll take me immediately, the other half hoping for true rest. He urges me to climb in first, then grabs his phone and selects some instrumental jazz to drift to us through the sound system. "Yes?" he asks.

"Perfect," I say, settling in.

He spoons me, completely naked, and I don't know how I'd resist if he wanted to take me again. But he doesn't, and soon I'm lying awake listening to him breathe peacefully in sleep.

I'm woken up by movement and realize Aidan is getting out of bed. There's no clock in here and I left my phone in the kitchen, so I have no idea what time it is. It's still dark out. I hear Aidan talk to the dog, asking if he wants to go out, and I smile to myself.

I should get up, though I could probably sleep a week straight if I had the chance.

I exit the bed and head for the kitchen. Aidan is coming in off the porch, Huck following on his leash. The dog leaves Aidan to come at me, giving me his usual enthusiastic morning hello by diving between my legs so I'll pet him.

"You're up early," I say. Aidan's wearing jogging pants and a t-shirt. His feet are still naked, but I spot socks and sneakers on a nearby chair.

"I thought I'd get a run in."

"What time is it?"

"Four-thirty."

My eyes go buggy and he laughs at my surprise.

"Do you always get up this early?"

"Before you, like clockwork. My schedule has been thrown off lately."

"Huh," I manage.

Maybe I am affecting him as much he's affecting me.

"Go back to bed if you want," he says. "Should I take Huck with me?"

"How far are you going?"

"Just down this side of the lake and back."

"I think that's almost eight miles."

"I haven't clocked it yet," he says, "but that's probably about right."

"He won't make it that far without tiring."

"Sorry, bud." He rubs Huck's head. "Looks like you're stuck here." He sits down to put on his footwear, and I stand in a daze considering whether I should just stay up. "Go back to bed, baby. I'll be back in an hour. Leave this on," he says, grinning as he tugs at the hem of my slip. "I'll wake you when I get back."

I nod as he gets up and kisses me sweetly, pulling me close. His hand slides down my back, the movement of the smooth fabric sparking shivers as the slip grazes over me.

"I'll be waiting." My words are more wistful than I intended. I wish he wasn't going.

He grabs his phone off the kitchen table and scrolls through the screen, then uses a strap to secure the phone to his arm. He puts one of the earbuds to my ear.

Springsteen. I break into a grin.

"Be back soon." He kisses me one more time and exits through the side door. I go to the window, watching him head down the long driveway at a fast walk, then picking up into a jog as he makes it to the road below, heading away from me.

Huck and I go back to our respective resting spots. I lay awake for fifteen minutes, thinking about Aidan, thinking about everything. I can't imagine what he's so afraid to discuss with me. I hope before long I can find out.

I *need* to find out.

He must know he can trust me. Why would he think anything would change between us if I learn more about him?

An idea comes to me in a sleepless 'a-ha' moment.

I can prove to him exactly how much he can trust me. I can't believe I didn't think of it sooner. I retrieve my phone from the kitchen and head back to bed. Huck is snoring, ignoring me as I pass by him.

I pull up a web browser and search through some case law, then make some notes in the app on my phone. I'll have to wait until I get to the office later to put my plan into action. I need my computer for that, but I'll have plenty of time after I meet with Myers and while Aidan is away.

I lay back in the comfortable bed, satisfied that I've finally thought of a way to get through to him. This has to work. I can't see any other way or consider for a minute the alternative of walking away from him.

I wake up to the sound of the shower running. Aidan slips into bed beside me. He's naked, warm, and sweaty.

"Time to get up."

"What time is it now?"

"Quarter after five."

I groan. "I think I just fell back to sleep. I thought you said you'd be gone an hour?"

"I would have been, but I got three miles in and couldn't get you out of my head. So I turned back."

I'm lying flat on my stomach, arms over my head. He throws the covers off, then straddles my back, bracing himself with knees on either side of my hips.

"Have I told you how beautiful you are in this?" His hands slide over the fabric. I can feel my chest tighten, my nipples harden into the mattress. He strokes my hair then massages my shoulders, pulling a moan from me.

"That feels wonderful. Please don't stop."

"I'd do this to you all day, but we have to get up. Come," he says. He lifts the fabric enough to reveal my ass, then smacks both cheeks, one after the other.

I yelp in objection, then flip over underneath him. He's hard and I take hold of him, stroking gently as I watch him. His breath catches, head lolling back, but in an instant he regains himself with his learned restraint.

"No you don't, my little siren," he says. "We don't have time. Let's hit the showers."

He gets off me, and I follow him into the bathroom.

The room is filled with steam, the mirrors and glass doors fogged up. He waits for me to reach him, then toys with the straps of the negligee. "*Bellissima*," he says. He puts his fingers beneath the straps and lifts upward, taking the slip off over my head and placing it on a hook outside the shower.

I don't wait for him to seduce me.

I grab behind his neck, kissing him, edging backwards. I pull him into the shower and turn him to the bench against the back wall, urging him to sit. I turn around, facing the opposite wall to leave my backside open to him. He's caressing me, only stopping to find soap somewhere within his reach.

He lathers my shoulders, then glides down my back to my hips. I lean forward a bit, and he slips his fingers into me, causing me to lose my breath.

"Yes," I mutter. "*More.*"

"Hold on baby, I want to try something." I'm not sure what he has in mind, but if it feels anything like this…

He slides fingers in and out, the rhythm becoming almost too much. His opposite hand is gliding over my behind. As he bites at my left cheek, I feel something foreign enter *there*, in previously virgin territory.

My mind is reeling. It feels so different and my brain won't ease. I've never felt so full.

"Stop thinking, Alexis," he commands. "It will feel good if you relax."

I nod, then breathe deeply to force myself to obey. He's working my front now while my backside is still full but relaxing around what I think is his little finger.

"That's my girl," he says. He begins to work me harder, and then all his fingers are working their magic. I am dangling on the edge of what I know will be a relentless orgasm when he removes everything, leaving me empty and aching. I moan in protest.

"Not yet, baby. Sit down," he commands. I do as I'm told, settling onto him with my back to him, my clit rubbing against the base of him as he fills me up.

"You're so tight," he says. "Move up and down. Slowly."

He reaches around, cupping my breasts, fondling them as he pleases. Again I comply, rising and falling in a gentle rhythm.

He groans, louder than I've ever heard him. He's close.

"Yes," he moans. "Come with me, baby." I'm not sure I can, until his right hand moves down past my navel, circling my clit with his usual skill and leaving me begging him not to stop.

He complies with my pleading, silent except for another loud groan as he fills me up. My climax arrives on the heels of his and shudders through me so powerfully that I almost lose my balance.

He steadies me, and I feel like my body temperature is a thousand degrees between the steam around us and the heat we've built between us. He leans forward into me, kissing my back, then massaging my inner thighs.

Desire has evaporated, replaced with a crazy heightened sensitivity to touch – so much that I can't stand it.

"Stop!" I holler. "I can't take it."

"Baby's ticklish, mmm?" He doesn't let up.

"Aidan *stop*."

He laughs, finally releasing me, and I rise off of him to duck into the jets and hose off. He joins me in the spray, grabbing for the shampoo. "Let me," he says.

I turn around, letting him massage and lather my head as it falls back in relaxation. I could stand here and feel this for hours.

"Time to get moving. For real this time." He says it as though I'm to blame for any delay, which is mostly true. He turns my back to the water and I let the shampoo spill off to wash down the drain. "Did you like that?"

I give him a quizzical look. I'm not sure whether he's talking about washing my head or…

"What I did to you," he says. "Did you like it?"

I nod, suddenly feeling embarrassed. I'm not sure I'll ever get over my modesty, as much as I know he wants me to. "It was interesting."

"Good interesting?" He's washing his face, his head, lathering his body.

His *fucking amazing* body. I'm staring at him without any shame whatsoever. His eyes are closed as he rinses and I find courage knowing he can't see me.

"Good interesting," I repeat. "I've never had that done to me before."

He scrubs his hand over his face, letting a spray of water rinse him off. He looks at me intently.

"You're very open to new things," he says, moving towards me. "I like that."

"I think it's you," I say. "You keep me open. I've never been this way before." I gaze up at him, held fast in his solid arms, enraptured by the man that stands in front of me.

"Miss Conservative is only open with me, hmm? I like that even more."

I shrug. "I suppose I could try it with someone else, if you wanted me to be sure." I'm teasing him, but he looks at me sternly.

"That's one thing you should know about me, Alexis. I do not share. If you're mine, there will be no 'someone else'."

I'm floored, only seeing this curt side of him in the context of serious business or when his temper takes over. Something about it makes me feel possessed. Against my usual controlling nature, I like it.

"Do you want me to be?"

His eyes don't leave mine. "Do I want you to be what?"

"Yours," I ask, willing myself not to flinch as I wait for his answer.

He pulls me tighter, kissing me eagerly, his tongue twisting with mine, nipping at my lips and neck before he comes back to rest his forehead on mine, closing his eyes as the water cascades over us.

"Yes," he breathes. "More than anything."

Aidan exits the shower before me to dress. He's gone when I get to the closet. The one suit that was here is also gone, along with the rest of his belongings.

I'm on some sort of happiness high as I get ready to leave the lake house. Thinking about what Aidan's said to me and how he's physically affected me, I feel like I'm floating as I dress and pack my bag.

I'm also eager to get to the office to secure the deal with Myers and to put my own plan into action.

I pull on a pair of dark jean capris that Byron packed and a snug button down blouse in the same purple color as the negligee. I pull out the belt and sandals that were packed to complement them, admiring the overall look. Just fine for a casual Friday at the office. The look Aidan gives me when I reach the foyer tells me it must be flattering.

He lets out a long, low whistle.

"You approve?"

"Yes," he says. "Definitely."

I'm admiring him while he looks me over. His suit is similar to the one he wore the first time we met – dark grey and freshly pressed, white shirt slightly open to bare his neck. He looks like he stepped out of a magazine.

I go to the front porch to untie Huck and put him on a lead to keep from brushing into Aidan. I wonder how we'll get the dog home in the Corvette, but as I move around the porch to the side entrance I see Aidan stowing the pretty car in the garage.

"No Corvette today?" It's five of six and I know he wouldn't tolerate being late. "What year is that anyway?"

"Byron's just arriving. And that car is my other baby," he comments with a grin. "She's a '67 Stingray. I'd drive her every day if I could but it's not the most practical mode of transportation. Besides, we need the SUV for Huck." He drops our bags on the porch and grabs his phone off the table in the entry, scrolling through it as we wait. Byron pulls up a moment later and Huck darts down the steps, barking and nearly dragging me along with him as he pulls the lead out of my hand.

The SUV is similar to the one Ivan drove me around in while I was in Arizona — a black Cadillac — though the model year is older. Huck is outside the driver door panting excitedly and wagging his tail. Byron steps out and gives Huck a hand signal, and the dog sits obediently. He reaches for the lead, smiling as he rubs the dog's head in approval.

"Good morning, Byron."

"Good morning, Ms. Greene. Sir," he says in Aidan's direction, "are you ready?"

"Yes, just these few things here," Aidan indicates our pile of belongings, "and the pooch, of course."

"Yes, sir." He opens the back of the SUV, points, and Huck jumps in. I'm floored, looking at Aidan in disbelief.

"Did you see that?"

"I told you." He smiles as he pockets his phone and locks the door to the house.

"I think I've been replaced," I joke.

"No one could replace you, baby." He plants a kiss on my hand and weaves his fingers with mine. He leads me down the steps, gesturing for me to get in the car first. I recall the way he'd been with Stella in the news clip, when he'd guarded her from the press.

I send the thought away.

He doesn't want her. He wants me.

Byron loads our things into the front seat and climbs in to drive us away.

"Another place I'd like to get back to," I comment. "I didn't make it past the first floor."

"You will," he promises with a smile. "In the meantime, we definitely won't forget it."

6

Aidan

On the plane ride to Manhattan I'm on edge knowing nothing will calm me until I follow the leads I have on the Irelands and get the gala details out of the way. This would have been so much easier if I hadn't met Alexis. I hadn't planned on her coming into the mix, upending my entire existence.

I regret the thought as soon as I have it.

The path may be easier without her, but I don't want it any other way. It doesn't matter that my life is more intense, that everything about her leaves me feeling an urgency I can't explain.

She made everything better, made me want to settle everything in California so I could focus on the here and now.

Byron looks up from his tablet. "The meeting with Miss Strauss is set. Tomorrow night before her set begins she can give you fifteen minutes."

"Great." I'd been lucky to get a meeting with the up-and-coming singer given her increasingly busy tour schedule. I hope to convince her to play at the gala since she'll be back in Manhattan for a show that same week. "Tell her I look forward to it."

"Bill Hoffman is ready to meet with you as soon as we land."

"Push him back to the afternoon."

I need to get settled at the hotel and follow up on the Irelands.

A conversation with Dimitri is my higher priority. He'd sent me a text last night that he was sifting through the list of names from Armstrong's cell in a last attempt to connect John Ireland to drug dealings.

By nine a.m., I'm checked into my usual suite at The Soho Grand. I had to wake Dimitri at dawn Pacific time, but I couldn't wait any longer.

Unfortunately, his research yielded nothing.

"There's nothing here so far. But I'm not done. I need a few more hours."

"Has every name been a dead end?"

"Most were. A few contacts were relatives – a sister in Oregon, an uncle in San Francisco. But there is one name I'm tracking. He's a known dealer on the streets, but he's a careful one. He doesn't partake in what he sells. It's going to take major digging to trace him to Ireland, if there's anything there at all."

"You might be right about switching tactics then," I say in resignation. "But I still say if we abandon the fishing expedition through Armstrong, the best idea is to go after Ireland himself."

"We talked about this. That's got to be a last resort."

"I can give you a few hours but after that we're at the last resort. If Stella gets out or decides she's fed up with being there, I need a plan ready to put into action."

"Let me exhaust this lead first. If we can connect the dots this way, there's far less risk for us both."

"Make it happen." I say. "I'll be in touch."

Byron is in a room one floor down, and I buzz him with the house phone.

"Sir?" he answers.

"Is Hoffman okay with one o'clock? I don't have the contracts yet, anyway."

"He tells me that's fine."

"Thanks, Byron." We disconnect.

I'm sure Alexis will come through soon with the signed contracts, but there's no rush. I have plenty to do in the meantime. I pull up Alanna's cell number and call to give her an update on her daughter.

"Good morning," she answers.

"How are you, Alanna?"

"Glad to be settled back in New York."

"Me too," I say. "Just got back from L.A. yesterday. And I'm in town, actually."

"That's wonderful," she says. "We should catch up. I'd love to hear how it went with Stella."

"I was thinking dinner?"

It's probably better I deliver this news in person.

"What time?"

"Let's say seven."

"That works. You prefer somewhere discreet, right?"

"Yes," I say. "That's best."

"Where are you staying?"

"Soho."

"I know the perfect place. I'll text you the address."

"Great. See you at seven."

I hang up and prepare myself for my meeting with Attorney Hoffman about Myers' sale, hopeful that will be one thing I can count on going right today.

At one in the afternoon, I'm in Bill Hoffman's office listening to him read me the riot act about conversing with Eli Myers's attorney without his knowledge. He has no idea that Alexis and I are romantically involved, and I intentionally omit that detail.

"Ms. Greene is going to be on our team, and I need you to get behind that."

"She represents the seller, Pierce. That's a line you shouldn't be crossing."

"You know I understand how this works, Bill. I can tell you with certainty that this situation is different. I've done my due diligence when it comes to her. She's not a threat. If anything, she's going to be an asset."

"You better hope you're right."

"Myers has accepted the contracts." Alexis and I conversed throughout the morning via email, and the contracts were signed by Myers as promised. She'd emailed them directly to Bill as instructed.

She'd also driven me into a state of dread.

First she'd awakened my libido, then proposed that she had something important to discuss that couldn't wait until I got back in four days' time. She avoided me for a solid hour while I'd tried to get out of her what the fuck she was talking about.

I'd been close to rescheduling my entire weekend just so I could fly back to Stanton to get her attention. Thankfully, we'd resolved things before I had to do exactly that.

"Can we move on with logistics now, Bill? This is a done deal. Eli Myers is selling to me, and R.E.E. is that much further out of the picture."

"I'm not so sure about that."

"You have new information?"

"Nothing confirmed, but there's talk of them making another offer."

"He won't accept it."

"Money talks. You know this better than all of my clients put together."

"Doesn't matter. My uncle is not interested in the money."

"So you've said." He's sitting in his chair, leaning back and pondering my certainty.

"Does the company have any other leads on how to get around Myers and acquire the land some other way?"

"Not as of now. But there are rumblings that R.E.E.'s reaching out to your nemesis to beat you at your own game, kid."

"Then we need to proceed immediately. The sooner we get the approvals, the sooner we can get the Center up and going, and it'll be too late for R.E.E."

"I'll need some time. I'm not well versed in the procedures up there. I do have an acquaintance that practices law in Lake County, but…"

I cut him off. "Ms. Greene will be handling that with Samira's help. And yours, of course."

He looks at me, not hiding his disapproval. "That's ill advised."

"Be that as it may, that's how it will happen." My tone is firm enough. He knows I won't be deterred. "You can review her work if you deem it necessary but she will run point there."

"I don't know what your reasons are for ignoring my advice, but they had better be good ones. I'm going on the record that I've advised strictly against this."

"Do what you need to, Bill. Make notes in your files. Ask me to sign something in blood. I don't fucking care. Now can we go forward with the details? We have other business."

"What kind of curveball are you throwing me now?"

"I need to review my agreement with Ireland. And I want him off the board for the Center."

He regards me with concern. "He's a thorn in your side again?"

"You could say that."

"That agreement is iron clad. There's no way you're getting out of it. Not unless one of you is dead."

"What if one of us is incarcerated?"

"You plan on being brought up on charges for something? I thought those days were behind you."

"Not me," I assert. "Him."

"You're going to be the death of me, Pierce." He shakes his head and gets up from his desk, heading for his disguised liquor cabinet. "Maybe you ought to be the one to take note," he says as he pours himself a brandy. "My hourly rate just doubled."

Not surprisingly, Alanna has chosen an Italian spot for dinner. I'm glad I didn't have to venture far to meet her. A ten-minute walk leads me to the doors of the restaurant where a chalkboard sign boasts a wine bar inside and garden-patio seating out back. A full menu is available until two in the morning.

Though the place is busy and square footage is minimal, the restaurant is not overcrowded. I can feel the eyes of a few people noting my entrance. Most of the patrons are absorbed in themselves though, not caring that I've stepped foot in here. I scan the room but don't see Alanna. I'm ten minutes early. I order a whiskey, taking the only open stool between two other drinkers.

When Alanna Rossi comes through the door, she turns more heads than I did. She's dressed casually in jeans and a white sleeveless blouse. Her low heels don't add much height to her small frame. Her dark hair surrounds her bare shoulders which are as freckled from sun as her cheeks.

She looks the part of a young Sophia Loren, more beautiful than her own daughter. Only upon closer inspection could you see her laugh lines or any indication that she was fifty-something.

She kisses both of my cheeks in silent greeting and I order her a glass of Merlot.

"Let's sit in the garden." She leans in and lowers her voice to a whisper. "More privacy out there." She turns her attention to the bartender. "May we take a table out back, Nick?" He regards her with a smile that tells me they're well acquainted.

"Of course. We'll keep it closed off for you for the hour, Mrs. Ireland." He passes her the glass of wine.

"Ah, Nick," she says, patting him on the forearm with a laugh. "You know it's Mrs. Rossi now."

"Yes, much to my dismay," he teases. He picks up her hand and gives it a quick kiss.

Nick is in his twenties at best. I'm sure his tastes are for far younger women, but I can appreciate how he charms her. Every male did. She was the source of Stella's outer beauty but she possessed a charismatic aura; a poise and wit that Stella never had the privilege of knowing or mimicking.

I follow her to the patio, admiring the garden and the quaint setting. There are candles glowing prominently on the tables as the evening settles in. Exposed brick walls are crowned with wooden lattice work painted black and adorned with climbing ivy. The atmosphere immediately reminds me of Italy.

"Isn't this place something?" she says, noting my admiration. "The food is wonderful, too."

We sit at one of the small bistro tables for two. I'm about to share some unsettling information, and there seems to be no good way to go about it. I'm suddenly at a loss for words, unsure how to go forward.

"What is it?" Alanna takes a sip of her wine, then holds the stem between her fingers as she relaxes and waits for me to respond. "You look pained. As though…" she pauses. "*Avere un piede nella fossa.*"

Like I have one foot in the grave.

I smile at her. If I went through with crossing her ex-husband, she was likely right.

"*Mi dispiace, Alanna.*" I apologize. "*Non voglio farti preoccupare.*"

I don't want to worry you.

"Is Stella safe?"

"For now," I say.

"Are you safe?"

"I don't know yet."

"You need to get your father involved. He'd never allow John to hurt you."

"Absolutely not," I assert. "You will tell him nothing of this." Dad may know John Ireland has a reputation, but I'm doubtful he has any idea what a bastard he truly is. If I had my way, he'd never know how mixed up with him I've been.

She sets down her glass and reaches for my hand. "Will you ever stop trying to carry the weight of the world on your shoulders, Aidan?" She never ceased to tell me I took on too much. "*Mettere troppa carne al fuoco.*"

Too many irons in the fire.

"I know, Alanna. But things are changing for me. I need John and Stella out of my life."

She looks at me in surprise, then with a scolding expression. "What's going on? If we're to discuss this you must explain everything, darling. I cannot advise you properly if I do not have all of the facts."

I reveal to her what I know, adding my suspicions about Stella's recent missteps being the result of John's illegal flow of income in California.

"I'm sure you're not surprised, Aidan. This is typical John."

"You knew about this?"

"No, of course not. But I always had my suspicions when we lived here in New York. He's never been an honest man and his actions have always been for himself."

"Did you ever have proof of anything illegal?"

"No. I purposefully removed myself from his business dealings – illegal or otherwise. I went to school, made my own way. Beat him at his own game. Except…" She pauses, lost in thought. When she speaks again she is quiet, her regret obvious. "Except when it came to Stella."

Alanna was no slouch in her field. She'd guided me through some hazardous turns in the market, always having the intuition on when to go all in and when to hold back. The investments she oversaw for me were my most profitable.

Yet, she had to give up Stella in order to get away from John. He took off for California when Stella was just six. I knew even to this day, Alanna regretted letting her former husband have his way.

"I warned you about him," she says. "That's all the help I could ever offer."

"I know. I should have heeded your advice. But I have my methods and with this information it's possible I can take him down permanently. I just have to keep Stella out of the fray if I can."

"I'd appreciate it if you could. But if she proves to be a lost cause, then you must find your own happiness. Don't let her hold you back."

"I'm not worried about that. Honestly, I'm just relieved you aren't upset with me."

"How could I ever be? You have done nothing but help her. You've done so much for my daughter where I failed her."

"You did not fail her, Alanna." My voice is stern as I look her in the eye. "He did."

She sets her glass down and fidgets with her blouse. A waitress emerges from inside the restaurant to take our order.

At the sight of the young woman with pen poised, Alanna perks up, her charming demeanor prevalent once more. "May I?" she asks, wanting to order for us both. "The eggplant here is simply heavenly."

"Please," I offer. She relays our order as the waitress jots it down. When she leaves, Alanna takes the opportunity to change the subject.

"So, what's it like up there in Lake County? You must find something about it appealing if you're willing to cut ties with John and still pursue the

Center, still ride things out there."

Pride swells thinking about what I've already established in Stanton and the project that lies ahead. My thoughts involuntarily shift to Alexis. Knowing she'll be at my side for the foreseeable future brings a grin I'm unable to stop.

"Aidan?" She pulls out a skinny cigarette from her small purse and lights it.

"Sorry," I say, composing myself. "I truly love it there. It's peaceful."

She lets a puff escape her mouth in an elegant ring. "Who is she?"

I give her an incredulous stare.

"You're not fooling me. What's her name?"

I blow out a breath. "No one knows about her, Alanna. Not Stella. Not John. Not even my parents. For her own safety, it needs to stay that way."

Accented with her French manicure, her index finger crosses in an 'x' over her bosom. "Cross my heart, I'll say nothing."

"Alexis," I say. I let go another involuntary smile just saying her name.

I fucking miss her.

"She's beautiful, yes?"

"Stunning."

"Smart?"

"Very. She's an attorney."

"Ah," she says, with a graceful laugh. "Well, none of us are perfect."

I smile at her humor. "She also drives me completely mad with her strong will."

"She sounds perfect for you, darling." She smiles, taking another puff, another sip of wine. "You wouldn't be happy with someone that didn't challenge you."

I sip from my glass, letting the burn settle through me. I'm realizing how it affects me just to talk about Alexis. I hadn't had an opportunity or a reason to discuss her with anyone. This conversation tells me more about how I feel than any prior self-evaluation.

Alanna was right. Alexis challenged me in a positive way.

Stella had never done that.

In fact, no one had.

Not since my brother died.

"I'm so happy for you, honey. You deserve this. Will I get to meet her?"

"I'm not sure how that might go," I say. "She isn't exactly Stella's biggest fan."

"We have that in common lately." The waitress brings us some bread and oil, then leaves us again. Alanna puts out her cigarette as I break the bread. "You'll know if the time is right. You should at least introduce her to your parents."

"I likely will, soon. They're just returning from Europe. In the meantime, I can't have John or Stella knowing anything about her."

"Stay out of the media, Aidan. That is key. There's far less concern for that Upstate than here in Manhattan."

"I know."

"She's not here in town with you?"

"No."

"Good. It's safer that way. If you want to introduce us, it can wait until John is out of the picture. I'll come up there."

"That's probably best."

"But I will meet the creature that's finally reeled you in," she emphasizes.

I dodge her gaze. *Had Alexis done that?* It certainly felt like it in this moment.

"You do realize how much this young woman is affecting you?"

Another easy grin comes over me. "I suppose maybe I do."

"Cheers," she says, raising her glass. "*Quando l'amore non è follia, non è amore.*"

When love is not madness, it is not love.

My smile is still firmly in place as I lift my glass.

"Madness, indeed."

7

Alexis

At ten Friday morning, I'm still on a high from my time with Aidan though we'd parted ways hours ago when he left for Manhattan.

I'm sitting in my conference room with Eli Myers, each of us browsing the last page of the contract Aidan has proposed. We've gone through every detail over the last half hour, and Eli objects to nothing in it. This has been the easiest negotiation I've ever been through with him.

I try to keep my relief to myself, but on the inside it bubbles over. Aidan is getting what he wants and helping our community. Myers is getting what he wants.

And Renewable Energy can take a fucking hike.

"Thanks so much, Alexis. You've been so great this last year. I know this was out of the blue for you but it's the right thing."

"I have no doubts about that, Mr. Myers." I smile at him as he signs the last contract and pushes it back to me across the table.

"Are things goin' well for ya? Mr. Young said you had a family emergency out west."

The way he calls Charlie 'Mr. Young' is somehow endearing.

"I did, yes. My sister's husband had an accident while hiking in Arizona. But he's okay."

I think.

I remind myself I need to text Jill today. She's probably keeping quiet to save me from hearing about our mother's visit.

"Well, that's good," he says, tapping the table with his pen. "You sure look happy. Somethin' seems different about you."

I blush. We never get personal unless it's to talk about my dad.

"Thank you. I am happy. And I'm happy for you, Mr. Myers. Is there anything else we need to discuss? It's my understanding there were some developments with your original buyer. Perhaps you'd like to talk about that?"

"Nah. I know what you mean. But it's water under the bridge. What's right is right, and this deal with Mr. Pierce is what's right. I know it. And I know you would never have steered me wrong if you knew about R.E.E."

I nod, again resenting such a close call. But I know better now and go on to warn him.

"Please let me know if they contact you. It's my understanding their company is not happy about your decision, and I don't want to see you swayed by intimidation. If you ever feel pressure from them, of any kind, you call me. Okay?"

He nods in agreement. "I sure will."

"Thank you, Mr. Myers," I smile, rising to shake his hand. "I'll get this off to Mr. Pierce's attorney right away."

He gets up from his chair. "Your dad's smilin' down on you, my dear. Don't give Renewable Energy another thought. You're doing just fine."

I fight back tears at his compliment.

I wish Dad was here.

"That means more to me than you could ever know."

Once Eli Myers leaves, I fill Charlie in on how the meeting went and head for my office to scan the contract and send it to Aidan.

I want to say so much but I leave the email professional, unsure who he'll need to share it with.

To: Aidan M. Pierce, President PPG
From: Alexis M. Greene, Esq.
Re: Myers Real Estate Sale to PPG
Good morning,
I met with Mr. Myers. He has accepted your contract terms and made no changes. The contract is in final form.
Would you like me to send it to your attorney?
Best regards,
Alexis
Greene Law Office | Alexis M. Greene, Esq.

It takes only moments for his response. I'm sure he landed in New York hours ago. The flight is under an hour, and we parted ways before seven a.m.

To: Alexis M. Greene, Esq.
From: Aidan M. Pierce, President PPG
Re: Myers Sale to PPG & Fundraiser Gala & This Morning
Hello beautiful,
Please forward a copy to me and one to my attorney under separate email at your earliest convenience. His email address should be in the contract.
Please also meet with Jade McCall to discuss finalizing plans for the Gala. Samira needs details for the website and other media outlets right away (yes, I realize it was my fault you had to cancel yesterday). Let's get this back on course.
I am meeting with a few prospects for the program today and tomorrow. We will decide on all details by Sunday so everything can be set into motion Monday. I will keep you informed.
Surprised at the sign off in your email. 'Best regards'? Is that all I am to you, a professional colleague? It certainly didn't seem so in the shower this morning. Can't wait to get back to you,
A-
Aidan M. Pierce, (Very Distracted) President
Pierce Philanthropy Group

I can't believe what I'm seeing on the screen as my cursor blinkety-blinks at the end of his email. I'm floating on air again at his greeting, at his sign off. The way he refers to us as 'we'.

Then there's the fact that he referenced this morning's shower.

Shock and awe for the win!

I fire off an email to his attorney with the contracts, as professional as the first one I sent, and forward it to Aidan. I send another just to him, resolving before I hit send that I won't check for any replies. It's the only way to win this little war.

To: Aidan M. Pierce, President PPG
From: Alexis M. Greene, Esq.
Re: Myers Sale to PPG & Fundraiser Gala & Shock & Awe

Mr. Pierce,

I will do as you asked with regard to the contracts and meeting with Ms. McCall. I will call her now and try to meet with her before the day is out.

My intention was to keep our emails professional, as I have no idea who reads them on your end. In fact, I have something pressing I would like to discuss with you and I'll need to know if this form of communication is secure enough to transmit a file to you.

In the meantime, it's clear you are not worried since you accosted me with such shock and awe in your previous email.

I consider you much more than a professional colleague considering what I let you do to me in the shower this morning. Incidentally, I'd like to know when you're going to do that to me again.

Oh, and one more thing. *Mi manca averti dentro di me.*

Yours,

Alexis

Greene Law Office | Alexis M. Greene, Esq.

Perfectly Level Headed, Undistracted Attorney

I dial Jade McCall's office. Her assistant puts me right through.

"Good morning, Alexis. What can I do for you?"

"I need to apologize for canceling yesterday. I'd like to meet with you today, if possible. Mr. Pierce does not want this to wait."

"I can certainly understand that. Is he coming to the meeting?"

Give it a rest, woman.

"No, just us. He is out of town. And Mr. Richardson is off the project. Mr. Pierce's personal assistant and I have taken over his duties. When is a good time for you?"

"I have a client here at two, but I can meet you at three. Your office?"

"Sure. See you then."

I disconnect and get through several files on my desk in preparation for next week. I've got a full plate of appointments after putting things off while I was in Arizona.

Just before noon, I'm able to move on to my pet project and get Gloria on the phone. I need to connect with her over the weekend but I also need her advice. I dial her cell and she answers on the first ring.

"What the hell took you so long? I was about to text and ask if you're alive," she teases. "You fell off the face of the earth for a week, then I saw that news report yesterday. What the hell's going on with that brunette twig Aidan was dating?"

"I know, I know. I'm so sorry. It's been a whirlwind. Can you come over tonight? Will Harry mind?"

"Yeah, I can get there. The Rebels are practicing in my garage and the twins are headed out. I'll bring some wine."

"Great. There's one other thing," I say. "Can you send me a sample Non-Disclosure Agreement?"

"That's out of your bailiwick, Lex," she laughs. "You expanding your area of practice?"

"No, smart ass. It's not for a client. It's…," I hesitate, "it's for me."

"And the plot thickens. I'll email a couple versions so you can tailor it to fit your needs. But only if you promise you'll fully disclose your ass off to me when I get there tonight."

"Deal. See you at my place. Is six okay?"

"Perfect. See you then."

I disconnect as my inbox pings with another email from Aidan.

Dammit.

I try forcing myself not to open it. Within seconds, I fail.

To: Alexis M. Greene, Esq.
From: Aidan M. Pierce, President PPG
Re: Patience Testing Siren
Dear Ms. Greene,
It would serve you well not to tempt me any further. I assure you I miss being inside you more than you miss having me there. If you're not careful, you'll find yourself collected and on a plane so I can put us both out of our misery.
What's so important to discuss? I would prefer important conversations happen in person, especially if I don't know what I'm discussing beforehand. We are secure here - to a degree.
I look forward to your reply.
Still can't wait to get back to you,
A-
Aidan M. Pierce, Severely Distracted & Now Stiff President
Pierce Philanthropy Group

Since email is not the best way to share what I'm proposing, I decide to mull it over tonight and come up with a way to delve into it with him tomorrow. That will give me time to review the agreement I've asked Gloria for.

I'm smiling at the effect the rest of my words have had on him. This method of flirting is new for us so that's probably part of it. But with him, it's more than thrilling.

It's him after all.

Everything is intensified when he's involved. A simple email exchange has left me notably aroused and, if I'm not careful, needing a change of underwear.

I fire off one last reply, the last I have time for if I'm going to get to lunch with Charlie on time. Once I hit send, I drop my phone in my bag and vow not to look at it again until after lunch.

To: Aidan M. Pierce, President PPG
From: Alexis M. Greene, Esq.
Re: Patience Testing and STUBBORN MEN
Mr. Pierce,
I liked your first greeting better.
Please stop talking about planes. I've recently found airplane travel quite exciting.
If you're going to be so stubborn about my undisclosed topic, I will find another way to communicate with you but it cannot wait until you return Tuesday.
I'm sorry I'm not there to alleviate your situation.
I can't wait to have you back.
Yours,
Alexis
Alexis M. Greene, Esq.
Mostly Levelheaded, Though Slightly Wet Attorney

Charlie and I are having lunch across the street again, now able to laugh about how yesterday's meal went.

I fill him in about my time with Aidan since then (at least the clean parts) and admit I'm more confident than ever about him and the beginning of whatever this is.

But what is this?

Sex? Infatuation? A silly crush?

I hear myself ask him out loud.

"I've never seen you happier. He is good for you," Charlie says. "Don't fuck this up with your insecurities and don't think so hard. In fact, don't think at all."

My response is non-verbal, a look of 'easy for you to say'.

"Does it matter what it is? Does it have to have a name? Three weeks ago, you were still lost in a fog and now look at you."

I tilt my head. "What do you mean?"

"You've never looked better. You're taking risks. And things are happening for you. Good things, babe. Just let go and enjoy it."

I hold in a breath as I fork through my salad. I believe he's giving me sound advice but conservative me is wagging a finger in her typical 'be careful' manner.

"I know what you're thinking."

I give him a look that begs more.

"You're thinking what happens if he breaks your heart," he says point blank.

I stare at him a moment. "Okay, yeah," I finally say. "So what if I am?"

"So what if he does?" he emphasizes, setting down his fork. "At least you'll have had the ride. Life is too short to be waiting on the sidelines for something to happen to you. You lost two of the people dearest to you in this life. You of all people should recognize that we don't know what tomorrow will bring. Isn't what you're feeling worth the risk?"

Butterflies dance in my belly thinking about what Aidan has made me feel in the last few days alone, never mind since the moment we met.

What I can't figure out is why.

Why *me*? Why not any other female that makes googly eyes at him every time he steps out his front door? I start to object, intending to spout more doubts.

"Don't," he says before I can speak. "Stop overthinking it. Ben would want this for you, Alexis. I want this for you. You deserve happiness."

"God, you sound like my therapist." But something within me clicks at his words.

I do deserve this. I do want this. And if the ship sinks, then I'll just have to go down with it.

"Yes, okay?" I finally voice, unable to stop smiling. "Yes, it's worth the risk."

"That's a girl. Now dish the dirt. I'm tired of the G-rated version of this soap opera."

I laugh out loud and nearly choke on a crouton.

"Oh c'mon, Lex. You don't really think I care about your feelings do you?" He's oozing sarcasm, leaning in close. "I just want to know if the man is as good in bed as he looks like he should be."

My ears flush with heat, but thankfully it doesn't spread to my face.

"Well, I'd have to say..." I pause, pretending to seriously consider. "I'd say yes, his skills definitely match his looks. And you could say..."

I stop again, regretting opening my mouth.

"*Ohmigod*," he prods. "What?"

"You could say that his equipment is," I pause again, "on point with his looks?" I'm waiting to see if he gets it.

"Holy shit! You mean he's?" He gestures with his palms placed in front of him, his hands set a distance apart. I lean forward over our plates and extend his hands further apart to demonstrate, giggling.

"I fucking hate you right now," he says, shaking his head and shoving his plate aside to feign disgust.

I clap my hands together, throwing my head back with a laugh.

"Why in the *fuck* do all the well-hung billionaires have to be straight?"

That does me in. I'm laughing so hard it's soundless. He's laughing too, drawing the attention of the people around us, but I don't care.

"Indeed," I say, trying to catch my breath. "Let me express my sincere sympathies to you, Charlie. I'm sorry that Aidan doesn't bat for your team. But, then again," I say, pulling a large French fry from his plate to wag it at him, "lucky me."

Charlie and I get back to the office an hour later, and I pull my phone out once I've retreated to the privacy of my office. I have an email from Dr. Flint scheduling me for an appointment Tuesday afternoon at four.

Just in the nick of time.

It's probably not a bad idea to keep that on my calendar.

There are two texts from Aidan and two emails. I read the emails first.

To: Alexis M. Greene, Esq.
From: Aidan M. Pierce, President PPG
Re: Stubborn Women

Hey Baby,
You REALLY need to stop tempting me. I've got Ivan on standby just in case you decide not to behave.
What is it you want to talk about? You know I am not a patient man. Please share.
Now.
A-
Aidan M. Pierce, Curious President
Pierce Philanthropy Group

Oh, shit. This does not bode well. I've been ignoring him for over an hour. I cringe as I open the next one.

To: Alexis M. Greene, Esq.
From: Aidan M. Pierce, President
Re: Stubborn Women THAT IGNORE ME
If you don't respond I will have to come up there. Ivan is ready.
Is everything okay?
It's probably not a good idea for me to miss meetings with my very expensive attorney who will charge me whether I'm in the room or not.
(What is it with LAWYERS?!)
I'd also have to miss a chat with a Grammy nominee that I'm trying to persuade to perform at the Gala.
But if I have to excuse myself from these obligations just to find out what you want to talk about, I WILL.
A-
Aidan M. Pierce, Turning from Curious to Furious President
Pierce Philanthropy Group

I check my texts.

Alexis, answer me. Is everything okay?

Five minutes later...

You have thirty minutes to reply.
Or else.

The last one came in about twenty minutes ago. I type a reply as quickly as I can.

Yes, everything is fine! Why the paranoia?

I hit send, so he'll know I'm not ignoring him anymore, then type another message.

What I want to discuss is personal. If you want it can wait until Tuesday.

His reply is immediate.

Thank God. DON'T DO THAT TO ME AGAIN.

I'm sorry I ignored your emails. The only way I can get one over on you is to ignore you. And what's with the LOUD CAPS? Someone told me that's RUDE.

Not funny, Alexis. And sometimes caps are needed TO MAKE A POINT. What do you want to talk about? What were you going to send me?

Aidan, let it go. We can discuss Tuesday. I promise it's nothing terrible. Trust me. Okay?

I do. It's other people I don't trust. Headed in to meet with Bill Hoffman to go over Myers deal. I'll let you know how it goes. Call you later?

Sure. Gloria's coming over to hang tonight. I'll be home.

Okay. Have fun 'hanging'. No more ignoring me.

I promise. And I meant what I said. I miss you.

Me too, baby. Talk soon.

Reluctantly I set my phone aside, trying to shut down my overflowing emotions and turn my brain on.

When Jade McCall arrives two hours later, I'm still wistful. Thoughts of Aidan have left me supremely dazed. Claudia shows Jade into my office and she takes a seat across from me, setting down her expensive bag and resting a large file folder in her lap.

She's disguised her big guns under a scoop neck today, but she is dolled up in her usual overdone makeup and dressed to the nines. Navy blue skirt, tight white button down blouse, gold jewelry covering her fingers, wrists, and neck. Her perfume is over the top and almost gagging me in my closed office.

"Thanks for coming, Jade. Again, I'm sorry for canceling yesterday. My holiday weekend was crazy. My sister's husband had a hiking accident in Arizona and I just got back Wednesday night."

"Oh my, really? Well I hope he's okay. Whatever it is you've been through, it agrees with you. You look like a million bucks," she says. "Is that really all that's going on?"

Yep. Nothing else. Aidan Pierce is just winning over every part of my being. No big whoop.

I can't hide my smirk or my happiness while thinking of him.

"Boy, you've got it bad young lady. Whoever he is, I hope he's worth it. Not many of them are."

I wonder if she's referencing that asshole Richardson with this remark but I don't ask.

"Let's get down to it, shall we?" I say, steering her to task. "We need to get everything to Pierce's PA right away."

"Right. I understand they've selected the second choice for the invites," she says, pulling a sample out of her folder. "I like it. Very elegant. And we've got the date and time set, as you know. Black tie. The menu is going to be the first option I presented, three courses. And there will be a vegetarian option."

"All of that sounds fine," I start, "except I might have a recommendation on the food. Do you know who the Sheridan uses for their food supplier?"

"I'm not sure. Is that important?" She looks overly concerned that she missed this detail.

"I think the hotel uses All Star Vending. They don't have the best reputation, at least not for food that knocks people's socks off. I'm thinking we should go with a farm-to-table type menu, as opposed to the typical dried out beef and crappy coffee the Sheridan serves. It would make more sense with the whole evening. Nothing too rustic though. Still suitable for a black-tie event."

"Yes, I'd agree. Should we get the Country Club to cater?"

"I'm thinking we source locally for everything. The meals, coffee and desserts, all of it. Local produce, local meats. Tell the Sheridan we will use their kitchen staff and their facilities, but we want to set the menu, bring in some outside caterers. A couple small businesses from Mirror Lake should be in the mix, too."

"Of course," Jade says excitedly. "That's where the Center is going to be, after all. This is definitely the way to go."

"Do you think the hotel will go for it?"

"I think they will. They won't want to lose this event bickering over who makes the dinner rolls. It will be their biggest event all year. Even with the short notice, they're expecting to be fully booked at the hotel."

"Great. So what else do we need to decide on?"

"Just the program," she says. "I have to be honest, I couldn't come up with anyone I thought would be worthy of putting in front of Mr. Pierce. But I have secured some rather large donors."

"That's wonderful. May I ask who?"

"Ashley Pharmaceuticals, for one."

Holy crap.

They're one of the oldest and largest companies in Stanton. No doubt her doctor hubby had some pull there, but it's for a good cause. I have to applaud her effort.

"Pleasing news, Jade. I'm impressed. Who else?"

"The doctors on staff with my husband have agreed to purchase a couple tables. I'm trying to get the hospital Chief of Staff to send around a memo to secure a large donation from the Children's Hospital of City General, so I'll let you know how that goes. I thought that would be in line with the project, being it's for community youth."

"Definitely," I say. "That's a great angle."

"And I might have a few smaller businesses that can contribute."

"It'd be great if we could get some local companies just to donate their time, their goods and services. This may go national and it would be great exposure for them too. Maybe the café up the street for coffee?"

"Absolutely. They have the best coffee in the city. I could ask Mrs. Cramer's Cupcakes in Falcon Lake to do some desserts. The owner is an old friend of mine."

"Wonderful. Please get me any other ideas you have on this. Email is fine. Of course we will compensate the vendors, but if they want to contribute their services as a donation that's fine as well."

She jots down some notes as she nods in agreement.

"As far as the entertainment, I guess we will know that by the weekend," I go on. "Mr. Pierce has agreed to secure that and his staff will deal with all the media. So I think the invites should be ready to have printed and sent out Monday."

"Great. I've talked to a local printer that can get it done for us in one day. You said his staff is handling the guest list and mailing?"

"Yes. But if you could put together a spreadsheet of local guests to be invited over the weekend, we can hand that over too. Make sure no one prominent from Lake County is left out."

"I'll get that to you by Sunday. I guess that's all for now then?"

"Yes," I say, thankful to wrap up this meeting. It's the end of my day. Relaxing on my deck with one of my dearest friends is all that's on my mind. "Excellent job so far, Jade. Aidan will be impressed."

She's grabbing for her bag off the floor when she stops and turns to me. "Aidan?" She looks at me with raised eyebrows, head tilted as she rests her bag on the chair. "I didn't realize you two were on a first name basis."

Oops. Shit!

I try to prevent myself from smiling.

"Ah, now I get it," she says as though she's uncovered a significant secret. I hope my expression confirms nothing. "Ms. Greene, you are one lucky woman."

I shake my head in an 'it's not what you think' fashion, but her smile widens. She's not buying it.

"Really, Alexis. You don't have to hide it from me. I'm happy for you. Your Mr. Pierce seems like a good – no, strike that – a phenomenal catch. Reel that sucker in, young lady."

She turns on her heel and goes, taking her strong perfume and leaving me with a dopey grin on my face. I don't have the chance to confirm or deny her suspicions or even say goodbye to her.

But I fully intend to follow her advice.

8

Alexis

Gloria and I are on my back deck polishing off our first bottle of red and a large pie from Brickyard Pizza. Huck is inside avoiding the heat of the evening. It's managed to stay warm and humid into the seven o'clock hour on Friday night.

After the wine, Gloria can no longer hold back her curiosity.

"If Aidan asked for a Non-Disclosure Agreement, why doesn't his lawyer do it?"

"He didn't ask," I say. "I just want to do it."

She sends me a puzzled look.

"There are things about himself he doesn't discuss," I explain, "things in his past. I want him to feel comfortable enough to tell me. I figured it would be the best way to demonstrate he could trust me."

"Seems to me he already does trust you."

"But this would make it legal."

"Do you think an agreement is going to trump instinct?"

"I don't know," I admit. "But he needs to know that I'm willing to sign one. That I wouldn't reveal to anyone what he shares with me."

"Not even me?" she teases.

"Not even you. Whatever he's not shared with me to this point isn't common knowledge. When the subject comes up, I get the feeling it's dark. Like something he's ashamed of."

"Sometimes the past needs to be left in the past, Lex."

"But it's part of who he is. If I'm going into this, I want to know everything there is to know. Did I tell you he did an extensive background check on me?"

"I don't think you mentioned that, no."

"Beyond personal details, he already knew me going into this. It's only fair I have the same courtesy."

"Maybe," she says. "He knows about your mother?"

"To a degree. I mean he could easily discern she has issues. And speaking of her," I begin. "Jill dropped a bomb on me while I was out there." I relay what I know from Jill and that I narrowly escaped running into our mother.

"What the fuck?"

"I know," I say with an eye roll. "Crazy, right?"

"So your mother and your sister live in the same state now." She's stunned. "Why didn't Jill tell you?"

"She thought there would be a better time to tell me. Up until Derek's accident, I think she'd only seen her a couple of times. It isn't like they live around the corner from each other."

"I guess I can see that. Still, it would have been nice to know that beforehand. Aidan flew you out there?"

I nod, swigging the last of my wine, a sheepish grin forming. "Yes and back."

"Ohh, girl. You're not telling me everything. Come on! Get to the dirty parts, would ya?"

"I don't kiss and tell."

"That's because you haven't kissed anyone since you've known me."

"That's not true. There was that one guy. What was his name? The blind date you set me up on. Carl?"

"Oh hell," she says in a fit of laughter. "Carl! You know how sorry I am about that. He was a friend of a friend, and I'm still not speaking to her over that whole thing."

"Well you couldn't have known he'd want to bring his lizard on our date."

"Or that you'd run into his ex-wife," she adds.

"And you're right, I didn't kiss him. He kissed me. On the cheek. I came directly in and washed it off." I shiver with a case of the willies.

"Let's be fair, Lex," she says chuckling. "It was an iguana."

"Yeah," I add. "A very large, very scary iguana."

"That thing was fucking huge," she laughs. "You sent me a picture of it that night, remember?"

"I do," I say. "It was practically a fucking dinosaur."

"He couldn't leave that thing home even if he wanted to. It would have eaten the contents of his trailer."

"Or it might have escaped and taken over Tokyo," I add.

We're both in hysterics.

"Shit," she says, trying to stop her giggle. "That guy was something else."

I nod in agreement. "Yeah. Something else all right. Please don't set me up again. Like ever."

"Doesn't seem to me you need any fixing up at this point. I take it Mr. Pierce is far more kissable than ol' lizard lips?"

"Uh, yah. And then some." I lean back in my chair and sigh. "I don't know how I got so lucky."

"Well I do," she says as she gets up. "It was all thanks to me. So don't forget me when he buys you a private island in the Caribbean or asks you to shack up with him in his fancy-ass loft."

"Oh as if, Gloria." My chest flip flops at her words. "You opening another bottle?"

"Only if you let me crash here."

"Sure," I say. "You can use Ben's room."

She pauses at the door before going in, obviously surprised.

"Charlie stayed in there while I was gone," I qualify.

"You were okay with that?"

"Not at first. But then I just decided it was time. It's just a room. Keeping it closed off isn't going to stop me from missing him."

"Or bring him back, Lex. You know that. You just needed time to realize it."

She heads inside and I follow. "Do you think Ben would be happy for me?" I let Huck out to do his business as Gloria pulls another bottle of red from the wine rack, coming back to join me at the island.

"I honestly do. He'd be over the moon. He could never love you like…" she pauses, "the way someone like Aidan can."

"Whoa. The 'L' word? Nobody's said anything about that."

"Get a fucking clue," she says. "That's exactly what's happening to the two of you."

"I guess I hadn't really thought about that."

"Oh Jesus, girl. Sit down."

I do, sliding my glass to her for a refill. She pours and then takes a seat next to me.

"I've barely known him three weeks," I defend. "I really wouldn't be comfortable describing it that way. Especially to him."

"Alexis," she scolds, "for someone so smart, you can be a complete dope. I knew Harold four weeks before we decided to get married."

I look at her in disbelief. "You did?"

She nods and sips from her glass. "My father threatened to kill him when he found out."

"Stop," I laugh. "You're making this up."

"Not a word of it. We didn't act on it at four weeks, but we went to Vegas after we'd been dating six months. My father was going to wait up with his hunting rifle until we got back – which would have been pretty dangerous considering he was a terrible shot. He spent more time falling asleep in tree stands than he did actually hunting deer."

I laugh at her recollection. Both of Gloria's parents passed away before we met, but she always had entertaining anecdotes about each of them.

"My mother, bless her soul, talked him out of it. She said if we were making a mistake then it was ours to make."

"Well, obviously it wasn't a mistake," I say. "Look at the life you have. You guys are so blessed."

"Because we didn't question what was happening. We just went with it. Don't you feel a certain way around him? Like you can't breathe? Or like some other force is at work?"

"Yeah," I sigh in admission. "I've experienced that."

"And then you see how your future is going to change, all stemming from one moment in time. Yours being the day you met him."

"That's exactly what it feels like." *And it scares the crap out of me.* "How do you know this?"

"I've been there, girl. It's overwhelming. When it happened to us we were young, but we were healthy adults that were sure about ourselves. We wanted the same things. Work, raise a family. And we were compatible, you know, in bed."

"Uh yeah, I don't need to hear that part." Gloria is like an aunt or a mother figure to me. I don't want to think about her having sex.

"Well I won't bore you with the details, but let's just say that department has never been lacking for us."

"Don't get me wrong," I say. "I know that part of a relationship is important. I just, I've never really had that or discussed it out loud with anyone. Know what I mean?"

"I do," she says. "But you need to get more comfortable with that side of you, Alexis. Especially if you're going to snag the likes of this guy. I mean, come on," she goads. "Women cream their jeans just looking at him. Don't you?"

Of course I do.

"Guilty."

"Well then," she says. "There ya go."

"He's amazing, Gloria." She beams at me as I go on. "He's attentive. And affectionate. And I have no idea what he wants with me."

"Shut up," she scolds. "Anyone can see you're a catch."

I twirl my wine glass by the stem as I let her words sink in. "Charlie says I should just stop thinking and enjoy the ride, even if it ends."

"Charlie is a smart motherfucker."

"Yeah," I say through my laughter. "He is."

"Stop undervaluing yourself, Lex. Aidan sees what the people closest to you see. You're a remarkable young woman. You're strong and independent and beautiful. And," she pauses. "I'm tired of talking about you. Tell me I'm pretty."

"You are pretty. And drunk too. This wine must be hitting you."

She smiles back at me. "Amen."

"And for the record, Harold is one lucky man. Let's drink to that." I raise my glass.

"No," she says. "Let's drink to love." She leans into my shoulder. "Let yourself fall, baby girl. I promise, it's totally worth it. And you'll never experience anything better."

"Okay," I nod in agreement. "Here's to love."

By eight-thirty, the pizza is gone (in part thanks to Huck) and we've had enough wine. Gloria has excused herself to Ben's suite to call Harry and let him know she's staying. She asks if I have anything she can wear to get comfortable.

"Borrow some of Ben's sweats," I holler. "Top dresser drawer."

"Thanks, babe!"

While she's occupied, I take the opportunity to text Jill. It's only five-thirty in the evening out there, but she's probably home. I'd rather call her, but I won't risk our mother being there to hear the call.

Hey! How's Derek doing? Is he glad to be home?

Her reply comes immediately.

Yes! And I'm so glad to have him home. So are the girls. He's still sore but soaking up the attention and being waited on.

I hesitate, then decide to find out what I want to know.

Did she come to help you?

Yes. But just for one day. She went back to Sedona.

Whew.

So happy to hear he's home. Keep me updated on how everyone's doing.

Will do. How's your rich boyfriend? Or is he back with his old girlfriend like The Tattler said?

He's fine, and no he isn't. Long story. I'll call you next week and we can chat. Ok?

K. But don't keep me in suspense too long! Love you.

Love you. Kiss the girls for me.

Will do. Talk to you soon.

Before I can get my phone back to its charger, it rings in my hand. Aidan's number appears on the display and I have a rush of adrenaline just seeing his name.

"Hey, sexy," I answer coolly. *Where did that come from?* Must be the vino doing the talking.

"Boy, it's good to hear your voice."

"What's wrong?"

"Nothing now," he says. "How's your evening with Gloria?"

"She's staying over. A few too many glasses of red to drive. How about you?"

"I'm better now. But I wish you were here."

"And where is here?" I ask, realizing I don't even know where he is.

"Soho."

"Ah. Hotel? Or do you own some over-the-top loft there too?"

"No," he laughs. "Occupying a suite at The Soho Grand. Just until

Tuesday. I don't invest in real estate here. Too pretentious for me."

I sigh. This is why I like him so much.

"Are you alone now?"

"Yes." *Where's he going with this?* "Gloria's in the other room."

"I wish I'd known that sooner. I would have let my best Italian seduce you through the phone."

My body responds to his words instantly. "Not now, Aidan."

"Isn't that what you wanted me to do the other day when I had a boardroom full of people waiting on me to hang up with you?"

"Yes," I admit. "But..."

"But nothing. *Mi manca il sapore di te, Alexis.*"

"Stop. Or I'll find a way to get to you. There must be a late flight to New York."

He laughs and my chest swells at the sound. I don't hear it enough from him.

"It's just a few more days," he says. "We can handle it. Right?"

"Depends," I say. "Tell me what you just said. In English."

"You'll just have to wait until I see you in person. And speaking of that, what did you want to talk about? I'd like to know what you were going to send me."

"It's nothing, don't worry about it. We can talk about it when you get back."

"If it's important to you, it's important to me. Besides, it's a nice distraction from the shit show I'm dealing with here."

"Wait, is...are you okay?"

"I'm fine. I'd rather not discuss it now."

I can hear his phone ping with a notification.

"Shit. I have to go," he says. "I'll call you as soon as I get a chance tomorrow. I think you'll like the lineup that's coming together for the gala. I should have it set by tomorrow night. Did you meet with Jade?"

"I did. She's got a big donor on board."

"Ashley Pharma. I heard something about that."

"Dammit, you're always one step ahead. Why is it you need me again?"

"It's my job to be a step ahead. And I think you know exactly how much I need you, never mind why."

I'm smiling through the phone, glad he can't see how his words leave me gushing.

"Well, just in case you don't have listening devices in my office, I'll email you the details Jade and I discussed. We should have a finalized guest list by Sunday for local people we suggest be included. Invites can be ready Monday, as soon as you reveal the details of your secret program. Should we deliver them to your office when they're done?"

"No. Just let me know where and when they're ready. Samira will get them. She's in Stanton."

"Okay."

"I need to let you go now. Sleep well, baby."

"You too."

"I will now," he says. "Good night."

I want to say something more, to let him know how much I miss him, but I don't. He disconnects and I'm left longing for him, frustrated by how much I wish for his presence. I feel a physical ache, discouraged that I don't know when I'll see him next.

Does he feel that way too? Even at all the reassuring signals he sends, I wonder if I might be in this alone.

Gloria emerges from Ben's room dressed in one of his old college t-shirts and sweats. Her fuller figure fills them out, but she looks comfy.

"Lex, you okay? You look like you've been wounded."

"Gloria, if this is falling in love, it is definitely not for the weak."

9

Aidan

At nearly nine o'clock, I hang up with Alexis to see who is messaging me. My evening had already been interrupted once when Dimitri called at the end of my dinner with Alanna. The leads from Armstrong's phone had been exhausted with no luck. We decided we'd both take the evening to think through some options and reconvene by phone tomorrow morning.

This text is from Lionel asking me to call him as soon as possible.

"Good evening, sir," he answers.

"There's news?"

"I've just been contacted by Gene Dobbs."

Damn. The *LA Times* reporter.

"And?" I ask.

"His informant has gone missing."

"We still don't know who the informant is?"

"I was not able to find out but, in light of this news, Dobbs has disclosed his source."

"Who is it?"

"No one I've heard of. He's an attorney. He was working for R.E.E. to acquire the Myers' land."

My chest tightens with dread. "Mark Whitmore?"

"Yes, sir."

"I'll call you back."

I hang up and dial Byron, rushing to speak before he can get out a hello. "Where was Whitmore when you last tracked him? Did he arrive in Florida?"

"He did. Yesterday at seven in the evening."

"Whitmore was Dobbs' source of information. Dobbs claims he's gone missing."

"I didn't track his whereabouts after his arrival in Florida. I'm on it." He disconnects.

I take a moment to think this development through. If Whitmore is missing – or worse – R.E.E. is behind it somehow. I consider calling Alexis back, but I don't want to panic her. It's likely she doesn't have any light to shed on the situation anyway.

I call Lionel back.

"Sir?"

"Where is Dobbs now?"

"He's in Pennsylvania. He went there to see Whitmore in person today but discovered his family left the state."

"Get me in touch with him."

"Yes, sir," he says. "I'll have him call your cell."

"Make it within the hour."

Despite Byron's objections, I've driven the hour and a half out of Manhattan to meet Dobbs at a halfway point, and I've done so alone.

The GPS of the rental car guides me to the all-night diner in the Poconos region of Pennsylvania where we agreed to meet. The diner is just off a county highway, some ways away from the nearest town. There's nothing but miles of asphalt cutting through fields in either direction.

Presumably the diner patrons pick up in the coming hours, after the bars have closed and likely again for early breakfasts. This is the most inconspicuous time we could have chosen to meet here. There are only two other cars in the parking lot.

Dobbs hadn't been forthcoming on the phone, but at least he agreed to see me now. I check my watch. It's nearly midnight, but I'm ten minutes early. I debate between going inside or waiting in the lot for him, finally deciding to stay put. It's better this conversation take place away from whomever happens to be inside.

Byron interrupts my thoughts with a call.

"Yeah?" I answer.

"Whitmore never made it home."

Fuck.

"How do we know?"

"His wife contacted the authorities. His plane landed on time. He made a call to her from the tarmac but that was the last call from his number. She has not seen him or spoken to him since that call."

"Has an official report been filed?"

"Just."

"Keep me informed, Byron."

"Yes, sir."

I disconnect as a sleek late model Honda Civic pulls into the lot. I shut off my vehicle and get out. Dobbs' headlights angle past me towards the diner's entrance several feet away. He shuts off the engine and parks even with me, giving me a chance to confirm there is no one else in the vehicle with him.

I lean back against my borrowed Lexus, waiting for him to emerge. As he comes towards me, I'm able to match up his build to his headshot, the same one I've seen plastered in newspapers and magazines throughout his distinguished career. We've never met, but I know he's in his early sixties.

His investigative reporting has earned Dobbs a respected reputation that matches his salt and pepper hair and dark eyes, but his slight frame suggests a less prestigious man. A disheveled suit hangs off him, and he looks tired. His wire-framed glasses are resting high up on the bridge of his nose.

"Mr. Pierce," he says as he approaches, extending his hand.

"Thank you for coming."

"It didn't seem I had a choice."

He's right, but I ignore his comment. "You have no recording devices on you?"

He expresses aversion at my question. "Of course not."

"What can you tell me about Mark Whitmore? Did he come to you?"

"I'm not sure I want to tell you anything about Mark. It's possible he's in danger. I have no way of knowing if you have something to do with that."

Oh, Christ.

I don't have the patience to be saddled with this task now. Convincing this guy I'm on his side is wasted time. I need to learn what he knows so I can act on it.

"We can stand here and debate that or we can get this over with so I can attempt to find Whitmore. I'm not certain you understand the urgency here. This guy may not have a lot of time if R.E.E. has gotten to him."

"I trusted you by revealing my source. What can you tell me?"

I'll have to give up something to crack this guy.

"I'm closely connected to someone Whitmore was working with for the last year. She'd want him safe. My interest goes beyond my own ambitions in Lake County," I say. "I need to know he's safe. For her."

He regards me with skepticism as he removes his glasses. He pulls a cloth from his suit pocket to clean the lenses, then puts the glasses back on as he speaks. "Who is she?"

"Doesn't matter."

"It does to me."

"It's irrelevant. If you want my resources to track down Whitmore and keep him out of harm's way, then you'll tell me what you know."

He doesn't respond but instead leans back on his car.

"Now."

"You can't bully me, Pierce. I've seen more shit in my lifetime than you can imagine. I'm not intimidated by your threats, violent or otherwise."

"I'm not threatening you, Dobbs. I'm trying not to waste any more of our fucking time." My jaw tightens. "Do you have information or not?"

He resigns, avoiding eye contact as he looks up into darkness. His arms cross over his chest as he starts. "Mark Whitmore contacted me a few weeks ago when the announcement about your project in Mirror Lake was released to local papers."

"What did he want?"

"To share information with me. About you, but moreover about the plans R.E.E. had to stop you and what they've been up to out of the public eye."

"He was your only source? You never had contact from someone at the actual company?"

"No. Just him. His firm didn't like that he had taken on R.E.E. as a client. They threatened to fire him, so he was hired privately by the company. He had no ties to R.E.E. other than being on retainer as one of their attorneys."

"Did he have a chance to disclose to you the company's plans?"

"No, just that he had the information. I reached out to your employee in California two weeks ago because Mark had turned reluctant, changed his mind about divulging anything. When you declined, I went back to him and persuaded him to meet. We planned for me to come here this weekend but when I got here, he was gone. He never told me he was leaving."

"He told someone," I say, more to myself than to him. My thoughts immediately go to Alexis. She knew this, knew Whitmore was hightailing it for Florida. And if he was missing, whoever caused his disappearance knew that too. "What other names came up in your research? Any other attorneys?"

I'm hoping he doesn't know Alexis had anything to do with this.

"No," he says. "Honestly, I hadn't gotten that far. I wasn't sure if Whitmore was even a legitimate source for a story. He had the right amount of paranoia when we talked by phone to concern me. It interested me enough to dig further. But I wanted to meet him in person to determine if he actually had anything."

Much like Dobbs was doing with me now. He'd refused to talk by phone and had insisted we meet in person, likely for the same reason – to see if I had anything worth pursuing.

"He was hesitant to agree to see me," he adds.

"Did you have a time and place set up to meet him?"

"No. I told him I'd call him when I got into Pennsylvania. I decided to visit his office without announcing myself ahead of time. I wanted to catch him off guard and gauge his reaction, but when I went there, the receptionist indicated he'd left the firm."

"I saw him just before he left town. He flew to Florida out of Stanton."

"What was he doing in New York? Did he come to see you?"

"No. It was by chance that I saw him." I intentionally omit that he'd worked with Alexis. "He seemed paranoid when he left Stanton. Visibly paranoid."

"And he had reason to be if he's gone goddamned missing."

I nod, lost in thought as Dobbs goes on.

"He seemed remorseful when he talked to me, as though he was trying to right a wrong. My gut told me what he uncovered with R.E.E. was something he hadn't been aware of going in."

"Highly probable." Alexis had been surprised that Whitmore went off the radar when my uncle's sale to R.E.E. fell apart. Whitmore hadn't accepted her calls to apologize for everything going to hell. She'd told me that was out of character for him.

If he uncovered something that didn't agree with his morals, exposing Renewable Energy through the media would have been his attempt to stop them. That he reached out to warn Alexis before his departure confirmed he had a conscience.

"That's really all the information I have," Dobbs says. "I'm sorry I can't offer more."

"Were there any other names mentioned in conversation?"

"Such as?"

"You'd have to tell me."

He gives me a distrusting glance as he shifts his weight from one foot to the other. He remains silent.

"John Ireland," I say. "John Ireland never came up?" His look of confusion tells me it didn't, and I don't wait for him to answer. "I appreciate your time, Mr. Dobbs." I'm already opening the driver door.

"Any chance you'd consider doing an interview anyway?" He pushes up his glasses, not yet departing for the opposite side of his car. "I'd be interested to hear about your motivations for the project in Mirror Lake."

"If that's something I decide to pursue, you'll be my first call." I get in without listening for a response, leaving him behind as I make my way back to Manhattan as quickly as possible.

By three in the morning I'm back at the hotel, unsettled and pressing Byron for information about Whitmore. Byron's contacts in Florida are keeping him updated about the missing person report, but so far nothing has led the authorities to Whitmore.

The security footage of Whitmore leaving the airport was not unusual. He hadn't appeared concerned, not looking over his shoulder as he'd been when I last saw him. He'd tossed his one piece of luggage into a cab and been driven away. Nothing in the grainy footage revealed any abnormalities about the driver or the cab itself.

"I'll contact the taxi company," Byron says as he closes his tablet. "Get in touch with the driver to see if he has information about where Whitmore was dropped off."

"I'm sure the authorities are on that. Let's wait until we get a report from your contact there."

"Very well. You should get some rest, sir."

Yeah, I should.

But it wasn't likely I'd be able to.

Byron leaves for his own room and I shower and climb into bed, naked and exhausted though my mind reels. I'm filled with apprehension and helpless in this situation

I never settle for helpless.

I also need to get back to Alexis to make sure she is safe.

The thoughts plague me until I finally drift off.

I wake with a start, my phone ringing at its highest volume on the table beside me. I shake myself alert and grab for it.

It's my attorney.

"Bill? What's going on?"

"I need you to come into the office. It can't wait."

I look at the display on my phone. "Jesus, it's six a.m. Does it have to be now?"

"Pierce, just get the hell over here and hurry up. I'm already late."

I disconnect and throw on jeans and a shirt, calling Byron as I make my way out the door.

"Any news on Whitmore?"

"No. The authorities are interviewing the cab driver within the hour."

"Keep me posted. I'm going to see Hoffman."

About what I have no fucking clue.

By the time I enter Bill's office, he's at the end of his rope. He's dressed down, which is not surprising on a Saturday. He's in golf shorts and a polo shirt and he's clearly pissed. Whether it's from being dragged in at the early hour or from what he's about to tell me, I can't discern.

"Well?" I ask. I take a seat in front of his desk, waiting for him to sit. "What's so pressing?"

"You're being sued," he says. He tosses some papers at me across the desk as he sits behind it.

"What's your point?" Litigation is something I'm familiar with. Over the years we'd had to defend patents or frivolous claims against me or my various companies and endeavors. It wasn't unusual. Definitely not shocking news.

"It isn't a bullshit lawsuit, Pierce. The Richardson Realty Group is suing for a cool million."

"And?"

"And you didn't tell me anything about this."

"There's nothing to tell. This guy feels he's been slighted a series of commissions and he's grasping at straws. This could have waited, Bill. I trust you to handle it."

"That isn't all," he says. He leans back in his chair, clasping hands behind his head as his elbows jut out from his white shirt.

"Can we get on with it? I've got a lot going on here, and I'm running on three hours of sleep. Are you really that hard up for billable hours?"

"Why would John Ireland suddenly want to let you out of your arrangement with him?"

I stop breathing for a moment.

What the fuck did he just say?

"Yeah, I thought so," Bill says. "You had no idea?"

"Get to the point, Bill."

He pushes another piece of paper across the desk. I scan it quickly and see it's a letter from John's attorney in California, indicating he's willing to terminate our arrangement if I sign the attached agreement. "I figured you were none the wiser. I stopped in this morning on my way out of town and found this in my inbox."

"Why the hell does Ireland want to offer this?"

"There's a catch," he says, "but one I think you should consider." He shoves yet another set of papers across the desk. At first glance I can see it's the termination agreement, but the terms are too lengthy to grasp without taking time out to read the whole document.

"Give me the short version," I say. "I'll read through this later."

"He wants compensation."

"He wants money? Fine. Whatever the amount, I'll pay it."

"No, he doesn't want money. At least not much. Only the half million dollar penalty called for, in the event the agreement is terminated."

"What else then?"

"Your uncle's land. He wants to buy it from you, once you've closed on your purchase of it. If you agree to that, he'll let you out of the arrangement with him and cut any ties between you and Stella. Permanently."

I'm completely thrown by his revelation, yet I answer without hesitation. "No."

Fuck no.

"Pierce. Come on. This is exactly what you wanted. Let Ireland have the land. You know how he is about acquisition, especially in New York. He thrives on it. You can go do your philanthropy somewhere else. Look around," he says, gesturing to the New York City streets some fifty floors below. "This city is crawling with need. It isn't required that you stay tied to Lake County."

"I don't care why he wants it, though I can assure you his aspirations are more closely tied to the devil himself than to his ego," I say. "This is not a mere conquest for him, Bill. It's personal."

Ireland's interests were about to align with R.E.E., if they hadn't already. That was the only plausible explanation.

"You'll be free of any obligation to Stella and out of his crosshairs. You should seriously consider this, Pierce."

"I'm not leaving Stanton, Bill. The land in Mirror Lake is mine." I get up and make my way to the door. "And if for some reason it isn't, you can bet your last bottle of Lenell's Red Hook that I'll be ashes scattered in the wind before Ireland ever steps foot on it."

10

Alexis

By eight a.m. Saturday morning, Gloria has deserted me to go home to her family, and I'm in my office putting together a Non-Disclosure Agreement for Aidan.

I plug in our respective names and business addresses with me as the 'Recipient' of Confidential Information, then get to the details. I take out what doesn't apply (any reference to proprietary or business-related secrets) and leave in the non-disclosure requirements for our relationship that require me not to speak about him publicly or post to social media anything about our relationship without his consent.

The rest I have to add on my own.

The Recipient shall receive Confidential Information regarding Aidan Michael Pierce, including but not limited to prior relationships, medical status, and any personal and familial histories as they may pertain to the current Relationship. Said Confidential Information will be provided at a time chosen by Aidan Michael Pierce, but shall begin on or before June 7, 2016.

The Recipient shall not distribute, disclose, or disseminate in any way such Confidential Information acquired from said Aidan Michael Pierce to any individual or entity, including but not limited to her colleagues, personal acquaintances, family members, employees, employees of Aidan Michael Pierce, or to any press or media outlet.

The last two provisions I add are personal and not so much legal, but I'm hopeful the document will remain private between us to demonstrate that he can trust me. If it never sees the light of day, so much the better. I don't intend to break the terms, but to me it's more than a binding contract. It's my request to know everything and a promise about what happens once I do – in the best way I know how to express it.

The Recipient agrees not to judge the giver of information or ignore him once said Confidential Information has been received.

The Recipient agrees to respect and abide by the terms of this Agreement for a period of:

I stop typing.

Should there should be an end date?

But I know the answer. I would never go back on my word.

The Recipient agrees to respect and abide by the terms of this Agreement in perpetuity.

I second guess myself as I finish typing, wondering if I'm doing the right thing. I don't want him to think it's too impersonal or cold.

Yet, this is me.

More than that, this is us. This is our way. We both live in a world of making things legal and binding, spelling out what's expected. The agreement is short and to the point at only three pages, but it protects us both. If I'm going headfirst into this, I need the full story about just who he is. It's only fair.

I'm jarred by my cell ringing on the desk next to me.

It's him.

Why is he calling so early?

"Good morning." I can't help my grin as I answer.

"Morning, baby. Did you sleep well?"

"I did. You're calling early. I thought I wouldn't hear from you until later."

"I took a break." He sounds tired, distracted. "I needed to hear your voice."

"What's going on?"

"Just hitting a wall. I'll break through it eventually." He sounds stressed to maximum.

"Is it John Ireland?"

"Please don't. I just...you need to trust me."

"I do. I just hate that you're going through this alone. Did you sleep last night?"

"Not much. But I'm talking to you now, so at least I'm not alone."

"I'm not sure how that helps."

"Just hearing your voice, baby. Though seeing you would be better. Do you want to come down for the night? I can send someone for you."

I'm torn. I want to be with him now, but I have no idea what else I'd be walking into.

"I don't want to get in the way or have you inconvenienced getting me there."

"You wouldn't be in the way. But I want you here for selfish reasons. It's probably better we wait. It's a risk, taking a chance we're seen together in the city."

"I understand. I can't..."

I halt my statement, unsure how forthcoming I want to be.

"What?" he urges.

I sigh.

Here goes nothing.

"I guess I'm just thrown off by how much I miss you. I'm scared to admit it because I don't know if you…if it's just me."

"It's not just you. If I had any choice, I never would have left you yesterday. You must know that."

"I know." Impulse overtakes me. There's one way I can demonstrate that I trust him implicitly, and now feels like the time. "I'd like to share something with you. How can I get a document to you securely?"

"What about?"

I'm not sure how to answer.

"What is it, Alexis?" His tone is irritable.

"An agreement. It's an agreement."

"For what? Something Myers wants?"

"No. I… it's for you. For us."

"I don't know what you mean."

"It's an NDA."

He doesn't respond.

"I want you to be comfortable telling me anything, Aidan. Telling me everything. I drafted one so you'd be more comfortable talking to me."

"That's unnecessary. Why would you do that?" His tone is bewildered, verging on angry.

"Because I thought you'd want this. We're both used to having things spelled out this way, to know what we're heading into. And I'd like the same courtesy you were afforded before you met me."

He's silent as I push on, hoping I can make him understand. So far this isn't going the way I hoped it would.

"Isn't that why you made Stella sign an agreement with you when you were together?"

"That was different," he says. "You're different."

"If that were true, you'd have talked to me openly already, without me having to persist. You didn't hold back with her. She already knows everything about you, doesn't she?"

He's quiet for a moment. I can't tell if he's resolving to my persistence or fuming in anger.

"Aidan?"

"I'm here."

I still can't tell. Mad or understanding?

Which is it?

"Could you just look at it? Please?"

"Send it by email, then delete it." His tone is clipped. "I'll take care of it on my end."

"You're mad."

I didn't want him to be angry.

"I'm not mad," he says. "Disappointed would be a better word."

Oh fuck.

This is definitely not what I was hoping for.

"Aidan, I didn't mean…"

"I have to go. I'll try you later."

"Don't hang up like that." I'm suppressing tears as I get the words out. "I just want you to trust me."

"I do," he says. "And to answer your question, Stella doesn't know everything. She never will."

He disconnects and I lose it to tears, hugging myself tight in my office as I grimace at the agreement on the screen.

Why did that go so horribly wrong?

I don't know what to do now.

Do I send it to him?

Do I keep it to myself?

I don't want to push him any further.

But if he obsesses about it, wondering what I was proposing because he hasn't seen it, I fear his paranoia will make this a bigger issue than it is.

I was surprised he'd never asked this of me to begin with.

I open a new email. I type then delete, type then delete. Four times I start over until I come up with something I hope will ease his mind.

To: Aidan M. Pierce, President PPG
From: Alexis M. Greene, Esq.
Re: NDA
Good morning (again),
I have attached a simple NDA that I mistakenly thought would help you trust me. Apparently, it has done the opposite. To be honest, I was surprised you hadn't asked me to sign one anyway.
I am not demanding that we sign it. Moreover, I'm sending it so you don't come to your own (possibly incorrect) conclusions about what I was offering to agree to.
I would like nothing more than to know the real you. The whole you - not just what everyone else sees on magazine covers or hears in news reports.
I thought this would help us get there.
I was off base and I'm sorry for that. I will not mention it again.
I hope you still trust me.
Missing you so much it hurts,
Alexis
Greene Law Office | Alexis M. Greene, Esq.

I hold my breath wondering if I'm baring too much.

Do I sound too vulnerable? Too weak? Too needy?

I read my email twice more and say "fuck it" out loud as I hit send.

Whether or not any of those questions could be answered yes, every word of my email is the truth. If I avoid being honest just for the sake of keeping my guard up, I can't see how we'd ever move forward.

I pace back and forth, waiting a solid five minutes for my phone to ring or indicate a text, or for a reply to come through. The wait is torture, each minute passing in slow motion.

Finally, a reply comes to my inbox.

To: Alexis M. Greene, Esq.
From: Aidan M. Pierce, President PPG
Re: My fault
I will read this later. I am on my way out.
I am sleep deprived and tense beyond reason. I should not have attempted to discuss this with you now. I was not in the right frame of mind.

In my defense, though - I was blindsided by the topic.
Let's talk about it later. Please don't forget to delete your email.
I miss you, too.
A-
Aidan M. Pierce, President
Pierce Philanthropy Group

I sigh.

He misses me too.

But he's not sleeping. He's beyond stressed.

And I've hurt him. I sense it in the level tone of his email. The slight lack of affection, no sense of humor at all.

I want to be with him. I need to see him.

Empathy crashes over me as I realize exactly how he felt the day Melanie's news report came out. All I want to do is make it right with him, and my options are limited just as his were when I shut him out.

I'm left with a pit in my stomach. He won't be back until Tuesday.

He doesn't want us to be seen together either, which is justified. Unless the Irelands are out of the picture, that part is understandable. But it also doesn't allow me to correct this.

I resolve the only way I can reach him is remotely and come up with something I hope will be better received. I open up my music library on the computer to make him a playlist, pushing away my thoughts that it might be too juvenile. Music has been an intense form of communication for us since we met. I know this won't be lost on him.

I start with the few songs I already have, download a couple and add two he's played for me, hoping this will convey my message and remind him of me. I log in to my internet account and create a new username and password just for his use, transfer the playlist to it, then start a new email.

To: Aidan M. Pierce, President PPG
From: Alexis M. Greene, Esq.
Re: What I Really Meant to Say
I would like to apologize again for ignoring you Thursday. I understand now exactly how you felt.
Since I can't get to you, which is what I'd really like to do, I thought this would be the next best thing.
Please use the link and login info below to access something I

made for you.
I hope you enjoy it.
Yours,
Alexis
Go to the netmusic website.
login: ifUtrustme
pw: iwilltrustU2

I hit send.

As the email leaves my computer, I let out a long breath, letting fear and anxiety go with it.

The only thing left is adrenaline.

It's after nine in the morning and I'm filled with a sudden desperation to get out of the house.

Upstairs, I throw on shorts, a tank top and sneakers, then take off for a run down to the lake. I take Huck with me for the easy mile down a grass trail to the shore.

The jog is just what I need. It's enough to clear my head and fill my lungs with fresh air, allowing me to breathe normally again.

In anticipation of summer, some guys in the neighborhood must have set the dock at the shoreline since the last time I was here. No one is here now. Not many residents use this area, the walk a bit far for some of the homes further up the street from me. The water is still too cold for swimming.

I'm grateful to be alone.

Huck and I walk to the end of the dock, and he lays at my feet as I sit on the metal bench that looks out over the water. The sky is a bright blue, the sun reflecting off the east shoreline.

I close my eyes and let the rays warm me until I can relax, confident that until I can lay eyes on Aidan again, I've done all I can do.

11

Aidan

I check my email and see the agreement from Alexis has landed in my inbox. I can't bring myself to open the attachment. I save it to my laptop and reply to her email, apologizing for my curt tone when we talked. I tell her I miss her but that we'd have to discuss the agreement later.

I'm on my way to meet one of my prospects for the gala in Brooklyn.

Even if I had the time, I have no desire to address this. I can't fathom why she's done this, why she thought it necessary.

Doesn't she realize the effect she has on me? That no one has ever gotten under my skin the way she does? I hadn't asked her to sign one intentionally. As much as it had conflicted with my past behavior when it came to women, I was damn certain I had not acted against my gut. Not when it came to her. I want to be with her without any conditions.

But I haven't told her everything.

I haven't opened up to her like she wants me to, but that was a line I never crossed with anyone. I can't make her understand everything I've been through. Even if I could, there is no need for it. All that shit is in my past. It doesn't define me.

I want to focus on the future.

The sooner I can make her realize it, the better.

Shawn Thompson is kicking my ass.

The NBA star is a beast in the paint. He's denied me under the basket several times, which is no task for him considering he's got nine inches of height on me. I've quit trying to keep up, and he damn well knows it.

"C'mon man," he goads. "You're younger than me. Get your ass in the paint."

"Funny, Thompson," I spout, "but this isn't my sport."

"What is?" He dribbles back behind the three-point line, turns, and shoots a basket without pausing so much as a second. I stand where it falls through the net and toss it back to him.

"Swimming."

"No shit," he says. "I thought you were just some rich Wall Street asshole."

"Never stepped foot on Wall Street. I'm just a regular rich asshole."

He laughs at my comment. "What event?"

I give him a look, wondering if he's feigning his interest.

"Swimming," he prods. "What event?"

"Crushed all of them," I say, "but my best was the 200-meter butterfly."

He huffs the ball to me. "I can see that, man. I can see that. You compete in college?"

"I did."

"No Olympics for you? Maybe you weren't crushin' it bad as you thought."

"I got distracted as an undergrad. Wasn't in the cards for me." I send the ball sailing back to him. "Will you come back to Stanton in July?"

I asked him to speak at the gala when we'd talked by phone last week, but he'd insisted on this powwow first. We're on his turf at a gym in Brooklyn. For me, this meeting is all about getting the yes.

I'm not sure what it is for him.

"I don't know, Pierce. The public speaking thing is my agent's idea. I ain't good at it. And I haven't been back in a long time." He shoots another basket.

"I realize that, Shawn." I grab the ball as it falls through the net again, positioning it under my arm while I try to hold his attention. "But you're always touting involvement, education for the youth of problem communities."

"I'm not playin'," he says. "I believe in that. I give back all the time. Financially."

"Then it's an opportunity to put your mouth where previously only your money has been. These kids need guidance. You want to do something for them? Show them there's another path."

"I'm no saint, Pierce. I can't be an example. That's why I've got you here. I'm hopin' you can help me get positive footing with the Lake County people. Folks weren't happy I left after freshman year to go pro."

"This gig is the best way for you to do that," I insist. "You are an example of success. This opportunity is the best thing I can offer to get you back in Lake County's good graces."

"I was hopin' more long-term."

"Like?"

"I want to coach. At Stanton U."

I can tell by his expression he knows this is a near impossible request to accommodate.

"Their staff has been lined up for years, Shawn. We both know the University isn't an option for you."

He bows his head and nods.

Stanton University had taken a sizable donation from Shawn after he'd gone pro. Improvements to their basketball facilities were accepted graciously, but the University made it public knowledge there was no place for him on their faculty. Shawn's reputation had taken a nose-dive in his first off-season. Women, illicit drugs and partying became his calling card until he'd switched teams and found himself a mentor in his last coach. Since then he'd been clean and effective for his pro team straight through retirement.

But he knows as well as I do the stigma of his past still followed him.

"Well then," he says, perking up, "what about running a program for you?"

I let the thought sink in and toss him the ball as I move closer. I hadn't considered this.

"It's a possibility, but one I can't commit to on the spot."

"I need ball in my life, Pierce. It's all I know. I'm too old to play. I can't hack it as an announcer. I've tried."

"You need some practice with it," I insist. "Give it a chance. This speaking engagement could help."

"What I need is to coach ball. College level is where the heart of the sport is."

"Come on board for the fundraiser and we'll consider it a step towards a coaching position somewhere. If there isn't enough interest to merit a program for the Center, maybe I can get you into one of the Ivy League schools."

He scoffs at my suggestion.

"Why not? You could take a Cinderella team to the big dance someday. Really make your mark in college ball. In the meantime, I'll pay you a speaking fee for your appearance and you'll get something out of it too."

"Yeah," he says, "what's that?"

"You'll be afforded an opportunity to speak. To get your message out in the hometown you came from."

He didn't need the money. He was set to retire at age thirty-four and had enough profits from endorsements alone to carry him through his lifetime. But I can see him wavering with each passing moment. He knows I can offer him more than money.

He's going to cave.

He shoots the ball again, and this time it bounces off the rim and rolls away. Neither of us move to get it.

"Sometimes the past gotta be left behind, Pierce."

Don't I know it.

"Forget the past. These kids are the future, Shawn. Things are falling apart, far worse than when you roamed the city streets at twelve years old. It's going to take effort to turn this community around. Don't you want to be a part of that effort? Pay it forward?"

"Pierce," he says, "you been watching too many movies."

"Maybe. But what a great way to end your pro career. To end Shawn Thompson's movie."

He tilts his head back and closes his eyes, grinning enough to reveal a single gold tooth.

I've got him.

"A'ight." He opens his eyes again as he concedes, reaching out to shake my hand. "I'm in, Pierce. I'm in."

I'm showered and dressed in a suit by one in the afternoon. I'm scheduled to see Marcus Neil at two, and I need to be prepared. I'm hoping he will agree to headline at the gala. This is one of the few meetings I've taken in my lifetime where I've felt intimidated.

Dr. Neil is twenty years my senior and a world-renowned self-help guru. His credentials are longer than my arm. He has doctorates in more than one field. He's taught as a guest lecturer and professor in universities all over the States, and he's written over forty books.

His advice is sought after by everyone from pro athletes to world leaders. People like me call on him hoping he will share his profound insight for a cause. Others have selfish motivations, hoping he'll counsel them one-on-one for their own gain.

I have no idea what approach to use. No matter what I say, he will see it coming a mile away. Beyond simply asking him to consider taking the paid gig, I'll be completely winging it.

Byron interrupts my anxious thoughts with a call.

"Yes," I answer. I'm hoping this is news about Whitmore. I've heard nothing since the pre-dawn hours.

"The police have exhausted their leads in Florida."

"Have they stopped searching?"

"No. As I understand it, his wife is from a prominent family there and every effort is being made to find him. So far, everything is a dead end. The cab driver reports he dropped Whitmore off at a hotel rather than at the home of his wife's parents as she had expected. We don't know why."

"Is there security footage at the hotel?"

"It's all been reviewed. Whitmore never made it past the lobby. He's shown going in, leaving his luggage there, then exiting the lobby out of the camera's reach. The vehicles that came and went all checked out. His luggage only contained his clothing. The police are canvassing, talking to hotel guests. But so far nothing."

This does not bode well for Mark Whitmore or his young family. His wife has to be beside herself with worry. I consider reaching out to her but decide against it. I am partly to blame for this. If somehow she knew that, I would be of no comfort.

"Will you be having lunch in the suite today?" Byron asks.

"Yes, I'm all set." I'd not eaten much of anything since meeting with Bill Hoffman. The bomb dropped about John Ireland being after my uncle's farmland ruined my appetite and only fueled my anger. I'd have to do something about my empty stomach before sitting down with Dr. Neil. "Have you returned the Lexus to the rental company yet?"

"No, sir. I can drive you to the meeting."

"Fine. The minute there is any news on Whitmore, I need to know. I'll see you downstairs in thirty minutes."

At two-fifteen I'm watching the second hand of a grandfather clock in Dr. Neil's reception area tick by in slow motion. He's late. I am growing impatient, wondering why someone so prominent can't be on time for an appointment.

The surroundings here are simple and clean with a relaxed, Zen-like undertone. Walls are beige, plants are botanical, and a water feature babbles in one corner. Dr. Neil's receptionist nods to me as she hangs up from a call. I'm surprised at the way this place hums with work on a Saturday afternoon.

"Dr. Neil will be joining you shortly, Mr. Pierce. He asks that you excuse his delay. It could not be helped."

"Thank you." My head is full of sarcastic comebacks I don't say aloud.

I have another meeting set up this evening. Before that, I need to think through John Ireland and somehow address Alexis' non-disclosure. But sure, I could sit here and waste an extra half an hour waiting for this guy.

Only because I don't have a fucking choice.

I need him. He'll be a huge draw for the fundraiser and I'm not about to give that up. At least my irritation at his tardiness has eliminated my nerves about taking the meeting in the first place.

I use the opportunity to scroll through email on my phone. There's one from Shawn Thompson's PR staff confirming the date and time for the gala. His representative asks to see my proposed contract and what amount I intend to pay his client. I forward the email to Samira and ask her to address it immediately.

There are several other emails from Samira and Lionel on different subject matters, but the one that grabs my attention is from Alexis. I must have missed it earlier. It came in this morning, not long after the first one she sent with the NDA.

I open it while I hold my breath, tense from anticipation.

What else is she throwing at me?

But it's nothing concerning.

In fact, it's adorable.

My baby made me a playlist.

I'm eager to know what's on it, but Dr. Neil has waltzed in through the front door of his offices.

Dammit.

"Mr. Pierce," he says as he comes towards me with a smile. "Welcome to New York."

He's shorter than I am but a commanding presence nonetheless. His black hair is woven with silver strands, cut short, and fixed in place with hair gel. He wears glasses with black rectangular frames midway down the bridge of his nose.

"Thank you, Doctor Neil. It's a great pleasure to meet you."

He's dressed impeccably, though he's not wearing a suit. Loafers, khakis, crisp blue button down shirt. His part-Indian, part-European heritage is prominent in his features and his light brown skin. Mixed with his American style of dress and a lack of any accent, his entire persona is approachable. As wise as he may be, in person he doesn't radiate the air of some holy leader you felt the need to bow to.

Yet, if he'd been dressed in robes like the Dalai Lama, that's likely what anyone would do upon meeting him. His insight is palpable.

"Shall we?" He nods to his receptionist, then leads me into his private office. The Zen motif carries through in here and I have to admit it has a calming effect. I take a seat in the vacant chair in front of his desk. "May I get you anything?" he asks. "I'm having tea."

"I'm fine, thank you. Please go ahead."

He moves to the kitchenette behind the desk, starting up a machine. I knew his teachings leaned towards the holistic side of medicine. This was likely a ritual he would not pass up for anything.

"I'd like to discuss what I proposed to your staff in our correspondence last week," I start. "I apologize for rushing into this, but I have additional items on my plate today and limited time to address them."

He turns to me as the contraption on the countertop whistles, indicating its job is done. He says nothing in response. He's taking me in, looking at me with wonder and interest. I wait out the silence, feeling intimidated once again. I don't want to say anything that will dissuade him. He brings his tea to his desk and sits down.

"I apologize for my tardiness, Mr. Pierce. I was delayed with a client emergency."

"I understand, Dr. Neil. It's no trouble."

"Before we talk about the speaking engagement, may I ask you a few questions?"

"Of course." I try to maintain a sense of calm, but it's growing more difficult. He wants to analyze my intentions and, though I know they are honorable, I'm concerned he might somehow misread me.

He sips his tea, then sets it back to rest in a saucer as he looks at me intently through his glasses. "Could you tell me what this project is that you're embarking on in Lake County?"

"I believe my assistant sent you an outline about that. If you've not received it, I could forward it now." I pull out my phone, but he stops me.

"I've read it. I'd like to hear it from you."

Here goes nothing.

"My project is an elaborate endeavor, Doctor. It's difficult to summarize, but in broad terms my concern is for the youth of the community. Prevention and treatment for drug abuse and the same for physical abuse, specifically for mothers and children."

"Why does that interest you, Mr. Pierce?"

"I have some experience with the issues."

"I was not able to find any such information about you in my research."

"It's not public record."

"I see." He considers me as another moment passes in silence. "Was this something you experienced personally or peripherally?"

"Both."

"And would you like to share any further detail?"

"Not especially."

"Very well." He lifts his chin, regarding me with interest again. "What do you hope to accomplish there?"

"Sweeping change. The City of Stanton and the surrounding communities are in a downward spiral, Doctor."

"As are many communities of the world. Why have you chosen Lake County?"

"It's where I'm from."

He gives me a slight smile and nods. "Yes," he says, "this is what I want to know. You feel you can correct the past by shaping the present and the future."

"In a manner of speaking."

"I admire your goals, Mr. Pierce. Yet the troubles of our times cannot be healed by money. It is hearts that need to be changed. Is financial assistance all you intend to contribute to this endeavor?"

"Of course not." If he's pegged me as an arrogant ass wanting to throw money at this problem just to say I did so, I'm not sure I can convince him otherwise. I make the attempt anyway. "My intention is to remain there, live in the community, and contribute in any way I can. Financially, of course. But also by learning what the root cause of the problems are. I feel immersing myself in the community is the only way to identify that need and steer help where it needs to go in order to make a difference."

"Do you have a woman in your life?"

What the hell? Where'd that come from?

"To be honest with you, Doctor, I'm not sure how that factors into our conversation."

"You're used to a single-mindedness in your endeavors to this point in your life. You've been quite successful in business, I understand. But success in this type of endeavor requires a different kind of strength, a vulnerability that many in your circumstances do not possess."

"I see. And if I have a romantic relationship that makes me vulnerable?"

"Without question. Don't you agree?"

I wait a moment and nod. "I do."

"You have drive, Mr. Pierce. In fact, you exude it. But brawn and intelligence, bulldozing through a project like this with only ambition? It will not work."

I sit in silence, letting him go on. If I'm about to get advice from Dr. Marcus Neil, I'm sure as hell going to soak it up and commit it to memory.

"Helping people requires emotion. Success in helping others requires you to open yourself to the same healing. To give is to receive, as I'm sure you understand. But to give only currency of paper without currency of the heart? Any such endeavor is futile and doomed to fail."

"I can assure you, Doctor, my ambition is matched by my innate desire to help."

The greater good. Always.

"You have yet to answer my question."

"About?"

"Have you someone important in your life, someone that's helping you in this work?"

"I have two parents that are very supportive of my efforts, both emotionally and financially."

"A strong family unit is a welcome cradle for the soul. This will be of great help to you. And as to a relationship?"

I let go a crooked smile as I bow my head briefly, then raise it again. "I've recently met someone, yes."

"I'm pleased to hear it." He smiles back a full grin, revealing a perfect set of white teeth. "Your energy said as much. She is worthy of your affections?"

She damn well is.

"More than I could have imagined. It's me that is not worthy." I mutter the last part under my breath.

He regards me with skepticism, having heard the latter part loud and clear. "How are you unworthy? Has she said so? Decided this?"

"I am not the best choice for her," I admit. "She is unaware of my past. She does not know me well enough to make such a decision."

"Then you must make her aware," he urges. "You are not unworthy. None of us is unworthy of love, despite our pasts. You already know this or you would not see this community as worthy of your time and kindness. If I'm left to guess, I'd say this same community was a souce of trauma for you or your loved ones in the past. Is that right?"

I nod.

"Yet here you are doing everything in your power to uplift that same community. It's an obvious parallel, Mr. Pierce."

I admit he has a point and tell him so.

"The past need not be hidden because it is not perfect. It is always there, whether it lies in wait underneath or rises to the surface. It shapes who we are from moment to moment. You must stop denying this. It is the only way to enlighten yourself, to free the soul to do what it was meant to do. You believe this is your chosen path, to help these people?"

"I do." I'd never uttered truer words. From the moment I'd begun this, I knew it was what I wanted. It put me in the zone, as they say. Made me forget to eat or sleep.

Being with Alexis is the only thing I've experienced that comes close.

"I believe so too," he finally says. "But you will need another to help you on this path. You cannot do it alone."

"I think I may already have that covered, Doctor." He smiles knowingly in response. "Does this mean you'd like to come and speak for us at the gala?"

He takes another sip of his tea.

"I will need to consider it a bit longer," he says. "I'm inspired, Mr. Pierce, and eager to see your success. Seeing someone step foot on their destined path is a thrilling experience for me, as much as for that soul. However, I will need time for self-reflection and to consider whether my involvement is necessary."

"Thank you, Doctor. I'll send your assistant the particulars and perhaps you could let me know by tomorrow?"

"I believe that will be time enough."

"And your fee, if you agree to headline?"

"One hundred thousand," he says without missing a beat. "But I will donate a quarter of that back to your organization if I decide to accept the engagement."

"That would be agreeable," I say. "Thank you for your time, Doctor."

"Thank you, Mr. Pierce." He stands to shake my hand. "I wish you every success."

As I'm riding back to the hotel, I scroll through my phone to find Alexis' last email while the Doctor's advice plays fluidly through my head.

You must make her aware. None of us is unworthy of love.

I didn't take the guy for a quack, but customarily I'd dismiss him as too spiritual for my taste. I usually craved concrete advice, numbered steps to take that would advance me to a desired outcome. The 'feed your soul' stuff I always took in small doses as needed but without directly pursuing it.

Yet the meeting with Dr. Neil had hit me hard, in a sledgehammer-over-the-head way.

I'd have been skeptical that ten minutes with anyone could do this to me, but this is Marcus Neil. People paid thousands of dollars for ten minutes with him because they knew it had the possibility to change their lives.

It isn't fair of me to keep myself from Alexis. If she wants to know everything about me, I'll have to reveal as much as I can – or at least tell her I'm willing to.

"Byron," I speak up from the backseat, "is there a set of earbuds in here?"

"Yes." He reaches into the glove box and retrieves a pair, handing them back to me.

"Thanks." I pop them into my ears and plug the jack into the phone, then log in to the website Alexis provided with her playlist. Or rather, my playlist – the one she made for me.

I recognize a couple of the songs from our time together, but there are a few others I've never heard. I open up the list and play it in order, wanting to hear the songs as she intended.

By the last one, I'm overtaken by her sentiment. When we arrive back at the hotel, I'm on a mission.

"Byron," I say as he parks in the nearby garage. "I need you to go back to Mirror Lake. Could you extend the rental on this car and drive it back to Stanton? Samira can meet you at the rental place for return so you can have the Lincoln."

"Of course, sir. Whatever you require."

"I just have one thing to do first."

By evening, I'm utterly exhausted. I have to meet Sicily Strauss before her set in an hour and hopefully secure her for the gala. If I can get her to say yes, the only remaining question mark would be Dr. Neil. If my instinct was right, I believed he'd be coming on board too.

I've already addressed Alexis and her NDA with Byron's help. There's been no further news on Whitmore. The police had come up with zip.

In the meantime, it's six p.m. and I'm trying to figure out how to handle John Ireland. I'd missed Dimitri's call late this morning. I call him back to fill him in.

"Yeah, bro. S'up?"

"Sorry I missed your call. Been in meetings all day. One of which you'll want to hear about."

"What now?"

"My attorney summoned me at six o'clock this morning. John Ireland approached him about letting me out of our agreement."

"Why the fuck would he do that? Did he have a near death experience? Some bad Chinese food?"

"No. He wants something."

"Okay," he says. "So give it to him."

"It's my uncle's land he's after. He wants me to sell it to him."

"Christ," he bristles. "What the hell for?"

I ignore his question. "I will not do that, Dimitri. Under no circumstances is he to get that land. If for some reason I leave this Earth, you're to make sure that never happens."

"I got it," he says. "But maybe we can use this to our advantage."

"I've been so preoccupied I haven't had time to think that through."

"Let him believe you're selling it to him." I can hear him light up a smoke.

"He won't believe that unless I put it in writing."

"Don't sign anything, obviously. But talk to him. Put up a fight, play the game. Then concede and tell him you'll sign something soon. At least it will buy us more time."

I consider it. At my silence, he goes on.

"It's worth a shot. It's a simple distraction, and you can't lose anything by trying."

"Maybe you're right." If I go into a conversation with him denying his offer, I might be able to switch tactics without him being wise to it. "Can you keep mining the dealing angle until then? I might be able to buy us a week." If that was all the time it afforded us, it would still be worth it.

"Absolutely. And I can pursue Armstrong, if you still think it's a good idea."

"I'll put Curtis on duty to tail him from a distance. I'll let you know if he uncovers anything we can use. Otherwise, he's probably a lost cause. You were right about him being unreliable."

"Okay. Good luck, man. I'm here for now. We'll be heading to New York for the convention in a couple weeks. Maybe we can hook up."

I had forgotten the tattoo expo coming up. He told me while I was in L.A. he intended to have a booth here. I knew he'd been considering opening another shop in New York since last fall.

"Nikki's coming too?"

"Of course. We're salt and pepper now, man. Not one without the other."

I laugh at that. "Maybe you can get up and see us in Stanton."

"Sure, if there's time. She wants me to meet her family in Brooklyn while we're there. Wait a sec," he says. "Who is 'us'?"

Damn that slip. I didn't want to tell him about Alexis over the phone. I hadn't mentioned her to him at all until now.

"You'll see," I say, "when you come out here."

"Things are starting to make sense now," he says. "You got yourself a woman, Pierce?"

I can't help my smile. "It's looking that way."

"You cagey fucker. Why didn't you just tell me that's why you were pushing the remove-Ireland-swiftly-from-my-ass agenda?"

"I don't know. It's early, I guess."

"I can't wait to meet her," he says. "Gotta jet. I'll call you the minute there's news."

"Likewise."

"And Pierce?"

"Yeah."

"Hold onto your hat, bro. It's one bumpy fuckin' ride."

12

Alexis

By Saturday evening, I haven't heard from Aidan. No emails in response to mine and no text messages.

Nothing.

I haven't shared what's going on with anyone, and I'm uneasy and restless. Huck can sense it, not leaving my side.

The weather is as unsettled as I am. Another storm is coming through, but this one is supposed to be quick. Just enough to decrease humidity a bit and settle the temperatures back to the seventies.

It's Ben's birthday today. Charlie left me a voicemail asking to meet up with him and Carter for dinner, but I haven't acknowledged it. I can't decide whether to get shitfaced to celebrate Ben's life or get drunk to avoid thinking about his death.

Or maybe I'll just keep sulking in sobriety.

I called Ben's parents this afternoon to apologize for not coming up this weekend. The Claytons confirmed Pam had called to let them know I'll be up to visit next weekend.

If Aidan is still speaking to me.

If he isn't, I'll go on my own.

The only other things I've accomplished today are a shower and putting together the notes from my meeting with Jade, which I didn't bother to send to Aidan. She sent her list of attendees a day early but I decided not to reach out to him again. I don't want to interrupt whatever he's in the middle of.

I haven't eaten much all day. I'm looking through the refrigerator when the doorbell rings. Huck barks with a few low *woofs,* and I head to the door after him, hoping I can bring him to heel.

I look through the sidelights before turning the knob.

As I open the door, Byron gives the dog his typical stern look, holding up his magic hand signal. Huck responds by sitting obediently.

"Byron," I say in greeting, "what can I do for you?"

"Mr. Pierce asked me to deliver this to you." He's holding a black folder in his hand, the same type that held the Myers contract.

This guy must get tired of moving at Aidan's whims.

"Please come in." He does, handing off the folder to me and giving the dog another signal, this one releasing Huck from his sit. Byron lets him lean in, petting him. I don't open the folder he's passed off to me. "Can I offer you anything?"

"No, thank you. I'll just wait until you have a chance to read what's inside. I'm supposed to take it with me."

"I'm not sure what this is."

"Shall I walk him for you?" He gestures to the dog, ignoring my comment. "The storm is not due for another half hour. Mr. Pierce indicated thirty minutes would give you sufficient time to read this."

I nod and head to the closet, get Huck's lead, and clip it to the dog's collar.

I hold up the folder. "Do you know what's in here?"

"Yes." He doesn't elaborate.

Okay, I'm not getting anywhere with Mr. Secretive.

"Fine. Please be careful. Don't get stuck in the weather."

"Yes, ma'am. We'll be right back."

He heads out the door, and I'm left staring as they walk off together.

I take the folder to the kitchen and grab a glass of red for my nerves and a snack to quiet my stomach. I'm anticipating the worst. I sit at the island and open the folder. Inside are two printed copies of the NDA I drafted. I flip to the last page.

Aidan signed them in blue ink. His signature is notarized by Byron.

Byron Santangelo.

So he's Italian.

Of course.

On the first agreement, there's a note stuck to the paper, underneath Aidan's signature.

Alexis,

You were right to suggest this.

I apologize for overreacting and hope you forgive me.

Please sign both copies and give one to Byron.

I can't promise how this will go from here. There is a lot you don't know. I can only assure you that I'll do my best. Once Byron has your signed copy, he has something else for you. It isn't much but, until I can get to you, it's a start.

Please call me after you've seen it.

Thank you for the playlist. I've listened to it on repeat all afternoon.

Yours,

A-

Relief collides with apprehension in the pit of my belly.

He signed it.

He likes the music.

He signed off that he's mine.

But what does Byron have?

I go to the drawer next to the refrigerator for a pen and sign both copies.

I'm on edge and pacing the foyer when he returns with the dog. It's beginning to thunder in the distance.

"Such a fine animal, this boy," he says coming through the screen door with his reserved smile. "Thank you for letting me take him."

I'm surprised at the change in him once again. These two are so good for each other.

"Thank you, Byron. Did Aidan ask you about next weekend?"

"He did. I'd be happy to keep the dog for you. He can stay with me."

"I…oh. Okay. Where will you be?"

"I'm staying in Falcon Lake at Mr. Pierce's other home there."

"Do you have a place for Huck to be outdoors? Maybe you could stay here with him if that's easier."

"No, ma'am. Not necessary. There is a fence for the yard. I used to have a dog myself. Mr. Pierce had the grounds outfitted to suit me while I was here last year."

"If you're sure. And please don't call me ma'am, Byron. I'm not a thousand years old."

He nods. "Do you have something for me?"

"Yes," I say as I hand over the folder. "I've signed it."

"Very well. May I witness your signature?"

"Please." I gesture across the foyer to my desk in the office. He pulls a pen and a stamp from the inside pocket of his suit and fills out his portion of both documents, then hands one of them back to me. It occurs to me he saw Aidan within the last several hours and may see him again tonight.

"You've been with Aidan today?"

"Yes."

"Is he well?"

"He is doing fine."

"I'm worried about him, Byron. He isn't sleeping. He's got so much to juggle. Are you going back to him today?"

"Not today. I am sure he will be better now that this has been addressed."

Oh.

I'm stung realizing part of his pressures come from me. Byron must be able to read it on my face.

"He can handle a lot, Ms. Greene. I will check in with him. Not to worry."

"Thank you. I appreciate that." I open my desk drawer and pull out an empty folder, placing my copy of the agreement inside. "Was there anything else?"

He returns his pen and stamp to his shirt pocket, then pulls a flash drive from the front pocket of his suit jacket.

"Just this. Please call Mr. Pierce once you've reviewed what's on here. It should not leave the house, and please do not save it to any of your devices."

Sheesh.

"Okay. I'll keep it safe," I promise him. "Don't worry."

He nods to me as he turns to go.

"Thank you, Byron. I'm sure I'll see you soon."

"Yes, ma'…Ms. Greene. Have a pleasant night."

And he's gone, leaving Huck and me to watch him get in the Lincoln and drive away.

A half an hour later, I'm on my computer reading the sole document on the flash drive Byron delivered – a report about the enigma that I am falling so hard for.

Name:	Aidan Michael Pierce (Adopted Surname)
Age:	32
Birth date:	06/21/1983

Height:	6'1"
Weight:	179 lbs.
Marital Status:	Single
Marital History:	None
Mother:	Victoria Ray Pierce (Nee: Davis)
Adoptive Father:	Reginald Watson Pierce
Biological Father:	Chet William Simmons
Siblings:	Thaddeus Raymond Pierce (Adopted Surname) (Deceased, June 21, 2007)
Adverse Medical History:	PTSD (Diagnosis January 2009): Resulting from: History of Child Abuse Automobile Accident 2007 Substance Abuse (Diagnosis: Nov. 2008): Various Recreational Drug Use Neuro-enhancers, Marijuana, Cocaine Period of Use: 2003-2008
Current Medical Health:	Patient is in good overall health No additional medical concerns at present
Current Mental Health:	Patient is currently managing PTSD without prescribed medication or medical intervention. Attending bi-weekly sessions as prescribed
Current Medications:	None Prescribed
Current Drug/Alcohol Use:	Occasional alcohol consumption
Other:	None
Current Physical Limitations:	None
Professional Status:	See Attached Résumé
Criminal Record:	Expunged 2009
Certified By:	Dr. James Mason Psy. D., CSAC, Board Certified A.B.P.P. Physicians Medical Complex 8000 4th Street, Suite 301 Newport Beach, CA 92660

Holy fuck.

On the surface, it doesn't seem like a lot of information. It's only one page. His résumé is not attached as the document claims. I could not care less about his employment history or about what his GPA was at Yale or how many accolades highlight his climb in the business world.

There are enough facts to digest without any of that.

I promised I wouldn't ignore him once I had this information. I agreed, per Byron's instructions, that I would call.

But I have no idea what to say or where to begin. I know where my thoughts are headed but that isn't helpful.

I'm sorry you were abused as a child.

Do you still have symptoms from PTSD?

Where is your biological father now?

How can I say any of these things without being a complete hypocrite, placating him like so many people did to me when Ben died? Or seeming like someone that just wants to pry out of curiosity?

I can see exactly why he didn't want to jump into this. Just this set of facts is overwhelming and I don't even have any of the details.

How was he abused? How often?

He was in a car accident *with* his brother when his brother died? How does someone even handle that?

My sad past suddenly seems tame in comparison to his.

The line I have to tread is so fine. My knee bounces in unrest, heart beating fast in anticipation of calling him. I know he won't want me to treat him differently, look at him as something less than I have before this moment. If I show too much concern, it will make him feel weak, as though I feel sorry for him.

He wouldn't stand for that, and I can't blame him. I understand why he tells no one these things, except some guy named Dr. Mason in California.

Apparently, that guy knows some shit. Idly I wonder what kind of NDA he had to sign.

I try to go through everything about my own therapy in my head. My past with my mother. Losing my Dad. Losing Ben. If I can pull to the forefront my own tragedies, maybe I can talk to him from a place of understanding without coming across as pitying.

I head to the kitchen to refill my wine glass then dial his cell, hoping I'm not interrupting his evening. The display on my phone reads eight o'clock.

He answers on the second ring.

"Alexis. Hold on."

I can't determine his mood. I hear some music in the background, then him talking to someone, but it's muffled. A few moments later, he comes back to the phone and there's no other noise. Just his voice.

"Hey, baby."

There it is.

The tone I've missed since this morning. I ache for him, wanting to be with him now, to hear those words in person.

"Are you still there?"

"I'm…yes, I'm here. Hey yourself," I say, recovering.

"I understand you had a visitor this evening?"

"Yes. Or Huck did." I force a laugh, trying to keep the mood light. "I can't believe how this mutt changes Byron's disposition. One brief walk and they…"

He cuts me off. "Alexis, don't."

"I…don't what?"

"It's okay. You don't have to do that. Let's just talk about it."

"Where are you?"

"Walking back into the hotel. Heading upstairs."

"I wish I was there."

"Me too."

"I don't know what to say to you, Aidan, except thank you."

"I understand. It's a lot to digest."

"Yes and no. I mean it is a lot. But the thank you was for trusting me. I understand now why you…" I stop, take in a sharp breath and let it go. "I get it now."

"I understand if it's too much. You don't have to humor me. If you can't...if you need time…"

Is he really thinking I would walk away just from learning this?

"Please don't say any more. When you're ready, it will come. When we're together. I can't stand being away from you as it is, but this – this makes it harder. I didn't intend to push you. I hope you know I wouldn't walk away just because you decided to be honest with me."

"You didn't push beyond what any rational person would want to know. You should know everything. But this is all I can give you. For now."

"I should have been with you, looked you in the eyes when you told me these things."

"I know that's what you want." He pauses, the silence lingering so long I wonder if we've been disconnected. "I don't know if I can give you that."

"You don't want me to pity you."

He hesitates again. "Yes."

"Aidan, I've been there. My past may not compare to yours, but I've been there too. People looking at you like their heart is breaking for you, trying to reassure you that things are okay. That life is full of roses and fucking rainbows. I won't insult you with that."

He's quiet. I can hear the sound of the elevator pinging in the background.

"When are you getting back?" I ask.

"I'm not sure."

"Oh." *Does he not want to tell me?* "I'll send you my notes from the meeting with Jade. She has the guest list done too."

"Great."

He is distant again, sounding removed and exhausted.

"Aidan?"

"Yeah."

"Are you all right?"

"I'm fine," he says. "Just tired."

"What do you have left to do?"

"I'm done for the day."

"Maybe you should get some rest."

"Solid plan, Greene."

I smile at that, not wanting to let him go. I know he's going to excuse himself to hang up at any moment.

"I miss you, Aidan. I can't…" I'm holding back tears again. I can't think of any words that won't sound contrived.

"I miss you, too. I think I'll take your advice and go to bed."

"Yeah, okay. I'll talk to you tomorrow."

"Good night, baby."

"Good night."

I hang up in tears, fearing I've completely screwed everything up. This beautiful man is already pushed to his limits and all I've done is add to his fears and anxieties, added to his already full plate with my insistence that he open himself up to me.

Huck is at my feet at the kitchen island, nosing under my elbow and trying to comfort his hot mess of a human mama. I love him up and pull myself together, wiping my eyes. He scratches to be let down to his couch in the basement and I settle him there, then climb the stairs to my room.

I take a bath to relax. When I'm clean and dry, I put on the slip Aidan gifted me, wanting to feel close to him somehow. After today, I don't feel close to him at all. I've pushed him too far, too fast.

Open Last plays through my phone. I don't even bother to put my earbuds in. I want his voice to fill the room around me, hoping I might dream about him.

I wish I'd never asked for more.

I finally fall into sleep, hoping a new day can undo what I've done.

My sleep is fitful, broken up by imaginary interruptions. I've woken up three times, each time having to fight to quiet the thoughts in my head.

As I doze off again, I'm startled by something buzzing. I wonder if somehow there's an insect crawling in my bed until I come to, realizing the buzzing is from the phone next to my head.

I look at the display. It's four a.m. and the call is coming from Aidan.

"What the hell, Aidan." My voice is weak as I answer. "Are you okay?"

"I'm about to be. Come downstairs and open the door."

"Wait." I bolt upright. "You're here?"

"Yes. Are you coming down or what?"

I disconnect and jump out of bed. I wonder why Huck isn't barking from the basement, then realize the dog is clueless about my visitor. No one rang the doorbell.

I run to the bathroom and brush my teeth for a matter of seconds, then take the stairs two at a time hoping I don't wipe out in my haste. I open the door quietly.

He's standing on the other side of the screen, freshly showered in shorts and a t-shirt leaning in the doorway.

My Aidan.

Before I can assess any further, he's through the door and on me. My lips blaze from the roughness of his kiss. His hands are around my back, holding me in his solid arms.

I hope I'm not dreaming and pull away to look at him, touching his face to make sure.

"You're here? I thought…"

"I know. I couldn't wait." He steps away and quietly shuts the door, coming back to me.

"I can't believe…how did you get here?"

"Does it matter?"

I smile in the darkness. I hadn't bothered to turn on any lights.

"No."

He pulls his phone out of his pocket with a pair of earbuds attached.

He places them gently in my ears, then pushes play on his screen, which is the only source of light in the foyer. One of the songs from the playlist I made begins – Nick Jonas' "Close" – and Aidan pockets the phone, pulling me to him.

His lips are on me again before I can say another word. I'm wet in seconds, the sensuality of the song pulsing through me.

Aidan is here, kissing me, reminding me of what he does to me, adding gasoline to an already raging fire. He lifts me up, wrapping my legs around him. My arms are locked around his neck, and his shorts are bulging in all the right places, revving me.

"Upstairs," I whisper in his ear. "Quietly."

He nods, then turns for the stairs, carrying me with him without a second thought about the effort. My lips roam his neck, taking in his scent through all my senses while the song continues to seduce me. When we get to my bedroom, he sets me down next to the bed.

He takes off his shirt and with music still in my ears, my hands roam all over him, caressing every inch of his shoulders, his chest, down his chiseled abs. He lifts my chin up with a finger, laying a kiss on me before he licks my lips.

I reach into his pocket for the phone, hearing the song is almost over. He moans as my hands find him beneath the fabric, stroking him until I abandon him to remove the phone. I slide the cue backwards, to the part of the song where the female lead starts singing. I take the earbuds out, lean up on tiptoe and place them in his ears. He's smiling as I start the song up again.

I can't help my own sly grin, undoing his belt and tossing it across the room. I unbutton his shorts and stop, waiting for a reaction.

He grabs behind my head, pulling me close and leaning into me, his tongue reaching deep in my mouth.

I've so missed this.

The taste of him, how strong he feels. I unzip him, letting his shorts fall off, leaving him standing there in boxer briefs.

Goddamn.

He could totally model that underwear professionally.

He tosses his removed clothing aside as I look down at the player he holds, seeing the song has ended. He takes the earbuds out, setting the phone on my dresser.

"I really like that song."

"You're liking a little Nick Jonas, huh?"

"You tell anyone," he says with a grin, "I'll flat out deny it."

I move to the bed to pull the covers back, neatening them after my restless night.

"Looks like you were sleeping about as well as I was."

"All I wanted was to be with you," I say, looking up at him as I sit on the edge of the bed, my hands falling to my lap in tired frustration. "I couldn't rest knowing how we left things, how I screwed things up. I'm so sorry, Aidan. I should have left well enough alone."

"Don't apologize. All I want is you. I don't care about all that. You're all I can think about." He stands between my legs, running his hands up and down my bare arms. "And you wore this," he says, toying with the straps of my slip. "It's like you knew I was coming."

"I needed to feel you, get near you somehow. My options were limited."

He lifts the purple silk over my head, revealing nothing underneath. His mouth is on my chest, roaming down until he gets lower. Before he can get too involved, I move away, back onto the middle of the bed to lay my head on a pillow. I don't want him to pleasure me. I want us to be as close as possible.

"I need to ask you a question now."

"Fine," I say. I can't wait to have him inside me. "But hurry up."

"Have you ever been with anyone else in this bed?"

"Never."

"Good," he says. "Another first."

He climbs over me and everything tingles in anticipation. My lips are parted, nipples erect.

"God baby, what are you doing to me? I can't get enough of you underneath me. Look at how ready you are. *Sei così bella.*"

He kisses me tenderly, softer than before. I kiss him back, ready to turn things up. I more than want him. I need him.

"Aidan, please. I can't wait any longer."

"Do you want me to make love to you now?" He's licking my neck, each breast in turn, kissing my sternum, trailing all the way down until I'm left begging.

"Yes," I moan. "*Please.*"

"You'd beg for it, hmm?" His lips trail back up my belly, and he's hovering above me, looking into my eyes with those mesmerizing baby blues that cut me to the core.

"Yes. I need you."

"Now?" he asks. He's watching me, his eyes dancing in anticipation, still hovering.

"*Now,*" I breathe. "*Please.*"

He lunges inside me before I can brace myself, as deep as he can, deep enough that it almost hurts. He stops abruptly, holding my gaze as he pushes himself up so he can look at me, still buried.

"I don't want to hurt you, Alexis."

"You're not," I say, my hand moving to his face, touching him. He's freshly shaven, his skin soft. "This feels so good, Aidan. I can't tell you how much I miss this when you're gone."

"I don't want to hurt you, Alexis," he says again.

I blink in the darkness.

He doesn't mean physically hurt me.

"Stop. You can't think like that. You haven't hurt me. I know you'd never..."

"People around me, they get hurt. I won't...I don't want that to happen with you."

"Then be here with me. That's all I want right now. Don't think anymore, Aidan. Do you want me?"

He comes down to me, kissing me almost with caution, as though he's afraid to break me again, like the first time.

"I don't just want you. It's so much more than that."

I move underneath him, finding a rhythm, hoping he'll stop thinking and just let us be us.

"Let it go, Aidan. I'm right here," I say, wrapping my legs around him. "Let it go."

He groans as he moves above me, his momentum starting to build as he glides in and out. I unwrap my legs, then nudge his shoulders with my hands as I push up, urging him onto his back. He complies with one swift, strong movement that takes me with him, and I find myself on top.

"That was impressive. And I like the view from up here."

His lips curve into a full smile and in that moment my whole world is righted. I let my fingertips move along his jawline in unison, then glide down his torso before resting my hands on his chest. I'm relishing this moment, enjoying just looking at him.

"The view from here isn't so bad, either," he says. "You have glorious tits, baby. Did you know that?"

"I didn't." I'm glad for the dimness to hide my blushing. "Do you know you have completely taken me over?"

"Have I? I thought it was the other way around."

"No way. I'm completely at your mercy."

"Doesn't seem that way now," he says, moving underneath me to demonstrate.

"I should take full advantage then, hmm?"

I lean down to him and take over his mouth. He responds with fervor, his arms circling me, pulling me close so our bodies are pressed together. I can't move this way, but the feeling of his arms around me, the closeness, it's what I've been longing for since we parted.

He's stroking my hair, hands gliding up and down my back as I nuzzle his neck.

I wiggle my way out from his hold, sitting straight up to rest all my weight on my shins. Slowly I rise, then move back down on him fast. My sight has adjusted in the darkness, and I can see his eyes go wide.

"*Oh shit, baby,*" he growls. "Do that again."

I do, sliding up slow, coming down fast. He moves his hands to my chest, gently working my breasts as he tweaks my nipples with his thumbs, keeping up with my rhythm. He moves his right hand down, his thumb finding my clit as I cry out, stimulated beyond rationality.

"Can you come this way?"

I manage a nod, my head falling back as I keep going, moving my hands to my chest. I can't stop the climb. I lose myself to sensation, letting go of doubt and insecurity. Climax takes hold and I'm shuddering as he grabs my hips, trying to keep me still. The effort now comes from him, pushing up from beneath me.

He's close, I can feel it.

"My God, Alexis…*shit.*" He's lifting me up and down his length, and in seconds he's exploding, filling me up as he moans in the glorious way he has, pulling me down and holding me in place until his throbbing inside me subsides.

I lean over him, kissing his chest, his neck, my hair draping over us as I relish the feeling of having him inside me. He wraps his arms around me tightly. His breathing is intense, labored as he tries to bring himself down from the moment.

He says nothing as I lay with him, rising up and down with the movement of his chest. I'm sprawled over him, my arms fully outstretched along his like the arms of a cross, our chests pressed together. We rise and fall in unison until his breathing needs less effort.

"Are you all right?" I whisper it, not wanting to break the quiet.

"Better than I ever have been."

I lean up to look at him, folding in my forearms to rest on his chest. He moves my hair away, and I can't take my eyes off his.

"When you wouldn't talk to me this morning..." I say.

"I know, baby." He strokes my hair. "I'm sorry. I just needed time."

"I'm the one who should be sorry. I wasn't even considering this would be another burden to you when you're already dealing with so much."

"I understand what you were trying to do. I thought about it, and I realized you've done nothing but trust me since we met. You're right, I always have the upper hand. More knowledge about you, no unknowns going in. If this is going to work, we need to have an even playing field."

"And exactly what is this? I know you said you can't answer that, but I..." I stop, starting again with a new breath. "Aidan, I don't even want to think about the next time you go. I'm becoming addicted. You're like..." I hesitate again.

I don't want to offend him with my current thought.

"I know what you're thinking. You can say it."

"Yes, okay?" I say, knowing he's figured me out. "You're like a drug. I've never felt like this before. It's so overwhelming. And scary. And beyond incredible."

"I agree with you, in every sense. That's exactly what a drug is, what it does. You get hooked on it, you think you can't live without it, without the next high."

"But people should live without that. It isn't healthy. Look how successful you are without it. You didn't need any outside vices. What if you don't need me? What if this is a detrimental addiction, something that wrecks us both?"

"It's not true that I have no vices. I have ways of coping, other things that replace the high. They're just not going to kill me."

"Like?"

"Running. Music. Sex," he pauses. "You."

"And who else are you having sex with?" I tease, sitting up astride him. I feign anger as I cross my arms over my naked chest. He lets out a lighthearted laugh, and I'm elated at the sound.

"I promise, baby," he smiles. "You're all I can handle."

I smile back as he lifts me up by my hips, withdrawing from me and settling me back down to lay next to him. The emptiness is more tolerable this time, maybe because I'm exhausted.

"I still can't define this for you, Alexis." I'm in the crook of his arm and he pulls me close, tracing my lower back with the tips of his fingers. "I can tell you I'm right here with you, as high as you are. And yes, just as addicted. But in a good way."

"Like being addicted to kale?" I joke.

He laughs softly, the sound a low hum in his throat. "Better than that," he says. He turns my face to him with his free hand, my eyes meeting his. "Like being addicted to someone that makes you feel more alive than you've ever been before. Someone that only makes you better than you were the day before."

His words take my breath, then relieve me to the point of fatigue as I exhale, letting them sink in. I run a finger below his navel, over the outline of his tattoo.

"I'm exhausted," I mutter.

"Me too." He pulls the covers up over us, urging me to turn over. He gets up to grab his phone and brings it back to bed.

"You liked the playlist?" I ask quietly. Sleepiness is taking over against my will.

"I loved it. No one's ever done that for me."

"It wasn't too cheesy? I figured I wasn't the first girl that ever made you something like that."

"Nope, another first. And sometimes I like cheesy," he says, stealing the words I'd spoken to him only days ago. He scrolls through the short list and finds Matt Nathanson's "Suspended". "I liked every song, but this was my second favorite. I'd never heard it."

"Mm-hmm. It's a beautiful song," I say. "Tomorrow is Sunday, Aidan. Will you stay? We can sleep in. Pretend we're normal." I close my eyes, relaxing as he spoons me again.

"Actually, today is Sunday. And yes, I cleared my day. Sleep, my love." His lips are on my shoulder, his arm around me.

I'm sighing at his words, at the music I chose for him filling the room. I'm content for the first time since we'd parted company on Friday morning, allowing sleep to take me over before the song can finish.

13

Alexis

I'm woken up by the sound of Huck barking from the basement.

I feel around for Aidan, but he's gone.

Maybe I dreamt last night.

I hear water running in the bathroom sink and sigh with relief. He comes out a moment later, dressed for a run.

"Morning."

"What time is it?" I sit up, pulling the sheet with me.

"Ten."

"Holy shit. I never sleep this late. And now twice in two weeks."

"Yeah," he laughs. "Me either. I've been up about ten minutes. Considering we went to bed at five in the morning, we're early."

"You brought clothes?"

"Yes. I left them in the car. I think I woke the dog up when I went out the front door a few minutes ago. Do you want to run with me?"

"No thanks," I say, rolling back over. "Wake me up when there's coffee."

"Can I take the pup? How far can he make it?"

"If it's still cool out, he can make it a few miles. If it's over eighty, don't bother. I'll let him out in a minute."

"He'll be fine. No humidity today," he says. "I just want to put in a couple miles. Where's the leash?"

"In the front hall closet," I mumble. I so don't want to get up.

He leans over me and plants a kiss on my head.

"I'll be back soon." He smacks me on the ass before he starts away and I turn over to watch him.

"What do you want to eat when you get back?"

He stops in the doorway and looks back at me, grinning.

"Oh *Jesus.*" I roll my eyes. "Go run it out of your system, stud. Or the only workout you'll get in this morning is from me." After the slap on the ass and his innuendos I'm sure as hell awake now.

"Tempting," he says. "But I'll consider that a cool down when I get back. *Addio per ora, splendida.*"

"English!" I shout to him as he takes off down the stairs, but he doesn't respond. I hear him let the dog up and listen to the sound of them greeting each other, flooded with emotion at the excitement in Aidan's voice asking the dog if he's ready to go. The closet door opens and closes, then the front door as they leave.

I take the opportunity to get up and shower, washing away the evidence of last night's reunion with Aidan. I'm still high on the fact that he's back, that he couldn't wait another second to be with me. Again confident we're on the same page, I head downstairs dressed in shorts and a t-shirt ready to spend a relaxing Sunday in his company.

I'm in my kitchen watching Aidan sit at the island and eat a plate of bacon and eggs. I've been assessing him for a few minutes as I sip my coffee, trying to determine if my opinion is biased.

I conclude that regardless of the fact that I'm sleeping with him, any woman alive would agree even the way he eats is sexy. He is just that pleasing to look at.

"Are you going to watch me eat all morning?" He asks the question without looking up from his phone as he scrolls through it.

"No, I'm good now."

"Good," he says. He smiles as he pushes away his clean plate. "What do you want to do today?"

"Really? My choice?"

"Your choice, baby." He sets his phone aside. "I'm all yours."

"I like the sound of that." *Maybe a little too much.* "How about we take a ride?"

"Solid plan, Greene. Where to?"

"I don't really care, Aidan. Wherever you want to go."

"Okay," he says, smiling his mischievous smile. "I have somewhere in mind."

"Great. You might want to shower first."

"Another sound idea." He gets up to clear the dishes. "Let's go."

"Oh no," I say. "You're on your own. Otherwise we won't leave the bedroom today."

"Good point," he says, coming over to kiss me.

"Hit the showers. I'll be at the computer."

Somehow I've managed to keep from following him upstairs while he showers and dresses, knowing it would only jumpstart both of us.

I spend the time composing the email I'd promised to send, with notes and ideas I had while sitting down with Jade. I attach the file she emailed to me yesterday. Aidan now has a comprehensive list of all the prominent people in the area who need an invite, along with names of local business owners Jade has already solicited donations from. Sometime today we can go over the details, unless he has yet to secure the entertainment.

Aidan comes into the office while fastening his watch. I force myself to ignore how handsome he looks so I can broach the topic.

"Did you get the gala entertainment secured while you were in New York?"

"Maybe." He comes at me, wrapping me up in his arms. He smells divine. His t-shirt is so white and tight in all the right places. His eyes are focused and incredibly blue today.

Apparently a roll in the hay, a few hours of sleep, and some exercise do this man wonders.

Huck comes in from the kitchen where he'd fallen asleep waiting for bacon to hit the floor. He jumps up on us both, and I push him off.

"Down!" I shout. "Naughty dog." He's aloof, disregarding my scolding.

Aidan gets his attention, lowering himself to the dog's head. "You wanna play, huh boy? Come here."

He taps his chest and the dog jumps up with his front paws. Huck would be looking me in the eyes if I'd done that. With Aidan, the dog lands at his chest – the human in control.

"I wouldn't recommend letting him do that."

"Oh, he's fine. Right, boy?" He ruffles the fur on the dog's head, then sets him down so he can rest on all fours.

"He might be fine. *You* might be fine. But I guarantee if Byron catches you letting him do that, it's your funeral."

"You might have a point there." His smile reaches his eyes, taking me out at the knees in the process.

I grab for Huck and take him downstairs. When I come up, I notice Aidan is going through his bag in the foyer. I'm temporarily dejected knowing he'll be gone before I know it.

I need to appreciate having him here now.

"Ready?"

"Just a sec," he says. He's fishing for something. He stands up, hiding something behind his back as he comes to me. "I have a surprise for you."

"What are you hiding?"

"Ah, ah. All in good time," he says. "First a little quiz. Do you know who the biggest singer-songwriter is right now?"

"I… no," I say. "Probably not."

"Just guess," he urges. "I promise you've heard of this person."

"It could be anyone. How about a hint?" I ask. "Male or female?"

"Nope, no hints."

"You're not playing fair."

"Sorry, Ms. Greene. My game, my rules."

I search the recesses of my brain, but I come up with nothing. "This is impossible," I say. "Russell from *Coffee Maniacs*, Jace from *Astro Lane*, that pretty songstress that has the new album, something with an S."

"You've almost got it, baby. Keep going."

"She sings with *Dead Set Against* sometimes. Oh hell, I don't know. I give up."

"Never give up, Alexis. Think harder."

I picture the album cover for her solo debut. I remember a rainbow on it, a cartoon drawing, and she's straddling it, rocking blonde pigtails as she licks a lollipop. For some reason, Italy pops in my head. Is her name Italian? I've been meaning to download the album, I just haven't had time.

"Sicily!" I say. "Is it Sicily Strauss?"

He's smiling smugly.

"Am I right?" I'm impressed with myself for remembering (and with him if he knows her). She is *ah-mazing*. She's written three hit singles in the last year for various musicians. Her career is taking off now that she's performing solo.

"That's the girl," he says with a satisfied smile. He knows I'm about to flip out.

"Holy shit, Aidan! You *know* her? She's beautiful! And her voice…she is definitely going to be huge before long." I'm totally gushing, but I don't care. Sometimes a girl can't help be a little star-struck. She must have been the Grammy nominee he was talking about meeting with. "Was she nominated for her songwriting?"

"She was," he says. "I love seeing you excited. It's fucking contagious. Here, she signed this for you." He reveals what he's been hiding - a copy of the CD encased in a cardboard sleeve. She's written on the face of it in black Sharpie above the cartoon rainbow.

Alexis,

Mr. Pierce is quite enamored with you. Go easy on him. Hope you enjoy the music.

#trackseven

xoxo Sicily

I'm totally floored.

"You got this for me?"

"I did. I just met her last night. Apparently all I talked about was you, hence the inscription."

"Aidan, I'm flattered. Thank you."

I throw my arms around him and kiss him with gratitude. When I pull back, he doesn't let me go.

"So you think she'll be a good fit for the gala?"

"Yes, definitely," I say. "She'll be amazing."

"Good. I offered her a hefty sum to do it, but it's worth it. She'll be back in New York for a gig the week before anyway, so it wasn't an inconvenience for her tour schedule."

"See?" I insist. "It was meant to be."

"I've been thinking about getting into the industry. There are so many talented people that don't get a chance now. Competition is fierce."

"So true. The internet has changed the game. It's hard for the standout talent to get noticed in a sea of new artists. I think you'd do well in that field."

"Really?" He takes a step back, trying to figure out if I'm being honest.

"I've seen you play. You're a talented drummer. You know worthy music when you hear it. And you definitely have rhythm," I tease. "Have you listened to this? She wrote 'track seven' on here."

"I have."

"And?"

"I think you'll love it. And by the way, I also got Shawn Thompson to speak."

"The professional basketball player? Isn't he a Stanton U Alum?"

"Yes and yes."

"Jeez, you have been busy. He's so accomplished, even after his bumpy start when he left Stanton. Didn't he just retire?"

"Yes, after his team won their conference in the NBA. I heard he intended to keep up his endorsements but was struggling to get speaking gigs, so I snagged him. The last person is just as amazing and hopefully will be confirming today."

"Don't make me guess again."

"Why not? You're good at it."

"Come on, don't keep me in suspense."

"Think inspirational speaker."

"Hmm...Oprah?"

"No," he chuckles. "Right church, wrong pew."

"Okay," I say after thinking a moment. "I'm totally drawing a blank."

"All right," he concedes. "I'll give you this one. Ever hear of Marcus Neil?"

"No way. Not *the* Marcus Neil?"

"The very same."

"As in, Doctor Marcus Neil? Author? Motivational speaker? Advisor to dignitaries and the Hollywood elite and the *freaking* Pope?"

"I probably wouldn't put it to him that way, but yes. And with any luck, you can add headliner for the gala on July second to his list of engagements this summer."

"My God, Aidan. This is going to be incredible! It's so good what you're doing. So, so good. I know it will help people," I insist. "It has to."

"If it only helps one, it's worth it to me."

"No, babe. It's going to be so much bigger than that. Everything you touch turns to gold."

"Except you, baby," he says pulling me into him again. "You're worth much more to me living and breathing. Not to mention much sexier."

"Well, thank you. Now let's get out of here. Can we listen to this on our way?"

"We could, but I'd like to save it."

"Buzzkill."

"Trust me, it's worth the wait. I want you under me when I play it for you."

Ohhh, shit.

How does he do this to me? It's like flipping a switch.

"Let's go upstairs," I say. Now he's all I can think about.

"You're totally serious, aren't you?"

"Yep."

"This is interesting," he says, stepping back and tapping his finger to his chin like a detective trying to solve a murder. "I wonder how long you can wait?"

"Not funny, Aidan."

"A lot funny, actually. I'm not putting out for you without a condition. What restriction can I impose that you'll struggle with most? You've done well with contemporary music trivia. There must be something…"

"Do you see that I'm not laughing?" He can't be serious.

"You need to learn some restraint."

"I'm not the one that flew here in the middle of the night just to get laid."

He looks at me emphatically. "You don't honestly think that." He seems hurt that I'm even suggesting it.

"No, I don't. And even if you did, I don't care. I couldn't be happier that you're here."

"Good," he says smiling his devilish smile. "And you're not getting laid again until you can name the first thirty Presidents of the United States without using the internet."

"You've got to be kidding."

"We'll see," he says, grabbing his bag and heading out the door.

History was my least favorite subject. Ever.

Right now, I absolutely hate it.

Unless I can convince him to drop his condition, this will be a sex-free zone for the foreseeable future.

Aidan drives us fifteen minutes away to the lake house where we'd spent the night on Thursday. This time we park at the bottom of the driveway and walk across the street to the sprawling lawn, down to the boathouse.

Floating at the dock is a large pontoon boat. It looks new and, of course, very plush. Byron is there, preparing for our impending arrival. He is removing the canvas from the seats at the bow of the boat and Aidan goes to help him.

"Good morning, Ms. Greene," he nods to me.

I nod back.

"Thanks for doing this," Aidan says. "I appreciate it on the short notice."

"She's all gassed up and ready. It was no problem."

I remember that Byron is staying in the other house Aidan owns, somewhere nearby. I'm happy he wasn't too inconvenienced to do something for us. I'm still not comfortable having someone available at a moment's notice.

Aidan nods at Byron then disappears into the boathouse, leaving me standing on the dock with his right-hand man.

"How is Huck doing this morning?"

It tugs at my heart how connected Byron is to my boy.

"He's fine. Aidan took him for a run this morning. He's home now."

"I would be happy to take care of him any time you like."

"Thank you, Byron. He is very fond of you."

I catch a glimpse of a smile before he replaces it with his usual rigid demeanor.

"Have a good day, Ms. Greene." He turns and walks away, heading down the dock as Aidan emerges with two fishing poles and a tackle box.

"Fishing, eh?" I don't withhold my surprise.

"Not your idea of a good time?"

"I don't mind it at all. My dad used to fish a lot. But I'm embarrassingly incapable of baiting a hook."

"Ever tried?"

"I can't get past the wiggling worm thing." I scrunch up my face in disgust.

He looks at me, grinning suggestively.

"Oh *come on*," I defend. "That wasn't a sexual comment." I'm still on the dock, watching him as he sets the gear on the boat.

"Do you want to get started on that list of presidents now?" He comes to the side of the boat, standing in front of me, leaning into my personal space. His eyes are filled with yearning.

"No. I'm good," I lie. He hasn't shaved today, and it's so fucking sexy.

"Fine," he says, using his mastered self-discipline to completely switch gears and shut me down. "Can you grab the lines?"

I don't know how he does that. I can't stop thinking about sitting him down and straddling him right here.

"Sure." I try to mimic his indifference but, as I untie the boat at the back, I have to ignore my physical response. As he starts the engine, I untie the front line then the last one at the mid-section of the boat.

"Come aboard, love. Let's see if we can catch us something." I take his hand and step on. He moves back behind the wheel, motoring us away from the dock. He's at ease there, as though he's an avid boater.

I sit beside him, looking out at the lake ahead. The water is calm today, with no wind to speak of and few other boats around. We pass one canoe with a couple of men fishing. They nod in greeting as Aidan waves back.

"You do this a lot?" I ask. "You seem very comfortable."

"Not a lot, but often enough." He puts an arm around me, pulling me in and inhaling through my hair.

We head for the middle of the lake, where we can see the east and west shorelines about a half mile in either direction. The north and south shores are not visible. The lake is several miles longer than it is wide.

The sun reflects off the water as it moves through a few high clouds. As we stop, I can see exactly why he loves this. It's peaceful out here, the sound of the boat rocking on the water, the warmth of the sun. The setting made it easier to forget about ex-lovers with drug addictions and multi-million dollar charity projects.

I let him up so he can drop the chain and anchor the boat, then follow him to the front. I'd rather be out in the sun than under the canopy at the helm.

He opens the tackle box. "You're in luck, baby. No fresh bait today. Let's see what this one will bring us." He baits a hook with an artificial minnow, then moves to the bow of the boat. There's a designated seat to fish from and he takes it, then casts the line into the water. "If you want to take this, I'll do yours."

"I think I'd rather just watch you."

"Suit yourself." He turns his attention to the water, as calm as I've ever seen him.

"You love this, don't you?"

He looks back at me from his seat. "It relaxes me."

"How many other girls have you taken fishing?"

"Before you? Let's see," he says, feigning an attempt to count.

"I'm serious," I persist. "How many?"

"None." He levels me with an intense gaze. "I told you, Alexis. You're different."

"Different how?"

"Come sit up here," he says, gesturing to the seat next to him.

I do as he asks, taking the second swivel chair that's meant for fishing. I watch him as he casts again. He's quiet, concentrating on the water. He is so capable, strong. Like he always is. I want to be wrapped up in him.

"I'm not sure I can explain it very well," he finally says. "I don't want to offend you."

"I've got a pretty thick skin. Go for it."

"Okay, then," he smiles. "You're independent. You don't need me."

That is getting further from the truth all the time.

I hold the thought in.

"You're intelligent. Smarter than most women I've been with. And you call me out on my shit."

"Come on now," I say. "I find it hard to believe you've never been with any smart women."

"It isn't just that you're smart. You're wise too. You have as much instinct and common sense as you have intelligence. Do you have any idea how rare that is?"

"I don't know. I guess not."

"I've worked with more people that aren't smart enough to follow an explicit instruction I've given them. Intellectual, accomplished people that aren't capable of handling a simple task, let alone deduce the solution to a problem on their own. Trust me, having your kind of capability is rare."

"Says you. Meanwhile you had to prevent me from tanking my career before it barely began."

"That's completely unfair to you and giving me too much credit. R.E.E. – the people behind the scenes – they are tactically deceptive, taking advantage of people like Myers. Neither one of you should consider yourselves less than because of what they tried to pull."

My response is silence. I know he has a point, considering the resources they have to hide their true intentions while acting on those same ambitions. It still bothers me what a close call it was.

He turns to face me, ignoring anything else.

"Alexis, I believe with everything I am that you would have found a way out for Myers if I had not stepped in. You are brave enough and smart enough and you would have figured it out on your own."

"I don't even want to think about it."

"Well then, let's not." He turns back to the lake.

"Can we talk about Stella?"

He looks back at me in confusion. "Why would you want to do that?"

"Because I've been wondering something," I start, "and now that we've signed our agreement, can you tell me about hers?"

"I'd rather not." His demeanor changes to irritated.

"If I'm going to be with you, isn't it fair for me to know what you expected of your last girlfriend?"

"I already told you it wasn't like that. This is exactly what I mean by you being different. There isn't a way to compare the two of you. Her agreement was more like one you'd have with a business associate. I wish you could accept that."

"The minute you stop seeing her and she has no control over what happens between us, I can accept that. But right now?" I sigh, exasperated that he can't see this from my point of view. "Right now, we can't even be seen outside of a fifty-mile radius together for fear that she or her father will find out. And in four weeks I might be face-to-face with them."

He exhales, setting his fishing rod into the holder in the floor.

"Please," I say, softening. "I need to know."

"Stella was not with me out of any sort of emotional attachment." He turns to face me, resting his elbows on his knees, hands clasped together. "Or so I thought. She wanted to further herself, move out from under her father's influence and control. I had known her for several years because I knew her father. I thought she wanted financial assistance more than anything, but I didn't care. I have it to spare. And like I said, she was a way for me to avoid social pressure."

I'm listening intently, silently urging him to go on.

"When we decided on this arrangement two years ago, it saved her from being a burden to her father. I helped her set up her business, which became successful with some of her ideas. I got her the right people to help her manage it, knowing her selfishness would hinder the growth of the business otherwise. And it worked."

"But eventually," he says, "it wasn't enough for her. What I gave was not enough. We both had spaces in each other's homes so we could live together but separately. Sometimes she would manipulate me into situations just to see how I would react, see if I would fix her mess. Ultimately, she admitted she wanted me to be emotionally available to her, and when I reminded her that wasn't the deal, she acted out in ridiculous ways. She broke the rules, if you will."

"How? What were the rules?"

He sighs. "This seems so malevolent. When I talk about it with you, I feel like you'll take it out of context. I'm not proud of my arrangement with her. I don't want you to see me this way, as someone who would impose rules on you – or on anyone."

"I understand you see me differently. Please just tell me," I plead. "I want to understand what your relationship was."

"Rules with her were necessary because she was unpredictable. I trusted her but only so far."

"You believed she wouldn't hurt you."

"Yes. I believed she cared for me enough not to. And that was as far as it went. I didn't trust her with the same things I've shared with you."

"What happened? Why did you break it off?"

"I just got fed up with her juvenile actions, with her selfishness. It became clear she wanted more, and I wasn't going to give her that. She had an allowance, a place to live – everything she could have wished for, materially. I agreed to let her keep the luxuries she'd been afforded as long as she agreed we'd go our separate ways."

"But you said you had sex."

"At one point, yes. We did have sex regularly. But I was never attracted to her in that way, I mean not organically. I know this sounds shameful, but it was only because she was there. I knew it was safe. I knew her complete medical history and she was held to certain standards and restrictions."

"Like?" I can't help it. I have to know, even as this tangent sparks a raging fire of jealousy in my chest.

"She agreed not to see anyone else. No drugs of any kind. She agreed to submit to testing any time I requested it. And," he adds, "she agreed to a mandatory sterilization."

My eyes bug out of my head.

What did he just say?

"Sterilized? Like, electively?"

"Yes. I did not want any children to come from our arrangement. It was my requirement and she accepted willingly. I felt strongly about it, knowing she'd have no idea what to do if she was ever faced with that circumstance. I didn't trust her to be responsible."

"So she can never have children now? With anyone?" I can't believe he would impose something so permanent on another human being. He made this woman agree to his demands about what she can (or can't) do with her uterus?

What the fuck?

"Of course not. I included a provision that I would pay for the reversal of the procedure, if she so desired."

"But there are risks with that, aren't there?"

"Yes, but it was the lesser risk. For both of us."

I'm just staring agape. I can't believe this revelation.

"Alexis, please say something. I feel like a jackass."

"As well you should." I can't help my accusatory tone. I'm saddened by this reminder of how he controls people, how far he can overstep. "Do you expect me to agree to the same thing?"

"You know I would never. I didn't even ask you to sign an NDA to spend the night with me."

"Is that typically a requirement to have a night with *the* Aidan Pierce?"

"Honestly? Yes. It is."

I don't know whether to be crushed, flattered or furious at his arrogance.

"Why didn't you ask me to sign one?"

"I couldn't figure it out at first. It went against what I'd always done in the past. But ultimately it was because I trusted you."

"And when was the last time you didn't trust someone?" He doesn't answer at first, and I realize it must have been recently. "Aidan, answer me. How many women were you fucking here in Lake County before me?"

"Jesus, Alexis. I'm not some kind of uninhibited bastard that fucks anything with a vagina. Why are you making it sound like I was sleeping with a city full of women before we met? And even if I had, it was before we met. Be reasonable."

I know he has a point. But when it comes to him, I'm not rational. I haven't ever been rational about him.

Why start now?

"How many, Aidan?"

"One, okay? One."

"And she signed something?"

"Yes. I got drunk one night. I took her back to my place. It was the week before I met you, and Stella had been pulling her shit. I was stressed beyond rational thought. I'll give you it was not a wise choice. But I handled it the way I needed to. She was a distraction."

"You only saw her once?" My stomach knots at the idea that he bedded someone at the loft before me. When he said Stella had never been there, I assumed I was the first.

"Yes."

"Were you careful?"

"Yes. You are one of very few I've not worn condoms with."

"And do you have these distractions on a regular basis? Is that what

I am?"

He looks at me with contempt, his blue eyes steeled in anger.

"Did you seriously just ask me that?"

"I have a right to know."

"Tell me you honestly believe that. That you're just a distraction to me."

"Well you said yourself I was an escape."

"I also said being with you is intense. For fuck's sake, I had Doc Mason prepare you a partial history on me simply because you wanted to know more. Do you think I would do that just so I could fuck you? Do you think I've chased any woman the way I have you?"

I suddenly feel like a jerk for questioning what he feels for me.

I've done it too often.

After the things he's said to me, the way he's treated me…

Dammit.

Now I'm the jackass.

"I'm sorry, Aidan. I…that was uncalled for. I just…" I stop myself. These are uncharted waters for me, and he needs to know it. "I'm not used to being jealous. I don't want to be a distraction, some sort of toy you toss aside when you're bored with it."

"Baby, come on. You know that isn't us. That isn't me. What happened when I got here to New York – it was a slip on my part. It isn't the way I would normally behave. It was more representative of my past. Not my present."

I nod in understanding. I can't fault him for things he did before me. It isn't fair.

"Can we please talk about something else?" He's rubbing his forehead, clearly stressed at this.

"Okay. Can we talk about the fact that you forced your ex to sterilize herself just to be with you? I'm still not sure I can get past that, Aidan. It's so overreaching."

"Enough, Alexis." His tone is commanding, impatient. "I don't see why that seems so unfathomable to you. Isn't that essentially what you agreed to, marrying a gay man?"

"No," I say assertively. "I did not agree to anything of the kind."

"So you don't see that marrying someone who would never touch you, where there would never exist any danger of you procreating – you don't see that as a sort of insurance policy for you?"

"No, I...I mean we," I can't help stumbling over my words. "We talked about kids. We decided it wasn't a priority for us. And we agreed we could look into options if our feelings ever changed."

"So how is my situation any different? I didn't force her to agree. Neither of us wanted kids to happen. Just like you and Ben. But for us the risk was still there because we slept together. She agreed she didn't want children."

I suppose he has a point, as fucking usual. But I don't admit it.

"If we are going to move forward, you have to accept this. Accept that the way I've lived my life is different. Just as I do for you. I don't judge you for your arrangement with Ben, even though it was unusual. It's who you are. It's brought you here, to this point." He leans down and looks at me, lifting my chin with the crook of his finger so I'll be forced to look in his beautiful blue eyes.

"Alexis," he says softly, "it brought you to me."

He moves towards me, laying his lips on mine, leaning his head onto mine. "I can't explain to you how glad I am that we found each other. We're both fucked up, can't you see that? Neither one of us fits in a mold. We've both survived the best we could with what we had. I think that's what drew me to you. I see myself in you. My strengths, my weaknesses."

I nod, trying not to cry as I rest my hands on his chest, feeling his heart beat fast.

"I know fear is what's driving your anger, baby. And I'm telling you, you don't need that fear. Not in this case. There isn't anyone on this planet that has affected me the way you do."

I'm taken back by his reassurance, by his sincerity. How does he always know what to say? He's called it right, as he always does.

I don't want to lose him to Stella or some girl he bedded before me. I want him to be mine and only mine.

And whoa, is that scary.

"Is that how you can always peg me so well? Because we're so alike?"

"Maybe."

"I don't want to think about you sleeping with someone else. You may as well torture me," I say. "I don't share either, Aidan. Tell me you are done with that, fucking random women that fall all over you. Tell me you won't see Stella without letting me know first. If she's the way you say she is, she's going to manipulate you until she gets you back into her life in whatever way she wants you."

"I am done with that," he swears. "I could never do that to you. And when it comes to Stella, I'm smarter than that."

"Yes, but you said yourself how difficult it is to be one step ahead. What if she and her father are two steps ahead?"

"I'm handling it. I promise to tell you as much as I can. And you must know I don't want anyone else. Alexis, you're all I think about. How you taste, how you feel."

He runs his hands up and down my bare arms, then holds the back of my neck. His lips are on mine, his tongue darting inside my mouth.

"*Here,*" I say into his lips, insistent. "Take me here."

"No way," he says, his forehead on mine again as he smiles. "You haven't complied with my rules. The first thirty presidents. You can start anytime."

"Fuck your rules, Aidan." I stand up, my waist now even with his head, and drop my shorts. His hands roam my hips, my belly, sliding up my shirt.

"You are so bad at this," he says. "You can't even wait six hours."

"I don't know what you're talking about," I say, indignant. "I'm just standing here."

He looks around to see if we're alone. There's not another boat or person in sight.

He teases me, his lips grazing my hip bone as he pulls the fabric of my underwear down, then puts it back where it was. He does the same thing on the other side. "Come on, Alexis. Start with George."

"No way," I say. "I'm not giving in. I'd fail miserably anyway."

He moves his hand inside the fabric, slipping a finger inside me. "I won't fuck you until you try," he insists. My head drops back as he fingers me. He bites at me over the fabric and I cry out.

"*I... will... not,*" I manage, panting between words. All I want is to feel him inside me.

He steps up his game, moving faster, moving my panties out of the way to lick me.

"Aidan, *please*. I need you."

He lifts me up into his arms, cradling me as he carries me to the back of the boat where the canopy and the fabric conceal us from view. He lays me down, stretched out on the bench seat as he stands at my side.

"You better hope the fish don't bite while we're back here," he says. "I'll have to leave you."

"I can bite, if that helps."

"You can do whatever you want. I'm still not going to make love to you until you pass my test."

"There's no way I can," I admit. "Unless you've decided never to be inside me again, I think we should consider this a draw and get busy."

"No," he says. "The point isn't to get it right. The point is not to give up, especially before you try to succeed. Come on," he urges. "You were a law student, baby. You know this. Every time you get one right I'll let you get closer. One wrong and you get punished."

Before I can agree, he leans over and slides my tank top off over my head then strips me of my underwear. He stands up and pulls off his shirt.

I exhale, already knowing I'm going to lose this little game of his. I will do whatever he wants to have him inside me. Just a glimpse of him shirtless makes me long for him to be above me so I can run my hands over his naked chest.

"Go," he urges.

"Washington," I start.

I feel ridiculous.

He climbs on top of me, his knees at rest on either side of my legs. He leans down, kissing me heatedly and I lose my senses for a moment. I let my eagerness for him take over, hoping he'll forget the stupid game. He moves down to my breasts, pulling back the fabric of my bra, sucking my left nipple. I'm wet already and unable to keep my legs together.

"Keep going," he says.

"Adams."

"Good girl." He moves to the other nipple, sucking gently as his hands move over me.

"Jefferson." He reaches beneath me, unhooks my bra and tosses it to the floor. He is sitting back up, looking at me as he uses both hands to cup my breasts before he leans down and assaults them both with his mouth.

"Madison," I breathe.

He moves himself backwards, then leans down to trail his lips along my midsection. He stops at my pubic bone, nipping and licking underneath my belly button. Chills chase down my legs. My clit throbs in anticipation.

"C'mon, baby. You got this."

"Monroe, Adams, Jackson."

"Ahh, see? You're holding out on me. A little reward, hmm?"

He dives into me with his tongue and I fight a convulsion at the sensation.

"*God, Aidan.* Please. I want you inside me."

He doesn't respond. He keeps up his assault briefly, until he stops only to get me playing again.

"Next," he says.

I'm stuck on the eighth, ninth and tenth, not wanting to get the order wrong. I try to recall a song one of my high school teachers had made up as an aid for his history students, but I can't remember the tune.

"Harrison?"

He bites my inner thigh. *Hard.*

"Ow!"

"Try again, love."

"VanBuren?"

"Good girl," he says, letting a finger slip into me.

"Harrison," I say again.

I think that's right.

He adds his mouth to the assault, sucking on my clit.

"*Do. Not. Stop.*"

As soon as I make the request, he halts his services.

"Come on, baby," he says. "I'll even compromise. If you get to fifteen, I'll fuck you."

"Tyler," I say. "Polk."

How many is that?

Eleven. Yes, I've gotten to eleven. My mind is reeling, wanting to get to fifteen so I can get what Aidan has promised. He lets two fingers in this time, and his thumb finds my clit swollen as he teases it. If he's not careful, I'm going to come now and I won't care about reciting the names of dead presidents.

"More?" he asks.

"*Yes*," I breathe.

He stops again.

"Tease."

"Next," he says. "You're on twelve."

"Fillmore," I say.

He bites me again, this time on the other thigh.

"Fuck! Stop that!"

"Try again," he says. He climbs off of me to remove his shorts, and now I'm so aroused I'm devoid of thought.

"This is getting harder."

"So am I," he laughs.

"Aidan, I can't think I want you so bad. Please," I beg.

"You're almost there," he says. "Don't give up on me."

I close my eyes, even my breathing and try again.

Ha! I remember!

I forgot Zachary Taylor.

"Taylor," I say. He kneels next to me, spreading my legs with his hands, diving full into me with his mouth.

"Gah....yesss."

"Three more," he pauses, then licks my inner thigh where he bit me a moment ago. "You can do it."

"Fillmore," I say. His fingers enter me again, and I'm wanting to laugh at the irony of the name and what he's doing to me. "Fill me more, Aidan," I breathe with a giggle.

"Two more and I will," he says. "The next one should be easy."

I repeat in my head the ones I've just recalled.

Polk, Taylor, Fillmore...

"Pierce!" I shout. Of course. The same last name as his.

Oh, this cocky bastard.

He keeps up his advances with his fingers deep inside me, then adds his mouth to my clit, and a pinky in my formerly virgin place. I squeal, not expecting it. He moves his mouth off me and removes his hand, leaving me empty.

"Come on baby, I want to fuck you."

Who's next?

I can't...oh...*I know!*

It comes to me like an answered prayer.

"Buchanan," I say. "It's Buchanan."

"That's my girl." He rises to climb on top of me and I move my legs apart. He lowers himself so we're face to face. "So smart, baby. Why don't you believe that about yourself?"

"Make love to me, Aidan. Please."

He smiles at me. "You're addicted."

"You bet your ass," I say. "Now give me what I want."

"I should make you wait. You only got to fifteen."

"Don't I get credit for trying?" I wiggle my hips in anticipation. "Besides, you promised."

"Yes, baby." He leans down and kisses me tenderly, then leans up. He slides into me, his eyes still on mine. "I can't get enough of you, either. You're the highest high I've ever had, Alexis."

I nod, too filled up from him, from his words, to speak any of my own.

He starts to thrust faster.

"Wrap your legs around me."

I do as he asks, then wrap my arms around him too, bringing him down to surround me as he pushes faster.

"*Baby.* I can't take it. You feel so good."

I slide my hands back to his chest, thumbing over his nipples, pushing him on.

"Come, Aidan," I say. "I want to feel you. I want to hear you."

"No, baby." His breath hitches as he drives faster, then slows. "You first."

He speeds up, then slows again, moving his hips in a way that leaves me almost breathless as I build momentum.

"Yes," I moan. "*More.*"

He complies in the same motion, quick then slow, gyrating in just the right way so my clit is stimulated while he's inside me.

"Let go, Alexis," he says. "I can feel how close you are."

My lips part, drying out from hot breath as I unravel. The world spins as I come, listening to him whisper my name over and over. He switches his tactic, thrusting in and out faster and faster until a moment later he fills me up, letting out his sexy growl as he collapses on me.

I smile, holding him in my arms, feeling the sway of the boat on its liquid foundation. My legs are numb in relaxation but still locked around him.

"God, baby, you are so sexy."

"Aidan?"

"Yeah," he says. His breathing is slowing as he comes down from his release.

"I think I have a new appreciation for fishing."

He leans up to look at me. "See? This is why you're different," he says. "This is the most unique fishing experience I've ever had. I couldn't even keep my mind on something that typically holds my attention, something that relaxes me. I'm so amped up with you around."

I laugh at his play on words, knowing he doesn't even realize it.

"I think I'm the one that's *amped.*"

He crooks a brow in question.

"A-M-P," I say. "Your initials. You're the one that's got me *amped.*"

"How clever, Greene." He kisses my naked shoulder. "But you're still not getting *amped* again unless you can recite the next fifteen presidents."

"I call bullshit," I say. "You can't wait that long. I promise I won't know the next fifteen like I did the first. This right here was divine intervention."

"Says you, baby." He leans down to whisper in my ear. "This game isn't over yet. *E io vinco sempre.*"

I push him up, giving him a look of pleading for a language I can understand.

"And I always win."

14

Aidan

An hour later, we've left the boat back at the dock and crossed the street to the lake house. As soon as we get through the door, all I can think about is getting her into bed.

"Bedroom or kitchen?" I ask.

"Hmm. You pick."

"In the kitchen, we eat. In the bedroom, I do."

Her lips curve into a sexy smile. "What's for lunch?"

I pull out my phone, checking a text from Byron about what he's left for us. "Sandwiches from Joe's Deli and fresh fruit."

"Is there dessert?"

"I don't eat sweets," I say, "except you."

"You're kidding." Her expression shifts to shock. "Nothing sweet? No chocolate? No whip cream? No pie?"

"No."

"Not even ice cream?"

"Nope."

"How did I not know this before now?"

I shrug. "I guess it never came up."

"Oh, babe, you don't know what you're missing."

"I do," I say. "I just choose not to eat it."

"Why?"

"No nutritional value. What's the point?"

"You could say the same about me," she says. "I can't believe you never give in to temptation."

"Oh, I do," I say while I stare her down. "I'm seriously considering letting you out of our dead presidents game so I can take you right here."

"Right here?" she teases, moving towards me.

"Right here. Right now."

"Nah," she says. "I'm hungry. Let's eat." She saunters off to the kitchen, leaving me and my semi-hard on in her wake.

We've finished lunch and are lazing on the porch in the swing. The late afternoon is as beautiful as the morning was.

"Should we get back to my place? I probably ought to get the dog out."

"Why don't we ask Byron if he'd mind taking care of Huck?" I suggest. "We could stay here again."

"Or you could come home with me," she says.

"That's an option. I should head back to Manhattan in the morning, though."

"Yeah, I figured." She fails to hide her disappointment.

"You could come with me."

"Are you asking me to come with you?"

"Yes." I don't care about the Irelands. I can keep her out of sight if she comes with me.

I don't want to be away from her.

"I can't. I mean I'd love to, but I have a crazy week after being gone four days. And I should be here, in case we need anything done on this end for the gala prep. Don't you think?"

I consider it as she curls up closer to me. I know she's right but I don't acknowledge it.

"I don't want to be away from you," she admits. "It hurts to think about."

"I know, baby. Me too." We're interrupted by my phone ringing. It's Samira. "I've got to take this."

I head inside to field the call. Samira gives me an update on the gala and reports that Stella is asking for me. Our call is brief and I go back to the porch to share details with Alexis.

"Good news or bad news," I say. "Which do you want first?"

She sighs. "The good, I guess."

"We got Marcus Neil." I can't help my grin.

"That's awesome, Aidan. That's better than good news. We can finalize everything tomorrow as planned. People are going to be really excited about this."

"I agree. Now the bad news."

"Go ahead," she says. "It can't be that bad."

"It is."

"Just tell me."

"Stella. She's called the office three times since yesterday. I just spoke to her Thursday when the news story was leaked. Her fellow inpatients had been fawning over her thinking we're back together."

"Why doesn't she just call your cell if she's looking for you?"

"I changed my number when I moved here. She doesn't have a way to reach me outside of calling Lionel or the office here. I didn't want the distraction."

"What does she want?"

"She says she's struggling in the program."

"Don't they have doctors for that? To help her?"

"They do. I don't know if this is a stunt, an attempt to get my attention, or if it has something to do with the Center."

"I don't understand."

"A lot has happened in the last couple of days, Alexis. I haven't had a chance to tell you all of it."

"I seem to have some time now. Go ahead."

"Some of it you're better off not knowing. What I predicted on the roof that night? It's happening. There are real threats here, and you promised me you'd follow my game plan."

"You just got through telling me how smart I am and that I call you out on your bullshit. Quit dodging, Aidan. I can handle it."

"John Ireland has offered to cut ties with me."

She gives me a look of surprise. "Isn't that good news?"

"You'd think so. But because of what it would cost me, it isn't."

"How much?"

"His primary goal has nothing to do with money. At least not mine." I sit in the swing next to her, take her hand. I know she's not going to like this. I'm about to turn her world upside down once again.

"Tell me," she insists.

"He'll let me out of the arrangement with him permanently. Including any obligations to Stella."

"In return for what?"

"Myers' land. If I agree to sell it to him after I acquire it, I'll be rid of him."

"Never." Her eyes dilate with rage. "I will never let you do that."

"Calm down," I assure her. "I don't intend to do it. When my attorney presented me with the offer, I told him I'd be dead before I let Ireland set foot on that land."

"Then what's the problem? We find another way out, that's all. Will you show me your agreement? The one with Ireland?"

"There's so much more to this. I really don't want you involved. I need to keep you safe."

"No one has threatened me, Aidan. I don't believe anyone would think to. Whitmore's warning to me was out of courtesy because we'd worked together for so long. I don't think either of us are in any real danger."

"Unfortunately, that's not true."

"What do you mean?"

"Did I tell you there was a reporter from the *LA Times* trying to interview me about this? That there was a leak within Renewable Energy?"

"No," she says. "I'd have remembered if you did."

"Gene Dobbs wanted to talk to me, but I declined. He reached out again Friday. I met with him and learned the source of the leak wasn't someone within R.E.E."

Her complexion pales. "Mark?"

I nod. "He's gone missing, Alexis. He's either in danger or on the run. We tracked him to Florida, but the police have no leads. He was last seen at a hotel, which he entered briefly only to turn around and leave without a trace."

She says nothing. She's white as a sheet.

"Baby, say something."

"I can't..." she says. "I feel sick."

I pull her into me, rubbing her back, trying to calm her. "It's all right," I say. "It's going to be fine. We'll find him."

"Jesus, Aidan. What the fuck are we going to do? He's got a family. A wife."

"I know."

"I don't want anyone to lose their life over this. It isn't worth it."

"What are you suggesting? We give in? Give my uncle's land away?"

"Your uncle?" She pulls back looking at me, bewildered. "Aidan." Her voice is strained from anger or hurt or maybe both. "Is my client your uncle?"

Goddammit.

I didn't want her to find out this way. I'm sure my silence confirms, but

I man up and reply.

"Yes. He was married to my mother's sister."

"Jesus Christ. You really don't trust me, do you? What the fuck else are you leaving out?"

"Nothing," I insist. "I was going to tell you. There just hasn't been a good time. And honestly, it's irrelevant. I'm trying to take care of him in all of this. He has benefitted from every action I've taken, or in the alternative been unaffected."

She pulls away from me and gets up to pace the porch. She stops to look out over the lake below, leaning on a large cedar log that serves as the railing. I go to her, wrapping myself around her from behind. I can't stand her upset with me.

I don't know why the fuck this is.

The emotion is unfamiliar. I just know my guts are twisting up like they're in a blender as I watch her lose faith in me. I'm relieved when she doesn't attempt to move away.

"Do you care about Eli at all?" She asks it so softly I can tell she isn't sure she wants to hear the answer.

"Of course I do."

I crane my neck back and let out a breath before I go on.

"The few good memories I have of my early childhood are because of him and my aunt. Their farm was a place for me to go when I had nowhere else. I'd never let anyone take advantage of Eli or acquire that land. It's my uncle's or it's mine."

I turn her around to face me.

"There are no other options I will live with," I say firmly. "None."

"I believe you, Aidan. I'm just…I don't understand why you didn't tell me in the beginning."

"I hadn't seen my uncle in over twenty-five years. I don't even know him, really. The first time I saw him after so long was the same day I met you," I say, "and since that day I've been a bit distracted."

She smiles reluctantly and I pull her closer. She smells so good, as she always does. The sweet aroma of her hair calms me.

"I'm sorry everything has been so fucked up. I already warned you that was the case. The details keep coming to you one at a time, and I'm sorry for that. It's not been intentional."

At her lack of response, I tilt her chin up and look into her eyes.

"Alexis, I was not trying to hide this from you."

"I understand." She sighs and nods in acceptance. "Now tell me why John Ireland wants your uncle's land."

"I have no idea. My guess is either he plans to convey it to R.E.E. at a marked-up price or he's after it just to spite me. Maybe it's just another property to add to the list of those he's muscled his way into owning over the years. But if he wants it, there's value in it for him. Even if it's just to be vindictive, to keep me from having it."

"Aidan, this is so messed up."

"I know."

She thinks a minute, still in my arms. Her face tilts to mine in a moment of revelation. "What if we expose them?"

"Who?"

"Renewable Energy. We expose their intentions. If word gets out about what was really going on, there won't be a chance in hell they can worm their way in here. Or anywhere in the state for that matter. Ireland wouldn't have a chance to buy from you, to turn around and sell to them."

"I've thought of that, about revealing what's been going on to the public." He considers me a moment. "But I always come back to a resounding no."

"Why? The people here deserve to know what's going on under their noses. They can handle it. And they have the fight in them to…"

I cut her off. "It's too risky. I don't doubt the morals of people here or their capabilities. But it's more than that. That would be an attack, not a defensive move. There's no telling what R.E.E. would do in retaliation. Not to mention Ireland provided the sources to uncover the information I do have, which is not solid proof anyway. But he won't stand for being caught in the crossfire."

"I don't see how else we can get rid of Ireland and R.E.E. And don't give me that shit about offense versus defense. As far as I'm concerned, the only thing we can do is defend ourselves against them. Don't you think it makes the most sense?"

"It's not only dangerous for us, but for Eli too. And for your firm. They could twist the story to be about you. Try to say you're playing both sides, or worse, try to get you disbarred. I don't like it."

She sighs in reluctant acceptance.

"The scary part is these two enemies' interests have aligned."

"R.E.E. and Ireland?"

"Yeah." I rub my temples. I can feel a monster headache coming on.

"I don't see how that works," she says. "How would they even know to reach out to him?"

"Just by doing their homework. Stella's tied to me, therefore so is he. I told you, his connections run deep. And he may very well have been the one to go to them."

"Even if it meant risking exposure? You just said he was the one that helped you uncover their ties to Waterman Oil. Would he really risk going to them, knowing they might find that out?"

Jesus, she has a point.

A major point.

"That's true. It leads me to believe R.E.E. definitely went to Ireland first."

She gives me a look. "So?"

"So, that means he's scrambling. He's trying to cover his tracks, to make sure they don't realize he helped me access the information about the bait and switch they were trying to pull."

"Promoting solar energy to Eli while planning to end up with a prime drilling site?"

"Exactly."

"So Ireland offers to cut ties with you in exchange for Eli's land?"

"Yes. Pushing me on this is the straw he's grasping at to save his own ass. He's dangling the carrot I'm after by offering to end our arrangement. He believes losing the land would be worth it to me, that my obligations to Stella are that much of a burden."

"He obviously doesn't know you very well."

"Oh, but babe, this is classic John. He's making damn sure there's something in it for him. He gets the land from me, marks up the price and sells it to the enemy. He's Renewable Energy's hero. Meanwhile he's made a profit and saved his own skin. He'll sell before the company can figure out he had a hand in tanking their deal with my uncle to begin with."

"Great angle he's got there, except for the obvious fact that you won't give up the land or the Center."

"Of course not," I insist. "But this means he's got something to lose. And I can exploit that to get him out of the picture. Thank you, baby."

"For what?"

"For being so damn smart."

"I didn't do anything."

"You got me thinking, love." I kiss her on the forehead and grab my phone off the swing. "We can run with this." Before I can make some calls and plot this all out, the phone rings in my hand.

"Yeah, Byron." I say. "What's the latest?"

"They found him, sir," he says. "They found Whitmore."

"And?"

"He's dead."

15

Alexis

I'm in the bathroom at Aidan's Falcon Lake house recovering from losing the contents of my stomach.

Mark Whitmore is dead.

I have no idea what the fuck came over me, but as soon as Aidan shared this news, I went completely clammy, nausea spreading through me so fast that I had to make a run for the toilet.

I look in the mirror after splashing water on my face and my hunch is confirmed.

I look as terrible as I feel.

"Babe? You all right?"

I had closed and locked the door. I didn't want Aidan to see me like this. He said he needed to make another call anyway.

"I'm fine." I search out the toothbrush I used the other day hoping a fresh mouth will help some.

"You wanna let me in?"

"I'll be right out."

I hear him move away from the door, grateful that he doesn't push the issue. I exit the bathroom to find him lying on the bed while his feet are on the floor. He sits upright, motioning me over. I let him wrap me up, settling in the comfort of him.

"I'm sorry, baby. Are you okay?"

"I'm okay." I pull back to look him in the eye. "I just can't believe it."

"I wouldn't have believed it myself," he says. "But Byron lent some details. I'm afraid it's absolutely true."

"Where did they find him?"

"A mile or so from the hotel."

"Yes, but," I hesitate as my voice dulls to a whisper, "what happened?"

"It's better if you don't know."

"I want to know how he died, Aidan. I worked with him for a year. Please tell me what happened to him."

He takes a deep breath. "He'd been shot. They found him in a lake not far from the hotel."

I fight off another wave of nausea, glad I have nothing left in my stomach to give up.

"How did they find him?"

"They tracked his cell phone. He still had it on him."

"That's risky for whoever did this, isn't it? What if there was information on there that would implicate someone?"

"For whatever reason, the aggressor was not concerned with that. I think Whitmore was acquainted with whoever did this. He was paranoid when he left you at the pub that day. He knew someone was after him. And if he left that hotel in Florida for a remote location, it was to meet someone he thought he could trust."

"I don't even know what to do from here. What now?"

"I'm on it. You don't have to worry, baby. You'll be safe. Byron is going to be with you any time I can't be."

I purse my lips together in irritation. "That isn't..."

"Don't argue. It *is* necessary," he says, objecting to thoughts in my head. "It's already done. He's going to your place to take care of Huck now. I've canceled going back to Manhattan. For the foreseeable future, whenever I can't be with you Byron will be."

I finally nod in acceptance. Maybe his concern is warranted.

"How is this even happening?" My rhetorical question hangs in the air. "His wife, his two kids. God, Aidan. They just lost their father."

He pulls me close again, urging me up onto the bed next to him. I lay there, listening to his heart beating as I let silent tears fall.

I know he's as knocked down by this as I am. Whatever his past held for him, regardless of specifics I had yet to know, nothing in our personal struggles compared to this.

We were dealing with corporate greed, with the pursuits of people who had means and money enough to wipe out whatever – or whoever – got in their way.

We spend the rest of Sunday back in Stanton at the loft. By seven in the evening, I've showered and redressed in a pair of familiar jeans and a t-shirt I'd left behind on one occasion, while Aidan is downstairs in his office working.

I call Charlie. I dread telling him this news, but he needs to know.

"Lex," he says. "Where the hell you been, girl? I wanted to take you out last night."

"Charlie…" I fight back tears as he carries on, oblivious to my impending emotional outburst.

"You'd be proud, though. I celebrated Ben's birthday plenty for both of us. We hit that new bar on Fifth Street, and you'll never believe what this one guy…"

"Charlie," I break in, not hiding my crying this time.

"Lex?" He listens as I sob. "Are you okay?"

"No," I manage.

"Where are you?"

"I'm at Aidan's. In Stanton."

"Did he do something? What's going on?"

"No, I… it isn't him."

"I'm home, babe. Only a few minutes away. Can I come over? Or do you want to come here?"

"No, I just…I have something to tell you."

"Lex. Tell me what the fuck is going on."

"It's Mark Whitmore," I say. "He's… he's gone."

"Gone where? We knew he was leaving for Florida on Thursday, right?"

"Yes, he did. I mean he was. He made it there, but they…they found him. He's dead, Charlie."

"Holy fuck." He inhales a breath in obvious shock. "Are you serious?"

"Yes. They said he was shot."

"Come over here, Lex. I need to see you. Make sure you're okay."

I wouldn't mind a hug from one of my best friends right now, but I know Aidan wouldn't want me leaving without him or Byron.

"I'm okay," I say. "I'm…Aidan doesn't want me to be left alone. He doesn't think it's safe."

"I won't argue with that. Do you want me to come over there?"

"Aidan is here. I'm fine. I just…I wanted to tell you before work tomorrow."

"This is crazy, Lex. What the fuck? I don't even know what to say. But I'd really like to hug you right now."

"I know," I say. "It's okay. I'll see you at the office in the morning. Byron has Huck for me. And if Aidan isn't with me, Byron won't be far away."

"That makes me feel a little better. You're sure you're okay?"

"Yeah," I say as my tears dry up. "I just feel terrible, like it's my fault. He had a family. And now…" I stop myself. It hurts too much to elaborate.

"It's not your fault, Lex. It's those bastards at R.E.E. We just need to make sure you're safe."

"Aidan is working on it. I think he has some sort of plan, I don't know. I just…I want it all to go away. None of it is worth this."

"I trust him, babe. He'll take care of you. But you know I'm here. Always."

"I know," I smile through my sadness. "Thank you, Charlie."

"Should you maybe take some time? Not come in tomorrow? I can handle things if you want to stay home."

"No," I say. "I've got a full plate, and I need to keep myself busy. Let's get through this week. We're heading up to Canada this weekend. I can wait until then for a break."

"You going to see Pam and the folks?"

"Yeah. Aidan's family has a place up there. He's not going with me to see Ben's family, though."

"I'm sure they'd love to meet him."

"I'm not ready for that. I just need to get through the week."

"We'll get through it. I'll see you in the a.m. Love you, girl."

"Love you, too Charlie. See you tomorrow."

I head downstairs to find Aidan. I exit the elevator and make my way through the cubicles, stopping short before I get to his office door. He's alone, but he must be on the phone because in between moments of silence I hear him yelling.

I've never heard him so angry.

I hear him say a curt goodbye to the person he's talking to. He lets out a guttural roar and my arms bristle with chills. I wait a moment, then knock.

"Yeah," he says, "come in."

I come through the door to find him trying to breathe himself into control. His neck is corded, his eyes wide. He makes no effort to hide his anger from me.

"What is it?" I ask.

"Nothing." He moves to the kitchenette and pours himself a whiskey.

I go to him, wanting to calm him. I hate seeing him like this. I lay a hand on his shoulder and he shrugs it away, leaving me wounded at his rejection.

He slams the shot, sets the glass down, and pours another.

"Is that necessary?"

He turns to look at me, his expression as hard as it was for whomever he was yelling at.

"Don't."

"What the fuck, Aidan? Who were you talking to?"

He shakes his head dismissively as he takes another sip, then walks away from me headed for the leather couch. He sets his drink down and collapses, his head resting on the back.

"Do you want me to go?" I ask. I haven't left the spot where he stood with me moments ago.

"If that's what you want to do."

I can't figure out where this coldness is coming from but it's starting to radiate through me. I'm absorbing his anger.

"It doesn't seem like I'm needed here."

He says nothing.

"Who were you arguing with?"

Silence.

"Aidan, what the hell? I thought we were done keeping secrets. I can't know who has the power to make you that angry?"

Again, nothing. He hasn't opened his eyes or turned around to look at me. His head still rests on the back of the couch. His body language is loud and clear. He's still pulsing with anger.

"Fuck this. I'll have Charlie pick me up." I start for the door, but he moves across the room in a hurry, reaching me before I can get there. He spins me around to face him.

"You're not going anywhere without me." He kisses me, letting his anger dissipate just enough to convey need. I kiss him back, wanting to bring him back to me.

I'm nestled between two chairs at the large conference table, my backside leaning up against it. I lean back and put a hand to his face, assessing him and waiting for him to speak.

"I don't like you seeing me like this," he says regretfully. He's still not calm by any means.

I kiss him again, running hands through his hair, down the back of him. I ache for him as I feel my body heat, wanting to feel something life-affirming in the wake of all that we're facing.

He strips off my jeans and underwear, lifting me up onto the table. He pushes me back, taking my clit over with his mouth before I can form any thought. I feel his tongue inside me.

"Aidan," I breathe, "come here."

He nips at my clit and draws a long suck, sending a shockwave through me before he rises. I lean up and strip him of his shirt. My hands worship everything before me and his head falls back as I run fingertips along his nipples. He undresses the rest of himself quickly and without his eyes leaving mine.

"I've wanted you on this table since the very first time you stood in this room with me."

I smile back at him as he removes my shirt and bra. "Don't let me stop you from getting what you want, Mr. Pierce."

He smiles his devilish grin. "Damn right." He places my discarded shirt under my head as he lays me back.

That's the last gentle gesture I'm granted.

In the next instant, he grabs my hips firmly, lifting them up and driving into me harder than he ever has before. He's head back, eyes closed, using my body at his whim.

This moment is all about him.

His satisfaction, converting his anger into need, controlling me solely for his pleasure.

And it feels too fucking good to stop him.

I spread my legs apart wider, giving him full access. He slows up some, only looking down at me as he moves hands to my breasts, then down to my clit with the same technique he knows will drive me over the edge. My back arches off the cold wood beneath me.

His hands abandon me to grab my hips again, pulling me into him harder. He slams into me as often as he wants as his climax builds.

The sight of him is so erotic to take in. My eyes go wide in amazement as he drives into me, each time harder than the last. I could care less if my needs are met this time. I just want to watch him, watch the way his muscles tighten as he fucks. I watch him satisfy his need, not caring if that need is for me or just for any release he can manage.

He comes hard as he calls out my name and fills me. He's more out of breath than I am. My hair isn't tied up, and it's slicked with sweat as I wipe it off my face. I drape my arms over my forehead, closing my eyes as he withdraws.

"Fuck," he says. He leans down, grazing his lips around my navel. "I'm so sorry, baby." He's kissing me all over, raking hands over my bare arms as far up as he can reach. "Are you okay?"

"Fine," I say. "I just need to sit up."

He moves off of me, offering his hand to pull me off the table. He lifts my naked body and wraps my legs around him, my arms resting around his neck as he carries me to the couch. When he sets me down, I stretch out lengthwise on my back. He leaves me to gather up our clothes and put his jeans back on, then sets everything else on the coffee table next to me.

"God, you're gorgeous." He hovers above me. "Do you want to come, baby?"

"I'll take one for the team this time," I tease him. All of my limbs are still numb. He smiles as he reaches for my clothes. He slides my underwear over my feet, gliding them up my legs and back in place. I wince as his hands move over my hips where he'd gripped them so tightly.

"Baby." He bows his head in regret before looking back to me. "Be honest. Did I hurt you?"

"No." I sit up and put my shirt back on. "Watching you was incredible."

He sits next to me and wraps me up in his arms.

"I shouldn't have done that. I just..." He stops his train of thought as he strokes my hair. It's a long, quiet moment before he starts again. "Alexis, you drive me completely mad. I was pissed from that phone call. I thought you were going to walk out on me, and all I could think about was having you just the way I did."

I'm at a loss for words. His regret might be warranted, given his actions were extremely selfish and in stark contrast to ways we'd been intimate before. I'd never experienced anything like what just happened between us with anyone.

At the same time, feeling possessed by him was more erotic than I'd ever imagined. Nothing he had done made me feel he cared for me any less. Gentle or not, he was still my Aidan.

"You're sure you're okay?" he asks again.

"If I wasn't enjoying it, I would have told you or put a stop to it. You know me. I won't put up with something I don't want." I look him dead in the eye. "Ever."

"I know, baby. But you deserve better."

"You were doing what you felt in the moment. I don't fault you for that. I know you'd never hurt me."

"Never," he whispers in my ear. "I could never."

"Do you want to tell me what that call was about?"

"It was Stella. She's considering granting her father a Power of Attorney. He's convinced her that I won't go there when her treatment is completed as I said I would, that I'm abandoning her."

"What's his angle?"

"I don't know," he says, "yet."

16

Aidan

As much as I'd tried to get her to eat dinner at a decent hour, Alexis hadn't been hungry after being sick.

Her appetite has now returned after I took her so crudely on my conference table downstairs. Long past eight o'clock, we're both hungry and contemplating what to eat in front of an empty refrigerator.

Neither of us is in the mood or has the energy to cook anyway. We're debating takeout in the kitchen when there's a knock at my door. I look through the peephole to see Mrs. Schmidt with a bag of groceries, and I open the door to her.

"Mr. Pierce," she says, "Byron thought you two might like a late dinner."

I welcome her in, and she follows me to the kitchen where Alexis is parked at a stool, wearing my Yale shirt. Thankfully, only I'm aware there's nothing underneath it.

"You're a godsend, Mrs. Schmidt." I move to Alexis and wrap myself around her from behind, my arms circling her. "My baby's starving and I am unforgivably unprepared."

Alexis looks up at me and smiles, no doubt caught off guard that I'm doing this in front of my housekeeper. I have to admit I'm surprised at myself.

"I should text Byron to thank him for sending you," I add. "You've saved us from starvation."

"Can I call him?" Alexis asks. "I'd like to check in on Huck anyway."

"Sure." I pass her my phone. "You should program his contact information into your phone while you're at it."

She takes the phone from me and excuses herself to find her own.

Mrs. Schmidt sets about her work, throwing together a dish of something on the stove. She grabs a cutting board and a knife and stands across the island from me, chopping fresh vegetables.

Her round face rests in a knowing smile as she looks up at me. "May I speak freely, Mr. Pierce?"

I give her a quizzical look as I steal a small carrot from her. She's never asked me this before. I smile back at this woman who has been a trusted part of my household for many years. I know she cares for me like a son.

"Please," I say. "I insist."

"You seem very happy these days. I'd just like to say I'm very happy for you." She lays a gentle hand on my arm, leaning in as she beams at me and lowers her voice to a whisper. "Don't you let her get away."

By Sunday at nine o'clock, Mrs. Schmidt has cleaned up and departed from the loft. A very tired Alexis has collapsed into my bed while I shower. Afterwards, I let her sleep and head down the hall to my home office in pajama bottoms.

Samira and I spend an hour by phone finalizing details for the gala. Contracts with Marcus Neil, Shawn Thompson, and Sicily Strauss were secured earlier in the evening before Stella called.

Stella.

I have no idea what John Ireland is up to, but I need to find out before he plays his hand.

I've spoken to Felicia Grimes, the woman that manages Stella's business dealings. She assures me she has not been contacted by John Ireland, and everything is business as usual. She emailed me the most recent sales reports to prove her assertion. The business is healthy, though growth has slowed some.

Felicia is concerned that sales will slump more with Stella out of the limelight much longer, but that can't be helped. Stella will be out of touch until the last week of June, right before the gala. I insist Felicia work around this and prepare a fresh marketing campaign to roll out upon Stella's return.

I try Dimitri by phone.

"Yeah, Pierce. This important? I was just heading out."

"It's very important, actually."

I explain to him what's transpired with Whitmore and, without hesitation, he agrees we need to do something now.

"What's your angle? I sense you've got something up your sleeve."

"Actually, Alexis lit the fire," I say. "We just need to fan the flames."

"Alexis? Is that your girl?"

"Yes."

"How's she fit into all this?"

"She's my uncle's attorney."

"Ahh. Another piece of the puzzle," he says. "That's convenient. What did the beautiful Miss Alexis come up with?"

"How do you know she's beautiful?"

"Because it's you, Pierce."

"Yeah," I say with a half-hearted laugh. "She's beautiful. And you'll keep your hands off her when you meet her."

"Duly noted. Now out with it," he urges. "I ain't got all night."

Monday morning comes far too fucking early. Alexis is motionless when my alarm goes off in the four o'clock hour. I know she's got a full day of appointments to catch up from her time away last week, so I let her sleep as I dress for a run.

Mobb Deep's "Survival of the Fittest" motivates me as my feet hit pavement, when otherwise I'd be dragging ass. Dimitri and I had a solid plan. He'd be diving into it today after we'd been up until midnight bouncing ideas off each other.

I'm five miles in and on my way back to the loft when my music is interrupted by a call from Byron. I slow my pace and come to a stop under a street lamp. It's still dark.

"Yeah," I say, breathing hard.

"Good morning, sir. Where shall I post today?"

"Alexis will need you here in Stanton. I don't want her left without protection. You can check in with her about where to leave Huck. Give her until seven before you call."

"Yes, sir. Should I post in her office?"

"No. Outside of it is fine."

"There's a back entrance as well as a front. I can't cover both."

"I'll make sure she keeps her back entrance locked. Charlie will be in the office with her today. You can watch the front."

"Very good. Let me know if you need me."

"Thanks, Byron."

Macklemore and Ryan Lewis continue their assault on my ears when the call disconnects. I finish my race for the loft, anticipating the reward of getting my hands on Alexis when I get there.

It's not quite six yet. At the loft, hip hop still plays through my earbuds. I'm drinking a bottle of cold water when my peripheral vision is graced with a welcome sight.

Alexis is in my kitchen, staring me down like she's a lioness about to tackle her next meal.

And she's stark naked.

"Damn, baby." I can't take my eyes off of her. She is stunning. "Now that's the way to greet a man."

I'm surprised at her confidence as she saunters over to me. I've never seen her like this but it's more than a fucking turn on. I'm already hard.

I pull the earbuds out and set my phone on the counter, then switch the music to play through the sound system. "My Love" from the Brown Study album fills the room.

She reaches her arms around my neck and drives her tongue into my mouth. I match her greed, pulling back only to strip my shirt off. I've left my sneakers and socks elsewhere, and she peels off the rest of my clothing, kneeling in front of me to take me over with her mouth.

I'm facing the kitchen sink and a wall of white cabinets, gripping the island counter behind me and unable to stop groaning with her technique.

Goddamn she's good.

I'm already close, but I tug on her hair. I need to make up for last night. I refuse to succumb before she does.

Not this time.

She looks up at me, no longer with those humbled doe eyes like the first time I experienced this from her. The hunger in her eyes hasn't faded a bit from the moment she prowled in here to find me.

I take her hand and pull her to her feet, then switch our positions in the aisle, her back now to the island. I lift her up onto the counter as she's kissing me, her hands roaming over my damp skin. She licks my bottom lip then bites it gently, stopping only long enough to speak to me.

"I woke up missing you," she says. "I was having a dream."

"Is that right? What about?" My arms are wrapped around her back, caressing her, then roaming through her hair.

"You," she says. "Taking me like you did last night."

"I can easily figure out if you're telling the truth." I slip fingers inside of her, finding her soaking. "Yeah, I'd say you're pretty amped, baby."

She smiles a mischievous grin at my words, and I groan as she wraps a hand around me, stroking.

"I'm not game for that this morning. You're getting off first," I say. "Now."

"If you insist. And I'm loving this song, by the way."

I make sure the music will continue, putting the slow jam on repeat as I grab my water bottle from where it sits next to her. I put a finger over the open top and drizzle some of the cold liquid over her left breast. She tips her head back with a moan, and I follow the drops of water with my tongue, then repeat over her other breast. Her nipples are extended to capacity, begging me to suck them.

As I let go of her with my mouth, she opens herself to me, wrapping her legs around my waist. I intended to taste her first but having her this close feels too good. I enter her gently, unsure how she's feeling after last night. She grabs at my ass, wanting me deeper.

I comply, relishing her tightness around me, but I have to stop in order to keep my promise.

I want her to get there first.

I transfer the music to the bedroom, then lift her off the counter, carrying her weight while I'm buried in her, feeling her lips roam over my neck, my collarbone.

"*Ti porto a letto, baby.*"

I carry her off and lay her down with a hand cradling her back, not wanting to remove myself from her. We manage to make it to the middle of the bed without an inch of space between us.

I'm kissing her neck, surrounding her, my arms still beneath her as I'm starting to pick up momentum with my hips. I can feel her tremor as I move in and out.

"*Aidan.*"

She's nearly out of breath. I pause to look down at her, unwrapping my arms from beneath her and resting my palms on the bed.

"I never want to be without this," she manages.

"I don't either. I'm right here, baby." I rest my forehead on hers, kissing her gently. "Same high, remember? I'm not letting go." I move my hips again and she gyrates beneath me.

"Yes," she breathes. She repeats it over and over, urging me on as I find the place deep inside her that drives her over the edge. I'm coming right after her, unable to hold back anymore.

I collapse on top of her, using what's left of my energy to roll her over and onto me while I'm flat on my back, trying to come down from the climb.

She pants as she rests over me and we rise up and down. She's silent, but I can feel tears leave her eyes and trail to my chest. I hold her tighter, my arms a cocoon for her while I rake fingers over her hair.

"Fall apart, baby," I say. "I've got you."

17

Alexis

Monday moves by in a blur. I've met with several clients about various topics from estate planning to real estate. One family is selling their second home in Falcon Lake because they can no longer afford the taxes.

I'm glad to be in the thick of normalcy, able to forget about all the craziness I've been surrounded with for the last several days.

Aidan has taken the gala prep off my plate for now, insisting Samira has plenty of time to handle it. They've taken off with my ideas for the evening, and the details are coming together. I've put Jade in touch with Samira at Aidan's insistence.

Now more than confident about his feelings for me, I wouldn't think twice about Jade contacting Aidan. But he preferred to stay out of it and let Jade and Samira go forward.

Thoughts of Aidan constantly creep in as welcome distractions. Recalling the way we'd been together last night and this morning left me physically aroused. I'd woken up so crazed for him that I'd walked into his kitchen in the nude, not caring if anyone else would find me that way.

I had to have him in that moment.

I smile as my phone pings with another text from him.

Day's almost over, baby.

You ready to come home?

I sigh as warm fuzzy feelings flood me.

He wants me to come home.

Byron has been posted outside all day, only taking a break when Charlie brought him some lunch from the café. Huck has been at home since this morning and I feel torn again. I want to be with Aidan, but I want to be home too.

I need to check on Huck and the house. Do you want to come with me?

I'd love to, but I'm in the middle of prep for meetings about the Center scheduled for tomorrow. I'd like you to join me for one of them. Are you free tomorrow at five?

I check my calendar. I'm scheduled to meet with Dr. Flint in the afternoon. Our sessions are typically forty-five minutes long.

Where? I have an appointment at four.

1150 Third Street

That's the County Office Building. What is it for?

I'm meeting with the Director of Probation. I'd like you there with me.

I'm warm fuzzies all over again.

I can be there. I think I'll stay home tonight, get some rest. That okay with you?

His reply doesn't come as quickly as the others. Charlie pops his head into my office.

"How you doing, babe?"

"I'm good," I say. "Tired."

"You going home tonight? Want some company?"

"I am going home, but I don't think I'll be alone. Aidan won't let Byron leave my side."

"Well, look at you coming into your own," he laughs. "You got your own Kevin Costner an' shit. Way to go, Whitney."

"Very funny." I crack a smile at his teasing. "So you'll be here tomorrow? Mrs. Loomis is coming in to sign her will. You know how she loves to flirt with you."

"Yes, ma'am," he says. "I'll be here for my sweet-ass Betty White look-alike. Her appointment isn't until eleven but I'll be here at eight-thirty on the button."

He turns to leave and pops his head back into my office, his hand holding the door open and grinning at me. "Delivery for you, babe." He opens the door wider to reveal Aidan standing next to him.

He's dressed in the same suit he had on when we parted ways this morning, but you'd never know he'd been wearing it all day. He looks as perfect as he did the first time we met.

"Good night, Charlie," I call to him. He's already heading for the back door.

"Later!" he hollers back.

"This is a surprise," I say as Aidan shuts the door behind him. I begin my end of day ritual, shutting off my computer, turning off my desk lamp.

"I wanted to kiss you goodbye," he says, "especially if I'm not going to see you until tomorrow."

He comes at me before I know what's happening. He smells so damn good and tastes even better. His soft lips have moved from mine to graze my neck, down to where my cleavage peeks through one of the blouses he bought for me.

"Aidan," I breathe. "Don't start this now. I won't be able to stop."

He pulls back, looking in my eyes. "You want to stop?"

"I never want to stop with you. But I should go home. Byron's been stuck out there all day."

He kisses me gently once more. "You're right. Byron goes with you. And," he emphasizes, "he stays over."

I groan internally. Part of me just wants to be alone. Then again, knowing Mark Whitmore is no longer living and breathing...

"Fine," I concede. "He can use Ben's room."

"You don't have to do that for him. I thought you kept that closed off?"

"I've pimped it out to Charlie and Gloria in the last week alone," I say. "What's one more?"

He chuckles, touching my cheek with a gentle hand. "I'm sorry it has to be this way. But I prefer you not be alone. Until I have more solid answers or action moving forward on R.E.E., this is how it has to be."

"I know," I say. "It's okay. I'll stay with you tomorrow night."

"Mmm," he groans as he kisses me again, leaning into me. He's hard, leaving me wondering how the hell he's going to take care of that when he's sending me away.

"I'll meet you at the Probation Office tomorrow at five."

"Good," he says. "Where will you be coming from?"

"I have an appointment next door to that building."

"With?"

I sigh. "My therapist." I cringe waiting for him to say something, to get upset or be concerned.

Instead he kisses me once more, sweetly this time. "I'll see you tomorrow."

Once he's gone, I lock up out back and leave through the front door to the sidewalk where Byron awaits.

Tuesday morning starts out with a bang. I'm glad for the extra space for Byron in Ben's room as he was able to stay out of my hair.

It's also allowed me to curse like a sailor without Byron overhearing when Huck jumps up on my outfit before I can make it downstairs. I'm now covered in dog prints and fur. I'll have to re-dress.

"Byron," I holler, "can you take the dog out please?"

He lets out a loud whistle, and the dog is off like a shot.

I welcome having Byron's help. I love my beast but, admittedly, Huck tended to be ignorant about the rules. I hadn't taken the time to properly train the big lug.

The only clean, suitable option that remains in my closet is a navy dress. Unfortunately, it's also too big for me to wear. I now have more clothes at Aidan's than I do here.

I wouldn't typically wear jeans when planning to meet with clients, but I don't have a choice. Huck's dirty paws ruined the outfit I'd just tossed aside. I dress up a pair of dark jeans as best I can with a belt, low heels and a short sleeve blue top.

By eight-thirty, we're back at my office and Byron resumes his post, parked out front as he'd been yesterday. I feel terrible that he's stuck on Alexis detail, but safer knowing he's not far away.

I'd heard from Aidan only twice by text since last night. He was busy trying to get us out of this mess, trying to juggle the gala prep, the Center, Stella. Idly I wonder if the stress is getting to him at all because he seems unfazed.

My intercom buzzes, shaking me out of thought. "Yes," I answer.

"Morning," Claudia sings. "Gloria Stearns to see you."

"Send her back."

Gloria comes through my door in the same pretty floral dress she'd worn to breakfast at the diner the day of her cousin's bridal shower. She looks beautiful, as always.

"Hey," I say. "What brings you here?"

"Just thought I'd kill a few minutes before court," she says. "Judge Cramer at nine-thirty." She gives me a look. "Everything okay? I haven't heard from you since I stayed over Friday."

"Things are a bit crazy but I'm fine."

"Lex, you know you can share. Are things with Aidan okay?"

I involuntarily smile. "Yeah," I say, "that part's great."

"Well then?"

"I suppose it's okay to tell you." It must be public information by now, at least in his hometown. "Mark Whitmore is dead."

"Shit." She'a taken aback. "Isn't he the attorney from Pennsylvania that worked for R.E.E.?"

"Yes."

"What happened?"

"We don't really know. He came to see me over at Reagan's Pub on Thursday while I was eating lunch with Charlie. I didn't mention it to you because I didn't think it was important at the time," I say, "but he was warning me."

"About?"

"Renewable Energy. He packed his whole family up to move to Florida in a hurry."

"Jesus, Lex. This is a big deal. Have you gone to the police?"

"No," I insist. "There really isn't anything helpful to share with them. Whitmore was in Florida when he…when it happened." I ignore the pain in my throat as I swallow hard. "Aidan is concerned for me, for my safety."

"Ah," she says. "So that's why Jeeves is out front."

"Yeah. Byron has been really great, actually."

"What's his deal anyway?"

"He's been with Aidan a long time. He's quiet. Polite. Amazing with animals. And punctual."

"Yeah," she laughs. "He must be one of the good guys then. Bad guys are never on time."

I crack a smile back. "I'll keep you posted on happenings as I can, but you should probably know I signed the NDA with Aidan."

"He signed it?"

"Not without an argument," I say. "But yeah, ultimately he thought it was a good idea."

"Has Pandora's Box been flung open yet?"

"Partly," I say, recalling the report of Dr. Mason he'd shared. "But it wasn't anything that changed my feelings for him."

"I told you," she says. "You're in deep, baby girl."

I sigh.

This much I know.

"I'm very happy for you, Lex. But as far as R.E.E. goes, please be careful."

"I think the people that ought to be careful are the ones that cross Aidan."

Dr. Flint is looking at me as though I have three heads.

Her milk chocolate complexion is flawless as always, but her pretty face is mixed up in astonishment. Her trademark rectangular blue frames rest high up on the bridge of her nose as she shakes her head at me in disbelief.

"Did you just say Aidan Pierce?"

"Yes."

"And you're dating?" Her expression is telling. She appears far younger than her fifty-something years, and she must appreciate gorgeous men as much as the next gal. She's looking at me like I've scooped up the best possible male on God's green earth.

"Yes?" My answer unintentionally comes out as a question.

"Uh huh," she says. She can't hold back her smile. "What's the problem then, Alexis?" Her head full of short ebony hair rests in her hand, her elbow on the arm of her chair as she waits for me to realize there shouldn't be a problem at all.

What I can share with her about Aidan is limited given our non-disclosure, so I change topics.

"That part is fine," I say. "It's work-related matters and my mother that are currently concerning me."

"Your mother? We haven't discussed her in quite a long time. Not even for the several sessions before your time with me ended in January."

"She reconnected with my sister in Arizona. My brother-in-law had a hiking accident. I went out there to help my sister and found out they now live only a couple hours apart. Connie has been calling Jill's daughters on the phone, visiting with Jill occasionally."

"Did you see your mother while you were out there?"

"No. I could have," I add. "I didn't want to."

"That's an entirely reasonable and acceptable position, Alexis. What about this are you struggling with? Are you envious of their relationship?"

I consider her question a moment. "That never crossed my mind," I admit, "but I suppose it makes sense. She was never a good mother to either of us. Maybe it bothers me that she reached out to Jill and not me. Or maybe it's the fact that my sister was receptive to it at all."

"You were the younger child," she says. "Your relationship with your mother was not the same as it was with your sister. They had more time together before you came along. Any bond with your mother was that much less and was broken long ago."

"You're right, of course."

"What if she'd shown up in New York living two hours away? What would you have done if she'd called you?"

"Ignored her." I say it without hesitation.

"You wouldn't have a relationship with her regardless?"

"No."

"I know we haven't delved into everything that you went through with your mother, but…"

"Because it isn't necessary. I didn't go through much of anything. She was just never there."

"So you've said. But you still feel the hurt because of that, Alexis. Feelings of abandonment, self-doubt, a lack of confidence. You were just overcoming that in our last few sessions. And I must say, you look much different than the last time I saw you."

"In what way?" I can't tell if it's a compliment or the opposite. I wouldn't be surprised if I looked more haggard than I did in January. Last night was only the second decent night's sleep I'd had in awhile.

"You're exuding a confidence I've never witnessed from you before. Maybe it's your Mr. Pierce. Or maybe it occurred before him and he was attracted to you because of it. Either way," she says, "don't let the lack of a fairytale past with your mother affect your present. If you want to reach out to her, now you know where she is. If you don't, so be it. The ball is in your court, as it always has been."

I nod. She has a fair point.

"Thank you for the compliment. I am definitely feeling different, but it's also been a roller coaster." She says nothing, waiting for me to go on.

I decide not to mention the crazy little voice that had been plaguing me until I met Aidan. My inner sex goddess has been awakened into reality and my head has been void of ramblings as of late.

"Our relationship is complicated. Especially since it's the only one I've had since losing Ben."

"Well," she says, leaning back in her chair and crossing her long legs, "we have another half hour. I certainly wouldn't consider it a waste of my time to hear about the world's most handsome, eligible bachelor and his attempt to court you."

At five o'clock, I'm waiting for Aidan outside the County Office Building. Byron is parked not far away and intends to go back to my place for Huck as soon as Aidan arrives.

It's unlike him to be late. I'm about to text him when I see him come around the corner onto Third Street about a block away.

He's drop dead gorgeous. Tight jeans in a dark wash, loafers, one of his signature t-shirts (this one is navy blue), and a navy blazer. I have to keep myself from barreling at him. It's only been twenty-four freaking hours.

He seems distracted but his smile is contagious when he catches sight of me.

"Baby," he says, wrapping me up in his arms, "you look amazing." He kisses me, leaving his tongue out of the mix but igniting me anyway. "I'm sorry I'm late."

"Should we tell Byron he can take off? Huck's probably crossing his legs."

"Yeah," he says. "I'll be right back."

He heads up the street and leans into Byron's open window, allowing me the pleasure of viewing his ass in those jeans.

Holy hell do I want to tackle him.

As soon as this meeting ends, that's exactly what I plan on doing.

The Director of Probation – one Ms. Hope Kennedy – has been irritated from the moment we walked in. I'm unsure why Aidan wanted to see her or why he has me here. I sit back and let him take the lead once he's introduced himself and then introduced me as Eli Myers' attorney.

"I can't give you much time," she says. "I'm sorry."

"Please excuse me for being late."

He doesn't elaborate or even smile for that matter. He's made no efforts to charm her since we stepped foot in her tiny office. It's hot as hell in here and there are no windows. The temps have been in the low eighties the last two days. Though it's early June, no one in the building has gotten the memo to turn on the air conditioning.

"What is it you'd like to discuss, Mr. Pierce? I was advised by my superiors that I had to take this meeting with you. I'll be honest," she says flatly, "if I wasn't required to do it, I would have declined to see you."

Aidan can sense as well as I can that Hope Kennedy won't take kindly to any bullshit. Her sweet moniker does not match her pessimistic persona.

Ms. Kennedy's face is free of make-up. Her dark hair would be in need of a dye job if she'd been a vain woman. Silver strands are apparent throughout her tight ponytail. Her brown eyes appear strained as she looks at us through her ordinary glasses. She's shorter than I am, a bit heavy in the chest. I can't see the rest of her as she sits behind the desk dressed in a well-worn business suit.

"I would like to discuss my plans for philanthropy here in Lake County," he starts. "I think we should work together, specifically on the drug problems being faced here."

"I'm not sure I can help you."

"I'm told you're quite effective in your job here and would be even more so if you were afforded more resources."

"Anyone can improve with access to more resources, Mr. Pierce. What can't be done is securing those resources to begin with."

"I would like to help with that," he says. "The Center in Mirror Lake is going to be a jumping off point, a place for learning and education for the community, especially young people. But I intend to invest far more than that."

He does?

This is news to me.

"Really?" I can tell she's more skeptical of his intentions than I'd ever been. It's not going to be easy to win this woman over, if she can be swayed at all. "How do you propose to do that?"

"That remains to be seen. I have to identify need before I can offer help."

"And you'd like me to help you identify the need?"

"Yes."

She rolls her eyes and blows out a frustrated breath. She removes her glasses, wiping her tired eyes with her right hand. When she looks up she not only appears disinterested, she looks flat out pissed.

"I'd love to sit here and discuss your pet project," she says, "but I've got far too much on my plate to be your go-to for this."

"I can appreciate you're overworked, Ms. Kennedy. That's what I'm trying to alleviate. You need more resources here. More staff." He waits a beat, then stands up and removes his blazer, revealing his well-defined upper body. "Maybe some fucking air-conditioning."

I'm surprised at his cursing with this stranger but figure he's got a method to his madness. He's been reading her the entire time. His attempt at humor catches her off guard, and I see her fight a smile. I don't hide my own amusement, but I say nothing.

"I admire your valiant efforts to make a dent here, Mr. Pierce. Who knows, maybe you'll end up doing some good. But I've seen projects similar to yours attempted not once, but three times. One gentleman was going to rehab a slew of houses in Stanton into eight-bedroom homes to serve as halfway houses. The city shut him down before he got started."

"I heard about that," I say. "The CEO of Ashley Pharma, right?"

"That's right," she says to me. "Ironic that pharmaceuticals are half the reason we face this problem."

"I would agree with you, and I'm aware of Mr. Wallace's attempts," Aidan says. "But plans like his fall short for a few reasons, one being location. Keeping these people in Stanton is a bad idea."

"What do you suggest?" she asks. "We send then on a Caribbean cruise?"

Aidan ignores her sarcasm.

"I've studied countless cases where users get out of jail after time served, maybe for their second or even third chance at rehab. Lucky ones might earn a place at a bootcamp in a remote corner of the state. They make some good progress, but once they're done they're shipped back here. They depart from a bus with no path forward beyond a requirement to check in here."

"They're also given tools, suggestions, recommendations. We can't do it for them, Mr. Pierce."

"I understand that. But you're returning them to the same city they left, where temptation is rampant. All it takes is one afternoon of boredom, one phone call to an old acquaintance to pull them back into bad habits they've just spent months learning to correct. Then it's another arrest and back to square one."

"So?"

"So we need a better plan, better post-care for those that actually have a chance once they've demonstrated an effort to get clean. The current housing the county provides is infested with bed bugs and outfitted with nothing beyond discarded mattresses and bare light bulbs. If those units are full, it's off to a motel filled with the same people they need to avoid – dealers, junkies, people from their past. Hardly an encouraging environment for someone trying to improve themselves. There's no support of any kind, and most of these people have no one left in their personal lives that trust them. They've burned all their bridges and go back to using within days of coming back here. You're setting them up to fail."

"Mr. Pierce," she starts.

I wait through an uncomfortable moment of silence, wondering if Ms. Kennedy is going to rant back to him about how wrong he is. Instead she releases a heavy sigh before agreeing with him.

"Your assessment is entirely accurate. You want to hear more?" She doesn't wait for him to respond. "Two of my officers – my best officers, mind you – are currently out on disability suffering from PTSD just because they showed up to do their jobs one day. Trouble is, while the suicide rate increases among our officers, the state refuses to acknowledge that PTSD is a legitimate concern for our department. My officers will likely fall into debt while they wait for treatment for their symptoms. Or they'll come back to work sooner than they should because they have no choice financially."

"Again," he says, "that's something I'd like to investigate."

"You going to get some politicians to pull some strings? Change how things run? Because that's what it would take. The problem isn't just with my staff or my lack of resources. It's with the system."

"I intend to build on what I've already begun. In the last few years I've met with political leaders and policy experts. Researched with clinicians, had conversations with educators and law enforcement. This is not an easy task, and not one I can do alone. This much I know, Ms. Kennedy."

Even with his assertions, she's unconvinced. "You may think you have that power," she says, "but even if you do, it won't help me now. I'm more than inconvenienced on a daily basis by the drug problems here. I'm short-staffed to the point I had to personally hold up the twenty-year-old single mother that came in here yesterday because her assigned probation officer is no longer here. Do you have any idea what her drug of choice was?"

"I wouldn't venture a guess." He's still reading her, still waiting for his moment to turn her.

"Cough syrup. The woman was on so much cough syrup she couldn't speak, or stand, or even manage sitting in a chair by her damn self. That was after I'd spent the morning demonstrating how to use NARCAN to my newest recruit because there was an immediate need when his first ever client dropped to the floor in our conference room while overdosing on heroin. Do you see the picture I'm painting here, Mr. Pierce?"

He says nothing. Neither do I. Hope Kennedy turns in her swivel chair to shut down her laptop before she speaks again. "I think we're done wasting each other's time, don't you?"

He leans back a bit and I can see what's coming. He's going to go for it.

"I appreciate that you think I'm only trying to gain media attention, Ms. Kennedy. To push for another irrelevant, piece of shit story you'll watch on the eleven o'clock news tonight when you fall into bed out of sheer exhaustion."

A look of surprise comes over her as he goes on, his tone becoming noticeably curt.

"Maybe you believe I'm just an asshole with nothing but money and time trying to make himself feel better about screwing hookers behind closed doors. But I can assure you," he says emphatically, "this is not the case."

The woman's eyes go wide.

"We are talking about a problem that does not discriminate by age or economic status. It's an epidemic, considering the number of lives being lost," he says. "I'm not only referring to the souls that have crossed the threshold of your office and ended up below ground. I'm talking about people in my own life that are gone because of the very problem you face."

He takes a breath, exhales sharply, and steadies his words.

I know exactly what he's doing.

He's trying not to go postal on Hope Kennedy.

"For me, this is personal. It's about time you wake the fuck up and realize I sincerely want to help. Whether you're acting out of pride or skepticism doesn't matter. Stop turning up your nose at the assistance I'm offering and accept it. You'd be a fool not to."

He stands up and grabs his jacket off the back of his chair, pulling out the silver case with his business cards. He tosses one on her desk and gestures for me to get up and exit ahead of him.

I'm in the hall already as I hear him utter a departing message.

"I appreciate the job you're doing here. Not everyone is cut out for it. To be blunt, it's near the shittiest position to hold in this city. You're a dedicated individual, Ms. Kennedy. But I'm telling you now, be a part of the solution," he says firmly, "or get the hell out of my way."

18

Aidan

Before we can get off the elevator at 250 Harrison, Alexis is all over me. I'm not objecting, but I don't think I've never felt this much carnal force radiating off her.

"Baby, what's gotten into you?" I break our lip lock. "You're insatiable."

"I wanted to jump on you the minute I saw you tonight. Then watching you in that meeting, watching you command a room. Even a tiny, too hot room with one person as your audience. *Fuck*," she breathes. "It's making me crazy."

"Damn," I say when she stops her rant. I'm resting my hands on her shoulders, my eyes looking into hers. "You're this amped just from that?"

"I guess. I don't know," she says, coming at me and sliding her tongue in my mouth. She pulls back when I don't respond. "Who cares why? Just take your fucking clothes off."

"Whoa," I say. "Let's get upstairs."

"No," she says. "Here. I've been fantasizing about this since we parted ways here that night you took me to the roof."

I can only consider her proposal for a moment before she's stripped off her jeans and top. She leaves on her lingerie and steps back into her low heels.

At that point I'm done like toast.

Fucking burnt toast.

I can't keep my hands or my mouth off her. I push the button to stop the car from moving as it reaches the third floor.

"Turn around," I order.

She does as I ask, quietly standing in front of me and facing the back wall of the elevator, her cheeks bared to me in her thong. I pin her arms above her head with one hand and smack her on the ass with the other, as hard as I think she can take it. She moans loud as I toss my blazer and shirt to the floor, kneeling on them. I'm at her from behind with my mouth, then let my fingers work every open space while I lick her from underneath.

"*Aidan.*" She says my name in a guttural moan, and my cock is straining to break free of my jeans. "Not this way. I want to come with you inside me."

I shush her as I pull my head back to speak. She may have started this, but I'm finishing it the way I want to. "You will," I say. "Trust me. You're capable of more than you know, baby. We haven't even started to test the waters."

I turn my back to the wall where I'm seated, using it for support as I sit beneath her and lap her up.

She always tastes so fucking good.

I can feel her start to climb, purposely driving her there faster, my tongue deep inside her as I work her ass with my free hand. She comes violently, trying to squeeze me out with her knees. I pull away, giving her a brief rest. She starts to sink to the floor into my lap, but I don't let her.

"Stay standing, baby," I say. "You're getting off again."

She arches her backside out so she can look down past her glorious tits to where I sit. "There's no way," she says. "I'm so done."

"You only think you are," I tell her. "Please trust me."

I'm caressing her inner thighs with both hands, letting her relax before I ramp her up again.

"I..." she breathes. "I can't. Your touch is driving me crazy."

"You're highly sensitized. Certain parts of you are going to feel like that, are going to shut down. Other parts will not. Just stay open-minded, okay? I promise you'll thank me later."

I watch her rest her head on her forearms as she leans against the wall above me, accepting my instruction.

Time to play.

"Take a deep breath." I reach my arm up and splay a hand over her belly as she does. "Again," I say. The moment I feel her inhale I insert my index finger and middle finger deep inside her, finding the magic spot I'm looking for. I can feel her fullness as I move my fingers back and forth. "You're so beautiful, baby. Does that feel good?"

"Yes," she moans. "What are you doing to me?"

"Just relax. All you have to do is feel." I keep at it, penetrating her and moving my fingers in a come hither motion. She's soaking all around me with minimal effort.

"Aidan, what the hell," she pants. "*I'm so wet.*"

"Mm-hmm," I moan into her. I suck on her clit and within seconds she's coming again, this time harder than she ever has for me before. Her hands are sprawled out over her head against the back wall, her breath heaving.

"See?" I say as I press my lips to her thighs. I haven't removed my fingers from her yet. "Again?"

She's tentative. "You think I can?"

"Absolutely."

"Then *yes,*" she breathes. "Again."

I start my assault once more, instead moving my efforts to her O-spot. She's moaning loud, begging me not to stop. I keep up as I remove my other hand from her belly so I can use a finger to enter her backside.

She's coming again. This time her legs almost buckle. "Oh my *fucking* God," she howls. She's practically yelling.

My jeans are wet where I'm straining through them. I move out from beneath her, dropping them to my knees along with my briefs. I could manipulate her to come again and again this way, but I can't wait anymore.

"Hold on," I whisper, "I'm going to fuck you now, baby." I move her hair away from her neck, sucking on the soft spot between her collarbone and her nape. "Hard."

She steadies herself as best she can as I grip her hips and drive at her, pounding into her as hard as I did when I took her in my office.

"You're so wet, love. *Dio mi piace essere dentro di te.*"

"English," she demands.

I can't respond. She feels too good, better than anything I've ever experienced. My vision is going blurry as I take her beneath the fluorescent lights. She leans into my thrusts, crying out my name as I hit her G-spot this time.

"That's my girl," I tell her. "This is gonna be a good one. Can you feel that?"

"*Yes,*" she moans. "I feel like I have to pee."

"Fight through it," I breathe. "It's a false alarm." I stop for a second, leaning over her to breathe in her ear and keep her from thinking. "Let go, Alexis. You're going to come again, and it's going to feel like you're ripping apart."

I suck on her earlobe then drive my tongue into her ear, knowing how she goes slack when I do it. It works as I predicted and she moans even louder. I pull back and start again, thrusting into her as hard as before.

"I'm almost there, baby. Come with me." I push into her with steady momentum, feeling her start to clench around me each time I tap her deep inside in just the right place. As she comes, she releases the sexiest growl I've ever heard from a woman. Her whole body tenses, convulsing in pleasure as she screams a string of profanities.

I slam into her one last time, pulsing deeper inside her when I allow my own release.

I'm shuddering in place for what feels like a full five minutes, though it's probably closer to one. I pull out of her and turn her around to face me, holding up her spent body. I push hair back out of her face, wiping sweat from her forehead. "Well?" I finally ask.

"Yeah," she manages, heaving a huge sigh. "Thank you. Thank you. Thank you."

I break into a smile. "Only the beginning baby," I whisper. "Only the beginning."

By eight o'clock, Alexis wants to call it an early night. After our elevator ride, I can't blame her.

We'd eaten some leftovers from Sunday night and showered together. She didn't think she could handle me again, and though I could push the issue (and shamelessly prove her wrong), I watch her crawl into my bed and don't follow her. She's reached a heightened level of exhaustion, as intense as her sex drive had been earlier.

Dressed in pajama bottoms, I pad to my office with a bottle of water and take a seat behind my laptop.

I'm pleased with the progress on the gala, nearly all the details now in place for the event coming up in less than a month. Jade McCall has proven capable and Samira directed her as needed. Invites have gone out, and before that, Mrs. McCall had secured several full tables. The event would surely sell out, especially once people got a look at the entertainment.

I had Samira gather the information Alexis would need for the approvals at the county and state level for the Center. I'd put that back on Alexis' agenda as soon as possible, but not yet. She was still shaken up by Mark Whitmore's death.

If I allow myself to think about it, so am I.

My phone dings with a text from Dimitri. I haven't talked to him since yesterday. My day had been full, and I hadn't had a chance to reach out to him yet today. I open the message to see only three words from him.

I've got something.

I don't hesitate to dial him or wait for him to speak when he picks up the line.

"What do you have?"

"Ireland. He's definitely making a move. I found a shit ton of communications between him and higher ups in R.E.E. as recently as yesterday."

"Fuck. How'd you manage that?"

"It's better you don't know. It was a risk, but I had to do it. I can't have him fuckin' up your life anymore, man. We're getting you out of this."

"And?"

"He's working out some sort of deal with them. It involves your uncle's land, just as you thought. The messages are coded, but I'm certain he's promised it to them, that he can get it through you."

"Like you said, let's let him believe that. Maybe it's time I reach out to him and play out that angle."

"Maybe," he says, "but how does Stella fit into all this? Or don't you care about that?"

I groan in frustration. "I still haven't figured out why he's pushing her to give him Power of Attorney. Does he want to control her assets? Or her?"

"You let him take over her shit, you can be free of her. But if that happens, you have no way of knowing her fate. It's your decision," he asserts. "Can you throw her to the wolves without the guilt killing you?"

I'm silent.

"I know you, man," he says. "This will eat at you if you don't go about it just right. Your new girl doesn't need to watch you self-destruct."

"I'll deal with Stella," I say. "Alexis is aware of how things are with her. We'll get through it."

"Let's get this underway then. Based on what I'm seeing here, I have an angle you might be able to use."

"Out with it."

"You're going to have to go into the lion's den," he says. "You need to go to R.E.E. directly."

"I have nothing on them that didn't come from Ireland, which means I can't use it. And I have nothing to offer them except Eli's land. You know that isn't an option."

"Not that," he says. "Give them something else they want."

"It would help if I knew what that was."

"Remember that parcel Gianni Rossi acquired downstate last year?"

"I do. He fought Ireland hard for that one. You know how he always takes the high road."

Alanna Rossi's husband had beaten John Ireland to the punch when he acquired the three hundred acres of land, the only remaining parcel of its kind within five hundred miles of New York City. It was a testament to his intelligence that he came away with it, even after Ireland used his typical tactics to bully the seller into changing his allegiance.

The seller had not been dissuaded and Gianni Rossi had walked away with the land.

"Are you catching on yet?"

"You think R.E.E. wants Rossi's land?"

"I know they do. It's right here in black and white. Ireland has offered it already. Claims if he gets nowhere with you, he'll muscle Rossi's parcel away from him and sell it to them."

"He can't deliver on that. Gianni Rossi wouldn't answer a text message from that bastard. He'd never negotiate with him. But it's possible Stella is coming into play somehow. That could be his angle."

"Manipulating control over her to sway Rossi."

"Yes," I say, "through Stella's mother."

"That seems entirely possible."

Ireland kept Alanna out of their daughter's life for over twenty years, but he knew when push came to shove she was still the girl's mother.

"If I want to prevent any of this, I have to act first."

"Agreed. That parcel of land is their Holy Grail," Dimitri says. "It's more rural than Mirror Lake. No existing population to rile up in protest. Less approvals required for whatever they want to do, whether it's solar panels or mining shale."

I wasn't sure I could convince Gianni Rossi to let that parcel go any more than John Ireland could. But if he knew the stakes, maybe he would consider it.

"I'm on it," I say. "Thank you, Dimitri. I'll keep you posted."

"Do that," he says. "And when we're out there in a couple weeks, I need to meet your girl."

"You've got a deal."

"Good," he says. "I hope it will be to celebrate the removal of the Irelands from your ass."

Wednesday morning, the alarm goes off and Alexis darts up to sitting, startled.

"It's okay, baby," I tell her. "I got it." I turn off the annoyance and settle her back down, cradling her in my arms.

I wish I could stay in this moment all day, but I have too many things to follow up on after hitting nothing but brick walls last night.

My call with Dimitri was informative, but I'd not been able to act on anything he'd offered.

I'd tried to reach Stella at The Meadows, to warn her that her father was manipulating her for his benefit even if I couldn't explain how yet. I was not allowed to disturb her. I was unable to get a progress report or find anyone that could help me. Stella's mother's friend, Director Jasmine Hernandez, had been helpful in the past, but I was informed the Director is on vacation until next week.

My next call was to Alanna, but she hadn't been available either. I'd left her a voicemail that it was urgent she call me back.

Alexis is peacefully back to sleep, and I take a moment to peel back the sheet and admire her nudity. I'm learning she's always covered up, even on hot nights.

My baby loves her covers.

I climb over her, turning her onto her back gently as I wait for her to wake.

"Mmm," she moans. "You looking to give me another education, Pierce? Because I sure liked the class you gave last night."

I love how open she's becoming, how she's giving in to becoming mine and learning her body. I smile down at her, though she can't see me with her eyes still closed.

"If that's what you want baby, I'm game." I discard my pajama bottoms, then climb over her again. "Open your eyes."

She does, revealing a hunger nearly as palpable as it was in the elevator. Her eyes are so arrestingly blue, so deep with meaning. They told her story, revealed her gumption and soul, her pain…

…and her pleasure.

Every time I look at her this way I feel like I can't catch my breath.

I'm slayed by her.

Burnt fucking toast.

I skip my run, choosing to work out my body with Alexis instead.

We've eaten breakfast, showered, and dressed in time to leave the loft early. I have something to show her before she goes to her office.

We walk with hands clasped the few minutes to our destination, the city blocks passing quickly without much activity on the street at seven-thirty in the morning. We stop in front of the one-story commercial building I'd purchased six months ago. The property became available while I was still planning my departure from California. My gut had told me to scoop it up.

I was damn glad I had. It will be the perfect spot for the next phase of my philanthropy.

"What is this place?" She's beautiful today, wearing the lilac dress I'd bought for her the first night she stayed in my guest room. Her hair is up in a clip, securing it from blowing around in the breeze. Another weather front is coming through today.

"You'll see." I pull keys from my jacket pocket as I unlock the front door. "Close your eyes."

She smiles as her eyebrows raise in doubt, but she does as I ask.

I open the door and prop it open, then take her hand again to guide her over the threshold. She steps into the space, which smells far better than it did when I bought the building. Evidence of squatters and drug paraphernalia are long gone. Cold cement block walls have given way to finished drywall painted in a clean white. The high celings are outfitted with new lighting and interior walls are partially constructed.

"Okay," I say. "You can look now."

"Wow." She looks around the vast space with interest. "This place is enormous. What is it?"

"The future home of Pierce Philanthropy Foundation. What do you think?"

"I think it's big enough to get lost in. You're not keeping the offices at the loft?"

"I am," I say. "That will be administrative for all of my business dealings. But this space is necessary to expand my philanthropy into the foundation. You didn't think I could run this kind of thing without a larger staff, did you?"

"No, it's just..." She considers it and smiles. "I guess I hadn't really thought about it."

"I'm handpicking board members now," I say. "That was part of my day yesterday. But there's one person I've yet to ask."

She tilts her head.

"I want you to be a part of this," I say. "Would you consider it?"

Her expression changes to surprise, her lips slightly parted in shock. "Me?"

"Yes, baby. I want you involved at every level."

"I…I don't know what to say, Aidan."

"You could say yes."

Please say yes. I can't do this without you.

"Yes," she finally says, nodding in enthusiastic agreement. "I would be honored."

"Good." I pull her to me, kissing her soft lips. "You'll have your own office in this building. Over there." I nod towards the back corner of the building where one of the larger offices has been carved out.

"God, Aidan. I can't even…this is so much to take in. How are you going to juggle this with everything you have going on back in California?"

"I'm dismantling my L.A. office," I tell her. "That was the rest of my day yesterday. I'm selling off assets out there, moving everything here. It will take some time to finalize, but the process is underway. Lionel is going to join me out here within the year. He's my right hand on the West Coast."

"You're staying here? Permanently?"

"This is home for me now, Alexis." My expression softens seeing her giddy at my statement. "I'm not going anywhere."

19

Alexis

Wednesday afternoon, I'm once again in a state of euphoria.

Aidan asked me to be a part of his philanthropy on a formal level. That he had the confidence in me to even ask, that he wanted me to be this involved in his life – I hadn't been able to wipe the dopey grin off my face all morning.

Byron is posted out front, as usual. I got the Huck report on my way through the front door this morning. Byron was happy to share that he'd taught Huck a few commands over the last few days. I was happy to see Byron happy.

Charlie and I are going over some files in my office when Claudia buzzes in.

"Chance is here," she says. "You need to sign for something."

Chance is our trusted overnight courier. I don't know his last name, but he came by the office regularly to deliver documents in his brown uniform.

"I'll be right there."

We chat about the changing weather as I sign my name to accept delivery and send him on his way. I look for the name of the sender on the envelope as I take it back to my office. I don't recognize the return address in Pennsylvania.

"Are we expecting anything from clients in Pennsylvania?" I ask Charlie as I take a seat next to him.

"Not that I know of."

"That's where this came from, but there's no name with the return address."

"You're sure it's for you?"

"Yes, it's addressed to me."

"Then what the hell are you waiting for?" he asks. "Open it."

I pull the contents out and find a handwritten note clipped to the top of some documents.

Ms. Greene,

My husband asked me to send this to you before he died. Please do not contact me. I'm only doing this because he indicated it was important for your safety.

Regards,

Laura Whitmore

I have no idea why Mark Whitmore's wife is sending me anything. We'd never even met.

I unclip the note and hand it to Charlie while I look through the documents, which appear to be messages between R.E.E. executives whose names I recognize. They're private messages between the players, discussing what would have been known only behind the scenes. One of the emails discusses at length how to go after Myers' land under the guise of a solar farm.

This is unreal.

How the fuck would Whitmore have gotten this?

Charlie hands me back the note once he's read it.

"What did she send?"

I don't answer him. "I need to call Aidan," I say. "Right now."

Half an hour later, I'm pacing my office while Aidan reads through everything Laura Whitmore sent.

"Well?" I finally ask. I can't take it anymore. "Are they legitimate?"

"I'll find out," he says. "It appears so on the surface, but I can't figure out how Whitmore would have gotten his hands on this."

"That was my question, too. But, then again, if he was killed for what he knew, it makes total sense. There may have been more information that he had, things he knew but didn't have proof of."

"I need to take these. Are you okay with that?"

"Of course," I say. "Do you think you can follow the lead without having to bother Mrs. Whitmore?"

"No."

I give him a stern look.

"I want to respect her wishes that she be left alone. Her husband is dead. Her children have no father. She's been through enough."

"I will handle this as I see fit, Alexis. Your safety is more important than protecting a widow from divulging what she knows. It's a matter of having one conversation. That's all I need from her."

"Fine," I say, knowing he won't be dissuaded. "But leave me the hell out of it. I don't want her thinking it was my idea."

"I'll be sure she understands that. You are not to leave Byron's sight. Do you understand?" He gets up to leave.

"I know, bossy-pants, I know." *I wouldn't want to if I could.* "Where are you going?"

"That's yet to be determined. I have a few calls to make first."

"Okay." I don't want him to go. He must sense it as he comes for me, setting down the documents to hold me in his arms.

"It's going to be okay." He looks down at me reassuringly. "This is good news, baby. We can use this to our advantage."

"I hope you're right."

Byron takes me home to Mirror Lake after work. I thought ahead and packed myself a few things while at the loft so I'd have multiple options for work tomorrow. I'm carrying two dresses on hangers over one arm and Huck bounds for me as I enter. Byron steps in between us before the dog can pummel me. He holds up his hand and Huck immediately sits.

Damn. I could kiss this guy. He's just saved me from another ruined outfit and bruised ribs.

"Okay," he says to me. He takes the dresses and puts them on a doorknob nearby. "I'm going to free him from his sit so you can pet him. Don't let him jump on you. No running through your legs or bowling you over. We're trying to break him of those bad habits. Agreed?"

Shit he's intimidating.

"Agreed."

Byron lets the dog go with another magic signal. Huck gently rises and walks over to me.

"Now ask him to sit. Like this," he says. He holds up his closed hand, but he's not making a fist. His fingers are pointing down, his thumb secured at the left of them. I mimic his gesture and Huck sits in front of me.

"Wow," I mutter.

What happened to my disobedient dog?

"Okay," he says. "Go ahead with the attention now."

He leaves me for Ben's room and I'm dopey smiles all over again.

Byron is definitely growing on me. His façade is gruff, but his insides are as sweet as sugar.

"Hey, handsome boy," I tell Huck. I squat down as tactfully as I can in my dress, rubbing his face between my hands. "That Byron's a keeper, isn't he, bud?"

The dog licks my face in agreement.

"Yeah," I say, "I thought so."

I pull out one of the frozen dishes Marta prepared a couple weeks ago so I can thank Byron with a proper dinner. I'm relieved Marta is due in again tomorrow. I haven't been here enough to keep the house up like I normally would. Dog hair is rolling around like tumbleweeds in the desert.

As I'm pulling the cooked meal from the oven, my sister calls.

"Hey, Jill," I answer. "How's Derek?"

"He's good. Starting to get the hang of his crutches. How are things there?"

"Crazy, but good."

"You still have a billionaire in your bed?"

"At this particular moment, no," I laugh. "Hopefully tonight, with any luck."

"So he's not back with Stella?"

"No. He was helping her out, the media spun it as if they were back together. She's out there, he's here. In fact," I say, "he's decided to stay here permanently."

"In Mirror Lake?"

"Sort of. The Center will be in Mirror Lake, but his home and offices are in Stanton. And he asked me to be a part of it. He wants me to be a board member for his philanthropy foundation."

"Wow," she says. "Did you accept?"

"I did." I'm sure she can hear my smile all the way in Arizona.

"Jesus, Lex. Your whole life seems to be changing right before my eyes. Are you okay with all this?"

"I am. I mean we're facing some hurdles with his project, but things are good."

"Lex," she scolds. She must sense I'm not letting her in on everything.

"I'm fine," I insist. "And I'm seeing Dr. Flint again."

"That's probably a good idea. Did you tell her about Pierce?"

"I did. She was blown away."

"I'll bet. It isn't every day her patient starts dating an Adonis with assets rivaling Mark Cuban's."

"Very funny."

I hear one of the girls break into a sudden scream in the background, followed by crying. "Ah, shit. I have to let you go. The girls are fighting over a Barbie."

"Okay," I laugh. "I'm glad to hear Derek's making progress. Please tell the girls I love them."

"I will," she says. "And please do me a favor?"

"Sure."

"Give that billionaire's fine ass a squeeze for me."

At eight o'clock, I'm in front of the television with Byron watching reruns of Seinfeld. He hasn't even cracked a smile.

I've heard nothing from Aidan this evening. I'm checking my phone for the hundredth time when the doorbell rings. Byron moves to see who it is before I can, and the dog is barking as he follows him, ready to tackle whoever is behind the door.

I hear Byron talking in a low voice to Aidan and go to the foyer to join them.

"Good night, ma'am," Byron nods to me from the doorway. I shoot him a disapproving look. Huck is now sitting perfectly still beside him, waiting for his next command.

"Byron, you're practically living under my roof. Stop with the formalities and call me Alexis."

He nods and almost cracks a smile as he leaves us. Huck nuzzles into Aidan briefly then saunters off, seeming disappointed that Byron is gone.

"What's the deal with Byron?" I ask. "He can't even call me by my first name. It's always ma'am."

"Habit," Aidan says. "He's ex-military and spent a lot of time in the South. You're not going to break him of it at this point."

"Ex-military? What service?"

"We covered this, baby," he teases. "I can't tell you. You'd have to be eliminated."

"Yeah, so you've said." I smile back at him, not hiding my sarcasm. "I wasn't expecting you to just show up. Is everything okay?"

"Yes. I've got some leads on Mrs. Whitmore. I'm hoping to see her tomorrow."

"Does she know you're coming?" I have a feeling I already know the answer.

"No. You need to let me handle this my way."

"I haven't said a word about how you've handled any of this. I just want you to be careful. And I don't want her upset. I don't even know when her husband's funeral is. It could very well be tomorrow."

"It was today," he says. "I've done some digging. I know what I'm heading into. You have to trust me."

I nod in silent reply.

"I'll be off to Manhattan early. My meeting is at nine, and then I'll be returning to Stanton. I'm hoping to see Mrs. Whitmore in Pennsylvania on my way back."

"Can I go with you?"

"I thought you wanted to stay out of this."

"I do."

But I don't want to be away from him.

He must sense my hesitation.

"I'll only be gone for the day," he assures me. "I'll stay here tonight. And I need you to cancel everything you have for Friday."

"Why?"

"We're heading to Canada early that morning. You said you have your passport?"

"Yes. I'll have to move up my appointments. There are two I can't put off until next week."

"Get it done, baby." He kisses me, and I feel the familiar heat intensify. "I'm whisking you off this weekend so we can leave this shit behind us for a while. We both need it."

20

Aidan

I call my mother while Alexis is sleeping upstairs. Huck is snoring at my feet. It's ten o'clock here but Mom's in California, likely returning home from dinner out with Dad.

"Well this is a surprise," she answers. "To what do I owe the honor?"

"Hello to you too, Mom."

"I'm teasing you, Aidan. How are you?"

"I'm fine. I need a favor." I never ask my mother for favors.

"Of course, darling. Whatever you need."

"I need you and Dad to fly out here tomorrow."

"What?" She utters in confusion. "To Stanton?"

"No," I say. "Sorry, I didn't mean 'here', here. I'd like you to come to Canada. Open up The Gables."

"Oh, Aidan. I don't know. It's such short notice. Your dad has a golf tournament this weekend he's been planning for weeks. I know he won't want to miss it."

"Mom, it's important." I don't want them in California. Between what Dimitri had uncovered and all the bullshit with Renewable Energy, my gut is telling me to keep my inner circle as close to me as possible.

"Can I let you know tomorrow?"

"I'd like you to commit now. Get your plans made tonight. I can have you flown here if Dad's not able to secure a plane to fly back."

"Aidan, it's such short notice," she repeats. "Are you okay? I feel like you're not telling me everything."

I decide to play the one card I know will flip her to my side.

"I'll be going up too," I say. "I've met someone."

"Have you?" Her surprise is audible. "What's she like?"

"She's amazing. Beautiful and smart. I can't wait for you to meet her, Mom. But it's kind of hard to do that if you're three thousand miles away."

"Wow," she says. Her surprise is warranted. I'd never spoken to her this way about anyone. "This sounds serious. Let me talk to your father and call you back."

"One more thing."

"Sure, honey."

"Can you bring Oates with you? I talked to him earlier, and he's free this weekend."

"Of course," she says. "We'd love to bring Daryl. Maybe we'll ask the Hamiltons and the Reeds to join us too. Really make a party of it. I haven't been up there in years," she says. "It would be nice to be back again."

My mother loved to entertain and she loved the Thousand Islands. She's realizing my request is not a chore for her. Rather it's like putting her in her element.

"We'll be getting there late Friday morning. I was hoping you could open the place up tomorrow."

"It was rented out for Memorial Day weekend, so everything is up and going. I'll call Nancy Lonergan and ask if their maid service can head over there in the morning. We'll get the place up to par."

"Whatever you'd like, Mom. I'm not telling Alexis that you'll be coming. I want it to be a surprise."

"How exciting!" She's almost squealing. "You're such a romantic, Aidan. Just like your dad. Alexis is her name?"

"Yes," I say, "Alexis Greene."

"Did you meet her in Mirror Lake?"

"That's where she lives, yes."

"Is she related to Bert Greene? The lawyer?"

"Yes," I say, taken off guard. "She's his daughter. But he passed away a few years ago."

She knew Alexis' father?

"Oh, Aidan, he was a wonderful man. I'm sorry to hear that. He was my lawyer when –" she stops abruptly, and I can hear her trying not to choke up. "For a brief time, he was a very big help to your dad and me."

"Wow," I say. "I had no idea."

"What does she do?"

"She's an attorney, like her father."

"I see," Mom says. "I expect she's as smart as he was."

I don't respond, but I'm smiling in silent acknowledgement.

"Well," she says. "I'll go and get these arrangements made. Your dad will be happy to pass up golf for this. He just mentioned to me a few months ago that he'd love to get to Canada again."

"Thanks, Mom. I'm looking forward to the break."

"Love you, honey."

"Love you, too. See you soon."

By nine o'clock the next morning, I've just made it on time to my meeting with Alanna Rossi and her husband. Alexis distracted me before I left, and I had to keep Ivan waiting for me at the airport for an extra twenty minutes.

It had been entirely worth it. I'd left my baby with a smile on her face, and she was still thanking me by text message up until a few minutes ago.

"Aidan," Alanna says as I enter their foyer. She kisses both my cheeks. She's beautiful as always in a black business suit, ever the professional. "Gianni is in his den. This way."

We enter a room just off the foyer. The space is an eclectic mix of modern and traditional furnishings. A cherry fireplace on one side of the room is decorated with a white marble mantle and flanked by two brown leather wingback chairs. A view of the Manhattan skyline is visible through floor to ceiling windows unimpeded by draperies. Central Park is easily recognizable in the distance, some thirty floors below.

Gianni Rossi is seated behind an imposing wooden desk that appears to be an expensive antique. He's focused on his computer screen.

"Darling," Alanna says, "Aidan is here."

He looks up, then stands to shake my hand. "Mr. Pierce," he says. "Always a pleasure. Please take a seat." He gestures to the straight-backed chairs in front of him.

He's a handsome guy, perfectly paired with Alanna. They look like they belong together. His Italian heritage is apparent. Dark hair, bronze skin. He looks younger than he is.

Alanna takes a seat next to me and I wait a beat before I begin. I'm not as intimated as I was with Dr. Neil, but Gianni is a powerful man. Even with his good intentions, his reputation and demeanor could be unnerving.

And what I'm about to ask of him will likely not be well received.

"Thank you for agreeing to see me. Unfortunately, I'm not coming here without necessity."

"I gathered that from what Alanna conveyed to me. Does this have something to do with John Ireland?"

"It does," I begin. "The last few weeks I have been working to remove him from my life, but I've been met with nothing but complications. I know he's involved in running drugs in California, but I can't tie him to it. I know he's attempting to acquire land in New York, land that is about to be mine. But I haven't been able to stop his efforts."

"I'm not sure how I can help," Gianni says. "You know Ireland and I are never on good terms. I don't like going to war with him. If I had my way I'd never have to, and currently I've got nothing on the horizon with him. I'd like to keep it that way."

"That isn't entirely accurate. He's got a hand dangling over one of your assets as we speak. You haven't been made aware of it yet."

"I find that hard to believe." His tone turns irritated.

"I'm certain of it. I can get you evidence, if you need it." Dimitri has proof available, but I'd asked him to hold off sending it to avoid risk of someone intercepting the information.

"Gianni," Alanna says. "If Aidan is telling you this is so, then it's so. We need to ask how we can help."

"This involves you too, Alanna. John intends to drag Stella into this."

"Oh for Heaven's sake." She starts swearing in Italian. I can't help my amusement at her word choices to describe her ex-husband. I agree with them all.

"Alanna has not been involved in her daughter's life for a reason," Gianni says to me pointedly. "John wanted it that way and he got his wish. The fact that she's Stella's mother should not play any part in your decisions about this matter. As for what you ask of me, consider that angle a non-starter."

"I understand, and I agree Stella should be kept out of this. But John is after one of these two parcels, yours or mine. I'm not sure how determined he is at this point, but..."

Alanna interrupts me. "We all know how he operates, Aidan. It's fair to say he's not going to let much stand in his way. Tell us how we can help."

"I'm not willing to give up the project in Lake County. My uncle's land is irreplaceable, and as you know the future home of something I've worked for years to bring to fruition." I turn my attention to Gianni. "Which leads me to ask if you'd you be willing to sacrifice yours."

"Depends on what property you're talking about and what the intended use would be once I let it go."

"Three hundred acres. The parcel you managed to acquire out from under John last year."

He thinks a moment. I'm glad he didn't immediately say no.

"I might consider that," he finally says, "as long as it isn't going to end up in John Ireland's hands."

"No, that would never be my intention."

"What is your intention?"

I'd planned to ask Gianni to sell to R.E.E., but in the moment consider another option.

"I'll buy it."

There's more than one way to skin this cat. If I buy it first, I'll have the Holy Grail to take to Renewable Energy. "Do you have any objection to solar farms on the land?"

"You want to sell to R.E.E." He states it as fact rather than inquiry, but I answer anyway.

"Yes."

"I'd consider that," he says, "but only given the position you find yourself in. And I would insist the land is never used for shale exploration."

"I agree completely."

Whether R.E.E. will is another question entirely.

"I'm firm on that, Pierce. No drilling. I'd want to see the contracts you make with them before I sell to you. I must be certain they cannot convey to an affiliate."

"I'd insist on the same. Of course if you prefer, you can sell to R.E.E. yourself."

"Out of the question. You're the middleman or this goes nowhere."

I can't help asking why.

"I'm quite familiar with their reputation," he says. "I never want to be associated with them. And if you want my advice, you shouldn't get in bed with them either."

Mrs. Laura Whitmore is less than happy to make my acquaintance.

Byron tracked her whereabouts last night. I'd reached her by phone this morning at her sister-in-law's home in Scranton, Pennsylvania to ask if we could meet. She had reluctantly agreed, I presume out of curiosity.

It's eleven in the morning and the large house is quiet around us – not unusual for the middle of a Thursday in an upscale suburban neighborhood.

We're on the back porch of the grand brick Colonial that belongs to Mark Whitmore's sister and her family. Everyone is out for the day. The kids are in school, and Mark's sister and her husband are back at work. Mark's funeral had taken place yesterday.

"Thank you for seeing me on short notice," I say. "I don't intend to take much of your time."

"I don't know how I can help you, or why you bothered tracking me down. I'm leaving tomorrow."

"I wanted to extend my condolences to you, for one thing. It's my understanding your husband was a good man, Mrs. Whitmore."

"He was." She's seated across from me at an iron patio table, not hiding her solemn demeanor. She's wearing jeans and a pink cotton shirt stained with coffee. At this particular moment, she's definitely not the put together debutante I'd read about.

Laura Whitmore is the daughter of a prominent government official in Florida, and she'd been afforded a proper upbringing. She'd met her husband in her home state and relocated with him to Pennsylvania after they married, when he'd decided to move his career back to his hometown. Mark had become a partner at the same firm he'd fled when R.E.E.'s deal began to collapse.

The Whitmores have two children. I can only presume they are with other relatives as no one else appears to be here.

"I'm sorry I never had the chance to meet Mark," I say. "But part of the reason I'm here is to help you carry out his good intentions. He was trying to help someone I care very much about, to keep her safe. My interests are the same."

She looks up at me. "You mean the lawyer from Stanton? Alexis Greene?"

"Yes."

"I've already sent her the documents Mark asked me to." She seems nervous, fidgeting with her shirt sleeve. "I don't know anything else. We never talked in depth about his work."

"I'd like to ask you a few questions. It's possible you could shed light on our situation. That you have details you deem unimportant which are actually pieces of a missing puzzle. Then I fully intend to leave you to your grief,

Mrs. Whitmore. I am not insisting that you become officially involved."

"Do you know why he was killed?"

"Not specifically, no. Nor do I know who his aggressor was. Is this information you have? Perhaps we should start there."

"I have no idea, Mr. Pierce. The police have uncovered nothing."

"Yes, I'm aware of that. I didn't know if you had any personal insights. A gut feeling about something."

"All I know is we turned our whole lives upside down in a matter of weeks. We beat a path back to my parents' doorstep in Florida. Mark stayed behind to put our house up for sale and was on a plane a week later. The day I left Pennsylvania a few weeks ago was the last day I saw him."

"He wouldn't tell you why this had to happen?"

"Just that he would be in some trouble if we stayed. He was unhappy at his firm anyway. And he didn't like working for R.E.E. He was ready to throw in the towel months ago, but the money was too good to pass up. They were a private client for him, outside of the firm."

"Was he fired by the firm?"

"No," she says, resting her elbows on the table to rub her temples. "He quit. Right before I left."

"He was licensed to practice in Florida too?"

"Yes," she says. "That's where we started our life together. He went to college there."

"When was the last time you talked to him?"

"He called me when he landed. He was still on the plane, I guess."

"What did he say?"

"He told me he'd see me soon. And he told me about the documents. The ones I sent to Ms. Greene."

"I'd like to know exactly what he said. Can you recall?"

"He said he'd sent documents to my parents' Florida house from here via overnight carrier. That's where we'd planned to stay until our house sold and we could buy a new one in Orlando. He said as soon as I got the papers, I should overnight them up to her in New York. It didn't make sense to me at the time and, honestly, it still doesn't. I just honored what turned out to be his last request, as a courtesy to my dead husband."

This poor woman.

"Do you have any idea why your husband went to that hotel? Did you have any friends staying there? Were you arguing and he planned to stay there to give you some space?"

"No," she says with irritation. "We were not arguing. We had a good marriage, Mr. Pierce. Not without our struggles, but he was a good man in everything he did. He was faithful. He was kind. He was an amazing father." She trails off, her eyes blinking back tears.

"I'm sorry," I offer. "I didn't mean to insinuate that he wasn't all of those things. I just can't understand his actions that night."

"He mentioned having to meet someone the next day," she says. "I don't see how that's relevant."

"It might be," I say. "Did Mark indicate he'd be right home once he got off the plane?"

"He didn't, necessarily. He just said he'd see me soon."

It was possible someone moved the meeting up to the same night he was killed. It would certainly explain why he'd not gone straight home.

"Do you know the person's name or the purpose of the meeting?"

"I think he messaged me the gentleman's contact information. I thought he was seeing someone about buying our new house down there. But I remember thinking it odd that he sent the guy's name to me at all."

"What was odd about it?"

"I didn't have anything to do with that side of our lives. He and my father always handled our business matters. I handled the kids and my own career in marketing. That was enough."

"Would you mind showing that message to me?"

She excuses herself to retrieve her phone. I check my messages while I wait. I have two texts from Alexis thanking me again for our rendezvous this morning. Another is from Byron telling me everything is fine in Stanton.

"Here." Laura hands me her phone with a photograph pulled up on the screen. "I guess he just sent me a screen shot of the gentleman's email signature."

"You're sure this is the person he said he had to meet on Friday?"

"Yes."

"To discuss real estate?"

"That's right," she affirms. "He sent me this before he got on the plane to Florida. You sound surprised. Do you know this person?"

I ignore her question. "Again, my deepest condolences to you." I pass the phone back to her and make my way to the front door.

"Wait," she calls after me.

"Thank you for your time, Mrs. Whitmore," I reply over my shoulder as

I leave. "I promise not to bother you in the future."

I'd committed the photo she shared with me to memory, though it wasn't necessary. I am quite familiar with the name.

The missing piece of the puzzle is John Ireland.

Ivan drives me from Pennsylvania to Stanton. It would have taken longer to head back to JFK and fly home. I've been on the phone the entire ride.

I field a call from Oates first, thanking me for hooking him up with the free ride to Canada that he's enjoying. We plan to discuss business over the weekend too, which I can do while Alexis visits Ben's family.

I was looking forward to seeing him again. With everything I'd been dealing with on my trip to California, I'd been able to mention Alexis only briefly at our last meeting. I knew even then I wanted to introduce them, though I'd only known her a matter of weeks at the time.

Oates was my closest friend before I'd lost my brother, and he's been like a brother to me since. We were roommates at Cal Tech and he is one of the few people I trust.

"I'm bringing a killer surprise, man," he says. "I can't wait. It's gonna be a rager of a weekend."

I laugh at his attempt to sound cool. He often goes out of his way to spout language he considers hip just to fit in. Outwardly he is a good looking enough guy, but he fits the classic definition of geek.

"Oh yeah?" I say. "What's the surprise? Because I can only afford to back one of your start-ups right now."

"Nah, man. Nothing like that. You'll see."

"Oates," I kid him. "Are you bringing a *girl* with you? You didn't mention any girl when I was in Cali."

"No way, bruh. I'm as single as they come. No woman's gonna tie me down. I'm gettin' too much action."

I let out a full laugh. There's no way this is true. He works eighty hour weeks and barely remembers to sleep, let alone go out and get laid. Neither of us even had time to grab the occasional meal together. He spent most of his time in Silicon Valley, writing code or running numbers or whatever other genius things he was hired to do by various tech companies.

"Well I look forward to your killer surprise," I say. "See you tomorrow."

We disconnect as I get another text. It's from my mother.

Mom never text messages me, and I can't help but smile. She and my father and Oates are arriving in Canada within a few hours. She says how excited she is to see me and to meet Alexis. She follows it up with a few heart emojis. I write her back telling her to let me know when they've arrived safely.

My first outgoing call is to Byron, telling him of my discovery after talking to Mrs. Whitmore.

"What's our next move?"

"Find out John's whereabouts for the last two weeks. I want to know where he's been every minute. If you hit any dead ends, let me know and I'll get Dimitri on it."

"Consider it done."

I dial Bill Hoffman next. His secretary tells me he'll have to call me back in a few minutes. While I wait, I send an email to Samira while another task is fresh in my mind in relation to Mark Whitmore. As I'm hitting send in the app on my phone, Bill Hoffman rings in.

"Bill. Thanks for getting back so quickly."

"Betty said it was urgent. Did you have a change of heart? You ready to forego the Mirror Lake project?"

"I told you that's never going to happen. I do have something new I need you to work on, though."

"Now what? Oh, and before I forget, we've answered the lawsuit filed against you by Richardson Realty. We have a conference set for next month."

"I couldn't give a fuck about that, Bill. Offer Richardson five hundred thousand as a settlement and see if he bites."

"It's only money, right?"

I ignore his dig. "I need you to draw up an offer for the latest parcel Gianni Rossi acquired outside of Manhattan, the one Ireland fought him on. Today. Then submit it to Rossi's attorney."

"All three hundred acres?"

"Yes."

"I don't work that way, Pierce. You have to get in line. I've got other fires to put out ahead of any new business. Not to mention some of those fires are yours."

"You doubled your hourly rate for a reason. I'll email you the particulars for the offer. Get it done today and send it to me for review before five."

"Is it that important?"

I consider my answer a moment and respond with the truth.

"Life or death."

21

Alexis

Thursday afternoon, I'm mentally drained. Charlie and I haven't even had a chance to catch up. I've had a full day of appointments already but, by the end of the day, my to-do list will be done. Tomorrow I'll be free to go up north with Aidan without leaving any clients hanging.

My intercom buzzes and Claudia's voice startles me.

"Gloria Stearns on line one."

"I've got it, thanks." I pick up the line. "Hey lady. What's up?"

"Not much. Thought you might like some company tonight."

"My bodyguard will likely be following me around and cramping my style. What'd you have in mind?"

"Let's go out," she says. "The Wall has karaoke tonight."

"I don't know if I can make it. I'm waiting for Aidan to get back. We're heading up to Canada tomorrow morning."

"Escaping for fun or out of necessity? This isn't about blowback from R.E.E. is it?"

"No. We both just need a break. And I want to see the Claytons."

"I'm glad you're getting out of town. You could use it."

"Even with all that's happened, I still miss Ben, Gloria. Is that crazy?"

"Of course not," she says. "You'll always miss him, Lex." A moment of quiet passes before she speaks again. "So do you want to come out with me tonight or what? We can catch up in person before you leave town."

"Maybe," I say. "Let me check in with Aidan and I'll text you. I don't know if he needs Byron to be pulled away from me for something else which would mean I'm stuck with Aidan instead."

"What a terrible fate for you," she laughs. "Harry's practicing again and as much as I love my husband and his rowdy boys' nights in the garage, I don't feel like hanging around for it tonight. I was going to ask Charlie too."

"Group message us and I'll let you know how it plays out."

"You got it, babe. Hope to see you tonight."

At five o'clock sharp, I leave the office via the front door. Charlie left through the back and locked up. He beeps as he drives around the building past me, headed home to change so he can meet up with Gloria. I haven't committed to joining them yet.

It's humid, the air thick and heavy though the temperature has only climbed to seventy-five today.

"Hi, Byron," I say as I approach him in the SUV. "You ready to go home?"

"Mr. Pierce would like you back at the loft."

"Would he?" I ask. "He didn't mention that to me."

Why does he think he can order me?

It irks me that he couldn't be bothered to call me himself, presuming that Byron will just bring me to him at his beck and call. "I'll be right back."

I unlock the front door and duck back into the office as I pull out my cell and dial Aidan.

"Baby," he answers. "God, I miss you. Are you on your way?"

"Miss you too," I say. "But I think I'm going out for a little while tonight. Can you come along, or do you want Byron to go with me?"

He says nothing for a minute, seeming distracted.

"Aidan, did you hear me? I said I'm going out."

"No, you're not," he says. "You're coming home to me."

Stop telling me what to do.

"Not, actually. I'm going out with Gloria and Charlie. Send Byron with me if you want, but I'm not coming back to the loft until later."

"We have to leave early," he says. "Do you really think it's a good night to go out and paint the town? Your track record for doing so and coming home in any state of preparedness for the following day is less than exemplary."

Oh, hell no.

He did not just play that fucking card.

"I can handle myself just fine, thanks."

"Alexis, don't pull this stubborn bullshit."

"I'm being stubborn?" I scoff. "You're the one insisting I follow orders.

You weren't listening to me a minute ago, and now you're commanding me like I'm one of your minions without even hearing me out. You don't own me, Aidan."

He's distracted again. He says nothing in response, and I can hear people talking in the background. He's too preoccupied to even finish an argument with me.

"In case you're still listening, I'm riding with Charlie, grabbing some dinner with him and we're meeting Gloria at The Wall. I'll have Mrs. Parker's daughter walk Huck, and I'll go home to my own house later."

Silence at first, then papers shuffling, people talking.

"Alexis," he starts.

"Have a good night, Aidan."

I disconnect and dial Charlie.

"Whassup, girl? You change your mind?"

"Actually, yes. Pick me up out back. I have to dodge Byron."

"Are you sure that's a good idea?"

"Yes, Mr. Buzzkill. There is no imminent threat to my safety as far as I know. And I know you can fend off anyone that tries to harm me, big guy."

"Be right there."

I hang up and lock the front door, peeking out the front windows. Byron is on the phone. I shoot Mrs. Parker a text as I head for the back door. She responds quickly with an affirmative that her daughter can walk Huck. Charlie pulls up behind the building as I lock up and hurriedly climb into the Cadillac, proud that I've not given in to one of Aidan's whims this time.

This time Alexis Greene is in control of her own fucking evening.

Charlie and I are eating a quick dinner in his kitchen. His offerings were limited to leftover Chinese food or leftover pizza. I opt for the pizza.

"You want to talk about why you're defying your billion-dollar stud muffin?"

"No."

"Alexis." He's looking down at me in judgment from where he's perched on his kitchen counter. "You're running."

"I am not," I insist. "I'm being assertive. I'm not a keychain he can attach to his belt when he wants it and set it aside when he doesn't. I have a brain. I have my own wants."

"What you want is him," he says. "Why are you fighting it?"

I sigh as I set down my crust. If Huck was here, I'd have tossed it to him.

"I don't know," I resign. "Maybe I am a little overwhelmed with all this. It's so much, Charlie. Everything I'm feeling for him is so intense. *He's* intense."

"You aren't walking down the aisle, Lex. You're dating. You have free will. No one is trying to hold you captive. And everything he's done for you with this whole Myers thing – he's protecting you."

"I know that, Charlie. And I'm not ungrateful. I'm just…" I drift off.

"You don't know what you are to him."

"I guess maybe," I admit. "Fuck. Dr. Flint would have a field day with me over this. Did I tell you that Aidan asked me to be on the board for his foundation? That commercial building he owns near the loft is going to be his new and improved headquarters for his philanthropy."

"Lex, that's amazing. You love helping people. It might as well have been your minor in college."

I don't respond because I know he's right. And I'm so proud of Aidan, of the way he just sets goals and knocks them off one by one all with the best of intentions. I just wish he didn't treat me like another marked-off item on his to-do list.

"Call him back, Lex. Tell him you just want to blow off some steam, that I've got your back and I'll deliver you safely back to his place. He either wants to keep you safe or he just wants to be in your presence. He didn't do anything wrong."

I can admit that, once again, Charlie is right.

Yet, I know I've pissed Aidan off and I don't want to face him if he's angry. I missed two calls from him already.

"I'll just go there when I'm done hanging out with you guys," I say. "It'll be early. It's only six-thirty now."

"If you insist," he says. "But if he comes for you, I'm staying out of it."

"Noted," I say. "Now let's go get our karaoke on."

The three of us are nursing drinks at a table some distance back from the stage while a guy is croaking out "Scarborough Fair". He looks like an extra from *The Wedding Singer.* His high-top sneakers are beat up and his pants are far too big. His brown hair is business in the front and party in the back.

Charlie is busting a gut laughing at the poor guy. His singing is worse than his appearance.

"I hate this fuckin' song," Gloria says. "When are we up?"

"You're first," I say. I'm practically yelling so she can hear me over the full barroom and loud background music. "Then Charlie, then me."

"Awesome." Gloria toys with the straps on her dress. She'd met with a client after hours in the city so neither of us had changed out of our semi-business attire. We're both in sundresses instead of suits today. Hers is a kelly-green with white polka dots. The color complements her red curls beautifully, but her straps have twice the heft of mine to hold up her husband's favorite body part.

My outfit is one of the gifts from Aidan and definitely leaned more towards sexy than conservative. My 'girls' are tucked into a strapless bra, the skinny strings of the white sundress the only thing on my shoulders. I love how the skirt floats around my legs, though it is a bit shorter than anything I'd have picked for myself.

I guess it's the kind of outfit a girl chose after a morning quickie with Aidan Pierce that resulted in four back-to-back orgasms, and all before he took off at the crack of dawn today.

"Charlie, can you get me another beer?" Gloria slides him some cash. "How about you Lex? You need another rum?"

"No thanks," I say. "I'm good." I have no intention of proving Aidan right by leaving here shitfaced.

Charlie saunters up to the bar while the current singer wraps up his warbling. The bartender is immediately batting her eyelashes at him, not realizing he's gay.

I watch as Charlie orders Gloria's beer and another gin and tonic for himself. The blonde bartender is dressed in a crop top, her navel exposed as she pulls a bottle of gin off a high shelf. I notice her belly piercing and roll my eyes. Before Charlie has a chance to cash out, the guy that runs the karaoke is coming over to hand the bartender a microphone.

"Let's give it up for Greg," he says, getting the crowd to clap for Eighties Guy as he departs the stage. "Up next, we've got your Singing Drink Slinger, Miss Robin!"

A lot of guys in the crowd cheer, including Charlie.

Except he doesn't cheer like a regular, run-of-the-mill bar patron. He brings out his inner fangirl with his I'm-so-totally-fucking-gay cheer. His eyes are open wide and he's clapping enthusiastically, squealing at the top of his lungs like he's about to be front row for Barbra Streisand.

I'm roaring with laughter, bumping Gloria with my elbow so she looks in their direction in time to see this. Miss Robin should now be quite certain that Charlie is a proud gay man.

Watching him shut her down is the funniest thing I've witnessed in days. Miss Robin's face goes slack as the karaoke DJ walks off to cue up her song, and I'm distracted by a text pinging on my cell. I close one eye, cringing as I swipe my phone to see who it's from.

Whew.

It's not from Aidan. It's from Ben's sister.

Hey sistah! Is it just ONE MORE SLEEP till I see you?! I'm so stoked! When are you getting here?

I can't help my grin. It will be so good to see Pam. I send her a message back telling her I'll call her tomorrow, as soon as I'm settled where I'm staying. I'm thankful she doesn't ask where when she responds. She replies that sounds like a plan and that she can't wait, followed up by a bunch of hearts and high-fiving hands.

Seeing nothing more from Aidan, I sigh with relief and put my phone back in my wallet.

Miss Robin now realizes Charlie does not play for her team and walks away from him. She continues to sing terribly from behind the bar while our friend returns with drinks.

"That was hysterical," I say. "You had her at hello."

"Right? Girl was all 'what are you doing in a place like this'? God, if I had a nickel," he says, rolling his eyes.

Gloria and I laugh at Charlie's impersonation. When the Drink Slinger is done, Gloria is called up to sing a Bonnie Raitt tune and Charlie and I are left alone.

"Did you text him?" he asks.

"No. Do you think I should?"

"Hey," he says, "it's your funeral."

I sigh with impatience. "I just want to forget about everything for a while. Sit around with my friends and pretend things are underwhelming and normal. Okay?"

Charlie nods back in affirmation and lifts his glass at me in a toast. "You got it, boss."

We clap for Gloria as she finishes. Charlie stands and whistles along with a few other excited bar patrons, and I catch sight of Carter coming through the door.

"Charlie," I say up at him. I tug on his shirt to get his attention over the crowd noise. "Carter is here."

He turns to see his sometimes lover sauntering up to us.

"Hey babe," he says. They share a chaste kiss. "I'm 'bouts to kill it on stage. Want to join me?"

"You know it," Carter smiles. He's dressed in his customary expensive jeans. The blue in his vintage t-shirt sets off his dark eyes. His black hair is immobile, perfected by product.

The DJ calls Charlie up and Carter joins him as they break into Run DMC's version of "Walk This Way". Charlie is doing all the rapping while Carter sings Steven Tyler's part. I'm surprised at the way he nails the vocals.

The whole crowd goes bonkers. Gloria and I are back and forth between laughing and cheering. They are quite a pair, neither of them looking at the screen for the lyrics. They have the performance down pat. I don't have an alcohol buzz, but I'm certainly high on my friends' performance.

It's shot all to hell when I glimpse who is coming through the door of the bar.

Fuck. I'm in trouble.

Ivan practically stomps up to me, his usual charming self.

"Mr. Pierce would like me to take you home."

The rest of Charlie's song is finishing out with an instrumental as the boys come back to our table.

"Guys," I say. "This is Ivan. Ivan, these are my friends Gloria, Charlie, and Carter."

Charlie reaches out his hand in an overly friendly handshake, obviously smitten with the Russian badass. Ivan just nods at each of them.

"Let's talk over here," I tell him. We move a few paces away to the bar as the DJ is calling my name. "Hold on," I tell Ivan. I go to the booth and tell the guy to push me back a couple songs and go back to Ivan.

"Where is Byron?"

"He's otherwise engaged, Ms. Greene. Would you come with me please?"

"I don't think so, Ivan. Tell your boss if he wants me, he can come and get me himself. I'm not chattel." He bristles, clearly put out by my refusal, but he doesn't move. "You're welcome to stay if you've been ordered to keep an eye on me."

Ivan sits down and orders himself a glass of water from the Drink

Slinger, who attempts to flirt with him to no avail. I see him pull out his phone before I head back to my friends.

"Who was that?" Gloria asks.

I'm fuming as I take my seat. "Another one of Aidan's robotic goons."

"I see," she says. "He's hot. Wasn't he at the meeting when we first saw Aidan?"

"Yep." I take a swig of my drink.

"Is he just here to keep an eye on you?" Charlie asks.

"I guess so."

Gloria and Carter strike up a conversation about Steven Tyler.

"Well he looks like he's the damn Terminator with that stoic mug," Charlie says as he leans close to me. "Can't he be a badass without looking so pissed off?"

I let a laugh escape me. "Not sure. I've never been a Russian badass. Maybe he's required by contract to look like that 24/7."

"Well, the dude's gotta get a handle on that," he says. "He's emanating bad chi left, right, and sideways. That shit will give a motherfucker cancer. And as fine as he is, that'd be a damn shame."

"Yeah," I say, forcing a smile. "Wouldn't it, though."

I'm irritated that Ivan is here, that Aidan is resorting to his overbearing habits once again.

And maybe I'm freaked out by the path my life has recently been careening down, just like Charlie said.

"I think I'm ready for that drink now."

"I'll get it," Carter interjects. "I'm going up anyway. What'll you have?"

"Captain and diet. Anyone else?" I ask. "I'm buying." No one else is in need, so Carter saunters away with the twenty I hand him. "You guys killed that song, Charlie," I say to him. "You must've planned that."

"I may have sent Carter a text to let him know we'd be here."

"What song did you put in, Lex?" Gloria asks me.

"Tedeschi Trucks Band," I say. "Made Up Mind."

"Ah," she says, "excellent choice. I think you're up next. The guy in the booth just nodded over here trying to get your attention."

Carter joins us again as the current singer wraps up her performance. We clap politely as she finishes a Jewel song and I'm called up.

I take a healthy swig of my drink and head for the stage as my pulse races, intending to take on my fears and frustrations by belting out this song like a fucking boss.

22

Aidan

I hesitate as I stand at the entrance to the bar. Ivan assures me Alexis is here and she's fine. She's not drunk. She's not out of control. She's just socializing with some friends on a Thursday night.

Whether she realizes it or not though, she's totally fucking up my plans. I'd handled so much today, come so far for us. All I wanted to do was share it with her and get ready to take off tomorrow. I was looking forward to finally being together without chaos around us.

Ivan has also confirmed that Robin is inside bartending. He was probably confused why I'd asked who was behind the bar, but I was glad he'd found out for me. At least I knew what I was walking into.

I hoped I could avoid the girl I'd once slept with and leave with the woman I came for.

I walk in hearing the DJ announce Alexis is about to take the stage.

My baby's going to sing.

Suddenly I'm anticipating that more than anything, forgetting I'm angry with her or that I'm here because she's too fucking stubborn for her own good.

I see Charlie and Gloria sitting with another guy and nod to them as I come in. I should probably join them, but they're in plain view of the bar off to my right. Where I'm standing a column is between me and Robin, blocking me from her view.

Ivan is seated at the bar nearby. I send him a text.

Stay seated. I don't want the bartender to see me.

When Alexis is done singing,
we'll take her home.

Yes, sir.

I stay stock still as Alexis starts to sing. My view is obstructed, the stage out of sight behind another column like the one I'm hiding behind now.

I don't need to see her to be physically aroused. I'm listening to her sing about her mind being made up and my cock involuntarily responds, stiffening beneath my jeans. I adjust myself and cross my arms over my chest in as rigid a posture as I can manage.

The music is high-power, crunching guitar, roots style blues. I don't know the song, but I'm watching the crowd eat it up.

I have to get a look at her.

I peer behind the column to see Robin is at the other end of the bar, towards the front of the building. I move forward into the crowd and duck behind the second column so I can get a look at my girl.

She doesn't need the lyrics on the flat screen ahead of her. She knows the song by heart.

She's fucking killing it.

Even from a distance, I can see her adrenaline rush as the song is climaxing and she sings about being in a higher place, about not being afraid. Her eyes are closed as my little force-not-to-be-reckoned-with crushes it right through a short instrumental. She looks over at her friends as they encourage her.

Except for Gloria, who has eyes filled with skepticism trained on me.

As the song finishes, the whole bar erupts in applause, including me. I can't help my grin as I watch her saunter off the stage with confidence, until I see the DJ pull her aside to whisper something in her ear. He's clearly complimenting her singing, but it's also obvious he's hitting on her.

I can see it in the way he touches her bare shoulder, the way he's looking at her. Before I can go tell him to keep his fucking hands to himself, Alexis gives him the brush off and returns to her friends. Gloria is sitting leaned back in her chair, sipping a beer. She smiles and says something in the way of an 'atta girl, but then she nods in my direction so Alexis notices me.

I stay still hoping she'll come to me, but she doesn't.

Fuck.

I take a breath and head in their direction.

"Aidan," Gloria says, "good to see you."

"You too, Gloria." I lean over and give her a quick hug. "Hey, Charlie."

"Aidan," he says, "this is Carter." Charlie's friend leans towards me offering his hand, and we shake.

"Good to meet you, Carter."

"Likewise."

Alexis is downright glaring at me. I can feel her eyes drilling into the side of my head.

"You going to sing for us?" Gloria asks. "I think they make it mandatory here at The Wall. Sing before you leave, or else." She smiles up at me. I'm not sure if she's truly pissed or if she's just fucking with me.

"Not tonight," I say. "We should probably get going. We have an early morning. Alexis?"

She lifts up her drink and tosses it back, setting it down empty. "Actually I think I might like to stay awhile. I can find my own way, thanks."

Oh, my little force is on fire tonight.

I feel like taking her home and thrashing her backside with my palm. Instead I make the decision to change tactics.

What I'm about to do is so terrible, but I can't see another way.

I'm sure Robin's noticed me by now. I feel my pocket buzz with a text and check it quickly. It's from Ivan, telling me Robin has commented aloud about my being here. He's probably going to be scratching his head for days over my next move.

"Sure," I say. "Ivan can drive you home when you're ready then. Can I get you another drink before I take off?"

She looks at me and blinks fast, bewildered.

"Fine with me," she shrugs. "Excuse us, guys."

I follow her as she sashays up to the bar in one of the sundresses I'd picked out for her. This one is white, and she looks amazing in it. I'm admiring her legs and the way the dress moves around them. She's as gorgeous from behind as she is from the front. Her hair is tied up in a high ponytail, exposing her neck and her flawless shoulders under the thin straps.

My pulse races as we reach the bar, anticipating an imminent, full-blown firework show, but she's left me no choice. I'm not going to force her to come home with me. I'm going to make her realize how badly she wants to.

She sidles up next to Ivan. "Hey," she says. "You want something stronger? I can imagine you need it working for this demanding prick."

Boy, is she pissed.

I would have thought her above name calling.

My plan is momentarily foiled as Robin is MIA. I can't ignite a real fire or let worlds collide unless Robin is present. Finally, she returns to her duties behind the bar, and I notice she has the mic in her hand.

The sky is about to light up after all.

I purposefully take a step back, away from Alexis and Ivan.

"Hi," Alexis says cheerfully. "Can I get another rum and diet?"

"Sure," Robin says. Flashes of the blonde being underneath me race through my mind, turning my stomach. Robin sends me a knowing smile but Alexis is focused on Ivan, not seeing it happen.

All I want is to take Alexis home.

Why does she have to be so goddamn stubborn?

Robin returns with the drink, and in the same moment, the DJ is cueing up a song and announcing from his booth that the Singing Drink Slinger is going to grace us with another song.

Gack.

"This one is for my friend Mr. Pierce," she coos. "Right, Aidan?" She winks at me suggestively.

That's all it takes to explode the room, just as I'd predicted. Carly Simon's infamous song starts as Alexis whips her head around to me.

Ho-lee fuck.

I've never (ever) seen her this mad. I'm involuntarily stepping back from her, wincing from the daggers she's shooting at me. It's possible I'm going to have physical wounds from that look. This plan of mine may have just backfired.

She comes closer to me, leaving her drink on the bar next to Ivan. I nod to him, hoping he'll get the hint that I'd like him to pay for it.

He does.

Alexis is standing in front of me, now so close I can smell the sweet scent of her hair. But she's no longer looking up at me. She's looking past me, speaking into my shoulder.

"Was that your one-time distraction?" Her words come out like poison darts, her anger growing when I don't answer immediately. "Tell me this second, Aidan, or I swear to God I'm walking out that door and you won't see me again."

"Yes," I say in her ear, "she was the one."

"Let's get the fuck out of here," she says. "*Now.*"

I feel overwhelming relief. Pissed or not, she's coming with me. I've obtained my desired result.

Before I can give her what we both want and get her out of this shit-hole, Robin has moved out from behind the bar to come towards me, still warbling into the mic about how this song is not about me. She's indicating the opposite with her suggestive body language as Alexis catches sight of her heading for us.

Dammit.

Before Robin can reach me, I grab for Alexis with my arm around her waist. I pull her as close as humanly possible and her arms fall back and away from her sides, her head tossed back.

The same way she's done a hundred times before when I take her this way.

She looks up at me in surprise as I lay a gentle hand on her face. Before she can catch her breath, I kiss her recklessly, without a single care that we're in public. We're in plain view of everyone in the bar.

It doesn't matter to me that anyone can see exactly how much I crave her, how much I need her.

The rest of the world falls away in the moment. The obnoxious wailing of Robin's song becomes distant as she takes the hint and walks away.

Alexis is responding with equal greed as I convey my message without words, powerfully enough that she won't forget it.

She's the only one I want.

Everything I am is becoming wrapped up in her.

I am unmistakably hers.

And she is mine.

In the few blocks we ride back to the loft, the car is silent. Ivan's contribution to this is expected, but Alexis and I have not uttered a word to each other.

In contrast, the sexual tension between us is palpable.

I want to fuck her into tomorrow and the next few days after that. The way she's tight up against me, the way her hand rests on the inside of my thigh as her fingers dance over the fly of my jeans – her body language signals with certainty she feels the same.

Ivan drops us off at the front door. He takes off with the Lincoln, and Byron is there to open the door to the loft for us, his SUV parked not far away.

"Sir. Ms. Greene," Byron nods.

"Please head to Mirror Lake for Huck," I say. "He'll need care from tonight on. We'll be leaving early."

Alexis speaks up. "Please call and let us know how he is," she says. She moves to Byron and gives him a warm hug and, though his demeanor doesn't reflect it, I'm sure he's flattered by the gesture. "Thank you, Byron. I appreciate you taking care of my boy."

"Of course. Have a pleasant weekend, Ms. Greene."

I let her walk in ahead of me, watching her dress sway back and forth as she moves, driving me wild again. We step on the elevator and, despite the continued tension surrounding us, we are both silent and still. We could fit another person in the space between us if it was required.

Meanwhile, I'm thinking about making her come in this elevator the way I did two days ago, the thoughts playing out in my head like a movie.

We arrive at the third floor. I let her exit ahead of me, then move past her to the keypad and unlock the door, still matching her silence. I gesture for her to go ahead, but as soon as the door shuts and locks behind us I grab her from behind, breaking the quiet with the sound of her moans as I kiss her mouth, her neck, suck her earlobe. My pulse throbs, heart pounding like a bass drum in my ears.

I take her face in my hands roughly, looking into her gorgeous eyes as we stand in the dimness of the loft, both of us breathing heavy. My want for her is intensified by frustration at the way she tests me, always doubting that I'm doing what's best for her.

For us.

If she'd just give in, let me do for her...

"Don't do that to me again."

"You have to stop ordering me," she says. "I'm not dinner."

"You might end up being my dinner," I tell her. "I wasn't able to eat thanks to your little game of chase."

"It wasn't a game, Aidan. Why couldn't you just call me yourself and ask me to come back? Why do I have to hear it from Byron? It's bad enough him carting me around all the time, but I find it supremely infuriating that you asked him to deliver me to you like a newspaper."

I let go of her, taking a step away.

Did she have a point?

I'd become accustomed to having my way in times like this, especially when I was in the thick of something important that needed concentrated focus.

Like the Center. Like the R.E.E. mess.

Like her.

If something overtook my time, required me to use the help of my staff to see to my other needs, I did it without thinking.

And what I needed was her.

When I wanted her, I'd make it happen, even if I left her out of the decision process.

All I can do now is admit the mistake.

"You're right," I say.

She looks at me blankly, surprised that I'm conceding so soon. "I am?"

"Yes. But you were also running. And you need to admit that you were wrong, too."

"I will admit I could have talked to you rather than blowing you off," she says, "but that dig you threw at me about not being able to go anywhere without being irresponsible was…" she trails off. "It was low, Aidan. It hurt. Almost as much as you flaunting that slut in my face tonight."

"I was angry," I say. "I'm sorry for that. You didn't leave me much choice when you refused to come back here. Once I got to the bar, I didn't want to shield you from mistakes I made before. I've done enough of that already. You said you want the whole me? Well that was part of the whole me. The week before I met you, I picked up a random girl in a bar. I'm sorry."

"Did you know she would be there?"

"Of course not. It was a one-time thing, Alexis. I don't even know her last name. After that night with her, I barely remembered her first name."

She sighs with an obvious ache that knocks me down. It's killing me to see her hurt, especially because of something I did.

"Can we move past that?" I ask. "I couldn't have known you were going there. I haven't stepped foot in that bar since that night. It makes me ill to think about it."

"Me too," she says flatly.

I lift her head, my hand behind her ear, my thumb grazing her bottom lip as I look into her eyes. "I will say this once more, because apparently you need reminding. You are what is important to me now. What's in the past doesn't matter."

She looks at me in quiet understanding.

"And you're leaving out the fact that you left Byron's sight when you promised me you wouldn't. I will not apologize for being angry about that. When it comes to your safety, you know the deal, Alexis. I will never allow you to risk it."

"I wasn't out roaming dark alleys alone, for hell's sake." She's got a fire in her again. "I was fine. I was with my friends."

"You don't know what we're facing here. Neither one of us fully does. Until then, it's better safe than sorry."

"I understand Mark's death is mysterious. It's unusual and scary. Horrendously sad. But I've thought about it, and we have no proof it was connected to R.E.E. It could have been something totally random. Something else he was mixed up in."

"I've got all the proof I need, but we don't have to get into it now."

"Fine with me," she says. "I'd rather not."

I pull her to me, thankful at last we can just be alone. The silence looms around us for a minute, the heat between us growing again as she pulls back and we stare each other down.

She runs her hands up and down my arms, then untucks my shirt. I pull it off over my head and let her drink me in as she always does.

I drop to my knees in front of her, lifting up her dress enough that I can get underneath it, caressing every inch of her lean legs. I massage her thighs from the outside in, then pull down the skimpy straps of her thong. I nip at each of her hips, then slide off what's in my way and toss it aside once she steps out of it.

I slide fingers into her, working her until she noticeably goes from wet to soaking as she moans my name. I dive into her with my mouth, my tongue teasing her in rapid strokes.

"Take me to bed," she finally says in a whisper.

I move out from under her dress and scoop her up in my arms, cradling her as her legs drape over my left arm, her head gently resting in my right.

As much as I want to talk, to tell her everything that's gone on today, tell her how much she means to me after she had to be faced with that random girl I'd made the mistake of fucking…

More than all of that, I want to be inside her.

As I'm moving towards the bedroom, she looks up at me.

"Not in there," she says.

I give her a questioning look.

"That's where you slept with her, isn't it?"

Oh, man.

I feel like I've been kicked in the balls.

"Alexis, don't."

"Take me to the guest room," she says. "I don't want to be in your bed tonight."

I set her down, wrapping her up in my arms in a gesture of comfort.

"Please don't let this become a thing, baby. It was before you." I look down at her, again trying to make her realize how off-base she is being concerned about this. "Nothing before you matters to me now. You have to put this out of your mind. I'm taking you to bed and we're not coming out until dawn."

She sighs in resignation, but I can tell she's still bothered. I kiss her gently, again taking her face in my hands hoping I can make her understand.

"You're the only one I sleep with, baby. The only one that's ever turned me on this much. The only one that's ever twisted me so fucking inside out. No one before you compares. As far as I'm concerned, that is our bed." Her eyes go wide. I'm blowing her away with this revelation, as much as I am myself. "And in a very real sense, no one was in it before you. No woman has ever been in my life before you, Alexis. Not the way you are. Don't you get it?"

She leans up on tiptoe and puts her arms around my neck, planting a kiss on me that reignites my libido. "I think I do now."

"Good," I say, leaning my forehead down to hers as I catch my breath. "It's about fucking time."

23

Alexis

At one in the morning, I'm unable to sleep at the loft.

I'm spent, physically exhausted after Aidan and I spent two hours making up tonight.

Boy, did we ever.

We still managed to fall into peaceful sleep before midnight, but I'd woken up twenty minutes ago beyond restless, anticipating our weekend away that was hours from beginning. I was looking forward to having Aidan to myself for an entire three days, to stow all this drama away.

But I had no idea what he was expecting.

Did he plan to work half the time? Spend our days in bed?

We hadn't even had a chance to discuss it.

I don't know what he's got up his sleeve on the R.E.E. mess or whether Stella has been continuing to cause him worry.

I also don't know exactly where we're going tomorrow (or I guess today). This fact is driving my controlling, Type-A personality batshit crazy.

I find my wallet in the foyer where I left it and pull out my phone, taking a seat at the kitchen island. I have a few texts I should probably respond to, though now is not really the hour for that.

The first is from Charlie asking me if I'm okay. I decide to respond so he'll at least see it when he wakes up. I tell him I'm fine, that Aidan and I are fine, and thank him for encouraging me to get the fuck over myself.

I add that I'll call him when I can, but I'm not sure when. He's got the office covered for Friday. I'll be out of cell range if we're on the St. Lawrence and wouldn't typically have my phone on with the roaming expense.

The second is from my sister asking how I am. It came in about the time Aidan was driving me mad beneath the sheets for a third time, around ten p.m. Given the time difference she's probably still up. I respond that I'm good and ask how Derek is. I add that I'm planning to be away to visit Ben's family and she shouldn't panic if she doesn't hear from me. She writes back that Derek's making a remarkable recovery and insists I call her when I get back.

The third is from Gloria and is verbose for her. Her messages are usually brief. This one takes up three thread bubbles on the screen.

I just wanted to tell you sorry for being skeptical of Mr. Big Bucks tonight. Charlie told me about the chat you two had and about Pierce asking you to be on his foundation board.

If I'd known what a dumbass you were being I would have sent my Doubting Debbie vibes to you, not him! Man up and take the reins, girl! He's crazy about you.

Have a great trip, I hope you have a shit ton of sex (so you can come back and finally share the X-rated version of Days of Our Rich-as-Fuck Lives!) LOL Love you!

Her words let my anxiety soften, allowing a moment of sheer joy sink in.

He hasn't told me he loves me, and I haven't uttered those words either.

Though I can count my relationships on one hand, I would have thought this a crushing sign of failure in the past. "I love you" was what you had to say.

But everything with Aidan is different. When it comes to him, clichéd expressions of endearment didn't seem strong enough.

I set myself a reminder to write Gloria back in the morning, then plug my phone into a charger on the counter. I'm at the refrigerator in search of a bottled water and a snack when I hear the most bone-chilling noise

I've ever heard.

It's coming from Aidan's room.

The sound sends shivers through me as I race for the bedroom, my skimpy purple slip doing nothing to support my chest or cover my bare ass as I run.

I reach the bedroom and realize it's him making the sound. My stomach flips in a rhythm matching the banging inside my chest. Aidan is gasping in one long, audible strain as though he can't get any air. He darts up to sitting in the middle of the bed as I enter.

I'm standing right in front of him at the foot of the bed, but he doesn't see me.

He's wearing nothing, his arms are outstretched at either side, his hands flat on the mattress. The sheets are a tangled mess around him. His eyes are dark and dazed, still not seeing me.

I call out his name, but again he doesn't acknowledge my presence in the room. His bare chest caves and fills with air so fast and often, I couldn't count how many times if I had to.

When his struggle to breathe eases, I stay completely still and whisper his name. I don't want to reach out for him, fearing he'll startle.

He's not here with me. I can sense it.

I let him relax before I say his name again. He shakes himself alert, feeling around and seeming to look for me. I climb up from the end of the bed and move towards him on my knees, staying a distance away, positioned in a kneel above him.

"I'm right here."

He looks over at me and I reach out to stroke his hair, slide fingertips down his steady jawline. I'm reeling at the concentrated fear in his eyes. He grabs for me, nearly hurting me with the force of his arms around me.

"It's okay," I whisper. "It was just a dream, Aidan."

I break free to untangle him from the sheets as gently as I can. I leave him exposed as I climb over him, wrapping my legs around his waist, my arms cradled beneath his, around his back. I kiss his bare shoulders, his neck up to the sensitive spot behind his ear. He's finally coming back to me, his head relaxing in agreement as my lips glide over him.

He tilts his head away to stop me after a moment, lifting me up by the hips just enough to settle me back over him, sliding himself inside of me. I expect him to start taking me over with thrusts or an attempt at pushing me to the brink, but he just holds me there in place, his arms wrapped around me, hands cradling the back of my head.

I can't bring myself to ask what he dreamt of.

I'm not sure I want to know.

He sways back and forth with me in his arms, whispering sexy Italian words I don't know, except for one simple word that's never meant so much to me until hearing him say it right here, right now.

Grazie.

He repeats it over and over again.

Thank you, thank you, thank you.

I groan when Aidan smacks me on the ass at what must be some unholy hour. I feel like I've barely slept.

He's sweaty from a run, climbing on top of me where I lay face-planted in bed.

"What time is it?"

"Six. Get up, sleepyhead. We're getting the fuck out of here."

He smacks me again as he departs for the shower, and I wonder if the guy that just spanked me is the same one that nearly fell apart in my arms last night.

It certainly doesn't seem it.

This Aidan is bright-eyed and raring to go, hooting in excitement on his way to the shower. Explicit hip-hop amps up through the speakers in the bedroom, interfering with my peace and quiet.

I take the hint and get motivated.

I pad to the guest room, figuring I'll shower and change there since that's where all my clothes are. On my way through the kitchen, I stop to reply to Gloria's text from the night before and see Charlie has responded with a smiley face, telling me to have a fan-fucking-tastic time.

After my shower, I come out of the guest bathroom dressed in capris and a t-shirt. Before I can make it to the closet to pick some shoes and pack for our trip, Aidan startles me from his position in the doorway. I grab my chest and swear as he stands there eyeing me.

He looks a different part today, and I'm slack-jawed once I calm down and get a good look. His snug jeans are tattered in a few places. His white t-shirt is different. A few silver buttons grace the top of it, but all of them are undone to expose one of the sexiest parts of him. The shirt is taut but his chest is slightly obscured by the dark flannel shirt he's layered over top. His sleeves are rolled up, exposing his strong forearms.

Damn. This version of Aidan could set fire to a girl without a match.

"Almost ready, babe?" His grin is contagious.

"Just have to throw some things in a bag, if I can find one in the closet. Did you pack cool weather clothes? It's colder up there than it is here, at least at night."

"I remember," he says, still smiling, "and I do have a weather app." He winks at me.

"I was just trying to be helpful."

"I've got all kinds of ways you can be helpful this weekend." He pulls me into his arms and kisses me. I want to wrap my legs around him and throw him on the bed, but that won't get me the information I'm after.

"We haven't had a chance to talk about this. Where are we going to be? I'll need to get in touch with Ben's sister to let her know. She's so excited I'm coming up."

"We can call her on the way. The rest is a surprise, baby. I can't wait to reveal it, but you have to have some patience."

"Not fair. You know I'm dying here."

"I know," he grins. "It's so entertaining to starve your obsessive need to have control."

"Hypocrite."

His grin widens. He knows I'm right.

"Can I at least know what's on the agenda while we're up there? Are we going to stay in bed for three days? Because I could get behind that."

"I could get behind you," he says, "and I would love nothing more. But we'll have a full weekend. I was thinking you could see Ben's family tonight or tomorrow morning, whatever suits them. I have a little work to do while you're preoccupied. Beyond that, I won't be leaving you alone all weekend."

I smile up at him. "I think I'm okay with that."

"Good. I had Samira pick you up a few pieces of luggage. Should be in there." He nods to the closet. "Pack light. And if you find yourself short on clothes any time soon, you should hit up The Red Door on Fifth and Main. There's an account set up for you there and at their sister store."

"The lingerie boutique next door?"

He just smiles as I try to blink the shock from my eyes.

"Come on, baby. I can't wait to get you out of the country."

When we emerge from 250 Harrison under blue skies and surrounded by a warm day, I'm finally as hyped as Aidan to blow off Stanton and Mirror Lake, even if it's just for a weekend.

Ivan pulls around from the back lot with the Lincoln. He grabs our bags from the lobby and throws them in the trunk while we climb into the back seat. I'm a little disappointed we can't ride alone, but I get over it realizing I can cozy up next to this stud for the two hours it will take us to get there.

We wind our way around the city streets but instead of getting on the highway that heads north, we're driving down a boulevard east of the city, passing restaurants and small businesses.

"I don't want to cost Ivan his job," I say, "but he's going the wrong way."

Aidan just looks at me and grins. His expression is pure wickedness. I can't imagine what he's pulling now.

Ivan signals to turn off the boulevard and starts north. We're going in the right direction to get to the Canadian border now, but I'm surprised when we pull into a car dealership.

"What are we doing here?"

He doesn't answer me. As Ivan pulls to a stop at the front door, Aidan exits the car and heads inside. I'm left sitting in customary quiet with Ivan.

A few minutes pass, and I'm getting antsy wondering where the hell Aidan went. My door opens without warning. I'm about to mouth off to Aidan when I realize it's not him opening the door. My emancipator from the Lincoln is a well-dressed gentleman with silver hair and a slight build. His name tag indicates he's a BMW Top Salesman and his name is George.

"Ms. Greene," he says, "please come this way."

I step out in time to see Aidan driving towards us in the most jaw dropping Beemer I've ever seen. He doesn't look too bad driving it, either. He's wearing his aviator shades and a sly smile as he pulls up. Ivan is already out of the Lincoln, switching our bags from one vehicle to the other.

The sun reflects off the Beemer's shiny black finish as a gull-wing door eases open.

My God.

This car is bananas and this guy looks movie-star-hot stepping out of it.

"Your chariot, baby."

I'm too astounded to do anything but nod. Top Salesman George rambles on to Aidan about the features of the 2016 BMW i8. Aidan is like a kid on Christmas as he takes turns listening and responding.

"I'll have it back Sunday evening," he says. "Do you have everything signed you need?"

"Yes, sir." George nods in my direction. "Have a pleasant weekend, Ms. Greene."

"Um yeah," I manage. "Thanks." I follow Aidan around to my side of the vehicle, stepping back as he opens the crazy-ass door. I'm thankful I packed only one bag. As gorgeous as the car is, I imagine trunk space is limited.

I settle into my seat, smiling back at him as he closes me in and moves around the back of the car. He sends Ivan on his way and climbs in, finding me admiring the cockpit. Even with the typical bells and whistles, the details in here scream vehicle-of-the-future.

"Aidan, this car is bananas."

He lets out a soft laugh. "It's not that rare. It's a hybrid. Lots of people drive these."

Yeah, right.

"Are you kidding me? I'm looking around for the flux capacitor like I'm Michael J. Fox. Did you just decide to swing in here and test drive it before you buy it?"

"Of course not," he says. "Please tell me you realize this car wouldn't be my style."

"Why are we taking it up north then?"

"Because it's hot as fuck and fun to drive," he says. "I actually like the last few model years better than this one, but you've got to admit this is a fine piece of machinery."

"Uh, yeah."

"We're borrowing it. For the weekend."

I just look at him, stupefied.

"You'd be surprised at the things you get for free when you have a lot of money."

"I still can't believe they just let you drive off in it."

"They're insured. I signed for it, set aside some collateral in the event of any damages. And the dealership wants to broadcast they lent it to me in a late summer ad campaign."

I laugh, dumbfounded that this is my reality right now.

"Well don't just sit there," I say. "Let's see what this thing can do."

An hour later, we pull off the highway. Thank God this car isn't a convertible because as fast as Aidan has pushed the i8, my hair would have become an absolute bird's nest.

We stop for breakfast at a diner Ben and I loved to frequent when we'd head to the river. It's a popular spot for big rig drivers and locals. Aidan parks the BMW far enough away from other vehicles that it won't be harmed, and I'm thankful we can be less conspicuous as we distance ourselves from it before going inside.

The place is humming with a full breakfast crowd at eight-thirty in the morning. Our waitress is brunette, probably in her early twenties. I'm about to ask her to put her eyes back in her head as she drinks Aidan in.

She finally leaves us after we order omelets and coffee.

"Are you hungry?"

"Starving," I say. "I was in the kitchen about to get something to eat last night when you..." I'm not sure how to go on. "You know," I finish.

"I know." He grabs for my hands across the table. "I'm sorry."

I look up at him with concern.

Why would he ever be sorry for that?

"I doubt it's something you can control, Aidan. It's fine. Do you have nightmares a lot?"

"Not really. They've recurred since I came to New York. It hadn't happened in a long time before that. And not much at all now," he says, "since you."

I smile down at our joined hands, then look back at him.

"You don't need to apologize. What are they usually about?"

Our waitress brings coffee and he completely ignores my question.

"What do you want to do first when we get up there?"

I sigh at his dodging the subject but choose not to force the issue.

"I have no idea," I say. "I don't even know where we're going."

"My family's place is called The Gables. It's smack in the middle of the river. You can see the Canadian span of the bridge from there." Moments later our food arrives, and we both dig in.

"Wait," I say between bites. "So we're going to an island?"

"I didn't previously mention that?"

"Uh, no." I set my fork down. "I think I would have remembered."

Ben's parents had a modest home on the mainland, across the street from a small plot of land on the riverfront. I'd never stepped foot onto one of the many islands. I'd only cruised through them by boat, and that was on the rare occasion we were up there in good weather between May and September.

"It's not really a big deal," he says. "Lots of people have islands up there."

"I know that. But most of them aren't gazillionaires," I say as I sip my coffee. "And I'm not sleeping with any of *them*."

"Ah," he laughs. "Point taken. Do you still need to get a hold of the Claytons?"

"Yes. I'll try when we're done here. And speaking of getting a hold of people, did you see Mark Whitmore's widow on your trip?"

"I did," he says. His demeanor shifts. "She wasn't overly excited to meet me. But she was cordial. She also shed some light on the circumstances surrounding his death."

I stop chewing as my stomach twists into a knot. "What did she say?"

"Mark was supposed to meet John Ireland the day after he died. She has no idea who John is but Mark had his contact information. Said he was meeting him about buying their next home in Florida."

"That makes absolutely no sense."

"I know. I'm guessing Mark was asked to take the meeting earlier, and when he did…" He doesn't finish the thought. "Either Ireland was there or he had someone there on his behalf. I've got Byron and Dimitri on it."

"Who's Dimitri?"

"A good friend," he says. "My brother's best friend, actually."

"Is he a detective or something?"

"No," he laughs, "but he'd think it was funny you suggested it. He's a hacker. Or used to be. Now he sells Harleys and owns a tattoo parlor."

"He sounds interesting."

"You don't know the half of it," he says with a grin. "You might get to meet him before the gala. He's coming out to New York the week before."

"Did he do your tattoo?"

He pushes his empty plate away. "Yes."

"And Stella?" I ask. "Is everything under control there?"

"Yes." He looks at me sternly. "I don't want you worrying about it. This weekend is about us. I refuse to allow that drama to interfere with it."

I nod, quiet and lost in my own thoughts.

He moves my empty plate out of the way and reaches for my hand again. "I've got a handle on it. Let's just put it out of our minds for now. Agreed?"

His charming smile is knee-weakening. There's nothing more I'd like to do than get lost in a bubble with him.

"Agreed."

24

Alexis

When we leave the diner, Aidan's excitement has returned. His phone is hooked into the sound system of the car and he asks me to select some songs.

"You go ahead," I say. "Let me just call Ben's mother. Reception gets spotty further north. Once we cross the border, my phone will be turned off. It costs me a fortune to roam up there."

He looks at me like I'm being ridiculous.

Okay, he could probably pay an entire month of my bills with a single day's interest off his investments. But I'm an independent woman, dammit. I can pay my own phone bill, and I don't want an extra hundred bucks coming out of my budget unnecessarily.

"If we don't have to race off to be somewhere on time, I'd like to call her now," I say. "Sit tight."

He nods, shaking his head and smiling at me as he's scrolling through his phone.

Ben's mother answers on the second ring. "Hello?"

"Hello, Mrs. Clayton." I'd never gotten used to calling her by her first name, though she often insisted.

"Alexis, dear. Are you on your way?"

"Yes. I was just calling to see when would be a good time to come by. Will you be home this afternoon?"

"Of course. You know Jerry will be outside doing something in that darn yard. So much for retirement. Pam can't wait to see you. Can you stay with us?"

Shoot. I don't want to disappoint her.

"Thank you so much for the offer. I'm staying with friends," I say, "but I'd love to come see you this afternoon. What time?"

"How about I fix us some lunch around one?"

"Just a sec," I say, muting the phone so I can talk to Aidan. "She'd like to invite me to lunch at one. Is that okay?"

"Should be. We'll have time to get settled this morning, then I can drive you over there."

"Um...I might have Ben's sister come get me."

"Can I ask why?"

"You. This car. It might be uncomfortable for them, me showing up there like this. Do you know how far it is between your place and theirs?"

"About ten minutes. Whatever you're comfortable with is fine with me."

"One would be fine," I tell her. "Would Pam be able to pick me up?"

"I'm sure she'd be happy to. She just ran out for one of those fancy iced coffees," she says. "You know how she loves those. Doesn't matter if the queue is out the door, she's there every morning. Shall I have her phone you when she gets back?"

"No, that's fine. Please just tell her I'll text her the address when I get there. I don't know it offhand."

"I'll tell her, dear. Customs shouldn't be too bad this early. And of course the holiday traffic was last weekend."

"Thanks, Mrs. Clayton. I'll see you soon." Aidan's still playing with his phone when I hang up. "I'm ready."

"Can you believe this car is running right now? My stomach is making louder noises after that greasy spoon."

"How is it so quiet?"

"Electric mode." He adjusts the fancy equipment, and the engine comes to life in its regular beast mode. The sound is not incredibly loud but there is a noticeable difference.

"I've got a few songs cued up here," he says. "You can scroll through the options on the dash to play whatever you want." He shoots me a playful smile. "As long as you let the first one play through."

I give him an eyebrow raise, scrunching up my face with curiosity. The car is idling as he hits a button to start the music. A cello starts the song, but it sounds more ominous than classical. A low voice comes through the speakers, and the bass kicks in as Aidan cranks the volume.

Okay, definitely not classical.

I look at the readout on the display. The song is "Remember the Name" by Fort Minor. I'm not familiar with it. I look back to him as he starts motoring towards the highway, picking up speed as we move into light traffic.

He's not singing out loud, but he's mouthing the words to a rap that's spewing at a pretty fast clip. The music overtakes the car, driving the song as the story unfolds about a rapper's formula to success.

Holy shit.

This isn't my choice of music, but everything below my waist is on fire while I watch him nail it. Though he isn't actually singing, he hasn't tripped up on a single word. His sunglasses are hiding his eyes while he slides through the song smooth as silk.

A skilled drummer and he can drop rhymes like nobody's business? Damn.

I can't recall seeing him this relaxed, enjoying himself like this. He hasn't paid me much attention since the song started. When it ends, I'm left flabbergasted. I hit the pause button on the audio.

"You wanna tell me what the hell that was?"

"What?"

"I'm ready to make you pull over so I can jump on you."

He smiles in amusement, a low laugh humming in his throat. He lifts his sunglasses up and eyes me.

"Oh yeah?"

"Absolutely."

"Play it again," he says, still grinning.

I ignore his request.

"Is that a new song? I've never heard it."

"That song was end of grad school for me. It's over ten years old. What rock have you been living under?"

"It's not my pick of genre," I admit, "but I did love it. And you're the one that's never heard of Tedeschi Trucks Band. How have you never heard of them?"

"Is that the band you were singing last night? The same one you played for me at your house that first night?"

"Yes."

"Sing it again," he says. "I've been dying to be your sole audience member."

Singing in front of a distracted crowd was no problem.

Singing alone in a car with him? Especially this car? I wasn't sure I'd be able to without feeling intimidated.

"C'mon, baby. You know you want to. Do you have it on your phone?"

"Not the one I sang last night, but I have a different one of theirs."

"Let it rip, love." He returns his shades to his eyes. "I promise not to bother you with my stalker stare."

I hook up my phone to the audio and select the song I want. "Come See About Me" starts playing at high volume, and he's right. I want to sing along as the song pours out to us impressively from the car's sound system. The lyric belts out from the start, and I lean myself towards the window and sing, pretending I'm driving alone.

As soon as I'm through the first verse, he's howling in approval, banging on the steering wheel with excitement.

"*Damn, baby*," he says. "I could hear that all day. Please don't stop."

I smile at him and just go with it. I so love this song, its lyrics urging a lover to come and get you, promising if he does you'll do anything he'd like.

Right now, that's exactly what I'm feeling.

There's been no chance to satisfy my craving for Aidan as we drive, but we've enjoyed the ride, laughing and playing music and talking. As we get closer to the border, he begins to recognize the landscape from driving through here in his younger days with his parents. He points out the exit for a small airport they used to fly into from California. We're both picking out milestones along the drive as we share stories about each of them.

At customs, Aidan answers questions with confidence, and we sail through without incident. As the Customs Agent hands back our passports, he tries to admire the fancy vehicle without breaking his rigid demeanor.

We make our way over the Canadian bridge as the familiar sound of the expansion joints passing underneath hums through me. I haven't been up here since Ben passed. Aidan must sense this is a solemn moment for me. He grabs for my hand and gives it a chaste kiss.

The car corners off the exit with ease as we head for the Thousand Islands Parkway. Ben's parents' house is this way too, except we would have gone left down the parkway. Aidan turns right.

We travel a few miles in silence until he turns off onto a side road, heading towards the river front. We stop at a marina with a large parking area and he cuts the engine.

"Are you okay?"

"Yeah, I'm okay." I smile up at him. "Don't I look okay?"

"You look gorgeous to me, baby." He eyes me with concern. "I just wanted to make sure you're all right."

I take a deep breath and steady my gaze on him.

"Ben meant everything to me at one time, Aidan. You know that. I will always miss him, miss our friendship. But what we have?" I shake my head with a smile. "I want to make new memories now. I'm just as excited about our time here as you are."

"I'm glad to hear it. And I have another surprise."

"Oh?"

I can't even fathom.

"Would you like to meet my parents?"

I blink fast, considering his question.

Holy shit. He wants me to meet his parents?

That is definitely not what I thought he'd say.

"I…yeah."

"Are you sure? Because you look a little doe-caught-in-headlights right now."

"I'm sure," I laugh. "I'd love to meet them. I think California is a bit of a hike from here though."

He's beaming at me now.

"They flew in yesterday."

"What?" I can't hide another wave of shock.

"I asked them to get things ready. My mother is over the moon that she gets to meet you."

"You told her about me?"

"Of course."

"What did she say?"

"That's the ironic part," he says. "She tells me she knew your father."

My eyes go wider. "In what context?"

"I haven't had a chance to ask. I got the impression she and Dad hired him once upon a time."

"How crazy is that?"

"I know," he says. "That was my reaction."

"Well I can't wait to meet her."

"You'll get to meet Oates too."

"Is he another one of your brother's friends?"

"I do have my own friends," he teases.

"Sorry," I laugh. "I didn't mean to imply…I've just never heard you speak of him before."

"He's in Silicon Valley most of the time. He works more than he breathes."

"It sounds like you've planned quite the weekend behind my back."

"I invited my parents and Oates. My mother may have invited the whole town to join us by now. She is so excited for this, to be back here in the islands. And she loves to entertain."

"Wait, have none of you been back here since you lost your brother?"

He looks away, his left arm resting on the wheel, his gaze focused through the windshield. "We've not," he finally says. "It's been a long time."

"I guess this is a milestone for both of us."

He looks back at me and grabs my hand again, repeating the sweet gesture of lifting it to his lips. "There's no one else I'd rather be here with."

"I'm flattered. And excited." A hint of disappointment creeps in anyway, realizing we won't be as alone as I'd hoped.

"Don't worry." As always, he reads my thoughts. "We have our own living space over there. I plan on making you scream loud enough so the fish can hear it, baby."

"Thank God." I can't help my grin. "I was ready to jump on you a hundred miles ago."

We take a boat similar to the one Aidan keeps at Falcon Lake for the short ride from the mainland to his parents' cottage, which he refers to as The Gables. Instead of docking at a slip along the island's shore, he drives us around the entire island first.

Calling this place a cottage is a gross understatement. The house is enormous and absolutely breathtaking. Despite its age, the home appears to be in pristine condition from where we float by it on the water. The bright white backdrop of the house is complemented with dark green shutters.

The family has aptly named it as there are too many gables on the front to count. The gigantic wrap-around porch and white columns pique my interest even more, and I pull out my phone to snap some pictures.

"Aidan. This place is…"

"Pretty amazing, isn't it?"

"It is. This is a realtor's wet dream right here." I take a few photos and pocket the phone again. "I'm in love with it already and I haven't even stepped foot on the island."

"Just wait," he says. "It gets better inside."

We drive past the back of the island where the main dock is. There are two other boats parked there. One is similar to this one – a high-end pontoon with plenty of room for people or partying. The other is a breathtaking wooden boat – a Garwood named "Victoria". It's just as head turning as the house.

"This is where you dock if you're staying at the main house. We're not," he says with a wink. We head beyond the slips to a boathouse that looks large enough to hold two watercraft side by side. The bay doors are up but nothing is inside. Living quarters appear to be above the empty space beneath.

"Is that where we'll be?"

"Nope," he says. "That's the guest house. It's a small studio space. Oates will be up there. We're over here." The boat motors along quietly past a small bay where two islands are joined by a wooden footbridge. "This property is actually one large island attached to a smaller one. The Gables sits on the large one. See there?" He points to a structure that's far smaller than the main house, but larger than the boathouse. It's a cabin, more informal than the grand home we'd just driven around. "We'll be on the smaller island," he says, "in Brat Cottage."

I shoot him a quizzical look. "Brat Cottage?"

"Yeah," he laughs. "That's what my parents named it when they constructed it for me and Thad."

"Was it correctly named? Were you brats?"

"I think it was more an ironic term of endearment," he says. "My parents do have a sense of humor."

Thank God for that.

"Let's take one more spin around the island," I say. "It's too beautiful not to admire one more time."

"As you wish, babe." He pulls away from the little bay and drives around again, confident as ever. "See that?" He points to a marker out in the main channel. "You have to watch out for shoals here."

"I'm aware. Ben's dad was famous for dinging props when he first learned to navigate up here. His River Rat status came after many years of accidental discoveries up and down the St. Lawrence."

"Sounds like he'd have some good stories to tell."

"He does. And a nickname to go with them. They called him Captain Crunch. Like the cereal."

"Clever," he laughs. "We have that in common. I banged up a few props myself as a kid."

This time as we drive by the grand house perched above us, we can hear laughter coming from the porch. The Gables sits on an impressive granite cliff, a good fifteen or twenty feet up from the water.

A man and woman whom I can only assume are Aidan's parents are waving from their seated positions at a patio table, and we wave back.

A younger guy (likely Oates) is hanging over the porch railing and waving. He puts his hands to his mouth to broadcast his hollering. "Pierce, you fucker," he yells. The shouting is unnecessary as his voice carries over the water easily on its own.

I see Aidan's mother turn from her chair and smack Oates on the shoulder in scolding, presumably for hollering obscenities. "Sorry, Mama-sita," he says to her before turning back to us. "Get the hell up here, man! It's time for cocktails! These old people are killing me!"

"We're coming!" Aidan says. "Stand down, you ugly bastard!"

I let go a peal of laughter. This says so much about their friendship. I'd never seen Aidan this casual. No drama, no big business. Just him being a regular person.

A regular, happy person.

Aidan pushes the throttle and drives around to the back bay in a hurry. He docks and I step out to get the lines, tying off the boat while he shuts off the engine and grabs our bags.

"Nice job with the lines, baby. I didn't realize you would be such a good first mate."

"I did grow up in an area full of lakes. Would you expect anything less?"

"With you?" he says. "Never."

We deposit our belongings inside Brat Cottage, which is an adorable two-bedroom cabin. I want to get a better look around but Aidan insists we head up to the main house to say hello.

My stomach is churning with butterflies about meeting his parents, but my worry fades as we walk hand in hand over the footbridge. I inhale the fresh air, listening to sound of boats passing and the resulting waves crashing up against the shore.

In the late morning warmth, the setting is just beautiful.

The island is thick with trees everywhere. Sun dances through the branches to light up a floor of granite and earth underfoot. The voices of Aidan's family trickle down to us as we get closer to the house.

"This is an amazing setting, Aidan. How lucky you were to spend time here growing up."

"I wish it had been more time," he says. "But yeah, it was the best few weeks of our summers every year."

I take a deep breath as we climb the steps to the porch. I can hear the men in a heated conversation. Mrs. Pierce is still seated, flipping through a magazine.

"Oh honey, you're here!" Victoria Pierce claps her hands together and abandons her seat to greet her son. She hugs him tight and he responds in kind, comfortable with the affection she seeks.

"Mom," he says, kissing the top of her head. Her hair is the same color as Aidan's. It's styled in a pixie cut that complements the regal features of her face. "It's good to see you. You look beautiful."

He's right. She's absolutely radiant.

She's dressed casually in white capris, a navy and white striped top, and flat sandals that grace her pedicured feet. Her jewelry looks expensive but not haughty. She's taller than I am, though not by much, but she is also very fit. Her skin is bronzed from California sun.

I'm trying to recall her age from Aidan's file – the one his doctor prepared for me about his personal history – but Byron had taken the flash drive back before I could memorize the document. I'm sure she looks younger than she is. I can see Aidan in her without much effort as I search her perfect complexion.

The resemblance is not so much in her eyes. Hers are blue too, but they're a lighter shade and definitely not as intense as her son's. The similarity is more apparent in her expression when she smiles and in her demeanor of grace and kindness. All the good things he possesses are emanating off of her in the same way.

This is a kind woman, not the type to be friendly to your face and cruel when your back is turned.

And she's coming at me for a hug right this second.

"Alexis," she says. She squeezes me briefly and pulls back with outstretched arms, her hands resting at my elbows as she looks me over. Her eyes meet mine again. "I am so happy to meet you."

"The feeling is mutual, Mrs. Pierce."

Because I'm falling face-first for your son.

Gah! Don't say that.

"Aidan speaks very highly of you." I smile graciously at her. "I'm glad we have the chance to meet."

"Please, call me Tori," she insists. "You are a beauty." My cheeks immediately flush. "Aidan, you said she was beautiful. You should have said gorgeous."

"Mom," he says, "stop now." He comes back and grabs for my hand, and I watch her notice the gesture. She gives me a smile, indicating she likes what she sees.

"Reginald," she says, turning to her husband who is several feet away. Her tone is scolding yet teasing at the same time. "Perhaps you and Mr. Oates could tear yourselves away from your conversation so Alexis can meet you."

"My apologies, dear," Mr. Pierce says as he gets up from his chair and approaches. "You know how I love debating with this wisecracker." Aidan's friend stays where he is, obviously wanting to let us get acquainted first.

Reginald Pierce is handsome to an intimidating degree. He and Aidan have that in common, though their features are nothing alike as they are unrelated by blood. His dad's nose is more pointed, his jawline more pronounced. Still, he could easily have a second career as a male model, albeit in the over fifty category.

He comes over to greet me first, before his son. "Tori is right," he says. "Beautiful, indeed. Now I see why it was so urgent for us to get out here." He takes my hand and gives it a gentle squeeze. "It's very good to meet you, Alexis." His smile reveals perfect teeth.

"Likewise, Mr. Pierce." He has kind, hazel eyes and a trim build. His full head of short silver hair is parted to one side. He's dressed casually in navy shorts and a white polo shirt.

"Please call me Reggie." I notice his limbs are lean and tan as he lets go of me and moves to Aidan. "Son," he says. He moves in for a quick handshake and a half-hug, his underlying affection doused with testosterone. "I trust you made the trip without a problem?"

"Yes," Aidan says. "It was an easy drive."

"Mr. Oates," Reggie says. "Come and meet this lovely young lady."

"Well I'm tryin'," Oates says, "but all you old timers are keepin' a brother down."

He puts some swagger on as he approaches, which comes across as silly given his looks. He is tall and fit but not built like Aidan is. His hair is dark and curly and, though it appears styled with product, some of it falls around his face. He pushes his black-rimmed glasses up the bridge of his nose as he greets me.

He takes my hand and lifts it to his lips. "Bonjour, Mademoiselle."

Is this guy for real? He's so adorable but nerdy and ridiculous all at the same time. I can't help it. I burst out laughing and then so does everyone else.

"Hi," I say through my receding laughter. "You must be Oates."

"The one and only," he says as he lets go of my hand. "Daryl Oates, at your service. And, apparently, the ice breaker for the welcome wagon."

"Well it's very good to meet you, Daryl Oates. And thank you for breaking the ice."

"My pleasure," he says. He lets me go and moves for Aidan. "So you're putting up with this pain in the ass, huh?" He puts out his hand and Aidan pulls him in for a strapping bro-hug as they smack each other's backs.

"I am," I say, still smiling from my fit of laughter.

"Have you two eaten?" Tori asks. "It's going on eleven."

"Yes, on the way up," I offer.

"Maybe a drink then," Reggie says. "I think I'll make us some Bloody Mary's."

"A fine idea," Oates says. "I'm sure you've forgotten where you left your walker and your glasses. You'll need my help."

Reggie gives him a nudge. "Very funny, whippersnapper. Let's go."

The two of them disappear into the house, leaving Aidan and me with his mother.

"Would you two like to sit?" she says. "Alexis, I'd love the chance to chat."

"For a minute, Mom," Aidan says. "I have to get Alexis back to the mainland. She's visiting some friends this afternoon."

"Oh, so soon?" Her genuine disappointment makes me smile.

"Just for lunch," I say. "I'm visiting my former mother-in-law."

She looks surprised. "You're divorced?"

"No," I say, "widowed."

"Oh dear," she says. "Aidan, you didn't tell me. How long ago did you lose your husband?" The three of us sit at the table, Aidan next to me with his mother opposite us.

"About a year and a half ago," I say. "It was unexpected."

"I'm so sorry, honey. I'm sure that was hard."

"It was, but I'm doing okay." Aidan squeezes my hand beneath the table. "Great, actually."

"I can see that," she beams. "And your father was Bert Greene?"

"Yes," I say. "Aidan tells me you knew each other."

"Briefly, yes. He was such a kind man. He helped Reggie and me before we moved away from Mirror Lake."

"I would love to hear more sometime. It helps keep his memory close," I say, "hearing people talk of him."

"How long ago did Bert pass?"

"About four years ago now. He was in his late seventies. Heart attack," I say.

"So much sadness," she says somberly. "To lose your husband and your father too. Yet look at you. You are overflowing with happiness."

"Thank you." I want to speak up and tell her that her son is the cause of that but I don't.

"Pierce!" Oates pops his head out the porch door. "Can I get a ride to the mainland around one-thirty?"

"For what?"

"I gotta pick up my surprise, bro. Can you do it or do I have to swim for it?"

"You can ride over with us," he says. "I have to take Alexis over close to one o'clock."

"Thanks, shithead," Oates replies.

"Language!" Tori scolds. Aidan and I share a smile as Oates shuts the door. "Well, I suppose we ought to have that drink and then let you two get settled," she says. "The Hamiltons and the Reeds are coming back later this afternoon. They just went into town for lunch."

"Mom," Aidan says pointedly, "who else did you invite?"

"That's it," she says defensively. "I told you I was asking them. They flew out from California with us. Oh, except the Lonergans," she adds. "They may drop by tomorrow night for dinner."

Aidan gives her a look.

"What?" she says. "They opened up The Gables for us, had their service stock the bar, the groceries, everything. The least I could do was invite them to dinner."

"What the hell?" he finally says. "The more the merrier."

25

Aidan

I pull up to the marina to drop Alexis off and feel an annoying sense of dread at the thought of leaving her. We also need to pick up whatever Oates is after, though I haven't figured out what that may be.

"Do we have to drive into town?" I ask him. "Because if we do, it's gonna be one hell of a ride."

"What are you driving now, bruh?"

"Beemer," I say. "An i8."

"Well then I'm sure pissed we don't need to go into town. But it's probably a good thing. There wouldn't be enough room for us and my surprise in that tin can."

"Tin can?" I bristle. "It's one fine ass machine. Isn't it, babe?"

"Sure is," Alexis says. She's not looking at us, her attention focused on the parking lot in the distance as we pull up to the dock. "Almost as slick as the driver."

Oates grins at me as though he's come to a revelation.

"I see Pam," Alexis says. She's waving to her sister-in-law, who's parked several yards away in a Mini Cooper.

"Who's Pam?" Oates asks.

"My sister-in-law," Alexis says. She's getting out, tying up the boat.

"You're married?" He's clearly surprised. Alexis doesn't hear his comment.

"Was," I say back to him. "Her husband passed away."

Regret washes over him.

"Jeez, I'm sorry," he says. "I didn't know."

I shoot him a look, but I know Alexis wouldn't be offended even if she had heard him.

"That's why you should keep your mouth shut, asshat."

"Agreed," he says mostly to himself with an embarrassed smile. I just shake my head at him. This is textbook Oates. Not always the smoothest guy to have around, but always entertaining.

"I'll just hang here, guys," he speaks up. "My surprise isn't being delivered for a half hour. You go ahead."

"I'll be fine," Alexis says from the dock. "You two should take a quick ride or something. I'll see you back here what, about four?"

I can sense she doesn't want me to meet Pam.

"That's fine." I don't want to push it. But I also don't want to let her go. Her safety is likely not in jeopardy here, but just the thought of harm coming to her because she's out of my sight nags at me. I step off the boat and walk her to the end of the dock where it meets the concrete of the parking lot. "I'll meet you here at four."

She looks up at me. "Aidan, it's only a few hours."

"You have your phone?"

"Yes, but it's turned off."

"Turn it on," I order. "I need to be able to reach you at all times."

"You're being ridiculous and controlling."

"Don't care." I reach in her back pocket, pull out her phone and turn it on. At the same time, my phone rings. I hand her phone back to her, then look at the display on mine.

"Don't run off just yet," I tell her. "It's Charlie." I answer and listen, responding that Alexis is with me. "Here," I say, handing her the phone. "He wants you."

"Hello?" Her expression tells me she isn't expecting the call. "Is everything okay?"

She listens for a moment, then speaks again. "That's good news. Wednesday is fine. I'll be catching up Monday and Tuesday anyway. And thanks for covering today," she says. "It is so beautiful up here, Charlie. It's going to be a great weekend." She shoots me a knowing smile as she disconnects.

"See?" she says. "No worries. Everything is fine."

"What did he want?"

"Just to tell me that he may have landed our first big client, outside of your uncle."

"Who?"

"No one I've spoken to before. I guess he's a big wig at Ashley Pharma in Stanton. Charlie said his secretary called to set up an appointment. Pickard is his last name, I think. Do you know him?"

"I've heard of him. I don't know him personally."

She gives me a look.

"Did you set this up?"

"No," I insist. "I had nothing to do with it."

It's the truth, but my gut tells me to dig further. Not that her skills are lacking, but with enemies circling us, I had to be sure someone wasn't trying to worm their way into her life through whatever means possible.

"It sounds promising," I add in assurance. I can check out Pickard on my own. She may kill me later but I would take the risk. I give her a quick kiss, knowing her sister-in-law is parked not far away and can likely see us.

"Enjoy your time, baby," I whisper in her ear as I look over her shoulder. "When you get back here, I'm going to bend you over the closest flat surface and fuck you senseless."

I can feel her break into a smile. "I look forward to it."

She turns on her heel and goes, leaving me standing there with an ache I've never known before.

Oates and I take the i8 out for a quick cruise while we wait for his mystery delivery. I keep it close to the speed limit because I don't need the hassle of Canadian Police, but we're cornering at a good clip as we head east down the parkway back to the marina.

"You're right," he says. "This thing is pretty hot. Maybe I'll get one."

"You could certainly afford it," I laugh. "Too bad it'd sit and collect dust with as much as you work."

"I've been thinking about cutting back."

I turn to him to see if he's serious. I can't picture him slowing down his work, but it certainly wouldn't hurt the guy. He spent more time in front of a screen than anyone I knew.

"Life's short, man. I say go for it."

"If I had a hot chick as a distraction, maybe I'd seriously consider it."

I can't help it. My grin widens.

"Yep," he says. "I knew it."

"What?" I ask in innocence as we pull back into the lot.

"Pierce, you dumb fuck," he says. "You're smitten."

I just laugh.

"Yes indeed," he says. "A smitten kitten. Aidan and Alexis, sittin' in a tree, bruh. I can see it comin' a mile away."

I look back at him without any humor this time.

"What is it you think you see coming?"

"To put it bluntly?" He pushes his glasses up then retrieves his phone from his pocket to check it. "Brother, you're fucked."

I just shake my head. Another vehicle pulls in the lot to park in the space ahead of us, but Oates doesn't notice with his head buried in his phone. It's a passenger van with the local airport logo on the side.

"I think your surprise is here," I nod.

"Yeah man!" He gets out of the car in a hurry.

I get out too, wondering what the hell this is all about. I see someone exit the van, and I throw my head to the side in an a-ha moment.

"Holy fuck," I say. "You didn't."

"I did indeed, man," Oates says over the roof of the i8. "Surprise!"

It's our Third Musketeer, my one other close friend on the planet that I've known as long and as well as Oates. We haven't seen each other in years, only speaking when one of us happened to have a spare five minutes. For him, the occasions were fewer than even I could afford.

"Nate Edwards," I say. "Ho-lee shit." He looks good considering he'd probably flown for several hours to get here from wherever he'd been. He's dressed down in jeans and flip flops, a pair of sunglasses dangling from the collar of his gray t-shirt.

"Pierce, you bastard. Did we get ya? Oates, tell me we got him."

"He had no idea," Oates says. "That was a solid plan, bruh."

"What the fuck, guys? You couldn't tell me we were having this little reunion?"

"I wasn't sure I could pull it off," Nate says. "It was last minute." He comes in for our typical handshake and bro-hug. "You look great, man. I hear you got a woman."

Jesus. Word travels fast.

"You'll meet her later. What the hell are you doing here?"

"Oates asked me. I'm headed to Florida from here, but I was able to score a couple days away."

"I'm honored." Nate Edwards didn't typically get time off for anything. He was single and had only his parents for family. His life was his work. "Heading to Kennedy Space Center?"

"Yeah," he says. "Duty calls."

Nate is undoubtedly the smartest of the three of us. He contracted with various government agencies, lending out his brain to whomever might need it. It wasn't unusual for him to be out of touch for months if he was working for NASA.

"Well I'm thrilled as fuck that you're here." He and Oates share a similar hug and we're all silent for a moment. It's the first time the three of us have stood next to each other in just shy of a decade, and it settles over me that Thad's funeral was the last time.

"Guys," Oates says clapping his hands together to break the sullen quiet. "We've got a short amount of time to catch up and rage out. What's first?"

I check my phone for the time. It's almost two o'clock.

"We've got two hours until I have to be back here for Alexis," I say. "Let's head back to The Gables for something to eat and some fishing. We'll rage out later," I promise Oates.

"All right, Pierce," he says. "You're lucky my brain could use some soaking up of nature and shit. But later," he says, "we're partying like it's fuckin' ninety-nine."

An hour later we've been well fed. My mother had lunch ready upon our return from a spin around the surrounding islands. Nate had insisted on the nostalgic ride to reminisce about past escapades hopping from one island to the next. The guys had been up for a few very memorable weeks during our summers off from college.

The three of us are on the main dock now, each of us in an Adirondack chair with a fishing pole in hand and a cold beer close by. It's the most relaxed I've been in recent memory.

"Tell me about this girl of yours, Pierce," Nate says. "Oates sent me a text me this morning after he met her and said you're in deep."

I recast and take a sip from my green glass bottle, letting my thoughts return to her as they constantly do. "So he keeps telling me. I cannot confirm or deny." I'm sitting between the two of them, and he turns to look at me while Oates punches me on the arm.

"Dude's fucking done for," Oates says. "Done-zo. Toast."

"Gone to the dark side have ya?" Nate asks.

"If you consider happiness the dark side, then yeah." I counter.

"Ohh, so she makes you *happy*?" Nate laughs. "You're burnt toast, motherfucker."

"Maybe," I say. "But I'm not the only one."

"Why?" Oates says as he reels in a perch. He unhooks it and tosses it back. "Who else is drinkin' the Kool Aid?"

"You'll never guess in a million years."

"Cameron Mays," Nate says, referencing his rival from Cal Tech. Cameron was the unfortunate soul on the receiving end of most of Nate's genius pranks. Oates and I share a laugh.

"Please," Oates says. "That guy's nerdier than I am. He couldn't score with a free hooker."

"Nope," I say. "Try again."

"I can only think of one other person we all know that we still have contact with," Nate says. "And there's absolutely no way it's him. Hell has not frozen over, and I can tell you for a fact the Earth has not stopped spinning."

"No way," Oates says. "That's gotta be it."

I smile. Oates has figured it out.

"I don't believe it," Nate says. "Dimitri?"

I nod, casting again. The fish are not biting for me this afternoon, but I don't care.

"Holy shit, man." Nate swigs the last of his beer. "It's an epidemic."

"Indeed," Oates says. "Nate, please save me from this zombie apocalypse. Do you have an antidote?"

"No one has an antidote for this," I say. "Once you're tapped, you pegged it exactly right. Burnt fucking toast."

"Goddamn," Oates says. "Please let me get my start-up off the ground before you go drowning in the river of love."

"Deal," I say. "Let's go up to the house and go over the birth plan for your baby."

After hashing out business with Oates, I retreat to the library alone. Nate's getting a shower after his hours of travel, and Oates is putting more thought into some suggestions I'd given him during our discussion.

Being here again has brought up so many memories of my brother. I needed a moment to regroup.

I'm sitting behind my dad's desk when he comes into the room, a newspaper under his arm.

"How are things going?" He takes a seat in a club chair in front of the fireplace. I get up and move to the chair opposite him.

"Can't complain."

"Are you ready to move forward with the Center?"

"Almost. We've got the land secured. I've got the gala underway. Did I tell you who I've asked to headline?"

"No," Dad says as he opens his newspaper. I always thought this was a charming quirk about my dad. It didn't matter how many electronic devices he had, he always read a crisp newspaper when he had a chance.

"Dr. Marcus Neil is our primary speaker." My statement gets his attention. He folds his paper back up and sets it aside.

"You're kidding."

"No. I met him last Saturday."

"I'm impressed, son."

"You should be. He's an impressive person."

"What did the two of you talk about?"

"It was a short meeting, but we talked about the Center mostly."

And Alexis.

"He'll be a great draw. I might just have to fly back for the gala."

"That'd be great." Though my mother wouldn't be there, it would be nice to have him attend for support, and to rub elbows with people in Stanton. "You can mingle and schmooze and I can take a backseat."

"It's your project. You'll still have to greet people."

"Never been my favorite part."

"I know. But you're good at it. You'll let me know if there's anything else I can do?"

"There is one other thing that has not been going well, actually. I'd like your take on it."

"John Ireland," he says. "I spoke to Bill Hoffman."

"I need Ireland off the board."

"I don't think that's a problem. We've got the votes. I understand Stella has had some difficulties?"

"She did. I believe she's on a better path now."

"She needn't be your burden, son."

"I know."

"If there's anything I can do, you just say the word."

"I've asked Alexis to be on the Foundation board."

He looks at me, a knowing grin forming as he speaks. "You believe in her capabilities that strongly, hmm?"

"I do."

"She seems like a remarkable young woman."

I don't answer. I don't have to.

"I'll be glad to second her appointment to the board. Let's get that done next week."

"How do you think Ireland will handle being ousted?" I've been anxious to get his perspective on this.

"I don't think it makes much difference to him one way or the other. He has no interest in your philanthropy. What I'm more concerned about is how Stella is going to affect what you're trying to do in Stanton. Does Alexis know about her?"

"She does. She knows a lot about me, actually."

More than any woman in my past ever had.

"Good. She should be aware of how the Irelands operate before she agrees to be a part of this."

We never discussed the Irelands in this way. I'm beginning to see my dad might know more than he'd ever let on, but I decide not to delve into it. The less we discuss, the better.

"Stella will be a non-factor. I'll make sure of it."

"Even without Stella being a problem, Alexis will have a lot to deal with if you go public with her on your arm. You realize that?"

"I do. We're being discreet for now. But I'm hopeful that won't be the case much longer."

He looks at me with concern. "You're very serious about her."

"Yes."

"All the more reason to be careful, Aidan. Pulling her into our world when things are status-quo is daunting enough. There's the press to consider. Your business. Your efforts in Mirror Lake, not to mention how this affects her life. Everything will be impacted once word gets out that the two of you are an item."

"I know, Dad. I don't care. Whatever is thrown at us, we'll face it together. To some extent, we've already been doing exactly that."

"You're aware the Irelands would abuse your vulnerability when it comes to this?"

"I am. And Alexis understands that just as much as I do. She's intelligent and intuitive, but she's also been through a lot. Her strength is incredible. She's unlike anyone I've met."

He looks pensive as he mulls over my assertions.

"I have no doubts about her, Dad."

"I'm glad for that," he says at last. "I'm happy for you. Just be careful. That's all I'm saying."

26

Alexis

The minute Pam drives us away from Aidan, my emotions are on extreme overload.

I'm so happy to see Pam. I haven't seen her since she came to the States for Ben's funeral. She might wonder who was kissing me goodbye at the dock, but she's said nothing about it.

The rest of me is overwhelmed by thoughts of Aidan. Meeting his parents and his closest friend had shown me a different side of him. Each of them reflects what is good about him in some way. I was grateful to see him through their eyes but also reminded how thankful I am to know him.

Add to that (as ridiculous as it seems even to me), I miss him already.

And now I'm going to visit Ben's parents.

While Pam is going on about her junior year at University and how well it went, I'm shedding quiet tears.

"Lex," she says. She turns down the music in her Mini Cooper when she realizes my state. "Are you okay?"

"I'm so sorry, Pam. These aren't sad tears." I try not to sniffle. "I'm just overwhelmed."

"It's okay," she says. "I get it." She lets me come around as I take a few breaths, then opens the glove box as she drives. "There's tissues in there, girl."

I pull a couple out and wipe my face.

"Better?" she asks.

"Better."

"What's up, eh? Are you sure you're okay?"

I dive into the events of the last few weeks, trying to get the details out in a hurry before we arrive at her parents' home a few miles away. Pam knew everything there was to know about her brother and me (though her parents didn't), and it feels good to finally get her up to speed. I fill her in about R.E.E. as much as I can, telling her how my career has been in flux since Aidan walked into my life, not to mention how he's affected the rest of me.

Her brown eyes dart to me in surprise at times, then light up with laughter at some of the anecdotes I've shared.

"Damn," she says. "You've lived a lifetime since we talked last. And all I've been doing is studying and trying to make it through my final exams."

"Well that's why I'm a bit screwy." I heave a sigh. "I've just been on a roller coaster the last few weeks. I'm so glad to be here though."

"*Hellz yeah*," she says. "I just wish you were staying longer. Do you really have to go back after lunch?"

"I should," I say. "Aidan's parents flew in from California. They made a special trip just for us to gather this weekend. I'd feel terrible if I bailed on them."

As much as I'd love to stay in Pam's company, I know a couple hours with Ben's parents will be enough. They are wonderful people, but we didn't have much in common. After a while, there tended to be more awkward silences than anything else.

"Where does his family stay up here?" She lifts her iced coffee from the cup holder and sips.

"They have an island," I say. "It's not far from here. They call it The Gables."

She turns her attention off the road for a moment just before we pull to a stop in her parents' driveway. "Get the frick' out. *The* Gables? As in the big white house on Fawn Island?"

"I guess," I shrug. "I've only just seen it for the first time a few hours ago."

"He's a member of *that* Pierce family?"

I'm not sure what she means, so I just shrug again.

"Lex," she says. "Their family was prominent up here for years. Then they just disappeared, stopped coming up here. Like poof," she gestures, her fingers flicking out. "Boom. Gone."

"They had a tragedy in their family," I say. "I think they just couldn't bring themselves to come back."

Her brown hair is tied up in a ponytail, and it bobs forward as she gives me a sideways glance, urging me to go on.

"Aidan's brother," I say. "He was in a car accident. He didn't survive."

"I'm sorry to hear that." She's quiet for a moment. "But it's nice they're back now. It's such a shame to see that house sit empty most of the time. It's always been my favorite one on the river."

"I can see why," I say. "The place is crazy beautiful. I haven't even gotten the full tour yet."

"*Gawd,*" she says. "I'd die to get a tour of that place."

"Why don't you come back with me?" I say. "There's plenty of room and Aidan says the more the merrier."

Her eyes light up. "Yes!" she shouts, elated at the invite. "*Abso-fricken-lutely* yes!"

We finish lunch on the Claytons' back porch, thanks to Ben's mom. Though I offered to help, Pam and her dad insist Mrs. Clayton and I visit while they clean up the kitchen.

"Care for a hand of Rummy?" Mrs. Clayton asks.

"Sounds great."

This would help pass the time. It's going on three already. I've extended the invite to Pam in front of her parents, and they were happy that Pam and I would get to spend more time together. I took the liberty of sending Aidan a text, and he agreed it would be good to have Pam join us.

Mrs. Clayton deals, then speaks again as she looks over her hand of playing cards.

"I'm so glad you came up," she says. "Please tell me more about these friends you're staying with."

Her silver hair is cut in a bob, framing her round face. She's a bit overweight but adorable nonetheless. She's wearing a pair of khaki shorts that go well past her knees and a cute top with flowers all over it.

Her eyes light up when she smiles, a trait she and Ben shared. It was this kind of friendly charm that made her son such a good candidate for broadcasting. In contrast, Mr. Clayton is gruff. I loved him like a second dad, but our conversations were always short and to the point. My talks with Mrs. Clayton leaned more towards heart-to-heart conversations.

Still, I'm not quite sure how to respond to her.

"I haven't known them very long," I admit. "But they're a wonderful group of people."

"Your turn first," she urges, gesturing to the remaining deck of cards between us. "And of course they're wonderful, dear. You wouldn't spend your time with anyone who wasn't."

I take my turn and discard. "I appreciate you saying so."

"So when are you going to tell me about the gentleman you've met?"

I sit in silence, completely stunned. Pam wouldn't have had a chance to tell Mrs. Clayton anything. I'd been with her since we came in the door.

"Um…" I stammer. "I'm not sure what you mean."

She discards, urging me to take my next turn. "It's written all over your face, dear. You're in love."

Whoa.

There was that word again. I hadn't considered it since Gloria had insisted the same to me a week ago.

"Mrs. Clayton," I blush, "you're embarrassing me."

"I'm sorry, Alexis," she says, "but I'm afraid that's something a girl cannot hide." She reaches out her plump hand to lay it over mine. "There's no need to hide it from us. We hoped so much that you'd move on after losing Ben."

I'm tearing up again at her words. I'm not crying like the car ride here, but I am genuinely moved. I never felt the need to ask Ben's parents' permission for anything, before or after he died. But the fact I had their blessing to move on carries a weight away like a leaf in a warm breeze.

"Thank you, Mrs. Clayton." I don't know what else to say.

"Is he a good man?" she asks. "I know Ben would want that for you."

"He is," I say. "His name is Aidan. Aidan Pierce."

"The Pierce family that owns The Gables?"

"Yes," I nod with a chuckle, "that family."

"Well, haven't you fallen into a bucket of luck. I think we need a fresh glass of pop to celebrate. Wayne," she calls to the kitchen, "bring out some glasses of pop. And heck," she says, "throw some rum in them, too."

At four o'clock on the button, we're back at the marina. Pam isn't literally jumping up and down with excitement, but that's the vibe she's giving off after she locks her car and tosses her duffel to the pavement.

"Do I look okay?" she asks. "I've never met rich people before."

I laugh out loud. "Sweetie, don't think of them like that. They're totally normal. I promise." I look over her outfit. She's in a sky blue sundress that accentuates her ample chest, though she doesn't have any cleavage showing. Her feet are adorned with cute strappy sandals that give her a little height.

Her skin is an olive color, like Ben's was, inherited from their father. "You look great," I say. "Honestly."

Pam is a bit heavier than me, but never what I'd consider unhealthy. She has emphasized curves in what most guys would consider all the right places. She often covered up her thighs, voicing she felt they were too big. This was likely the reason she preferred sundresses over shorts. But she is cute, even sexy in her own way.

She is also extremely bright. I knew she often had dates that she turned away before they could become boyfriends. She was too involved in her studies to be bothered.

"I am so excited," she squeals. "I gotta get a grip!"

I come over and give her a squeeze. "Relax," I tell her, resting my hands on her shoulders. We're the same height with the sandals she has on. "It's just a weekend with friends, okay? No biggie."

"Right," she says. "No biggie." She lets out a breath as I hear the boat pull up.

Oates is tying up the boat to the dock. Aidan is in the driver's seat and there's another guy with them I've never met.

"Who is that?" She looks in the direction of the men.

"The guy tying up, or the other guy?"

"Not the guy that was kissing you goodbye," she says. "Obviously that was Aidan. And not the guy in the salmon colored shirt that stayed behind on the boat. The one that's coming this way with Aidan. He's got glasses."

"That's Oates," I say. "Aidan's best friend. I have no idea who the other guy is."

As the guys get closer to the parking lot, I notice Pam is looking at Aidan. Oates lags several feet behind.

"So that's Aidan, huh?"

I nod.

"Wow," she says under her breath.

I just nod again. I should access her glove box for more tissues to wipe my drool.

He has his aviator shades on and a more casual outfit – low sneakers, a pair of khaki shorts and a gray t-shirt that's tight around his chest. The sleeves are ripped off and tattered at the edges, a washed-out beer logo gracing the front.

He looks *ah-mazingly* hot.

And he's running for me.

He comes at me to lift me up and spin me around. Before he lets me land, he plants a kiss on me that leaves me aching for more.

Dang.

I suddenly find it hard to stand up.

"Baby," he whispers in my ear. "Please tell me I don't have to let you out of my sight for the rest of the weekend."

"I'm all yours."

"Thank God." He spins me around again and sets me back down, leaving me glad that he's standing close enough to hold me upright. "Oates!" he hollers over my head towards his friend, who is walking slowly up the inclined pavement towards us. "Hurry up! There's an unescorted female here that needs a hand down to the boat!"

Oh, jeez. This should be something. Aidan turns his attention to Pam while we wait.

"Hi," he says, extending his hand. "Aidan Pierce."

"Pam Clayton," she says timidly. "Good to meet you, Mr. Pierce."

"Please call me Aidan," he says. "Alexis tells me you're off from University for the summer."

"I am," she says. "I just completed my junior year at OCAD U."

"Great school," he says. "Toronto, right?"

"Yes," she says. She gives me a look that begs to know how he would ever know that. I just shrug. I can tell her later than Aidan seems to know everything before you even realize it's something to know.

Oates saunters up to us, his swagger on full throttle.

Until he catches sight of Pam.

As he drinks her in, he goes completely slack-jawed.

In my head, I'm roaring with laughter. In reality, I introduce them and wait for Oates to start in with his king-of-the-ladies demeanor, but he doesn't. He clams right up.

"Pam is heading into her senior year at OCAD U," Aidan offers to break the silence.

"No kidding?" Oates finally says. "What are you studying?"

"Digital Futures."

Oates is visibly taken aback, audibly appreciating this information. She's studying in a field that he's more than a master of.

"Right this way, Mademoiselle," he says. "I'd be glad to escort you to our watercraft."

Aaaand he's back! Game on.

I'm elbowing Aidan in the side, trying not to burst out in laughter. He's smiling ear to ear.

"Babe," I whisper, "this could be very bad."

He leans down to lay a kiss behind my ear.

"Or," he says, "it could be very, very good."

27

Aidan

I introduced Alexis to Nate on the boat ride back. By the time we get through cocktail hour and dinner, he's had a chance to chat with her a few times. He pulls me aside at the first opportunity.

"Dude," he says.

"What?"

"She's amazing. I don't even care that she's a lawyer."

I can't help my reaction, grinning like an idiot in response.

Shit. Maybe Oates is right.

I'm smitten.

And utterly fucked.

"You're different," he says. "It's good to see you happy, man."

I thank him and make my way back to her, feeling him eye us the entire time. It felt good not to have to hide it. Back home, we were suffocating under worry and conflict. Here we could just be us.

I'm becoming more comfortable with the notion of us together and realize it's something I won't allow anyone to interfere with.

After dinner, I field a call from Byron. I asked him to get information from Charlie about Alexis's potential new client, and he's reporting back.

"I wasn't able to find out much," Byron says. "Charlie only had the name and phone number. I've found his profile on Ashley Pharmaceutical's website, but there isn't much solid information. Do you want me to dig deeper? Maybe ask Charlie to cancel the meeting?"

"No. Let it play out. We'll be home Sunday night and we can reevaluate then. If it is a true threat, we don't want anyone alerted that we realize it. I'll be in town Wednesday. I won't let her take the meeting alone, if it comes to that. If the appointment is legitimate, she can meet with Pickard and get the new business."

"Understood. I have asked Charlie to keep this between us."

"Probably a good idea. What about the Rossi agreements? Has Gianni accepted yet?"

"Yes. Just. That was the other reason for my call."

"That's good news." I'm that much closer to getting R.E.E. off the scent of my uncle's land and removing Ireland from my life. "Have Lionel reach out to R.E.E. and set up the meeting as we discussed." I move to the refrigerator in the kitchen for a bottle of water. "And California is under control?"

"As far as I'm aware, sir. Curtis tells me she's still in-patient at The Meadows."

"How is Huck?"

Alexis has been enjoying a glass of wine with my mother at the kitchen island. This left both of them feeling chatty, and I excused myself to answer the phone in private. We're in the same room now, close enough that Alexis overhears me say her boy's name. She makes her way over to join me.

"Is that Byron?" she asks.

I nod.

"Please," she says, "can I?"

"Byron, Alexis would like to speak with you." I hand her the phone. "You can disconnect when you're done," I tell her. "I'm all set."

She greets Byron in such a cheery demeanor, I know she's working on a good buzz. I hear her ask about Huck as I cross the room to join my mother.

"Aidan," she says, gesturing me closer. She lays a hand on my shoulder. "I absolutely adore her."

"Good," I say. "So do I."

"Well that much is obvious. I've never seen you so happy."

I roll my eyes at her. "Don't go all Mom on me," I say. "You're so much cooler than that."

She laughs, uninhibited after her glass of wine. My mother is not a big drinker. One is usually her limit.

"I can't observe that my son is happier than I've ever known him to be?"

I smile. She's right, but I'm thrown off hearing it from everyone.

"Listen," she continues. "I know you thought we believed in your relationship with Stella." She looks at me in earnest. "But I must tell you, your father and I tolerated that relationship. It was never our intention to encourage it. I know it may not have seemed that way at times, but your father was often trying to keep the peace with John Ireland. And I know you were, too."

"How do you mean?" I can't help wonder what she knows.

"John Ireland is not a good person, Aidan. That's all I'm going to say. And I have a feeling you know this. I'm just glad your dealings with him are done."

I suck in a breath. I'm relieved she doesn't know the full story. Hopefully it won't be an issue for much longer. I don't know what she's referring to when she speaks of Dad's dealings with the bastard, but I don't ask more.

"Everyone loves Alexis," she says. "We support you one hundred percent this time, honey. Trust me and trust yourself." She smiles and pulls me down to plaster a kiss on my cheek and speak in my ear softly. "You're a perfect match."

By dark, I'm a bit lit. My parents and their friends are upstairs relaxing on the porch. I'm sipping whiskey as the five of us are sitting around the fire pit on the brick patio, down near the water. A discussion has ensued about music, and Alexis and Oates are debating personal preferences.

"You're kidding me," Oates says. "I can't believe you'd pick The Beatles over The Stones too. You're my people."

"Hands down," she says. "Any day of the week." She's noticeably buzzed too, but not as out of her own control as she'd been the night I accosted her at Mac's. She sets down her glass of whiskey (rocks, not neat as I've chosen) and leans in towards him. He's seated noticeably close to Pam, who is looking on with admiration. "However," Alexis says, "we can have the Paul vs. Paul debate, and I'd change my tune."

"McCartney vs. Simon?" Oates says. "No way." He pushes up his glasses, leaning forward to rest a hand on his knee, his elbow cocked out in challenge. "You prefer Simon over McCartney?"

"Yep." She sits back in her chair, crossing her legs. "Paul Simon wins that head-to-head in my book every time."

"*Bah*," Oates says in frustration. "Pierce. Tell me you don't agree with her on this. This is a character flaw that should not escape your attention.

A short-sightedness of epic proportions."

"I don't know," I say. "She's a lawyer. She must have something to back up her claim. Hear her out."

"McCartney was a fucking *Beatle*," he says. "There's no arguing with that. Simon is just..." he trails off. "He just doesn't compare."

"Oh come on," Alexis insists. "He's a master at writing lyrics. He's in a league of his own."

"Bullshit," Oates says. "The Beatles were the ones in their own league. You can't compare the two. It's just a coincidence they're both named Paul. It's like comparing a legit music legend to...shit, I don't know," he says exasperated, "to a washed-up hippie that happens to go by the same name."

"Says you," my girl asserts. "I happen to think Paul Simon is a genius."

"But McCartney collaborated with John fucking *Lennon*, Alexis. You know, the same guy that wrote "Imagine"? I mean," Oates shakes his head, then makes a swirling motion with his finger near his temple. "You're loco, girl."

"Lennon wrote "Imagine" after being inspired by Yoko's poetry," I offer. "McCartney was a non-factor."

"Lennon was also notoriously abusive to his wives," Nate pipes in. "Not exactly a role model for peace."

"Damn, guys," Oates says. "You sure know how to throw a brother under the bus."

We're all laughing at his expense now, but Alexis puts a hand on his in reassurance.

"It's okay, Daryl," she says. "I admit my personal opinion is biased."

I can't help but ask. "Why's that?"

She looks at me with a shy smile.

"Simon and Garfunkel were one of my dad's favorites."

"Well that's no reason to have such a strong opinion," Oates says.

I wait for her to continue. She's so fucking adorable. And sexy. She's wearing one of the skirts I'd picked for her when I shopped online at The Red Door.

Her gorgeous stems are visible. The soft cotton fabric is slit high up the middle. When she stands up, the navy and white striped garment flows around her, swaying as she walks. But as she's sitting down with legs crossed, I'm getting a killer view.

Her tits are perfection in the tight white tank top with thin straps that grace her shoulders. She must have a strapless bra on underneath.

Fuck.

Now I'm sporting a semi-hard-on.

"Maybe not," she replies to Oates. "But I used to listen to their music with him a lot," she says wistfully. "They bring up good memories of him. That's reason enough for me."

I squeeze her hand.

God, I want to take her to bed.

"Fair point," Oates says. "I concede."

"Good," she says. "And I'd think someone named after an eighties rock duo would have done so long ago."

"You told her?" Oates throws his empty plastic cup at me and I catch it, then toss it in the fire pit. "Damn, man. Not only did you throw me under the bus, now you've gone and backed over a brother twice."

"Relax," I laugh. "I didn't tell her anything. But you just confirmed it for her, shit for brains."

Pam speaks up. "Who were you named after?"

"It isn't the exact same name," Alexis says. "How did you end up with it, Mr. Oates?"

"Yes, okay? I admit it. My mother was a diehard eighties music *fah-naaa-tic*. My dad's last name is Oates. And she loved Hall and Oates. End of story."

Pam is still in the dark, too young to realize the connection.

"Daryl Hall and John Oates," Alexis says. "Hall and Oates. They had a lot of hits in the eighties."

Nate busts into "Rich Girl" and we all laugh (except for Oates).

"I know that song," Pam says. "Didn't they also sing the song from *Flashdance*?"

"Yeah," I say. Pam is a cute girl. She may be young, but she's smart. Her pleasant personality made her a great addition to the evening. Watching her throw my friend off his game is also enjoyable entertainment.

"We used to play that song in our warmups for volleyball. That's so cool."

The two of them share a smile, and I can see Oates' embarrassment fade quickly to pride.

"Yeah," he says. "It's not so bad I guess."

"Your mother didn't want to take it all the way and name you John Oates?" Alexis finishes her drink and sets it aside. "Why'd she use Daryl instead?"

"My grandfather's name was John and she was not too fond of him.

He was kind of a bastard. So," he says, "she settled for the next best thing."

Alexis flashes my friend her killer smile and Oates responds in kind.

I have to have her.

Now.

"Should we call it a night?"

Everyone looks at me as though I'm crazy, except Alexis.

My baby knows exactly what's on my mind.

"I am kind of tired," she says.

"Actually, I've been up nearly twenty-four solid," Nate says. "Point me to my bed and we shall reconvene this round table tomorrow night."

"You and Oates in the boathouse," I say. "Alexis and I in Brat Cottage. Pam, would you be comfortable staying in a guest room in the main house?"

"Really?" Her eyes fly open wide. "Mr. Pierce," she teases with an elated smile, "you, kind sir, have just made my freakin' year."

We barely get in the door of the cottage and Alexis takes the lead before I can. We don't make it past the small kitchen, which is the first room beyond the front door. It's dark, the only source of light coming from a bulb over a small, old-fashioned stove.

She's taken everything below my waist to the floor, dropping to her knees and taking me in before I can object. Thankfully, my body is swimming with drink and I should be able to hold out longer than I would otherwise. I intend to fulfill my earlier promise and bend her over until she can take no more.

Her tongue is doing something different though, and my willpower is fading fast.

"Up," I tell her. "Come here."

As she pulls off, I step out of my shorts, then strip my shirt off. She's got a look in her eye I've not seen before, not even during our most intimate moments. Apparently, there's a just-right amount of liquor my baby can indulge in – just enough that her inhibitions fade while not becoming fall down drunk.

"Someone is feeling it tonight," I comment.

"You bet your sweet ass, babe," she says. "I've wanted to jump on you since our ride up here this morning. Take me to bed."

I lick my lips. "Not yet."

She looks at me with inquiring eyes. "Are you telling me you don't want to take me to bed?"

"I'm telling you I'm giving you exactly what I promised earlier. This way."

I head for the dining room in the dark, using my memory and hoping I don't run into any newly placed furniture on my way. We arrive in the room unharmed, our hands clasped, and I get the first glimpse at exactly the surface I was hoping for – the dining room table.

The walls on two sides of the dining room are floor-to-ceiling windows facing the river, where this part of the cottage teases the end of a granite cliff. We're far lower than the main house, only ten feet above the water below. The bare glass provides a full view of stars and a first quarter moon in the night sky. The single panes are thin enough that we can hear water breaking softly on the rock below.

I can hear her lose her breath when she catches sight of the view.

The only room of the single-story cottage we'd previously seen today was my bedroom, where we'd deposited our bags in a hurry and changed clothes before dinner to join everyone else. We'd both wanted to stay here and devour each other then but had dutifully decided against it knowing time would be short with everyone.

But now she is mine for the taking. As slow or as fast, as soft or as hard as I wanted her, we had the time. And I want to be at her hard, to possess her as I previously have not done.

"Aidan, this view." She walks to the windows and my breathing intensifies just watching her stand there. Her silhouette in the windows, the way her hair falls on her bare shoulders, the moon shining in on her.

She's other-worldly.

A myth.

A fucking unicorn.

Mine.

She turns around and I nod for her to come back to me, to the other end of the long, polished oak table. As soon as she's within inches, I grab for her, kissing her as I've wanted to do since the last time I had to stop. I lick at her salty lips, biting the bottom one before I take over her mouth again.

"Aidan," she breathes, breaking our kiss. "I need you come to bed with me. Like yesterday."

I don't answer her. I strip her of her tank top and toss it on the table where her head's about to be.

But oh, holy God in Heaven.

It's the first time I've seen her in a strapless bra and she looks damn amazing. It's white and lacy and sexy as sin. I pull one cup down at a time, teasing her nipples in an attempt to further rile her. My method is accepted as she drops her head back, moaning until I replace the fabric and stop only to instruct her.

"Keep this on."

I don't remove her skirt either, instead spinning her around quickly and guiding her forward, splaying her flat on the table.

"Oh," she says, "this is what you meant."

"That's right, baby. Senseless." I lift her skirt up from the bottom, gathering it up over her hips, then relieve her of her thong by ripping it off her. "Hope you've got more of those."

She lets out a throaty laugh and it sends me into a tailspin.

I need to be inside her.

She tries to stand and lift her upper body off the table but I lean over her, settling her back down. I'm draped over her back as I encourage her to stretch her arms out above her head and lay flat. Her head rests to the side with her shirt as a cushion.

"Keep your arms here," I whisper in her ear. "You're okay?" I suck at her earlobe, then drive my tongue where I know it makes her crazy.

"Mm-hmm."

"If you're uncomfortable, tell me to stop."

She just nods. Her pouncing-like-a-panther mood has suddenly shifted. She's still breathing heavy, still anticipating my every touch. But she's also nervous.

"This will feel good," I tell her. "We'll start slow. I'm not going to hurt you, baby."

"I know," she breathes. "I trust you, Aidan."

I can't remember her ever saying these words to me before. They send me soaring with emotion, wanting to claim her more than ever.

I lean up from her, then bend to kiss her shoulder blades where they peek out from under the clasp of her skimpy bra, trailing my lips down the center of her bare back. She moans when I run my tongue from the indentation at her lower back, moving out to each of her hips in turn.

I drop to the floor on my knees to be underneath her while I hold her skirt up, readying her with my tongue, working her with my fingers. She's wet in seconds, and I bring her to soaking before I stand back up. I grab for her hips and pull her close roughly, but without entering her. She gasps and, hearing the sound, I can't wait anymore.

I enter her slowly at first, wanting her to become used to the position.

I pull back, then move deep inside her again, my hands on her hips.

"Yes?"

"Yes," she moans again. "Don't stop."

I start at her faster, wanting her to feel every inch of me, as deep as possible. I rest a hand on her back and keep one on her left hip as I start to drive harder.

"Oh, God. *Yesssss,*" she says.

There she is.

My baby is here with me, relaxed at last and letting her body fall into my rhythm. I pick up my pace and move both hands back to her hips, then circle one around so I can work her clit.

She blurts obscenities as she comes hard, all while I'm watching her heave up and down in front of me, rising and falling on the solid wood beneath her, mesmerizing me. Once I get my bearings and she's sufficiently relaxed, I pull out and take a step away.

"Take one step back, baby."

She nods as each exhale of breath becomes less labored, complying as soon as she's able.

"Lean over," I tell her. "Like you're going to touch your toes." Again she follows direction, her arms down, hands easily falling flat to the floor beneath her.

Damn she's limber.

I'm ready to explode just looking at her ass. She's the perfect height for this position, the perfect fit for me. I take hold of her hips again and enter her as she screams my name. She is so tight this way, even as wet as she is.

"Sei mia, il mio amore." I say. *"Si prega di dire che sei mio."*

I explode into her after only a few more driving thrusts, and she stands up trying to steady herself as soon as I let her break away. She leans her hands on the table, her back to me as she catches her breath.

"English," she finally manages. She's not looking at me. She's absolutely spent, and I lived up to my promise. I may have let her off a little easy, but she can take no more tonight. She's pretty damn close to senseless.

I peel her skirt to the floor, leaving her standing there in just her white lace bra. I pick her up, cradling her in my arms as I carry her to bed. I lay her down and she stretches out to capacity. Every limb is a sexy extension, from her fingertips where they touch the headboard to the tips of her toes.

I whisper her name as I make my way from her feet all the way to her neck with soft kisses, not wanting to miss an inch of her. I'm enjoying the sounds of her soft moans of appreciation. She is satiated, as content as I've ever seen her.

"Mine," I tell her. "That's what I said. Please say you are mine, my love."

"Yes," she says. She holds my face to hers, her eyes cutting through me. "A thousand times over." She urges me to collapse on her, her arms surrounding me as I start to drift, the motion of her fingertips gliding over my back calming me towards sleep. "I'm yours," she whispers. "Never question it."

28

Alexis

I wake up to the sound of something hitting the bedroom windows, the noise loud enough to wake me out of a sound sleep.

I'm wrapped up in Aidan, who is vocally sharing he's unhappy as I untangle myself from him, curious about the noise. I get up, taking the sheet with me. I open the bedroom curtain to see Oates cruising by in the water below. He's driving an old Boston Whaler as he tosses pine cones at the window from a stockpile next to him.

"This guy cracks me up," I say to Aidan.

"Wake up in there," Oates shouts from afar. "You two lovesick puppies gonna sleep the day away?"

Instinctively, I duck at the next toss of ammunition, though there's glass between us. I wave to him as he continues to float by. Aidan is hollering back in his most polite tone that Oates should fuck off as I move away from the window and crawl back in bed.

"What time is it?" He's face down, completely naked, his muscular arms perfect triangles folded on either side of his head. His hands are hidden under a massive pillow. I'm studying his body, admiring everything in my sight. I have the sudden urge to smack him on the ass but, fearful of the repercussions, I don't.

"I have no idea," I say. "But the sun is up. Oates is up. And, apparently, we are not."

"He needs to get out of my Whaler," he says. "That maiden voyage should have been mine. She's been put away for years. I didn't know Dad got her going again."

"Maybe Daryl didn't know," I offer. "How about you take me out in it later and make it my maiden voyage?"

"You're such a problem solver, baby." He rolls over and pulls me into him, nuzzling my neck. "Such an admirable quality."

He leans back, revealing his typical I-just-woke-up greeting which is unhindered by boxers this morning. "You are rising and shining as always," I say.

Damn.

His favorite muscle is straining towards his perfect upper body.

He is too much to resist.

I climb on top of him, taking full advantage yet surprised I'm not sore from the night before. Rather than let me take control, Aidan is helping me, moving me up and down by my hips, then moving underneath me at his will.

"God damn," he says. "You are so fucking sexy in the morning."

I smile and lean down to him, kissing his bare chest, relishing in the way he feels beneath me, skin to skin. He moves me in a different way and hits a place so deep I gasp.

"There it is." He repeats the motion again, and my reaction is the same. "Let go," he urges. "Come for me."

It takes little effort with this technique and I'm following orders like he's my boss. I'm coming hard, trying to stifle my screams not knowing who might be outside within earshot.

He lets me come down only for a brief moment before he lifts me off of him and flips me over. He pulls my hips up to meet him, taking me from behind similar to the way he did last night, but without the benefit of a dining room table beneath me. He's tugging at my hair, driving into me with enough force that I move forward on the bed each time. Finally, he's filling me up, collapsing in a heap on top of me, pressing me into the enormous feather bed.

"Holy fuck," he manages. "At this rate you're going to kill me. You realize that?"

"I thought men needed this sort of release regularly to keep a clear head," I insist. "Surely it's me that's going to an early grave."

He rolls off me and pulls me into him.

"Did you enjoy that?"

I give him a look that says don't be ridiculous, but he doesn't answer. "You really don't know?"

"Just making sure my baby is satisfied." He kisses my forehead. "Now let's get motivated. I know that look," he adds, reading me. "You need coffee and you're hungry."

"I am," I say. "Between the alcohol and you last night, I'm ravenous. I could eat anything you put in front of me."

He smiles his shit-eating grin. "Much as I'd like to test that, it's Saturday. Mom's got bacon and eggs up there," he says. "I can guarantee it."

We've finished a wonderful breakfast put together by Aidan's parents. He was right, his mom had cooked the same meal she had for her family every Saturday of the summers they'd spent here. Bacon and eggs, along with fruit and bagels and every other thing you might wish for at the first meal of the day.

Nate and Oates have eaten three plates full of food. In contrast, Pam has eaten like a bird. She hadn't been expending as much energy as Aidan and me, since she slept alone last night. I loved the way Aidan had taken control of that situation, like he was her big brother. He hadn't given any opportunity for his friend to make a play for Pam, even though she probably would not mind if Oates had tried.

My heart swells as I watch Aidan's parents move about the kitchen together. They have a great affection for one another, teasing each other as they tackle domestic chores.

The guys are not witness to this as they've now left us to take a spin in the Whaler. Pam is upstairs getting a shower, which I'd done before Aidan and I made the walk up from the cottage.

"Thank you for breakfast," I say to his parents as they're cleaning up. I offered to help many times but they refused.

"Glad to do it," Reggie says. "It was easy with this small group. Our friends left early to head to the mainland. They're taking one of those boat cruises today." He looks so handsome, showered and dressed in tan shorts and a short-sleeved button down.

"Honestly, this is one of the things I miss most about being up here," Tori says to me.

She's putting clean dishes away and hasn't yet readied herself for the day. She's wearing a lightweight robe that looks expensive, yet she still seems the type of attentive mom you'd want to come home to at the end of a school day.

"I never had help when we came here. We hired caterers for parties, bartenders, things like that. But when we were here as a family, I was in this room doing exactly this for all my boys." She smiles wistfully at her husband as he pulls her up to his side and kisses the top of her head. "I wouldn't trade those times for anything."

I'm sure they're lost in recollections. From their expressions, I can see they're happy ones.

"I'm heading to the porch with my laptop for a bit," Reggie says. "When you're dressed, let's take the Victoria out for a spin, hmm?"

"Sounds wonderful." Tori kisses him on the cheek and he leaves us.

"Can you tell me a little about Thad?" I ask once we're alone. "Aidan doesn't like to talk about him much."

Tori sighs. "Oh, honey, I could go on about my son straight through tomorrow." She shoots me a smile and lays a hand on mine. "Let's talk about it after lunch, okay? We'll have some girl time."

"I'd love that."

"Be patient with Aidan," she says. "He'll come around. It's not his brother he doesn't want to talk about. It's the fact that he's no longer with us."

I nod politely, feeling remorseful for bringing it up. "I'm sorry," I say. "Sometimes I need to learn to keep my mouth shut."

"Oh no," she chastises. "Don't ever feel bad for talking about my boy. That's one thing Aidan just never came to grips with that talking about him is a good thing. I love to tell stories about the two of them. It keeps Thad with us, keeps him close."

"That's how I feel about my dad. But it's different with Ben. I find that harder to talk about. Maybe because it's so recent, I don't know. But I can relate to his hesitancy."

"When it comes to his brother, Aidan blames himself. He probably always will." She looks away a moment, then back to me as she lays her hand on mine again. "That loss nearly killed him, darling. In fact," she adds, "it nearly killed us all."

I go upstairs to find Pam, almost getting lost in the giant house. I only find her when I call out for her and she shouts back to me.

"In here."

I make my way down a long hall in the opposite direction from the master suite, which is to the left at the top of the grand stairway. Pam's voice has come from the right. I move past the open doorways of two empty bedrooms, likely where the Hamiltons and Reeds are staying.

She pokes her head out of the third door I come to.

"Get in here," she says. "You're not even going to believe this room!"

I laugh at her enthusiasm, following her into a medium-sized bedroom with a bathroom attached where Pam is now drying her hair.

A four-poster cherry bed is angled in the corner of the bedroom. A fireplace is tucked into the opposite corner and next to it is one of the gable windows that looks out over the river.

The view draws me in and I walk to the window in time to see the Victoria glide away from the island. Aidan and the guys pass by his parents and everyone waves to each other.

"The boys are back," I holler towards the bathroom. The hair dryer cuts out.

"What?" Pam asks.

"I said the boys are back."

"Awesome!" she shouts as she fires up the appliance again. "I can't wait to get a look at that boy again. Did you see him at breakfast? He's so cute!"

I laugh, heading to the bathroom to join her. The hair dryer is put away and she's applying mascara in front of the mirror.

"I saw him," I say. "He could barely eat his gigantic breakfast he was so busy staring at you."

I'm blown away by the amenities of the bathroom as I walk in. A floor to ceiling marble wall is smack in the middle of the room. The white and gray stone is accented with a two-sided gas fireplace, revealing a gorgeous clawfoot tub on the other side. Pam is standing at the sink, in the aisle between the vanity and the tub.

"Wow," I say. "You were right. This room is over the top."

"Freaking amazing, right?" She's pulling her hair up into a ponytail. Her outfit is similar to yesterday, a dress in a lime green color with the same shoes she had on the day before. Her chest fills out the dress noticeably and is accented by the pretty silver chain around her neck. Oates will be drooling when he sees her.

She looks at me through the mirror.

"I'm so happy to see you happy, Lex. And Ben is happy too," she adds. "I can feel it."

"Thank you," I tell her. "I hope so."

"He is." She turns around to face me. "He was always so grateful for having you in his life. But he felt like you deserved more. He wanted this for you. Don't ever think he didn't."

She hugs me, and I well up with tears.

God, I'm such an emotional wreck lately.

"Thank you, Pam. I'm so glad you're here."

"Right?" she says, pulling back and holding me at arm's length. "I cannot thank you enough for this weekend. I needed this break at the end of school and this place," she says, looking around. "Just that I got to set foot in it has made my little girl dreams come true. It's off the hook!"

I smile at her. "I know," I say. "The great thing is the people that live here appreciate it as much as we do."

"They *so* do," she says. "The Pierce family is a great bunch. And speaking of bunches," she turns to the mirror and dots her lips with some gloss, "let's go get me some Honey Bunches of Oates."

By afternoon, we're lazing on the sun deck in chaises some twenty feet above the water. It's hot for early June, but I didn't bring a bathing suit, knowing how cold the water is this early in the season. I'm soaking up the rays anyway in shorts and tank top. Aidan is stretched out next to me. Pam and Oates are fishing off the lower dock, and Nate is nearby in an Adirondack chair reading.

I turn my head to look at Aidan and notice he's dozing off.

"Are you a bit hung today, babe?"

"Nope." He smiles and grabs for my hand without opening his eyes.

"I call bullshit. You have a hangover. You never sleep as late as you did today."

"Must be the fresh air."

"Oh yeah?" I ask. I know he's full of it.

"You cannot prove that I have a headache raging through me like a bullet train right now," he says, "and I'll never admit it."

"Babe. Don't be a hero. Get some ibuprofen."

"I'm good," he says. He pulls his shades from his shirt and puts them on.

"Why are you letting yourself suffer? I'll go up and get you some."

He lifts the sunglasses to look at me. "I'm fine, baby. Really."

"If you insist," I say. "I don't know why you have to be so fucking stubborn."

Nate laughs from across the deck.

"That's Pierce," he says. "Get used to it, Lex."

I smile at his informality when he shortens my name. Nate Edwards is a serious individual. He exudes intelligence. But he's also kind and witty, and he's one of few people that seem to understand the inner workings of Aidan Pierce.

"Me?" Aidan sits himself up. "You're calling me stubborn?"

"No," I say, correcting him. "I'm calling you so *fucking* stubborn."

"Oh that's it, woman," he threatens as he stands up. "You're in trouble."

I'm afraid of what I've gotten myself into. He's got that mischievous look in his eye.

"Lex," Nate says without looking up from his book, "you should run."

"Nate," Aidan says in a raised voice. "What do we do when we're challenged on this deck?" He tosses his sunglasses on his chair.

Nate looks up and smiles. Now his grin matches Aidan's, and I'm regretting whatever I said to start this.

"Oates," Nate hollers. "Get your ass up here! Someone's gonna be jumpin'!"

What the hell did he just say?

I grip the sides of my chair, unwilling to move. My regret has morphed into bone-chilling fear.

"Aidan, what the hell is he talking about?"

He just smiles back at me as Oates and Pam come running up to the deck out of breath.

"What's going on?" Pam asks. "Daryl says somebody's gonna jump off the deck?"

I look at Aidan, not hiding the sheer panic in my eyes.

"No," I say. "No. Fucking. Way."

"Oh yes, baby." He strips off his shirt as Oates and Nate do the same.

These fuckers are crazy.

"Pam," Aidan says. He hands her his phone. "Run in for some towels, then down to the lower dock to take some pictures of my baby jumping."

Pam sees my expression as I shake my head violently.

No.

"Um, somehow I don't think she's going to go along with that," Pam says. "Do you know how cold that water is?"

"Sixty degrees tops," he says as he stares me down. When she doesn't move, he turns his attention to her. "Go," he says, "or she's going to freeze her ass off down there without a towel."

Pam has gotten a glimpse of don't-fuck-with-me Aidan. She's off like a shot.

Dammit.

"Aidan, you know I hate heights." When he'd taken me to the rooftop at his loft, I'd been unable to go anywhere near the edge of the building.

"Babe," he coaxes, "you're doing it."

"Actually," I say in defiance, "there's no way in hell I'm doing this. It's like fifty feet to the water. I don't even have a suit." I dismiss him as I wave my hand towards the water. "You guys go ahead."

"It's less than twenty feet," Nate says. "Child's play."

Aidan comes at me, wrapping me up and charming me with his concern. He tucks a hair that's come loose from my ponytail behind my ear.

"You are doing this. You called me stubborn, and here you are throwing down like you're the queen of it. Prove me wrong, babe. Prove yourself wrong. I hate it when you limit yourself."

As much as I'm endeared by his attempt to get me out of my own head, I refuse to budge. I am deathly afraid of heights, and I'm not a big fan of freezing cold water either. Nate moves to the edge of the deck, and I realize there is no railing on the far side of it.

How did I not notice that before?

"There's no railing," I whisper. "Isn't that against code or something?"

Aidan just smiles.

My palms are sweaty. I haven't even moved close enough to the edge to look down at the water.

"I'm ready," Pam hollers from the main dock below.

Nate turns back to us. "It's no big deal, Lex. Watch," he says. "I'll show you how it's done."

He turns around with his back to the water. His toes are the only thing left in contact with the solid deck. He bounces a couple times, then does a backflip.

A freaking full-on, I'm-a-professional-diver backflip.

I move closer to the edge to watch him plummet below. He reaches the water, his body perfectly straight as he dives headfirst with minimal splash.

"Holy fuck!" I say to Aidan. "Did you see that?"

"I did," he says. He's standing next to me now.

"How did he do that?" I watch below as Nate emerges from the water. He swims effortlessly to the ladder of the dock where Pam awaits.

"We swam together in college," Aidan says. "His event was diving."

I throw my hands up in the air. "You expect me to jump off this ridiculously high platform like it's my chosen Olympic event?"

"Do you know how to swim?"

"Of course," I say. "It's not that, it's just..."

"Hey, chica," Oates says. "I'm not a diver or a competitive swimmer, but I see my lady down there waiting and I'm going for it." He takes a few long strides back as Aidan and I step aside. He runs for the edge and jumps, falling to the water below in a perfectly formed cannon ball. As he drops the million feet down, he's hollering something to Pam about coming for his princess.

I chuckle at him, though I'm still nervous as all get out.

"Your turn, baby."

"Aidan, please don't make me do this."

"I'm not giving you a choice."

I turn to look down, making sure Oates has arrived at the dock safely. Pam is handing him a towel. Even from up here, I can see her admiring his body. He is a pretty handsome dude if you're into that kind of geeky charm.

"Let 'er rip, tater chip!" Oates shouts up to us.

"No way!" I holler back.

Before I know what's happening, Aidan charges me. Just as he reaches the spot where I stand dangerously close to the edge, he stops dead in his tracks. "You must believe in yourself, baby," he tells me. "I'll never let you give up."

He pulls me tight into his chest and just as I think he's letting me out of this little dare, he takes a firm hold of me and shoves us both out over the water.

We're falling, falling, falling, and I'm screaming my fool head off the whole way down.

He lets go of me somewhere around the halfway point, and I can't bring myself to look down. I instinctively curl my legs up into my chest, cannon balling like Oates as I splash into the water below.

The freezing cold water.

Oh. My. God.

I surface out of breath, treading water and looking around for Aidan. I can't see him anywhere, and I have no idea how deep the water is here.

Did he hit his head on a shoal and sink to the bottom?

Bubbles rise to the surface as he comes up from beneath me. He cradles me under my legs and drapes my arms around his neck. I'm pissed enough to let him do all the work as he kicks behind himself, pushing both of us to the dock.

The guys and Pam are cheering, hollering congratulations that I did it. I'm not sure they realize I didn't have a choice. But I am secretly happy that I took the leap.

Though I'd been forced, Aidan made me realize I could do something I didn't think I could, the way he always does. I plan to withhold this fact for as long as I can out of sheer spite.

"I knew you could do it, baby," he says. "How do you feel?"

"Exhilarated. Pissed," I say. "And like my life was just shortened by ten years."

"I know," he smiles. "Isn't it great?"

We reach the dock and he plants a kiss on me in front of everyone, then hefts me up under the arms towards the ladder. I'm shivering, probably as much from adrenaline as from the cold water. Pam wraps me up with a huge fluffy towel when I get out.

"I can't believe you did it, Lex," she says with hands on my shoulders. "That. Was. Awesome!"

"Yeah, chica!" Oates hollers. He throws up his fist to bump mine, and I can't help my smile.

He and Nate are standing there in towels with their very handsome chests exposed, nipping out, and crawling with goosebumps.

We're all cold, apparently.

"Congrats," Nate says. "Nothing like taking that first leap. Want to do it again?"

"No way," I say. "But thanks for the offer."

Aidan climbs up after me, thanking Pam as she passes him a towel.

"Hot tub," he says. "Let's go, guys."

"Damn," Pam says. "That I could handle. But I didn't bring a suit."

"Me either," I spout. "Apparently that isn't a requirement."

"You can borrow one of my t-shirts," Oates tells her. "Come on, we'll stop by the boathouse and get one. The hot tub is in that direction anyway." He gestures towards the opposite side of the island.

"We'll be right behind you guys," Aidan says.

Everyone heads in the direction of the main house, up the path that criss-crosses the island and leads to the boathouse. Before I can follow, Aidan pulls me to him and rests his chin on my head.

"You still pissed?"

"Maybe." My grin says otherwise.

"Well there's an easy way to correct that." He tosses me over his shoulder. "Let's get you out of these wet clothes."

29

Alexis

By four o'clock Saturday afternoon, I've forgiven Aidan twice. Once in a hot shower at the cottage and a second time when he made a meal out of me in bed.

We're now in the kitchen back at the main house getting things ready for dinner. His parents haven't arrived yet, and neither have their friends. Aidan sent his dad a text telling them to take their time and arrive for appetizers and cocktails by five-thirty.

The five of us 'kids' have taken over, handling designated chores to prep a dinner party for all of us including the couple that opened up The Gables. The Lonergans are due here at five-thirty too, and Aidan wanted to keep his mother from having to do everything herself. We're slated to eat dinner at eight.

I'm learning that wealthy people tend to sup late.

Oates marinated enough chicken to feed a small army and basted a ton of skewered shrimp. Pam is on the porch, throwing together whatever appetizer was planned, and Oates excuses himself to help her. Aidan is boiling potatoes on the stove, I'm chopping veggies for a salad, and Nate (much to my surprise) is baking a cake.

From scratch.

"What's up with that," I whisper to Aidan. "He likes to bake? Is he gay?"

Aidan lets out a laugh, thankfully not loud enough to draw attention.

"No," he whispers back. "He loves the science of it. It's math. A formula. Fuck it up and you end up with a hot pile of goo and not a delicious cake. Get it?"

I nod. I do. Nate is seriously a neat guy.

"What's his story then? No girlfriend?"

"Not anymore," he says. "Bad break up once upon a time. And now he has no free time." He lifts the carrot I have in my hand to his mouth and bites it. "Therefore, no opportunity. Even if he met someone, he'd never see her. His line of work is pretty top-secret."

Dang. Neat and mysterious.

"That's unfortunate," I say. "Look what he's missing out on."

"Trust me, babe. I know." He sends me his charming smile. "I'm just glad Oates told my mother Nate was coming. He would've been pissed if he had time off and didn't get to make his world-famous cake. She must've planned for all the groceries knowing he'd be here. How are you coming on that salad?"

"Good," I say. "All set." I cover up the metal bowl and place it in the enormous Sub-Zero fridge. "What time are the Hamiltons and Reeds getting back from their day tour?"

"Any time," he says. "I think the Hamiltons were looking to buy a place up here. Maybe they found something and decided to look into it further."

"Why here?"

"Well, because it's here," he says. "It's beautiful. Don't you agree?"

"Yes, definitely. But it's quite a hike from California."

"It's close to Manhattan. That's where they typically live in the warmer months. It was luck that they were in California when my parents invited them to fly out here."

"I feel like that name is familiar," I say. "What does Mr. Hamilton do for a living?"

"He co-owns a pro football team," Aidan says matter-of-factly. "But he was a Hollywood producer by trade. Back in the day, that is. He's been retired a long time."

Holy shit.

"Wait," I say. "He's *that* Donald Hamilton?"

I'm so out of my league here.

I urge Aidan to give me the backgrounds of the rest of the guests that have been on the same island as we have for the last twenty-four hours, as well as the couple showing up here in acceptance of gratitude for opening The Gables. I'm dying to know what I'm going into at dinner.

As it turns out Mrs. Hamilton was an actress in B-movies once upon a time, which is how she met Mr. Hamilton.

Mr. and Mrs. Reed own an organic dairy farm and a winery in California as well as a resort in Mexico often frequented by the Hollywood elite. They spend most of their time traveling now, having handed down their day-to-day business operations to their children.

The Lonergans are distant relatives to British royalty and are local real estate agents for high-end properties here in Canada. They also manage three marinas along the St. Lawrence River.

"Jesus Christ, Aidan. You could have told me all this sooner. I feel like an idiot."

"Why?" He looks at me as though I'm crazy. "They're just people, Alexis. I thought you were above that."

"I don't mean because they have money or prominent careers that they're any better or any less than the rest of us. I'm just…God, I think I told Mr. Hamilton a joke at dinner last night that was a bit off color. I never would have done that had I known that he was, you know, *that* Donald Hamilton."

He's smiling at me in amusement now. "From what I recall, he found your joke very funny. He was laughing straight through dessert. I heard him repeat it to my father on the porch before we went down to the fire pit."

"Really?"

"Really. Just relax, babe. It's not a big deal. Peoples is peoples, as they say."

"But you're used to running in these circles. I'm not. And you're as comfortable with this group as you are on a boat in the middle of Falcon Lake waving at two grumpy old farts in a canoe. Or speaking to a room full of strangers and asking them to approve of your dreams and invest their time and money into them too. How do you do that?"

"You misread me," he says. He gives the pot of boiling potatoes a stir, then replaces the lid.

The oven beeps that it's preheated and Nate enters the room again, coming towards us with his cake pans. He'd been in the foyer on a phone call and now places the pans in the oven. He's still listening through his earbuds and talking into the microphone hanging around his neck. He mutes his call to speak to us.

"Check it at twenty-two minutes. And for fuck's sake," he says more to Aidan than to me, "do *not* let it overcook."

He retreats again, talking numbers and science and NASA jargon. I turn my attention back to Aidan after setting the timer on the microwave.

"What is it I misread about you?"

"That I'm comfortable in any situation. I can adapt to anything, yes. But I'm much more comfortable alone with you than having to address a crowd of nameless strangers about money or politics or the plight of youth facing drug problems."

I'm floored. I've never heard him say something like this.

"I thought you thrived in those situations," I say. "You can't come as far as you have, built what you have without that being the case."

"Being capable and having it be what you want or where you're most at ease are two different things."

He takes a step away from the stove, standing in front of me, looking me in the eyes. He rests his hands on the counter on either side of me, much like he did the first time he kissed me at my house. My breathing is shallow as his baby blues bore into me.

"We've been surrounded by brewing storms since we met," he says. "But I need you to know, I surround myself with peace as often as possible. I much prefer shutting out the negative buzz of the world whenever I can. And when I involve people in my life, I don't take it lightly."

"I can see that. Everyone I've met has been an absolute joy to be around," I say. "Perhaps with the exception of Ivan."

He smiles at my wisecrack. "I told you it's taken years to get here," he says. "I meant it. And I'd shut them all out to stay in a bubble with you. I just can't afford to do this often and actually accomplish my goals. See the difference?"

I silently nod.

"It's not that I'm more comfortable surrounded by accomplished people or in a business setting. It's not what I prefer. It's just always been necessary."

"I understand," I say.

"That's why I got out of it to pursue philanthropy. It's far more appealing to me than earning money just because I can."

"So essentially, you're retired?" I laugh.

His smile is endearing. "In a manner of speaking."

I lean up to kiss him, not waiting for him to do it. I am completely taken over once again by all that he is, all that he wants to do in this life, while underneath it all we are so much alike.

"I would prefer seeing all the world has to offer on a day when the entire population is somewhere else. Especially if I can have you there with me."

"Really?"

"Anywhere you want to go, any time we can get there. Where haven't you been?"

"Everywhere."

He smiles at me again, and I'm just as bowled over by it as I was seeing him on a magazine cover.

"Seriously," he says. "Where?"

"I haven't been anywhere," I admit. "Here in Canada, New York City a few times. Arizona to visit Jill. That's about it. And I had some cousins in Massachusetts I used to visit with Dad."

"You're kidding. No studying abroad? No crazy trips with college girlfriends?"

"Nope," I say. "Never. Not that I didn't want to. I just never had the means or opportunity."

"Oh, babe," he says, tossing back his head before he rests his eyes on mine again. "This is exciting. I can't wait to take you to some of my favorite places. *Voglio mostrare al mondo di,* Alexis. "

Good Lord.

I feel like I need Nate in here to help me throw up some kind of NASA-worthy force field to defend myself.

"English," I plead.

"I said I want to show you the world, baby." He lowers his voice to a whisper near my ear. "If you'll let me."

Yup. I'm done like dinner.

He lifts my legs up to wrap around him, holding onto my backside. Now he's gotten us both worked up. He's hard, even wet through his shorts. He starts to carry me out of the kitchen.

"Dinner," I say in objection, "and Nate's cake. He'll kill us." Aidan is kissing my throat, my bare shoulders in my strapless sundress. "He might literally have us shot off into space if that cake burns."

"Totally worth it," he says, carrying me up the stairs of the grand house. "Nate," he hollers down. "Get your single white ass in the kitchen and tend to the food. My baby and I are off to conquer the world."

Thankfully, Aidan and I recover from our brief rendezvous upstairs within a half an hour, with twenty minutes to spare before everyone is due back. I'm in the kitchen pouring a glass of wine to use as an excuse if anyone asks why my face is so flush.

Aidan took me to one of the many bedrooms upstairs, and it was only after he'd ravaged me to the point I could hardly stand up that he mentioned we were in the room he once shared with his brother as a kid.

It was the first time he brought Thad up voluntarily.

Before we left the room, he spent a long moment looking out the window staring down at the river. Their old bedroom was in the back of the house and faced the main dock. You could see Brat Cottage if you craned your head to the left. I stood in the doorway, watching him get lost in what I hoped were fond memories.

Then he'd turned back to me cheerful again, as much as he'd been carrying me up the stairs. I didn't push the issue, following his mother's advice. I'd be as patient with him as he needed me to be.

Upon entering the kitchen, we see Nate rescued his cake in time. He insists it came out perfectly. Aidan is now at the stove, working with his cooked potatoes.

"What are you doing to those?"

"Olive oil," he says. "Fresh basil. Salt."

"That's it?" I ask. "Sounds boring."

"No way, baby." He's rubbing his hands together in anticipation. "Simple. Clean eating is not boring. Trust me. I know what I'm doing."

"Did you learn this in Italy?"

"Mm-hmm." He's ignoring me now, tossing everything together in a giant bowl as Oates and Pam stroll in.

"Aww, bruh," Oates says in Aidan's direction. "Are you making Mamasita's favorite taters?"

"I am."

"Wait till you taste these, Pam," Oates says. "They are crazy-sexy good. You'll never want potatoes another way again."

"They're okay," Nate speaks up from his stool. He's tapping away at his phone, presumably working. "But nothing's as kick-ass as Nate's Best Fucking Cake You Will Ever Fucking Taste."

I laugh at that. His sense of humor seems to come out at the most unexpected times.

"Can we help? Apps are all set on the porch," Pam says. "I covered them with those fancy screens to keep out the bugs."

"Ask Aidan," I say, "but I think everything is set."

"Bar," he says over his shoulder. He's a mad man, tending to his dish like he's a world class chef. "Someone could head for the library and get some drinks going."

"Great idea," Nate says. "Let's get the rentals liquored up tonight. C'mon, Oates. You can help me."

"Where are we eating?" Pam asks. "I can set the table."

"Dining room," Aidan says. "Nothing's too good for my peeps."

Pam shoots me a look and we both burst into laughter.

"You've been hanging out with Oates too long," I say.

"For realsies, Pierce," Pam says as she takes a stack of plates and silverware to carry off as instructed. "Even I can see that, and I've only known you twenty-four hours."

As she leaves the room, Aidan laughs to himself while he finishes fussing over his masterpiece, pouring the food into a huge glass dish. He slides it into the oven to keep it warm.

"Let's adjourn, baby," he says. "It's cocktail hour."

I am having the most relaxing evening I can remember in a long time. Dinner came out perfectly, and Aidan's mother was vocally appreciative of all of our work. Everyone loved Aidan's potatoes. Just as Oates promised they were crazy-sexy good.

The older crowd is as tipsy as we were the night before. Raucous conversations have ensued throughout the evening about interesting and random topics.

From law to music, from the field of science and digital technology (thanks to Oates, Pam, and Nate) to American politics (not out of debate but purely for the entertainment of the Canadian couple that's dining with us), we've covered just about everything.

I've managed not to tell any more embarrassing jokes and held my own anyway, probably because I've limited myself to one glass of wine. I don't care how well-received Aidan says my humor was last night. I refuse to have a repeat of that faux pas.

I've taken his advice and conversed with each of the guests as I would anyone else. When you got right down to it (and as usual), Aidan was right. "Peoples is peoples."

At nine o'clock, Nate serves his self-proclaimed "best fucking cake you will ever fucking taste" which Aidan passes on. I notice he hasn't had as much to drink tonight either. He's sipping a whiskey now, but he'd only had water earlier and the thirteen of us have eaten every bit of food that was prepared.

"Well, darlings," Tori says, "since you put on this lovely meal, I'll clean up."

She rises and again I notice how absolutely regal she looks. The sun has kissed her cheeks and neck today. She's wearing a flowing white skirt and a navy top with capped sleeves, the fabric clinging tight to her belly. She is in such great shape. The only jewelry she wears is her wedding ring, a pair of diamond earrings and a few silver bangle bracelets.

"I'll help," Reggie offers. He moves to get up from his seat at the head of the grand mahogany table. We're all seated around it comfortably with room to spare.

"No, dear," she says. "Isn't this when you and the men adjourn to the porch for cigars or something? Alexis and I can handle the clean up." She smiles at me with a wink. "Right?"

"I'd love to." I hadn't had a chance to chat with her privately after lunch. She and Reggie had been gone all afternoon.

The rest of the ladies affirm they'll help, too. The guys break away from the table except for Aidan, who leans in to whisper in my ear before he leaves with the rest of the men.

"I can't wait to take you to bed, baby," he says. He plants a kiss behind my ear. *"Mi manca il modo di gustare."*

I give him a scolding look, but before I can insist my usual command he leans in again.

"I miss the way you taste." With that his tongue finds its way to my ear, and I'm noticeably wet underneath my dress.

I turn to respond, but he's already gone.

Within a half hour, the six of us ladies have managed to get everything cleaned up. Pam has abandoned us in search of Daryl and the three other ladies are enjoying a brandy in the library. The men are on the porch, their laughter carrying to us through the open windows as their conversation ebbs and flows.

Tori and I have seated ourselves at the kitchen island again, each with a glass of Malbec.

"I'd love for you to tell me about meeting my dad," I say to her, "if you're comfortable sharing."

She twirls the stem of her glass between her elegant fingers, considering me.

"Has Aidan told you anything about his childhood?"

I'm surprised at her forward approach, but not at all inclined to be dishonest.

"Some," I say. "I know that your sister was married to Eli Myers, who is essentially my biggest client."

"Emma and Eli were married, yes. He was always very kind to me, though he couldn't offer much help with our situation."

"He still is kind," I say. "My dad always held him in high regard."

"I haven't spoken with him since Emma died," she says. Her tone is wistful and sad as she speaks. She doesn't look at me when she inquires how he's doing.

"He's doing well," I say. "I think he's ready to slow down his operation, though. He's been selling equipment off a little at a time, and as you know he doesn't have any children to pass things on to. His sister's children are his pride and joy, though."

When she doesn't respond, I continue.

"Aidan also told me that Reginald is not his biological father. Beyond that, we haven't discussed many details. I can sense it's painful for him." I don't mention the nightmare I'd woken him from the night before we left New York.

She looks at me as though I've made a grand revelation.

"He told you that?"

I nod.

Was he not supposed to?

I decide not to voice the question.

"He also qualified that by saying Reginald is his one and only dad. He made it very clear to me that he loves your husband as much as any son loves his father."

"Oh, Alexis." She sighs as a gentle smile comes over her. "I'm so glad you and Aidan are not starting out in turmoil the way I had to. And as a young mother no less."

She must know nothing about the Irelands or the craziness we've been facing back home.

"When I met your father, it was at the insistence of Reggie," she says. "Reggie helped me escape the life I was living when Aidan and Thad were just innocent children. Without him, we never would have survived, never would have ended up here. And your father," she says. She lays a hand on mine, looking at me intently with the same soft expression I've seen from Aidan so many times. "He was a very big part of that."

"How so?" I can't help it. My curiosity is on overload.

"He helped Reggie adopt the boys."

My heart stops.

Dad did that?

"I had no idea he'd ever handled such cases."

"We were his first and last adoption case, from what I understand," she says. "Your dad's firm was new at the time. He was taking any case he could while getting things off the ground. Reggie offered him a good sum to move things through the courts quickly and Bert did that for us. Back then, it was an option. People could get around red tape depending on who they knew. Your father knew a lot of good people that were eager to help us."

"My dad was always more about helping people than earning money," I say with a smile. "He made a good living, but he worked many cases where the pay didn't compensate him for the time he put in. He also told countless stories about those early days when he could get more done with a handshake than a typed contract. He hated red tape if it was to the detriment of common sense."

"I can hear Bert saying as much," she grins. "He was stubborn, but in a good way."

"That's very true." Regardless how little time this woman spent with my father, it's clear she knew exactly what kind of man he was.

"When Bert was successful in helping us and we'd made our way to California, Reggie kept in touch with him for a time. He asked your dad what kind of work he preferred and your father insisted real estate was his truest passion."

"It was. He always felt it made most people happy, unlike divorces or criminal matters where someone was either forced to compromise or showing up in a bind to begin with."

"Reggie knew your father was a good man just as much as I did. Any time we knew of someone selling property back east we referred them to your father. He and Reggie lost touch over the years, though. I was busy with my nursing career and with the boys, but my sister told me your dad built up quite the firm."

"He did," I say. "But maybe that was thanks to your husband, at least in part." Wherever Reginald Pierce is at this moment, I want to go throw my arms around him in gratitude.

"I don't know how much of that is true," she says. "I'm sure Bert would have made his own way regardless. He was so kind to us through everything we went through trying to get out of there, away from Aidan's biological father. Reggie felt your father was worth his salt as a lawyer, or he wouldn't have made even an occasional referral. My husband may be soft-hearted underneath that veneer, but he's also a damn good businessman."

"I can see Aidan learned from that," I say. "You must be so proud of him."

"I am. But more so because he is a good judge of people. He picked you," she says, "and I knew the minute he told me you were Bert's daughter that I'd just love you."

"I miss my father so much," I sigh. "Every single day."

"I know what you mean. Not a day goes by I don't miss my Thad."

"Tell me about him," I say. "Any silly little thing you loved about him."

"He was as handsome as Aidan. And I'm not saying that with a mother's bias. I'm saying that because when he was a teenager, my home telephone rang more than the local pizza parlor's did on a Friday night," she laughs. "That was before cell phones, of course. All the girls just went crazy over him."

"I'll bet. Was it that way with Aidan too?"

"No," she says. "He was typically more confident with girls, and once he picked one, he stuck by her until they became incompatible somehow. I never witnessed him misleading a girl into a false sense of exclusivity. I'm not as familiar with his choices as an adult."

"Oh?"

"He's never introduced us to anyone. He never had time to date much once his business took off. And of course we already knew Stella."

I sip my wine and keep listening, trying to hide my distaste at her name being mentioned.

"He is a good boy, Alexis." She shakes her head. "A good man, rather. He'd hate that I called him a boy. But my point is, he's loyal. Almost to a fault."

"I've seen that side of him," I say. "It's one of his qualities I most admire."

"That's why he's pursuing his cause in Mirror Lake. Stanton would never have been on his radar if he wasn't trying to be loyal to me and to his brother's memory. He wants to make up for past sins, though he had no part in committing them. I've tried to dissuade him, tell him there are other ways he can help. But I can't get that through to him."

"I agree, he is stubborn. He about drowned me this afternoon to make a point that I'm more stubborn than he is. I'm still not sure who won that battle."

She laughs aloud. "Oh my, I hope you weren't hurt. He made you jump off the deck?"

"Yes. I was not entirely happy about it at first but, in the end, he was right. He always makes me see that I'm capable of more than I think I am."

"He cares very much for you, Alexis. Anyone can see that. Even his father. But," she adds, "sometimes his stubbornness gets him in over his head. If you see that happening, please know you can come to us. He often takes the weight of everything upon himself, thinking he can handle it all. He can't," she says. "No one can."

"Of course," I promise. "I'll keep that in mind."

"Good" she says. "Now let me tell you a story about the boys and the summer of 1993. You'll never hear another like this one."

At nearly eleven o'clock, the elders of our crew have all retired to the porch for a night cap. The Lonergans have decided to stay rather than drive their boat home in the dark after tipping a few too many.

Dave Matthews is playing softly from a couple of speakers between Oates and Nate when I join our group around the fire. Everyone is sitting in the same Adirondack chairs they occupied last night.

"Finally," Nate says in my direction. "We can reconvene now that we're all here," he teases. "It's about time, Miss Greene."

"Hey baby," Aidan says. "I saved you a seat."

Oates and Nate look at each other and, in the same moment, burst into an exaggerated "aww".

"Shut up, assholes," Aidan says. "You guys can stay over there in the single-and-lame-as-fuck section."

"Ouch," Oates says. "That hurt, bruh."

"Agreed," Nate says, "and I don't even have feelings, Pierce. That was low."

"No feelings, huh, Nate?" I laugh.

"No," he says. "Life is too short to have fucking feelings." Nate is on his second glass of whiskey and seems a little more forthcoming than he's been so far.

"Some girl do a number on you?" Pam asks from her seat near Oates.

Nate doesn't respond, his silence confirming that maybe Pam is onto something.

Maybe a change of subject then.

"Who's controlling this music?" I ask. "I think we need something with a little more kick."

"I am the Lord God D.J. Master tonight," Oates says. "Who else but

Daryl Oates would be in control of the music?"

"Alexis could sink your battleship in that category any day," Aidan pipes in. "She even knows who Tedeschi Trucks Band is."

At his sarcastic dig, I smack Aidan on his muscled arm as hard as I can. He laughs without so much as a flinch.

"Everyone knows them," Nate says.

"See?" I say to Aidan. "You're the ignorant one this time."

"Except when it comes to hip hop," Aidan adds. "You'd kick her ass at Final Jeopardy on that one, Oates. You too, Nate."

The three of them share a knowing look.

"Can you all rap?" I ask.

Aidan just smiles and lets Oates reply.

"We've been known to throw down a rhyme or two."

"You should hear Alexis sing," Aidan says. "Her game's as good as yours, man."

"No way," Oates says. "Really? What's your poison? I'll play anything you want."

"Not tonight." I wave off his offer. "I just thought I'd see what you had for playlists. It says a lot about a person. But I like what you have on."

"Totes," Pam says. "It's Dave. Everyone loves Dave."

"Not everyone," Nate pipes in.

"Ignore him," Oates insists as he squeezes Pam's hand. "I've got anything you want to hear," he says to me. "Pierce, you didn't tell your lady about our business venture?"

I wouldn't normally ask, but beverage bravery is in play right now.

"What business venture?"

"Daryl is developing a new music app," Pam says. "It's going to be huge."

"Aww, thanks, Princess. Of course, you're all sworn to secrecy. Like we should probably take a blood oath. This shit's highly confidential. Only my closest posse has the privilege of hearing me drop this knowledge bomb."

Nate rolls his eyes as he sips his drink. "Oh please," he says. "You've been saying that for years."

"This time I mean it. It's gonna be bigger than anything that's out there now. Music sharing will be changed forever. For reals."

"Sounds amazing," I say. "Is this a side gig for you or something you're working on in Silicon Valley nine to five?"

"It's all mine," he says. "A project I started years ago that's finally coming to fruition." His expression turns more serious than is characteristic of him. "Thanks to Aidan."

This must be the business Aidan had to handle while we're up here.

"That's so cool," I say. "I'm sure you'll slay the market with it."

"Like dragons for a princess," he says. He turns back to Pam and smiles, and she returns the gesture. "I don't have the ability to demonstrate right now. But I can play any song you want. Just name it."

"Oates, let's throw down," Nate says. "You know the one."

"Oh babe, see what you started?" Aidan says. I'm smiling as I shiver in my seat. The evening air is cool with the sun having gone down hours ago. The fire isn't quite close enough for me to get warm. "You're cold?" he says. "Come here."

I abandon my chair to settle onto his lap and he wraps me up. Oates monkeys with his phone, then Macklemore and Ryan Lewis begin streaming through the speakers.

Oates is rapping from the get go to "Can't Hold Us". He's doing it just like Aidan did in the car yesterday, except he's more than lip-syncing – he's vocalizing and not missing a single word.

"Turn it up," Aidan says from behind me. Oates raises the volume as the next part of the song brings Nate to life. He's singing during the more lyrical chorus, and (of course) he's got a smooth and perfectly in-tune voice. He belts out from his position in our circle, seated at the edge of his chair. I've never seen him so animated. He's a handsome guy, but even more so when he's in the zone like this.

By now, we've attracted the attention of Aidan's parents and their friends who are up on the porch looking down at us.

"I love this song," Tori shouts. "They play it in my spin class! Turn it up, Daryl!"

Now we're all cracking up. Oates does as he's asked. Pam and I jump up to dance in place, pointing up at the porch at Aidan's mom like this song is our anthem. When the song finishes, Aidan pulls me back to his lap.

"Keep shaking that ass in front of me and we're cutting this party short."

"No way," I say. "I'm not leaving until you participate."

"More!" The porch tribe shouts. "Play some more!" They're probably enjoying a laugh at the guys' expense more than the music, but I love that they are so into it.

"That was awesome!" Pam says. "Do another!"

I'm too wired to be sitting, getting up in anticipation of what could possibly be coming next. I pull out my phone intending to shoot some video of these clowns.

Oates looks at Nate. "Go for it," Nate says. "I'm in."

Oates just nods and grabs for his phone again. "All I Do Is Win" starts playing, DJ Khaled starting off with his winning chorus (which Nate belts out). Again Oates is trading parts with him, and I am teary-eyed from cracking up. They are nailing it, but in my head I keep thinking about Charlie.

If he were here, he'd be commenting on how ridiculously white these two rapping gangsters are even as they sing explicit lyrics along with Ludacris.

As I stop taking video of the two of them, neither Oates or Nate are fielding the next verse. Oates passes Aidan his make-believe mic, which Aidan immediately fake-drops as he leans back in his chair and Snoop Dog's part of the song begins.

He nails the lyrics without tripping up at all, just like he did with the Fort Minor song in the car. The verse is a mellow style, and his lip sync is smooth as Snoop's voice flows from the speakers.

Nate takes over again for the chorus but my eyes haven't left Aidan. He's so hot when he does that. Everything below my waist is buzzing again, and I'm aching to relieve him of his clothing.

Dammit. I have no willpower.

The song ends and everyone on the porch is hooting with laughter, clapping in appreciation and shouting for an encore.

"I can't think of any more at the moment," Oates says to us. He's out of breath. "Someone pass a brutha some water, yo. I'm parched."

Pam jumps at the chance like she's his backstage groupie.

"That was so awesome," I say to Oates. "I can't believe that came out of the same guy that argued with me about Paul Simon. A guy this cool should know better."

"If you mean I'm as cool as Paul McCartney," he jokes, "I'll take it."

"Alexis, I think it's your turn," Pam says. "Do that Norah Jones song Ben always loved."

"Sweet of you to ask, Pam. I'm afraid it would be a mood killer after all that."

"No way," Oates says. "We can always bring the mood back up with the next one. I say go for it."

"I'd love to hear you," Nate says. "Music is one of the few things I trust Pierce to judge."

"Go on, babe," Aidan says. "If you can't open up here with us, then who with?" I give him a look and he shoots me one right back. His is far more powerful than mine. "Let go, Alexis."

"Okay, okay," I concede. I'm all kinds of mixed up hearing him say those words, the ones he usually says to me during our most intimate moments. "But I'm doing this for Pam. Aidan's heard me enough lately. I'm sure he's sick of it."

"Never," he says. "Do it up, baby."

"Yeah," Oates says. "Let 'er rip, tater chip!"

I head over to Oates and whisper the song I want as Aidan shouts up to his parents. "Mom and Dad!" he hollers. "Get down here!"

I shoot him a scolding look as my cheeks flush. Intimate audiences are not my thing. Barrooms full of drunk people who don't care about much of anything are far less intimidating.

"I've even got a karaoke version here for ya, chica," Oates says.

Great. More pressure.

"One Flight Down" begins as I take a seat near the fire pit by the speakers. I move forward in my chair so I can sit up straight, my music teacher's voice dancing in my head.

Posture is important for projection.

The second glass of wine I had earlier allows me to get the song out stronger than I thought I could. I'm soaking up the starry night sky and, by the end, I'm lost in the music with eyes closed, not caring who is listening.

Pam picked the perfect song. It's in my preferred range but also short and sweet, not lingering with long instrumental breaks or boring parts. It's all lyric, a pretty short story.

As the song ends, my shoulders tense as I open one eye in anticipation of everyone's reaction. I'm more at ease when everybody claps and whistles in appreciation. I'm surprised the loudest whistle comes from Tori who is standing next to her son.

Damn, his mama can whistle.

Aidan is still sitting back in his chair, relaxed but with an expression that tells me he's proud of me. His dad is on the other side of him, and all three of the other couples are down here now, too.

Sheesh.

Oates and Nate are bowing at my feet in a "we're not worthy" fashion, leaving me mortified.

"I wish I could have you guys as an audience while I croak these tunes out in my convertible," I say. "You're too kind."

"I'd pay good money for that," Nate says as he grabs for his empty glass.

"Me too," Oates says. "You got a crazy set o' pipes, chica." He fist bumps me like he did after jumping off the deck today, this time adding an explosion at the end. "Killer. Just fucking killer."

"I told you," Pam chimes in. "She's amazing. And you're welcome."

"Yeah," Oates says. "I would've hated missing out on that. Thanks for encouraging her, princess."

Pam smiles a lovesick grin in response.

Oh, boy.

I have to stifle a laugh.

"What about you?" Oates asks Pam. "You hiding a beautiful voice behind that smile?"

"Afraid not," Pam shakes her head. "My brother had the musical talent between the two of us. But I guarantee I can keep up on the dance floor like nobody's biz-nass."

"I'd love to test that claim," he grins. The two of them step away as Tori comes up to me.

"Beautiful, Alexis." The rest of the couples are saying good night and heading back to the house. "I could listen to you sing all night," she says, "but I'm afraid the old folks are going to bed."

"What time is it?" Nate asks.

"Almost midnight."

"Damn. Pierce, I need a ride to the mainland in the morning." Aidan is still seated, just taking everything in. "Shuttle is taking me to the airport at nine."

"No problem," Aidan says.

"Sweet. I've got time for one more." Nate jiggles the ice in his glass. "I'm heading up to the house for a nightcap."

"Good night, darling," Tori says to me as she kisses my cheek. "I'll see you in the morning."

"Good night."

Reggie comes up to me next, giving me a side hug and kissing me on the forehead. "Good night, kiddo."

I manage a good night in response, completely thrown off.

Theirs is the only parental affection I've had in years. My heart sinks knowing I won't see them much at all when our time here ends.

Aidan calls me over and I stroll up to him, standing between his knees.

"Are you ever getting out of this chair?"

"Are you ready to call it a night?"

I smile down at him. "You read my mind."

He gets up and stretches while standing an inch from me, his shirt lifting up just enough that I can look down and get a glimpse of his abs.

Oh, yeah. I'm so ready to go.

He squeezes me in a bear hug. "It's been six hours," he says in my ear. "I'm sure you're ready to go again. But maybe I should resurrect our presidents game."

"After you hurled me off that deck today I think I've passed enough of your tests. They're dead, Aidan. I promise they don't care if I remember. And besides, we're in Canada. Outside of the U.S. that game should be tabled."

I pull back to read him and see he's seriously contemplating the stupid game. I stand on tiptoe to whisper in his ear.

"Would you really deny me a big 'O' at bedtime over my lack of knowledge about the founders of our country?"

"Okay, you win," he laughs. "You'll get what's coming to you, baby. Don't you worry."

30

Aidan

We leave the guys and Pam to their own devices, but only after I pull Oates aside and tell him to be on his most gentlemanly behavior.

"Of course, man," he'd said. "You know I'd never disrespect a princess."

I knew this much to be true. Oates was a good guy through and through. But I felt like I had to vocalize my hope that he'd not take advantage of Pam. She was important to Alexis, and she felt like a little sister to me already.

If you tallied up the pros and cons, the two of them made a good match – but I didn't want Oates to lead her on. Given their current paths, there was a remote possibility they'd be able to see each other much at all, if ever.

We'd stepped foot into Brat Cottage not ten minutes ago and Alexis has just emerged from a hot shower to get warm. She pulls me out of my thoughts by asking me what's going on in my head.

"Nothing important."

Now that I've had a glimpse of her, I'm unable to form any thoughts at all. She's naked, her wet hair pulled taut in a plastic clip to keep her mane off her neck.

"Damn", is all I can manage to say.

She had me worked up all evening. I'd watched her socialize with ease and grace earlier tonight, but then her uninhibited, chin-to-the-sky laughter while we were hanging out with the guys, the unbelievable way she sang that made people shut up and pay attention.

I hadn't been able to do much but sit back and let my surroundings calm me as a life-altering revelation became more clear.

I was falling in love with Alexis Greene. Every single part of her.

The same woman who, at this very moment, is not paying any attention to me as she's slathering her gorgeous stems with lotion.

"Why don't you let me do that?"

She stops and looks over at me. "Yes, why don't I?"

She tosses the lotion at me where I lay on the bed. My shirt is off, but I'm still wearing jeans, which are fitting tight in the crotch right now as hard as I am. I bite my bottom lip as she comes at me, staring me down in that way she does when she looks at my chest.

"I think you need to lose those pants," she says.

I stand up and drop them to the floor along with my briefs. Before she can make the next move, I lift her up and toss her into the middle of the bed on her stomach.

"You have any Norah Jones on your phone?"

I need music.

"Yes," she says. "It's over there," she points above her head. "On the nightstand."

I grab for it and pull up a playlist of Ms. Jones, letting the music fill the room. I straddle her, stretch her arms out, then grab for the lotion. I start with her shoulders, out to each arm in turn, all the way to the tips of her fingers. She's moaning softly in appreciation.

"If you keep this up, I will fall asleep on you," she says. "That feels amazing."

"Go ahead if you want." I've ravaged her so much the last two days and nights, her body likely needed the rest.

"No way," she says. "You're not getting out of your promise. You said I'd have a bedtime orgasm and I'm holding you to it."

I move down her back with more lotion, moving myself to kneel above the backs of her thighs. "One?" I ask as my hands work over her backside. "How about several?"

"One would be sufficient." She groans as I begin my assault. She's more relaxed than usual. I flip her over with one quick motion, smoothing lotion from her neck to her glorious tits as her nipples harden beneath my touch.

"Baby, you have the most beautiful body." I glide my hands up her arms, move them out to her wrists then back down, all the way to her tight belly. "So soft and sexy."

She smiles her demure smile at me. "I look better with you on me."

I switch my position to hover over her, holding a plank as I look her in the eye. "Like this?"

"A little closer would be better." She opens her legs to me and I enter her, more gently than I have in recent memory.

She feels so goddamn good. I tell her so, but in a language she can't understand.

"English," she whispers. Her breathing is halted, her skin slick beneath me from the lotion.

"Not this time." It's far easier to get out the words when she doesn't know what I'm saying.

I've never spoken to a woman this way.

I've used my preferred romance language to my benefit many times, whether to entice a woman when I met her or to compliment her in public.

But with her, the words are not the same.

Having her is a necessity. I feel something every time – something intangible I couldn't describe if it was required. Italian feels right in these moments, the language the only one sexy enough to convey what she makes me feel.

"*Permettetemi di fare l'amore con te*, Alexis."

She looks at me again, her hand resting on my cheek as she pleads with her eyes.

"You won't know what I'm saying in the literal sense. Just trust me." I move myself out briefly, then slide back into her, groaning at how good it feels. "All you have to do is feel and listen," I tell her. "You'll know what I'm saying."

I kiss her throat, moving my lips up to her ear. I reach a hand over her head and remove her hair clip. "*Quando è giù i vostri capelli sono così sexy*," I say. "Leave it this way." She just nods, enamored. I smile at her, glide the back of my hand over her cheek. "*Sei così bella*."

"Okay," she says. "I'll leave it down."

"*Grazie*." I move my mouth over hers, lost in how sweet she tastes, how her body feels beneath me. "Are you ready to come now, baby?"

She moans, speechless as my lips trace an imaginary line between her breasts before moving over one, then the other.

I move out from inside of her just long enough to grab my pillow from where it lies unused next to her head, placing it under her hips. I push her knees apart as I kneel in front of her, then move closer to her, entering her again as gently as I did before.

At the same time I'm circling her sweet spot with my thumb and her breath hitches immediately. I push into her faster and she's already close, so wet around me. Before she can climax, I stop, resting inside her while my thumb keeps up.

"Aidan," she breathes. "I can't take it. Let me come." Her eyes are closed as she tries to wiggle beneath me.

"Now?"

"Yes," she says. "Now would be good."

I keep up my technique. Without warning I drive into her with force, deep enough to hit all the right angles. She curses and releases unintelligible words as she tightens around me.

Watching her come undone, I can't hold back anymore. I'm coming inside her even as her body goes limp beneath me, exhausted and satisfied.

I collapse on her and roll over, bringing her with me. She lays on top of me, quietly recovering as I whisper more Italian, telling her how much I need her, that I wasn't living before her.

All the things I can't bring myself to say in English I let fly out in foreign words.

I don't want to think about leaving here tomorrow, stepping outside our bubble and going from a place I love so much to the mess I had to get us out of back in Stanton.

Sharing this with her, being here with her – it's been more affirming than I could have predicted.

"*Aidan.*"

"Mm-hmm." I'm eyes closed, spent and unable to form words.

"Whatever happened to your biological father?"

My eyes snap open.

"Why?" I can't hide my irritation at her question.

"I don't know. I was just curious, I guess. Is he still alive?"

I don't want to talk about that bastard.

"No."

My single-word answer must escape me firmly enough. She changes the topic.

"Can you tell me something about your brother then? About your time here?"

She lays her head on my chest and I fold her up in my arms, recalling Marcus Neil's advice about opening myself up to her.

"Like what?" I ask.

"Anything."

I'm quiet and lost in thought for a moment, but she doesn't push. She just waits, her bare chest rising and falling in time with mine.

"He loved it here. He was the first ever to jump off the deck the way we did today."

She looks up at me with a warm smile. "He was?"

I nod. "I was going into my junior year in college. He was just starting his college career. We'd been arguing about the creation of my first company, about whether I should take the leap and do it."

"And?"

"And I told him the day I'd go all in on such a risky endeavor was the day he jumped off that deck."

"And he did it? Just like that?"

"He asked if I was challenging him. I said I was. And he jumped. Got a running start and that crazy fuck jumped clear off the deck. My mom was on the porch and about had a stroke when she realized it."

"I can't blame her. She seems very protective of her boys."

"She was. And she would get so flustered with Thad's antics. He was always the more daring of the two of us. He always pushed me to do crazy shit like that."

"The same way you push me."

"Yes," I grin back at her. "We all need someone like that. To remind us that we're capable of more."

"And he was that for you?"

"We were that for each other," I say. "I was his tie to reality, a reminder that sometimes it was a good idea to slow his roll. He was my reminder that sometimes I should take the dare."

She nods at me. She gets it.

"Jumping off the deck sort of became a tradition after that, especially when there was some sort of debate to resolve."

"You miss him terribly," she says. "Why don't you talk about him more?"

"I don't know." I'd been over this with Doc Mason several times. He always encouraged me to talk about Thad, but I never heeded his advice. "I guess it's just a way to avoid the pain that he isn't here. That he'll never be here again."

"But he is here," she says. "The more you talk about him, the more he's still here."

"You don't talk about Ben. Don't you think it's similar?"

"I don't talk about him with you because I was married to him and it feels inappropriate."

"But you were just friends. I wouldn't mind hearing about him, if you're comfortable with it."

"Stop deflecting, Aidan," she scolds. "And as practical as I might be, I am a firm believer that people we lose are not gone forever. There are things we pick up on, reminders that come at just the right times. You just have to be open to it."

I close my eyes and pull her tighter.

"Being here brought a lot of memories back to me. But talking about him..."

"I understand." Her tone is remorseful. "You don't have to."

I tilt her head up to look at me. "Please don't regret that you asked. I want you to know who he was. In time, you will. Okay?"

She smiles up at me. "I'm not going anywhere." She kisses me before resting her head again. With her curled up in my arms, exhaustion settles over me once again.

"Do me a favor baby, hmm?"

"Anything."

"Whatever song comes next, please sing it."

She looks up at me in question.

"*Per favore*," I say. "*Voglio addormentarmi sentire la tua voce.*"

I want to fall asleep hearing your voice.

"Okay" she whispers. A song about nightingales begins and her sweet voice surrounds me as I lose myself in sleep.

I wake later than usual, but earlier than the morning before. I take a shower while Alexis is sleeping, wrapped up in the covers as she always is. I kiss her before I leave, but she doesn't stir.

I head out in search of Nate to see if he'll be ready to leave for his shuttle, but no one is in the boathouse. I go up to the main house and find it's full of life. Soft laughter echoes out to me and the smell of breakfast wafts out to the porch, coming on stronger as I go in through the front door.

My mother is coming down the stairs, dressed and ready for the day.

"Good morning," she says as she hugs me. "Where's Alexis?"

"Still sleeping. What's for breakfast?"

"It's Sunday," she says. "What's always for breakfast here on Sundays?"

"Pancakes, Mamasita," Oates says as he comes through the door behind me. Pam is at his side. "Everyone knows that."

Mom smiles and heads for the kitchen.

I wonder if my friend did not heed my advice and spent the night with Pam, but resolve there's not much I can do about it.

"I'm starving," Pam says. "Where's Alexis?"

"Sleeping," I say. "Could you go and wake her? I don't want her to miss breakfast."

"Sure." She plants a kiss on Oates' cheek and departs.

Once Pam's gone, I shoot him a look.

"It's all good man," he says, slapping me on the shoulder. "We're on the same page, brother."

I nod and follow the smell of food to the kitchen along with him, hoping his statement is the truth.

As he mixes up a second batch of pancake batter, Nate gives Dad a detailed explanation about one of his latest projects, leaving out details that might breach national security.

Pam reports that Alexis is headed up this way after a shower. Nate and Pam will head back to the mainland after breakfast, and in the meantime Pam and Oates head down to the main dock to fish one last time. The rest of the couples are chatting over mimosas down on the patio by the fire pit which is a heaping pile of ashes after last night.

Mom and I are standing on the porch, looking out over the river.

"I've so missed this place," Mom says.

"Me too."

"We have Alexis to thank for this, you know. For getting us all back here."

I smile. I know.

"I think we ought to make this a regular thing," Mom goes on, "especially if you're going to stay in New York. It would be a great way for us to spend time together."

"I agree. Though you're always welcome to come to Stanton and visit."

"Thank you, honey. But you know I just can't."

I give her a silent nod, letting her know I understand.

"How is Byron?"

"He's doing well. Glad to be back in New York. I wish I'd been able to get him some time off to enjoy it more, but that hasn't been possible lately."

"Does he still have a place in the Adirondacks?"

"Yes. That's where he's headed as soon as things calm down."

"Please tell me you're not in any danger, Aidan."

"Everything is fine, Mom. I don't want you to worry."

"I'll do that anyway."

I ignore her comment. "Alexis has a dog," I say. "Byron has been in his glory training him. By the time we get home, Huck will probably be obedient enough to star in movies."

"Oh, that Byron," she laughs softly. "He was always so good with animals. Remember that odd little dog we watched for the Dillon family when their son went away to Denmark for a semester? It was a cross between two very unattractive breeds. The thing didn't weigh more than six pounds."

"I do," I say with a smirk. "That dog was so annoying. The Dillons went with Craig overseas for two weeks and they had no one to watch it. I think they left just to avoid the damn thing."

"You must've been a junior at Cal Tech by then," Mom says. "Oh, that dog was an ass. I couldn't thank Byron enough for offering to take him. How he found time to do it between training athletes I have no idea."

"He likes most animals better than people," I offer. "Sometimes I can't blame him."

"By the time that dog went home, Byron had trained it to stop peeing on the carpets."

"And not growl at everything that walked by it," I add.

"That's right," she laughs. "I'd forgotten that. He had those weird little teeth that jutted out in an underbite." She's shuddering at the recollection.

I can't help but laugh now. She's right. It was an ugly dog.

"Janice Dillon couldn't thank me enough after that. I still get a Christmas card from her."

"That's comical. Their whole family was odd."

"What's more, until the dog died, he would sit on their laps for that Christmas card photo every year. I think they even had him stuffed when he passed. Ah," she laughs, "to each his own, I guess."

We're both quiet for a moment. I'm lost in thoughts of my brother. He'd been in the same class as Craig Dillon in high school.

"So tell me about Alexis' husband," she says. "She seems very fond of him."

"From what I know, he was a good guy. Died too young from an undetected heart problem."

"So tragic." My mom shakes her head in sympathy and sips her coffee. "The poor thing."

"Their relationship was complicated. Ben was from Canada. His parents – Pam's parents – they live not far from here. Essentially Ben and Alexis were just friends." It would make no difference to my mother that Ben was gay, and I omit the detail. I'm unsure if Alexis would want me to share that anyway. "She was still a college student when they were married. She wanted to help him stay in the States and work in broadcasting, get his citizenship easily."

"That sounds like something characteristic of your girl," she says, still looking out over the water. "Unselfish. Kind."

"It very much is." I can't help my grin when she calls Alexis mine.

"Is she close with her mother?"

"Not especially, no. She lives in Arizona."

"She was somewhat absent back when I met Bert," she says. "That was the rumor anyway. I never heard him speak of his wife."

"How did you know Alexis' father?"

Mom is quiet for a long moment. When she answers me, she looks away. "He helped Reggie adopt you and Thad."

I'm not sure what to say in response. I'd never considered this a possibility. I'd never asked my parents about what they went through to leave New York.

"Are you going to go public with this relationship?" Mom asks, switching gears on me. "Is Stella aware of her?"

"Eventually it will be public knowledge, yes. But I need to tell Stella first. She's in a bad place right now. I didn't want to send her over the edge."

"I understand your hesitation. But you can't live your life for that poor girl. Whatever she's been through, whatever she's yet to go through – don't let it be your problem long term."

"I know, Mom. I've got a handle on it."

"Does Alexis know about Stella? I mean, beyond what the media reports?"

"She does. I'm doing my best to keep the Irelands away from Alexis. I just need a little more time." I look out over the water. "She knows a lot about me, too."

"Aidan." She lays a hand on my arm so I'll turn my attention to her. "You realize you're head over heels in love with her, don't you?"

I lean over the railing, gripping my coffee as I let go a cleansing breath. I say nothing.

"You won't be able to hide it for long," she says. "Especially if the Irelands ever lay eyes on the two of you together."

Again, I'm silent.

"At least tell Alexis how you feel," she urges. "A girl needs to hear the words, no matter how strong and independent she is. Trust your mom on this one." She leans into my side. "You'll both feel better if you tell her."

We're hurrying to finish eating before we have to take Nate and Pam back to the mainland. As Alexis is clearing our plates, I'm watching her, unable to shake my mother's advice.

She's in capris and a fitted t-shirt that's the same color as the slip I bought her. The plum color is flattering on her. Whether from the rest she's gotten or what caused the need for it in the first place, she is damn near glowing this morning.

Oates fires up some music, interrupting my zone-out. "Sinatra Sundays," he says, sending me a nod. "I didn't forget, man."

My college buddies learned this during their past visits. Every Sunday was pancakes, sausage, and Sinatra, without fail. Thad loved these classic tunes, always dancing and singing into the closest kitchen utensil to whatever song struck him in the moment.

Oates is doing a similar gig right now to "At Long Last Love", putting a spin on it that is all him. He's gliding around the kitchen in his socks as the few of us left in the room look on. He stops only long enough to pull Pam into a dance, and I can see it from here.

They're both *done-zo* too, as Oates would put it.

Alexis stands next to me where I'm seated on a stool, wrapping her arms around my waist. She nods towards the dancing couple. "They're cute."

"Indeed they are. But never tell Oates I said that."

"Deal." She leans up to whisper in my ear. "Thank you for last night."

A smile comes to me easily. "My pleasure."

She rests her head near my shoulder and her demeanor shifts in an instant. "I don't want to leave here." She sounds pained by her admission. Empathy rolls over me like a tidal wave, changing my mood to match her reservations.

"Neither do I."

The first part of our ride home is quiet. We'd parted ways with Pam and Nate at nine a.m. and left the rest of our clan after lunch. Mom and Dad planned to fly home this afternoon with Oates, and their friends were flying to Manhattan out of an airport in Ontario at four o'clock.

Our departure had been emotional, especially for my mother and Alexis. Alexis had a hard time holding it together when she said goodbye to my parents. My mother broke down in tears when she hugged me.

Alexis falls asleep as soon as we've crossed the second bridge over the St. Lawrence, now on U.S. soil again. I use the quiet to contemplate how I'm going to move forward and get us out of this mess with R.E.E.

Byron reported by email that Dimitri needs to talk to me at my soonest availability, though it was nothing truly urgent. He hadn't wanted to contact me while I was away.

I have a meeting set up with R.E.E. at their headquarters downstate on Wednesday. On short notice, Lionel wasn't able to get me in with any of the higher ups.

It might mean an extra day in the city to make the company realize what I had to offer, to get in front of a decision maker. But I could be patient. What I now had to bargain with would be making their greedy corporate dreams come true, so long as they could resolve that it came with conditions.

We're more than halfway home. I've just put my earbuds in, intending to give Alanna's husband a call when my phone rings. I'm not connected to the sound system in the car, and Alexis is unaware that Byron is calling.

"Yeah," I say. "How's it going?"

"I need to go to the office. Are you on your way back?" His tone is hurried, more informal than usual.

"Yes. Why?"

"I've left Huck at Ms. Greene's home. If you're headed back now, he should be fine there until you arrive."

"Byron, what the hell is going on?"

"The alarm went off at 250 Harrison. I'm headed there now. The police are on their way. Samira is headed there too."

"Jesus. We're on our way. Huck will be fine. We'll come to the building first."

"No," he insists. "I'll handle it, sir."

"We have to go through Stanton to get Alexis home anyway. We'll stop there first."

"Fine." He knows I won't be dissuaded. "I'll see you there."

I tromp down on the accelerator, glad for this vehicle's capabilities and hoping I won't pass any speed traps as we haul ass the fifty miles it'll take to get home. Alexis wakes up at the increased speed. We're doing ninety-five.

"Whoa," she says. "Slow down, Ace."

"Byron called. There's an alarm going off at 250 Harrison. We need to get there."

She eyes me with concern. "Is everything okay?"

"I don't know" I say. "I hope so."

I don't stop at the dealership to return the car, instead calling the salesman's cell to explain there's been an emergency and I'll come by in the morning instead. We arrive at the loft as two city police officers question Samira and another pair talk to Byron.

Everyone looks our way as we pull up in front of the building.

"Stay here," I tell her.

"Oh come on," she says. "It's fine. I'm getting out."

I shoot her a look stern enough that she stops objecting immediately.

"Okay," she says. "I'll wait here."

Good girl.

I head over to Byron first and meet the two male officers he's been talking with.

"You're the owner of the building?" the first officer asks. His uniform indicates his last name is Bennett.

"I am. I'm just returning from a weekend away. What happened?"

"Your security agent here says he was alerted to a break in. We've been through the first floor and found no evidence of any intrusion in the building. The elevator and the stairwell doors have not been accessed according to the alarm company."

"Just a broken window in the front, sir," Byron says. He nods to the window of the cell store, which is shattered. "We believe that's what caused the alarm."

"This could have been a case of vandalism," Officer Number Two says to me. "We'll be canvassing the area, but it's pretty quiet out here on Sundays. We'll let you know when we're ready to file our report."

"Fine," I say. Vandalism or not, I need to know who did this. I neglect to mention to the officers that we have our own cameras disguised on the building. I'm certain Byron is waiting for them to depart so he can check the footage.

"They're giving your assistant the name of someone who might be able to clean up and secure the window for you," Officer Bennett says, nodding in Samira's direction.

"Thank you. I appreciate that." I grab for my wallet. "Please take my card. You can reach me on my cell if you have anything significant to report."

"We'll do that."

I talk with Samira and her set of officers too. When everyone departs, I contact the gentleman the police referred to secure the window. Samira is calling the cell store manager to alert him to the break-in, and Byron is preparing to drive Alexis home in the SUV. I don't want her left alone while I stay behind to figure this out.

I get back in the i8 and Alexis is non-stop questions as I'm angling the car into a space out back.

"Baby," I turn to her, "I don't have any answers. As far as I know it was some kid breaking the window to snag a cell phone. Don't panic, okay? Things like this happen here all the time."

"I know, I'm sorry. I just hate this feeling of dread. Can we turn around and go back to Canada?"

"If only," I say. "But you're going home with Byron."

She gives me her typical laser stare full of sass, the one I detest and love all at once.

"Don't start. Huck is there waiting for you both. Let me catch up with this and I'll come down later on."

She finally sighs in resignation. "I suppose there's not much I can do to help you anyway. I'll go home and unpack, get ready for my crazy day tomorrow."

"That's my girl." I kiss her on the cheek. "See how much easier things are when you're not being stubborn?"

"See how much easier things are when your requests actually make sense?" She punishes me with another of her smart ass looks. "Don't mistake my willingness for weakness, Aidan. I'll never stop being stubborn," she says as she exits, "and neither will you."

31

Alexis

On the ride home from Aidan's loft I'm utterly spent, contemplating the weekend for a few short minutes before I fall asleep.

Our time in Canada has tossed my emotions into a spinning tornado.

Leaving Aidan's parents had been heartbreaking. I already missed them and seeing the way he was with them. Watching him be a son as well as an amazing lover had been another layer of intensity for me.

Aidan's friends were just as easy to miss. They showed me so much of who he was, how he took care of the people in his life. And their larger-than-life, sweet and quirky personalities were hard to forget.

Then there'd been Pam, who was over the moon for one Mr. Daryl Oates. Our conversation as I'd walked her to her car was short but full of revelations. They had spent the night together but had only talked. She was giddy telling me they discussed everything under the sun and almost until the sun came up. They'd fallen asleep cuddled up in the huge hammock in the boathouse, floating over the river as they slept.

"Am I crazy?" she asked me.

"Crazy for what?"

"Liking someone I'll probably never see again."

I didn't want to burst her bubble, as much as I knew she was calling it right.

"I don't know, Pam. With modern technology what it is, you guys can stay in touch. You can Skype and have a meal together every day if you want."

"Yeah, I can eat lunch while he forgets to eat breakfast."

"Well, so what," I'd said. "The time difference shouldn't matter."

"I guess," she'd said wistfully. "But seeing him in person is so much better."

"I'm going to tell you what your brother would say. If something is meant to be, it will find a way. Don't force it. Don't count on it. Just let it be."

She had let out a hearty laugh then, going on to tease me. "You realize you've nearly quoted a Beatles lyric? Daryl would have your butt in a sling over that. You're wavering in your Paul Simon devotion."

I laughed too, leaving her with the only piece of wisdom I could think of that she'd actually want to hear.

"The heart wants what the heart wants, Pam. There's not much any of us can do about that."

I stretch with a yawn as we pull up to my house. I lean up to the front seat and see Byron is on the phone.

"I'll get my own bag," I offer. "It's just one suitcase. I'll see you tomorrow?"

I don't wait for his reply, already out of the car as he disconnects his call. I want to be left alone for a while and hope to hell Aidan hasn't ordered him to stay.

As I shut the tailgate, I notice the front door to my house is ajar.

That's weird.

I come around to Byron's side of the car and gesture for him to roll down his window.

"Did you leave the front door open?"

"No, of course not. Huck would get out."

He follows my gaze and sees the front door has indeed been left open. He orders me to stay put and opens the door of the SUV, barreling past me.

I don't follow his instruction.

I drop my bag to the pavement and race after him, calling for the dog as I run.

Huck hasn't bounded out to the porch. I can't spot him in the side yard.

And he doesn't come up to us when we reach the door.

I fly past Byron, going into the house without hesitation. I don't care who was in here, or who might still be in here.

All I want is my boy.

I look towards the kitchen and my hand instinctively goes to my face as I suck in a breath. I blink fast, my throat tightening to choke back a scream.

My dog is laying on the foyer floor.

Blood pools on the tile next to him.

He's motionless.

"Huck!"

I scream his name so loudly, my voice doesn't sound like my own. Huck lifts his head when he hears his name, and relief washes over me when he gets up to greet us.

But his effort is brief.

After two steps, he lays down again. A grunt escapes him as he rests his head back on the cool tile.

Byron is shoving me out of the way. I can't force myself to move.

"Call the vet," he demands. "Then Aidan."

I hear his words, but I don't understand what he's saying. I'm shaking as the world spins, fuzzy and soundless.

Who would do this to my boy?

"Now!" Byron hollers.

I nod my head furiously as I snap out of it. I feel around my pockets for my phone and fumble with it. I dial Aidan first, panicked that harm may be coming to him in this same moment.

He doesn't answer.

I hang up and scroll for my vet's number.

"Wait, Byron," I stammer in tears. No one answers at the vet's office. "It's Sunday. The office is closed. I don't know...I've never had to use the emergency vet service."

Byron ignores me as he looks Huck over thoroughly.

"Is he going to be okay?"

"I need to stop the bleeding," he says. "Go get some clean towels."

I take the stairs two at a time and do as he asks. As I come back down, I notice my office is completely ransacked. I ignore it as I sit down next to Huck and stroke the fur on his face, willing him to be okay.

"Put your hands here," Byron instructs. "Press firmly. It looks like a knife wound."

I nod, unable to hold back tears any longer.

"This must have happened in the last hour. If we can get him stitched up, he'll be fine. It looks worse than it is."

Oh, thank God.

"Okay," I say through my sniffling. I press the towel to the wound behind his shoulder. Byron connects with whomever he's calling, speaking hurriedly in another language I don't recognize. When he hangs up, he addresses me again.

"Did you reach Mr. Pierce?"

"He didn't answer."

Byron dials his employer, who must pick up this time.

"The footage taken at the building," I hear him say. "You need to review it now. I'm here with Alexis. Someone's broken in."

He listens for a moment. I can hear Aidan yelling on the other end.

"She's fine, sir. It's the dog. I'm taking care of it."

More listening, less yelling on the other end. I can't help a sigh of relief.

Aidan is okay.

"The break-in at 250 was a distraction," Byron says. "Yes, I've got it. Ivan is coming."

"Ivan?" I look up at Byron as he disconnects and pockets his phone. "Was that Russian you were speaking before?"

"Yes. Ivan will take care of Huck. Don't worry."

"I didn't know Ivan had a medical background."

I also didn't know Byron spoke Russian.

"He was a medic in the service. Do you have an electric razor?"

"No, I don't think," I can't stop shaking. "Wait. Ben did. In his bathroom," I nod towards Ben's room. Byron makes his way to the room he is now familiar with. He emerges with the razor in hand.

"You'll not want to see this, Alexis. Where can I take him?"

"Take him for what?"

"We need to stitch him up. Where can we set up a table?"

Oh, God.

A wave of nausea comes over me. I'm not good with this kind of thing. I'd known early on in my life that I would never make a good nurse.

"I don't know. The basement I guess? There's a table down there and a utility sink too, if you need it."

Please let him know what he's doing.

"That's fine," he says. "Go."

I head downstairs and clear off the long folding table piled with Christmas decorations and random stuff of Ben's that I'd boxed up. I can hear the electric shaver going as chills climb up my spine.

"Do I need to clean the table?" I holler up to him.

"I'll take care of that," Byron yells back. "Come back up here."

I do as he asks. He gestures to the office with a nod of his head. "Is anything missing in there?"

I move to the room and take a closer look. "My computer." The monitor and keyboard are unmoved, but the tower itself is gone. My desk is untouched. My tall filing cabinet is the source of the mess, the drawers open haphazardly with contents strewn across the hardwood floor.

"Tend to Huck," Byron says. "I doubt the intruder is still here but I need to be certain." He withdraws a small pistol from beneath his pant leg.

What the hell?

This feels like a nightmare.

Am I having a nightmare?

Byron moves about the first floor in a hurry, then upstairs. I can hear him go through all the rooms while I'm kneeling by Huck, pressing a white towel to him. It's covered in blood already.

It seems like an eternity, but ten minutes later Ivan is coming through the wide-open front door.

"Did you clear outside?" Byron asks him.

Ivan nods.

"Bleach," Byron says. "In the kitchen?"

"Garage," I say. "I can get it."

"I'll do it," Byron says. "Ivan, we're set up downstairs. Alexis, take his bag."

Ivan says nothing as I stand. He hands me his medical kit which is nearly bigger than I am.

Without a word, he scoops up Huck as though the dog weighs nothing more than a single feather and carries him off to the basement. I feel like I'm living a movie as I follow the burly Russian down my basement steps with the medical bag.

He rests Huck on the couch with his wound face up, kneeling next to him as he speaks firmly at me.

"Set up my kit on another table."

I wipe streaked tears from my face and open the bright orange bag onto an old card table. I'm thrown at how elaborate the equipment inside is.

Jesus. This guy doesn't fuck around.

"What now?"

"Out," he says. "You see him when I'm done."

I just stand there, staring at my boy who isn't moving. Byron arrives with an empty bucket and the container of bleach I had in the garage.

"Please go upstairs," Byron urges. "He'll be fine."

I plant a kiss on Huck's face and take off up the stairs, sobbing as I go.

Aidan calls me three times, but I can't bring myself to answer. I've poured myself a whiskey over ice. I'm numb, sitting on the steps of the front porch as I text him back.

Byron and Ivan are working on Huck. I'm okay. I just don't want to talk.

His response is immediate.

I'm on my way.

I dial Charlie and fill him in.

"My God, Lex. I'm coming right over."

"No, it's okay. I just wanted to let you know. I'll call you when I know more. Let's not worry Gloria."

"Whatever you want," he says. "You know I'm here. Kiss our boy for me and call me back."

"I will, Charlie."

Aidan pulls up moments later in the i8. He runs for me and I stand up, letting him take me in his arms as I lose it once more. He's laying kisses in my hair, only stopping to ask if I'm okay. All I can do is nod. He guides me back up to the porch and makes me sit on the swing.

"Where are they?"

"Basement," I say, finally composed back to the hot mess I was when he pulled in.

"Wait here, okay?" I nod again and he disappears inside. Ten minutes later, he's coming out of the house on a mission. He heads for the driveway and picks up my bag from the pavement, then throws it in the tiny trunk of the borrowed Beemer.

"Come on," he says from the driveway.

"I'm not going anywhere," I say. "I need to know Huck is okay."

He comes back to the porch, frustrated at my refusal. "They're stitching him up now," he says. "We need to go."

My head pounds as I get my words out as sternly as I can manage.

"I'm. Not. Leaving."

"Alexis, it's not safe here. Did you see your office?"

"Call the police then. I'm not leaving. Besides they won't come back. Whatever they were after, clearly they got it. Or they were interrupted while trying."

And they hurt my beautiful, innocent boy in the process.

"I don't care," he says. "It's a risk I'm not taking. Get in the fucking car."

"Stop ordering me, Aidan. This is my home and my dog, and I'm not abandoning either one."

"This is no time for you to be difficult. We need to go. You could be in danger."

"Yeah, thanks to you."

Oh, shit. I hadn't meant to say that out loud.

But there it is, and he knows it as much as I do – it's the truth.

He paces in front of me, running his hands through his hair as he often does. I can't tell if he's angry or frustrated until he speaks up again.

"I warned you about this from day one," he says in accusation. "I told you it might come to this, that you'd have to let me do things my way."

"This?" I spit back. "You seriously thought harm might come to my dog? That someone would want to break into my home?"

He stops and stands at the railing overlooking my front yard with his back to me, not saying a word.

"Maybe you should set up your ambitious project elsewhere."

He turns his head to speak at me over his shoulder.

"You don't mean that."

"What are you trying to make up for, Aidan? Something your father did when you were just a boy? Because I can't understand how putting me – or putting us – in this situation is going to correct any of that."

He's silent. I stand up, intending to further drive my point home.

"Just tell me what is so fucking important," I plead at his back. "What is it that drives you so much you're willing to ignore people close to you that are hurting here and now? Your mother is worried sick. My home has been invaded, your property vandalized, my dog hurt. Mark Whitmore lost his life. What else has to happen for you to walk away?"

He says nothing. At his silence, my anger only intensifies.

"Aidan." My voice comes out louder than I expected. "*Answer me.*"

More quiet.

"Does this have to do with choices your brother made that caused him to lose his life?"

He turns to me, his words weighted with a thousand times more malice than mine. His eyes are sending just as clear a message.

"*Do. Not.*"

I immediately regret opening my mouth. For a brief moment, fear of the power he has behind his temper rushes through me.

"You will *not* bring my brother up to me. You have no right."

I look around for neighbors that might be outside, close enough they might overhear. Thankfully, there is no one. We stand there, both of us riled and angry.

My heart is pounding so hard it physically hurts.

I realize then I'm at a crossroads, making a life-altering decision in this split second of time.

Either I walk away and leave him to figure this out without me, or I dive in. I jump off the deck blindfolded, knowing he's the reluctant one this time, knowing I need to find a way to take him with me. I visualize it, seeing myself gear up with a running start to dive into the depths of what is driving this man.

But there's only one way I can get him to take the leap with me.

I have to push him.

"I have every right," I yell back. "We are standing here while your employees try to save my dog's life. This is personal for me, too."

He's quiet again.

He knows I'm right.

"I'm supposed to be in this with you, Aidan. Remember? The Foundation, the Center, all of it. I'm in it with you. You just have to tell me what the hell you're trying to fix. Tell me why it's worth all this."

He's shaking his head, walking away from me, walking back to me.

I'm watching him struggle, standing on the edge, not knowing what to do.

I stop him on his third pass by me, pushing his back to the porch railing, resting my hands on his chest as I look into his eyes.

"Just tell me," I say softly. "Tell me why other people's mistakes are your cross to bear."

Jump with me, Aidan. Please.

"They weren't his mistakes." He pulls me tight to him, holding me, moving his hands over my back. His voice is low, strained by emotion. "They were mine."

I'm quiet, more tears falling as I let him get his bearings, waiting for more.

"Thad looked up to me. He did everything I did. If it hadn't been for me, for the bad decisions I made that he outdid, he'd still be here."

I don't voice my objections, as much as I know he may be taking unnecessary blame.

Though he's looking over the edge with me, he isn't going to make the leap.

Not yet.

For now, standing here with me had to be enough.

I rest my head on him, standing in silence as the tension between us finally eases. All I can hear is his heart beating. After a moment, he guides me backwards to the swing and sits me down, kneeling in front of me with concentrated patience he didn't have mere seconds ago.

"I know you're upset. But it's not safe to be here. As soon as everything is cleaned up and Huck is stable, Byron is going to bring him back home to Falcon Lake. Ivan will keep an eye on things here. And we will find out who did this."

"Where are we going?"

"We'll go to the lake house. Byron and Huck will be close by." He wipes my wet face, pulling me to him. "I will take care of both of you, baby. You just have to let me."

My head is still pounding three hours later when I wake up in the huge bed at the log cabin in Falcon Lake.

I agreed to go with Aidan because his logic had been sound. I wanted to be near Huck, and I didn't feel safe at home. After a quiet drive here, I collapsed into bed and told Aidan to wake me only if there was urgent news.

It has to be seven o'clock by now. The sun has moved to the other side of the house, but I can see through the open drapes that it hasn't set yet. Whispy clouds glow an orangey-red as daylight fades.

I get up and pad to the kitchen. "Do we have any ibuprofen?"

Aidan is on his laptop at the kitchen table. He looks me up and down when I enter the room. I'm waiting for him to tell me I look terrible or give me orders to go back to bed, but he doesn't.

"I have some in my travel bag," he says. "I'll get it."

I pour myself a glass of water. When he returns, I swallow the two pills he hands me as he retakes his seat.

"Are they back?"

"Yes," he says. "Just. Huck is doing okay. Do you want to walk over there? Maybe it'll do you some good."

I nod, staring off into space as I stand in front of the kitchen windows that look over the porch and down to the lake. I hear Aidan's laptop close and then he's behind me, rubbing my shoulders.

"I'm sorry, Alexis." His tone is guilt-ridden and sad. I turn into him with my head down, buried in his strong chest. "If I had any idea things would go this way, I never would've..."

"Stop," I interrupt, tears coming again. "You couldn't have known. I don't want you to be taken away from me too, Aidan. I can't have you thinking that way, that us not being together would have prevented anything. Would fix anything."

"I'm not going anywhere," he assures me. He lifts my chin up with a finger. "Let me take you to see your boy. Byron says he's just fine. No internal damage."

"Okay."

"I think it'll make you feel better."

"You want me to feel better?" I say. "Find the cowardly bastard that did this and let me go at him with a knife."

The next morning I'm up before dawn, even though it's a dreaded Monday.

Aidan was right, as usual. Last night, we walked the half mile down to Byron's place and the fresh air did improve my mood. It was a beautiful night absent of rain and enhanced by a warm breeze.

Byron's temporary home is a slightly smaller scale of the house we stay in. There's a beautiful fenced yard, which I recall Byron saying had been installed for his own dog. I presume the dog died sometime in the last year. There was no evidence of another dog in residence.

Huck had been resting when we arrived, but he was alert when we came through the door. Byron went out to pick up dinner, and I was able to relax and love up my boy.

Huck's wound looked well cared for, but it was disconcerting to see him shaven with stitches exposed. More comforting was that his demeanor was unchanged. He was still my huge, goofy ball of fur.

Byron insisted the dog see the vet today and that he be the one to take him while I go to work. I agreed knowing Byron felt responsible, though I don't see it that way.

I feel indebted to Byron and Ivan. I have no idea how I can express enough gratitude for what they did.

Aidan busied himself with Byron after we ate, making calls and reviewing video footage of the break-in on a laptop. They'd been able to glean nothing from the footage, other than the size and build of a hooded male stranger. The guy had come up to the front of the building, thrown a rock through the window of the cell phone store, and taken off out of view of the cameras. Aidan asked me if I recognized the perpetrator, but I didn't. He looked like any random hoodlum you might see in the scarier parts of Stanton.

We left Byron's at nine o'clock, walking back to climb the stairs and fall into bed, both of us exhausted. I was certain I didn't dream. I don't know if that was the case for Aidan, but at least he hadn't woken up with any nightmares.

He's not in bed now, presumably out for a run. It's only five-thirty.

I intend to call the vet's office as soon as it opens and set up an appointment. This will leave me with Ivan today, but given the events of the last twenty-four hours I'm okay with that, especially now that I've seen him act in a crisis.

The dude is a certified badass.

He'd been ordered to stay at my house last night, after going into Stanton to make sure my office was undisturbed. No one had tried to break in there. He and Charlie had done a sweep and made sure everything was copacetic.

I'm about to get out of the shower when Aidan comes in, naked and sweaty and bearing the gift of music. Survivor's "High On You" starts playing through the music genie speakers, and I'm looking at the sexiest cure for stress a girl has ever laid eyes on.

"Feeling in a cheesy eighties mood this morning, hmm?"

"Yeah, baby. This song came up on my run. That's actually the name of the playlist on this app. 'Eighties and Nineties Cheese'. Can you believe that?"

"That's hysterical. What else is on it?"

"I don't even know," he says. He's lathering up in a hurry, rinsing off. "I couldn't help but think of you when I heard this one, and I turned the fuck around."

I know the song well. I've always loved it.

"That's a very swoon-worthy compliment. Thank you."

He lifts me up, my legs wrapped around him as he presses me into the cold shower wall.

"It's true," he says. "The highest high ever, baby." He overtakes my mouth with a heated kiss, then lifts me up to slide me over him.

Oh, sweet Jesus.

He feels ah-mazing.

He's driving into me as the jets spray us clean, washing off the stress of last night, rinsing away all the anger and pain I've felt since we got home.

"*Yes*," I moan. "Harder."

His mouth dives to my breast as he throws my hands over my head. I leave my arms pressed up against the wall as he moves his around to cradle my back, holding me up as he complies with my request and forces himself into me harder than before.

God, this feels so fucking good.

I beg him not to stop.

His vocal response is a grunt as he keeps going, not as fast but just as hard with each thrust. He hits that magic spot deep inside me, groaning in his carnal growl. He fills me up and I'm coming right after him, and with such force I have to concentrate so I don't throw him off balance.

He's holding me up, carrying all of my weight with one arm, leaning his other above my head as he kisses my neck, my collarbone, my bare chest. "Alexis," he moans. He says it as though it's a sacred utterance.

"Mmm." I'm unable to speak coherently. I let my legs fall, my toes barely touching the floor.

"I love you."

I'm not sure I heard him right. The water is flowing all around us and the music continues as Aidan's playlist moves into a ballad. It's Bryan Adams' "Do I Have to Say the Words?"

The song might be on the cheesiest playlist known to man but, right now, hearing words about a man begging his lover to rescue him, wanting to prove how perfect they are together…

…even with the hot water, my limbs have goosebumps everywhere.

He's still carrying some of my weight, still comfortably inside me, the way neither of us can seem to get enough of. I lift my face to his.

"Say it again."

He smiles and my insides are officially mush.

"I love you, Alexis Marie."

I return his grin, throwing my legs up around his waist, my arms around his neck as I look into his eyes. "I love you too, Aidan Michael." I kiss him gently, taking his bottom lip between my teeth briefly until I can speak again. "Now take me to bed."

"Bossy little siren, aren't you?"

"But I'm your bossy siren," I say. "And you L-O-V-E me now. No take backs."

"Never," he laughs. "I love you, baby."

"Enough to slay dragons for me?"

"That's exactly what's on my agenda this week. I'm slaying dragons right and left for my princess," he says, stealing Oates' ridiculous line.

I can't help my laughter. "Your princess whom you love," I tease.

"Yes." His happiness is contagious. "Do I have to yell it?" He asks it just after the song begs the same question.

"Yes," I insist.

He yells the words at the top of his lungs, courteously directing them away from my ear as his voice echoes off the tile walls.

"Yeah, you do." I turn my words to a whisper in his ear. "And I love you back."

32

Aidan

I drop Alexis off at her office by eight in the morning on Monday. The only way I'd been able to do so without hesitation was knowing Ivan would be with her.

That, and recalling what a great morning we had.

I'd finally let go of the words I'd been holding in.

And she said them back.

As we're saying goodbye, we're both feeling ridiculous and giddy, not wanting to part company. My resolve steels when she mentions Huck and his injury. Someone is a very real threat to us and that has to be addressed now.

"Byron will bring the pooch by to see you after the vet appointment," I promise.

"I feel like I should be there."

"He's going to be fine. Let Byron do his job. You know he feels responsible."

"Okay," she resigns. "And you'll tell me as soon as you have information about who did this?"

"Of course," I insist. "No secrets."

She nods in response.

"Ivan is stationed outside. Make sure you lock the back door."

She kisses me insatiably and we part ways, resolving we'll see each other when she is done for the day. It should be a routine departure, similar to what regular couples must do any day of the week. But it never seems that way with us. I am always hesitant, always wondering if someone is going to interfere with us. The panicked feeling is one I am hell bent on eliminating.

If I can execute my strategy, the Irelands and Renewable Energy will no longer be a concern before the week is out.

I deliver the i8 back to the dealership and head back to the office to dive into work and find out what we're facing after the break-ins.

I return Dimitri's call from the weekend. He'd been attempting to uncover new information from the emails Mark Whitmore's wife had delivered to Alexis. Unfortunately, he has no good news. All of his digging had resulted in countless dead ends.

"There's no trace of this information anywhere, on any live system of the names you've given me. Either they got wise or intended all along to get rid of it. It's a miracle that Whitmore ended up with this."

"Understood. If you uncover something new, let me know immediately. And while I've got you here, could you check something out for me on Shane Pickard? He's a V.P. at Ashley Pharma. Alexis got a call from someone claiming to be with his office."

"About?"

"His assistant set up an appointment for Wednesday, alleging it's about a real estate purchase here in Lake County. Byron hasn't been able to confirm Pickard's motives or whether his office actually set it up. I thought it sounded odd but I don't want Alexis to think I'm questioning her abilities. If he truly wants to hire her, I don't want to get in the way."

"Got it. Better safe than sorry."

"With the break-ins over the weekend, I'm more concerned than before. I need to confirm this appointment is legit."

"Consider it done. I'll text you if it checks out. Call you if it doesn't."

"Thanks."

"How was your weekend at The Gables?"

"Great." I break into a grin just thinking about it.

"Did Mamasita make pancakes?"

"You know she did. With Nate's help, of course."

"I heard he was there."

"Yeah, Oates pulled one over on me."

"Damn," he says. "I'm sorry I missed that. I'll have to get up there again someday if Mama will put up with me. I'd love to show Nikki around up there."

"Of course. In the meantime, we'll try to catch up while you're in New

York, hopefully to celebrate."

"Count on it, man."

By the afternoon, I've had confirmation from Dimitri that Mr. Pickard of Ashley Pharmaceuticals checked out. His appointment with Alexis shows up on the calendar of his personal cell phone which was synced as recently as this morning. I have no doubt Dimitri accessed the information illegally, but I was also sure he left no trace of his access behind.

With his assurance, I'll be free to keep the meeting in Manhattan on Wednesday without worrying about Alexis. I may require until Thursday to get in front of the C.E.O. of Renewable Energy. If he won't accept my terms, negotiating over the Rossi parcel might take even longer.

Byron took Huck to visit with Alexis before securing the dog back at his place in Falcon Lake. He's just arrived back at the loft so we can review John Ireland's whereabouts over the last two weeks.

"Nothing I found indicates he left California in that time. In fact, he hasn't left the state since January."

"Then we have no leads about who Mark Whitmore went to meet the night he died or whether he thought it was going to be Ireland."

"My contact in Florida was able to forward the video footage from the hotel. I reviewed it over the weekend. There was nothing amiss, no evidence of anyone Mark was going to meet. Whatever happened, it happened out of plain view and away from any cameras."

Fuck.

"I can't defend myself against this, Byron."

"My biggest concern right now is enemies we cannot identify. I have no leads on the footage from our break in here. The police are treating it as a random act of vandalism, given their lack of information about Ms. Greene."

"I don't want her dragged into anything with the authorities. Ivan will keep Alexis protected. Did you speak to any neighbors on Peaceful Drive?"

"I did. No one in Ms. Greene's neighborhood saw any suspicious activity that night. I left the dog there for only one hour. The intruder was in and out fast."

"Tell me what we should do, Byron." I'm at a loss. I've never felt so vulnerable, and it's throwing me off. My usual capability to be several moves ahead feels compromised by what's at stake.

"We may have to draw the threat in to identify it."

"I won't use Alexis as bait."

"I don't see that as necessary, sir."

"Good. What do we have then?"

"Myers' land. It's the one commodity everyone is after. We know Ireland is involved. We just don't know whether it's him or someone from R.E.E. that's the aggressor right now. Call all the players together, get them in the same room, and put this to bed."

"You have a point, but Ireland will never agree. I have R.E.E. lined up for Wednesday already. I say we wait Ireland out. I might have a way to take him out of the picture by going to R.E.E. with the Rossi parcel. And Alexis will be kept safe until this blows over."

"Do you think Ireland will retaliate?"

"I don't know," I admit. "But I think this is my only option now. Until I can confirm what his angle is, he's unpredictable. At least this will remove him as a player where the land in New York is concerned."

"Agreed, sir."

"I'll call Lionel and have him keep his ear to the ground in California. Curtis should be watching Stella. I'll try to get through to the staff at The Meadows this afternoon."

"Please let me know if there's anything else I can do."

"If you get any further ideas," I say in exasperation, "make me the first to know."

Ivan delivers Alexis to the loft promptly at ten after five in the evening. The lobby is quiet when I greet her, the storefronts both closed up for the day. I had the broken window replaced at eight o'clock this morning so the cell phone store conducted business as usual.

Alexis saunters up to me in the same outfit she put on this morning. The pale blue dress complements her eyes and hugs tight to her body in all the right places, and the low-cut neckline reveals just enough to bring me to attention.

As beautiful as she looks in the dress, I can't wait to relieve her of it as soon as possible.

"Hey, baby. Good day?"

"Great day," she says. "Huck is going to be fine. The vet called me after Byron was there. He's on antibiotics as a precaution, but Dr. McMahon said whomever worked on him saved his life and did a remarkable job. I don't think Byron revealed that he or Ivan had anything to do with it."

"No," I say. "Probably not."

"I don't know where you found them, but I have been thanking God all day that you did."

I smile at her. "You think we should keep them around, hmm?" I pull her close, giving her a chaste kiss. "Because you say the word and I'll terminate their employment right now."

"Very funny," she says.

"Anything for my princess."

"Oh yeah?" Her laughter lights up her eyes. She perks up, her breasts lifting up to tease me. "I could use another educational lesson," she says. "You game?"

"As long as you have the rest of our founding fathers from fifteen to thirty memorized."

"Come on," she protests. "Not this again."

"Rules are rules."

"Then I'll make my own rules. I won't let you touch me unless you can tell me the name of the song that was playing this morning when you told me you love me."

I can't help my grin.

You're going to lose this one, baby.

"I'm ready. You go first. You left off with Buchanan."

"How do you even remember that? And the answer is no way. I'm not doing it, Aidan."

I pull her into the elevator, ready to make her climb faster than it takes the car to reach the third floor. I pin her up against the wall and unzip her dress down the side, then pull the straps off her shoulders so the dress falls to the floor.

"Here?" she asks.

"No," I say. "Not unless you get them all."

I'm insistent she play my game until I stand back and look at her.

She's wearing the strapless white bra again, along with a white lacy thong that might as well be made of dental floss.

She's amazing.

A fucking unicorn.

"Goddamn, babe. Fuck it." I'm all over her, possessing every inch of her with my hands, taking her lips over with mine. "I don't care if you know the name of the current president, let alone the first thirty. Let me take you upstairs and make love to you."

"Ah, ah," she says. "My rule stands. You should take your hands off me now, unless you're ready to fail."

"You sure you want to push me?" I take a step back and release her. "You know I always win."

"Stop stalling and admit it." She crosses her arms in defiance over her chest, leaving her belly exposed. "You have no clue what song it was."

"It was Bryan Adams."

"That would be the name of the artist, not the song." She bats her eyelashes, teasing me with her nearly naked body. "Sorry, Mr. Pierce. You lose."

She's about to lean down and tug her dress back on, but I stop her. I use the crook of my finger to tilt her chin up as I look in her eyes.

"I wasn't done."

I pin her arms up, my grip holding her wrists together as I press up against her. Her breath catches as her bare skin touches the paneled wall at her back.

"The title of the song is "Do I Have to Say the Words", and it's from his 1991 album."

My free hand glides down her left side, her skin reacting with goosebumps as I trail down her arm, over the side of her breast, along her midsection to her exposed thigh.

"The title of the album is *Waking Up The Neighbors.*"

I rest my hand on her hip, underneath the string of her thong. I kiss her neck and move lower, pausing as my lips reach the lace that covers her nipple.

"He won a Grammy for another song on that album," I whisper over her skin, "but that single made the Billboard Hot 100 too. And in case you were not aware..." I slide my hand off her hip, reach behind her and pull her in tight, knowing she'll feel how hard I am. "Bryan Adams is Canadian."

She's speechless.

And panting.

I lean back to look her in the eye and she just stares at me, smiling.

"Anything else you want to know?"

"Guess not." Her grin is adorable. "So you were paying attention."

"Baby, I won't forget what I said to you this morning for as long as I live."

She's taken off guard once again. I release her wrists, letting my forehead gently drop to hers as she wraps her arms around my neck.

"I've never said those words to any other woman. Never even felt like

I might want to say them to someone someday. Trust me," I say with certainty, "I know what I said, what day and time I said it, and exactly what we were experiencing in that moment."

I kiss her as if I've not seen her in months until she pulls her lips away and jumps high enough to wrap her legs around my waist.

"I love you, Aidan."

"I love you more, baby." I add her words to my declaration in a whisper, the ones she'd said to me at the cottage when she agreed to be mine. "Never question it."

33

Alexis

June 13, 2016
Monday Evening

I'm rattled from sleep by a dream about Mark Whitmore.

More like a nightmare.

I'd been talking to Mark but, instead of the scene playing out as it had the day he'd found me in the pub, this time the situation is reversed.

I'm the one trying to warn him, begging him not to go to Florida as he planned. But in the dream I have no voice, no ability to move. I can't stop him from leaving the pub the same way he'd done in reality.

I wake up clammy and unnerved, searching for the comfort of Aidan's arms.

He isn't in bed with me.

I pad to the kitchen in the darkness, but he's not here either. I call out for him, thinking maybe he's in his office.

Again, no answer.

I'm about to go back to the bedroom and dress so I can look for him, presuming he's downstairs. Instead, I'm startled out of my skin by Ivan as he emerges from the guest bedroom fully dressed.

"Ivan." I fight to catch my breath, clutching my chest and thankful at least I was wearing Aidan's t-shirt when I walked in here. "Where the hell did you come from?"

"Mr. Pierce assigned me here tonight. He was called away unexpectedly."

Why didn't he wake me?

"Is everything okay?"

"Fine, Ms. Greene. Can I get you anything?"

"No, thank you. Did Byron go with him?"

"No. I'll be joining Mr. Pierce in the morning, and you'll be with Byron tomorrow."

"Okay," I concede. "Go to bed, Ivan. I'm headed there myself."

He doesn't leave the kitchen. "Good night, Ms. Greene."

I go back to the bedroom in search of a note or some indication from Aidan about why he had to leave.

There are no notes in the bedroom and no messages or voicemails on my phone. I dial his cell, but he doesn't pick up. I don't bother leaving a voicemail, but send him a text asking him to call me as soon as possible. My phone indicates it's three a.m.

I dial Byron and he answers on the first ring.

"Yes, Ms. Greene."

"Where is Aidan?"

"Manhattan."

"That's all you can tell me?"

"I'm afraid so."

"What time will you be arriving here? And what about Huck?"

"I've had Samira outfit my apartment in Stanton for the dog. We're at your home this evening. I'll be arriving at the loft in four hours."

"Where will Huck be while I'm at work?"

"He'll be at the apartment. I've got a kennel set up for him. He'll be thoroughly exercised before I leave him for the morning. I'll walk him again in the afternoon."

"Byron, why can't you tell me what's going on?"

I'm freaking the fuck out here.

"You are not to leave the loft until the morning when I arrive. Ivan will be there until I get there. Is there anything else?"

Byron is under strict instructions. It's clear I'll get nowhere with him.

"No. Good night, Byron. Hug my boy for me."

"Good night, Ms. Greene."

I've heard nothing from Aidan three hours later. I tried to fall back to sleep, but it was futile.

Something is going on, and being out of the loop is wreaking havoc on me.

What am I supposed to do now? Go about my day like it's a regular Tuesday?

Not fucking likely.

I head for the bathroom at six o'clock to shower and ready myself for the day. Hopefully, Ivan will have left the guest bedroom by the time I'm ready to get dressed. All my clothes are in that closet.

When I come out of the shower of the master bath wrapped in a towel, I notice something on the counter next to my toothbrush. I pick up the napkin that's been crafted into the shape of a rose. There's a note next to it in Aidan's impeccable handwriting.

I've been called to slay some dragons, baby

Please don't worry. I'll be back as soon as I can.

Ti amo, splendida.

A-

He told me he loves me in Italian, called me gorgeous, and left behind a gesture he knows I'll swoon over.

An audible sigh escapes me.

I can't follow through on his instructions. Of course I'm going to worry. It's either that or take action – and I'd have no idea what action to take.

I don't know where the man I love is or what the hell is going on.

Any hope that seeing Byron would put my mind at ease about Aidan's whereabouts was squashed like a nuisance insect within ten minutes of his arrival.

Byron and Ivan powwowed near the elevator at the loft while I waited inside. Try as I might to hear their conversation, I could not make out the words they were uttering in their low voices.

For the short time I'm in Byron's company, I learn nothing beyond the fact that Huck was happy to collapse in his kennel at Byron's city apartment after his three-mile walk this morning.

Ivan left in a hurry at eight o'clock and Byron escorted me to my office building immediately after. I'm sitting at my desk now, barely listening as Charlie goes on about the latest backsplash trends on HGTV. He's switched topics to tell me about Carter being a pain in the ass when he claps his hands together right in front of my face. He startles me so much that I jump.

"Girl," he snaps. "You're a space cadet this morning."

"I'm sorry. I don't know where Aidan is, and it's driving me crazy. He told me he loved me yesterday. And right now I have no idea where he is."

"What the fuck did you just say?"

"I said he's gone. To who knows where."

"No, no, no." He waves off my statement. "He told you he loves you? And you didn't tell me this yesterday?"

"I'm sorry," I say with a slight smile. "But if it makes you feel any better, I haven't told anyone." I had enough to talk to Charlie about yesterday as I'd gone on about our time in Canada and revealed more detail about the chaos we'd come home to.

"Holy shit, Lex. So you don't know where the lovesick stud muffin is?"

"Just that he's in Manhattan. But I don't know why or for how long. He left me a note but all it said was that I shouldn't worry. I haven't heard from him since we went to bed last night."

"Jesus. This sounds serious. Jeeves won't divulge anything?"

"It's Byron," I correct him. "And no, he won't."

"Maybe you should let me talk to him."

"It won't do any good. He's a vault."

"I can be very persuasive," he says with his coy smile.

"I just have to wait this out. If Aidan's not getting to me, there's a reason. I just have to trust him."

"You sure he's not ghosting on you?"

"Ghosting?" I have no idea what he means.

"He told you he loves you. You don't think that scares a man to death? Sometimes we tend to run in the opposite direction after that kind of declaration. You know," he says, "turn into ghosts."

I roll my eyes.

"I'm just saying, a man might disappear after that kind of revelation."

"I don't think that's the case, Charlie. There's definitely something going on. I could tell by the way Ivan and Byron were talking this morning."

"That Ivan is something," he says, his mischievous smile returning. "You should have seen him sweep this place the other night after Huck was hurt. It was right out of a James Bond movie."

"He does have that air of a Bond villain, doesn't he?" I ask, my grin matching his.

"I'm just glad he's on our side. What can we do while we wait for Aidan to materialize, then?"

"This," I say as I shove him a stack of files. "We have Mr. Pickard from Ashley Pharmaceuticals coming in tomorrow and we need to clear the decks first. Let's get to work."

At lunch hour, Byron comes through the front door while I happen to be out front talking to Claudia. I haven't heard from Aidan all morning.

"Is everything okay?"

"Yes, ma'am. I thought we might take a break, tend to Huck, and get you something to eat."

"I really can't, Byron. I'm in the middle of a few things here. Could you take care of him this afternoon?"

"I can't leave you alone, Ms. Greene."

Charlie comes out front, overhearing our conversation. "I can take care of our girl," he says, laying a hand on my shoulder. "I won't let her out of my sight."

Byron thinks a moment and finally resigns.

"Do not leave the office. I'll bring you something to eat."

"I'm fine," I assert.

"I'll get you a salad."

"Fine." I shake my head in frustration, giving in. "But I'd like Huck and I to stay at my place tonight."

He nods in affirmation. "I'll post outside again in forty-five minutes. We'll head to Mirror Lake when you're through for the day."

He leaves to tend to what should be my responsibilities and my heart is tugged in so many directions.

I'm overcome with guilt wanting to handle everything myself, yet full of gratitude that Byron watches out for me.

And Huck.

And Aidan.

All of which is getting to be more than a full-time job.

I arrive home to find no evidence of the break-in. The floor is spotless where Huck's blood had been, and my office has been cleaned up too. I spend a few minutes going through my filing cabinet and, thankfully, find nothing missing. The NDA agreement with Aidan had been hidden in the back of a desk drawer and is still there. My desk had been untouched, likely thanks to Huck interrupting the intruder.

Byron insists that we ask Charlie, Gloria and Harry over for dinner, then exercise Huck and ourselves on a three-mile run while we wait for them to arrive. It's weird seeing Byron dressed down in jogging pants and a t-shirt. After our run he goes to Ben's suite in favor of a shower, and I start throwing dinner together.

The gang arrives and I'm glad for the distraction. I'm sure this is exactly what Byron intended. I send the guys outside to grill meat and ask Gloria to stay so I can catch her up on everything that happened over the weekend.

"Girl, this is too much. I gotta sit." She squeezes into the banquette and gestures for me to join her. "I can see why you didn't call me. I'm not sure I would've believed you. Your time in Canada sounds amazing, but multiple break-ins? Knife wounds to your baby boy?"

Huck plants himself on the floor next to us.

"I wanted to call you. I just...I didn't have the energy to get into all of it over the phone. And I didn't want to worry you."

"You're entitled," she says, twirling her glass by the stem. "But I'm definitely going to worry now. What's being done? Do the cops have any leads?"

"No. We have some video footage of the loft vandalism, but nothing has been determined yet. We didn't report what happened here."

Gloria gives me a scolding look. "You think it's wise to withhold that information?"

"I didn't at first, but I don't think there's anything the authorities can do. It happened so fast. No one in the neighborhood saw anything, and only my computer was taken, which is really not a big deal. There wasn't much on it. Huck being hurt is my biggest concern."

"Yes, and that whoever did this is still out there, Lex. You need to be careful. I really think the authorities should be involved."

"Well I'm never left alone now, so they'll have to get through Byron first."

She hesitates, then nods in agreement. "I still can't believe someone would do this to your baby. " She looks the dog over as he pants away. "That's a pretty rough looking wound. He's okay, though?"

"The vet says he's fine."

"Thanks to Byron?"

"Yeah," I nod as I rub the dog's head. "And Ivan. I don't know what I would've done without them."

Our conversation halts as Charlie calls from the deck that dinner is ready.

Byron makes sure the dog minds his manners while all of us break bread around my patio table, but I have little in the way of an appetite. I can't ignore the nagging feeling in my stomach. I have not heard from Aidan at all today. My only comfort is knowing Ivan is with him, watching out for him while he does whatever the hell he's doing.

Harry and Byron start in about motorcycles and, after the meal, a discussion ensues about the armed services. As usual, Byron reveals few details about himself. Charlie, Gloria, and I take the opportunity to head into the kitchen for a second glass of wine.

We're laughing about our karaoke night last week and the way the bartender had been repeatedly shut down, especially when Aidan kissed me right in front of her. I don't let on the reason she'd been so upset, though I am sure Charlie might have figured it out.

"I tried to cheer her up after you left," he says. "I got behind the bar with her, helped her make drinks while she croaked out a Mariah Carey song. "

"You're such a sweet guy," I coo with sarcasm.

"I am, dammit," he insists as he tops off his glass. "She sings like a moose being castrated. It was torture."

Our light-hearted conversation is interrupted as Byron comes through the back door of the kitchen to hand me his phone.

"For you," he says.

"Hello?"

"Hey, babe. Are you behaving?"

At the sounds of Aidan's voice I'm relieved, but pissed that he couldn't have called me even once today. My pissy demeanor wins out as I reply.

"Where the hell are you?"

Gloria shoots Charlie a look, and everyone excuses themselves back to the deck so I can talk in private.

"I'm in New York. I thought Byron told you."

"He wouldn't tell me anything beyond the fact that you're in Manhattan. I've been anxious all day worrying about you. What's going on?"

"I'm sorry," he says. "I didn't mean to upset you. I've been in meetings with R.E.E. all day."

"What the hell for?"

"Slaying dragons, baby." He sounds downright excited now. "I have to go back in, okay? I'll be home tomorrow."

"Aidan, please tell me what's going on."

"I will, I will. I just can't get into it right now. Trust me, okay? Everything is working out better than I hoped."

I sigh in exasperation. "You can't expect me not to worry," I say. "This is killing me. Are you safe?"

"I'm fine. Ivan is here. Go have fun with your friends. I'll see you tomorrow."

"If that's my only choice," I concede.

"I love you, baby."

"I love you, too."

He disconnects and I bring the phone back to Byron.

"Your employer is infuriating." For the first time in my presence, Byron reveals a full smile. "Please tell me he knows what he's doing."

"He does." Byron's usual stern demeanor is back in place. "I'd bet my life on it."

Wednesday morning, I wake up with a slightly pounding head after a few too many glasses of wine. Charlie and Gloria had even more than I did. Harry assisted his wife home and, when Byron retired to Ben's room, Charlie crashed in my bed with me.

At six-thirty, I shut off my alarm. Charlie's already out of bed, ready to go back to Stanton and get on with the day.

"See you at the office," he says. He blows me a kiss and makes his way downstairs. I hear him say goodbye to Byron and Huck as he leaves.

"I'll be ready shortly," I yell down to Byron.

"Very well," he says. "I'll walk the dog."

I shower and dress in a hurry and head downstairs for a huge glass of water and some ibuprofen. Byron is coming in the door with Huck.

"Can we leave him here today? I think he'd be more comfortable at home."

"Yes, ma'am. I've asked your neighbor to keep an eye on things and advise me if there's any suspicious activity."

"What neighbor?"

"Mr. Dingham."

"He hates everyone. How'd you get him to agree to that?"

"We were both in the service," he says. "He's doing it as a favor to me."

Further proof Byron possesses some magic voodoo to get people to do whatever he wants. Mr. Dingham couldn't be bothered to wave hello to me once in the few years I'd lived here. He isn't known for being nice or accommodating to anyone. Still, I trust Byron's judgment. If Dingham wants to play chairman of neighborhood watch today, so be it.

"Okay," I agree, "but if something happens to Huck on Dingham's watch, I get to be there when you string him up and beat him to a pulp."

Claudia buzzes in to let us know my potential new client is twenty minutes early. I hurry to clear off the large conference table in the library from all that Charlie and I were working on.

I send Charlie out front to introduce himself and bring Mr. Pickard back to where I sit in the library, in the same chair I sat in to negotiate with Eli Myers.

I stand as the two men enter. Mr. Pickard is shorter than Charlie and his frame is round. He's wearing a navy blue suit with a green tie and he looks a bit flustered. He's bald with the exception of the two tufts of reddish-gray hair above his ears that are combed away from his full cheeks.

He is not someone I'd picture as the VP of a pharmaceutical company. I'd sooner envision him in a blue uniform collecting change at a toll booth.

"Mr. Pickard, this is Alexis Greene," Charlie says.

"Pleased to make your acquaintance," he says. He shakes my hand, then seats himself in one of the upholstered chairs on wheels as he adjusts his suit coat.

"Likewise, Mr. Pickard. Charlie, thank you," I say. "I think we're all set for the moment."

"Good to meet you, sir." He nods to Mr. Pickard, then looks in my direction. "I'll be in my office if you need me." He exits, closing the door to the hall behind him and leaving us in silence.

I retake my seat across from the gentleman and wait for him to take the lead, but he says nothing. His hands are folded on the table. He looks pensive.

"I understand you're interested in buying some land in Falcon Lake?" I ask.

Again, I'm met with silence. The guy hasn't looked up from his hands since he sat down.

"Mr. Pickard? Are you all right?"

"Yes, fine. Sorry," he says. He pulls some folded letter-sized papers from his inside suit pocket and slides them across the table to me. "I must apologize, Ms. Greene," he says. "I didn't want to take this meeting. It wasn't my idea."

I pull the papers away from him gently and unfold them. There are three sheets of white copy paper.

"Where did you get this?"

"I printed them from an email," he says.

The first sheet is a typed note to me. I ignore it as I look at the second of the three pages – a printed photo of Aidan kissing me.

It must have been taken at The Wall the night before we left for Canada, when he claimed me for the benefit of the bartender he'd bedded before we met. More disturbing is the fact that this is a screenshot from a cell phone and snapped from a video clip. The photo has a pause button visible at the bottom.

I flip back to the front sheet of paper. The only thing written on it is a telephone number, an address in Stanton, and a time – four p.m. The address is on Seventh Street on the southwest side of the city, a sketchy area I've never been brave enough to frequent in the past. I pick up my phone to check the time. It's now quarter to three.

The third sheet is a printed list of all the documents that were on the hard drive of my computer. I can easily dismiss this as a concern. Even the encrypted client files that may have been opened were insignificant. Anything saved on my hard drive would have been public record anyway.

All that effort to break in and you assholes found nothing worth knowing.

Meanwhile this person hurt my dog and likely had something to do with Whitmore's death. I need to investigate this lead so someone can run with it.

"Who gave you this?"

"I don't know," Pickard says. "It was emailed to me anonymously and I was instructed to deliver it to you today at this time."

"You arrived earlier than the appointment you made," I say. "What was the exact time you were asked to bring it to me?"

"Three o'clock," he says. "I couldn't wait any longer, though. As soon as I got the email, I rushed over here. I didn't want to be late."

I might be fifteen minutes ahead of the person that gave him these instructions. They hadn't counted on Pickard's paranoia, on the human factor when they instructed him. People in this situation never followed plans to the letter.

If I want to take advantage of this, I have to act now.

"Is there anything else?" I ask with as much nonchalance as I can. "I'm sorry you had to come across town for this, but it really isn't anything you should be concerned with."

"Are you sure?" He looks at me with his fuzzy caterpillar eyebrows raised in doubt.

"It's a photo of me being kissed by my boyfriend. I'd hardly say that's worth writing home about."

At least not for regular people.

I don't reference the rest of the information he's handed me.

"I was under the impression this was very serious, Miss Greene. There was one more part to the email besides the attachment."

"Which was?"

"The body of the message. The sender asked me to deliver this to you and asked that you go to the address and call the phone number once you get there. As I'm sure you know, that is not a safe part of town."

"Was it mentioned whether I had to go alone?"

"No," he says. "But I would not recommend that you go at all."

"Mr. Pickard, why did you do this? Why are you even entertaining some stranger's request to contact me?"

He rubs the back of his neck and leans closer to me, looking around before he speaks.

"Are we completely alone in here?"

"Of course," I say. "You should feel free to speak your mind."

Mr. Pickard clams up again. His head tilts back as he swivels in the chair and grips the arm rests tightly, considering me for a long moment.

"For the sake of formality, why don't you pass me a dollar and we'll call it a retainer? Whatever you say to me will be confidential under attorney-client privilege."

He sits back and looks at me skeptically, then nods in agreement as though I have a fair point. He passes me a twenty, which I did not literally intend for him to do. I take it anyway and encourage him.

"Go ahead," I say. "I am officially your attorney, Mr. Pickard. Please tell me what you wanted to say."

"Whomever sent this email is not someone to be trifled with, Miss Greene. The only reason I agreed to do this is because I was being threatened. I have no trace of the email that was sent to me. My computer at the office crashed after I received the email this morning, an apparent result of being hacked. I've been unable to recover anything."

"Would I be able to get a look at your system?"

Oates might be able to recover something from it. Or maybe Aidan's hacker friend in California, whose name escapes me in this moment. My heart is pumping so loudly I'm sure Pickard can hear it.

"I'm afraid our IT department has it now. Because of the nature of my business, it's under lock and key until they either fix the problem or dispose of the device altogether. Shortly after that, I got a text from my daughter. Or at least, I thought it was from her. It turned out to be a virus. Now my phone is hacked too, rendered useless. It is the equivalent of a paperweight, so I can't access my email there either."

Shit.

I'm trying to keep my knees from bouncing underneath my dress.

"I understand," I say. "And the senders never revealed themselves?"

"No. The first email came in last Friday. I had my assistant call your office and make an appointment because my family and I were being threatened bodily harm if I did not. Since that's all that was required of me, I complied. I received the second email today with what you see here," he nods towards the papers I'm holding. "The threat was the same. I was told there would be nothing more asked of me, but I have no proof of what was sent Friday or today. I'm sorry. That's all I know."

"If any further threats come to you, Mr. Pickard, I insist you go to the police. I'll follow through on this and leave you out of it. But I cannot protect you from an unknown threat. Do we understand each other?"

"Yes," he says as he rises to leave. "Please be careful, Miss Greene. Whomever sent this is no one I'd ever want to meet in person. And Seventh Street is no place for a young woman."

"Thank you for your concern," I say. "I'll take it under advisement."

As soon as the door shuts behind Pickard, I buzz Charlie and ask him to join me in the conference room. He hurries in, anticipating good news.

"So? Do we have ourselves our next humongous client?"

"No. I need you to go home and be with Huck. He's at the house."

"Now?"

"Now."

"What's going on, Lex?"

"I don't know. But I need to know the house and the dog are safe. Can you do it?"

"Of course," he says. "I was going to meet Carter for dinner but I can cancel. Wouldn't be out of line considering what a crabby bitch he's been lately."

"Thanks, Charlie." I'm smiling at his crack about Carter. "I'll let you know what's up as soon as I have more information."

"You swear you're not in danger?"

"I'm not," I assure him. "Byron won't leave my side, remember? I'll be fine."

"Just promise me that whatever you're doing, you'll be careful."

"Always," I say. "It's my middle name."

At ten after three, I close up the office for the day and send Claudia home, telling her it's too nice a day to stay cooped up inside. She takes off in a hurry without questioning me.

I can see why. The temperature is seventy-five degrees, and a warm breeze is bringing forth summer. It's a perfect weather day.

The weather outside my office may be innocuous, but my mood is not. I'm sitting in the front seat of the SUV next to Byron after showing him everything Pickard brought to me.

"Ms. Greene, we should head back to the loft until I can get through to Mr. Pierce."

"No. We're going to this address, Byron. Right now. If we get there early, maybe we can surprise the person. Get the upper hand somehow."

"I can't do that alone," he says.

"You have me."

He ignores my comment. "We should not leave your home unattended."

"Charlie is going there," I say, "and the dog will be with him. He can handle himself. Can't we just call Aidan now?"

"I'm afraid he's unavailable." He's staring straight ahead through the windshield, practically ignoring me. I can tell he doesn't intend to budge from this spot or honor my request to drive to this mysterious address.

"I want to know what the hell is going on, Byron. An innocent man has been threatened. My dog was fucking stabbed." I'm trying not to cry as I go on. "Whoever this person is will not stop until they get what they want. I have no idea where the hell Aidan is or if he's in any danger. If you don't tell me something or drive me to this address this minute, I'm going there by my goddamn self."

He turns to me with a concerned expression, but he's quiet and unflinching at my anger. He's cool as a fucking cucumber floating in an icy drink.

"I already called the number," I admit. "The call wouldn't go through."

"Alexis, it does us no good for you to get upset or act irrationally. I will not take the chance and put you in harm's way. If this person is dangerous, I will not have you face them – especially in an unknown location – without considerable thought and some backup."

"If I don't show up at this place on time, this person could have a Plan B that blows up everything. They have evidence of Aidan and I being together. If it's not Ireland, then Ireland could be the person they intend to reveal this to, which brings on another set of problems. And if it is Ireland doing the threatening..." I trail off, shuddering in dread at the thought of Aidan's enemy.

Byron stays silent.

"They have my computer."

"Is there anything important on it?"

"No. But if this person has my computer, they're also the person that hurt Huck."

He turns his attention back to the windshield for a long minute.

"Byron," I plead. "We have to do this. Aidan will understand."

He starts the vehicle and backs out of his now customary parking space in front of my office building.

I played the right card.

These people hurt my boy. They'd threatened an innocent man just to get to me, and I was almost certain they had something to do with Mark Whitmore's death.

Whether or not this sets Aidan off, Byron isn't going to sit idly by any more than I will.

Samira was asked to remain at Aidan's office. She's been cautioned to be on alert. Charlie is home with Huck and reports that everything on my street is boring suburban bullshit as usual. Mr. Dingham almost shot him on sight, but Charlie put me on the phone with him so I could tell him to stand down.

Byron and I are parked two blocks away from the address I'm supposed to go to at four o'clock. We're fifteen minutes early. The SUV idles at the curb near one of the local hospitals – the one where ambulances are typically dropping off gunshot victims.

"What are we doing?" I ask. "The address is two blocks up."

I'm in the front seat, watching Byron fiddle with the navigation on the dashboard.

"I need to scope out the surroundings," he says. "It will just take a minute. You're early anyway."

He pulls up the address and scans the surrounding streets on the map, then pulls out his phone.

"Now what?" I'm impatient, more anxious than I've been in my entire life. I have no idea what I'm heading into. "How do you handle the stress of a situation like this so easily?"

"Relax," he says. "I need to pull up the satellite imagery for the location."

He fiddles with his phone some more, scrolling through whatever information he's after.

"Byron, can we just get this over with?"

He looks at me sternly enough that I shut my mouth and look away, focusing my attention out the window. "Sorry," I say. "I'm being a pain in the ass. I'm just nervous. I feel sick."

"Take a breath," he says. "I'm not going to let anything happen to you. If I can't get the information I want here, we're turning around to head back to the loft."

"No, Byron." I do as he instructs and breathe deeply several times to steel my resolve. "I'm okay. I can do this."

I glance at the clock on the dash. It's 3:50 p.m.

"We have to go now," I insist. "You can come with me. There were no instructions that I had to come alone. Let's just go together."

He pockets his phone, scrolls through the map illustrations a few more times, expanding the view before he zooms in again.

"See this?" he asks, pointing to the screen. "This is the address you were given. I'm comfortable letting you go alone."

"You are?" I'm dumbfounded.

I'm going to meet some potentially volatile character alone?

"Yes. I'll be here." He points to an intersection shown on the screen. "Program the phone number Pickard gave you into your contacts and I'll do the same. Leave the papers with me."

I do as he asks, then hand him the sheets of paper.

"Why are you making me go alone?"

"See this icon?" He points back to the address I'm going to and I look closer.

"Ah," I say in understanding.

The address I was given is a Baptist church on the corner of Seventh and Market.

It's in the middle of one of the worst neighborhoods in Stanton, but still. Church is church. People respect church.

Right?

I don't want to go in.

The church is a two-story building, but the building itself does not feel ethereal or religious in nature. It was an office building in a previous life.

In defense of the make-shift house of worship, there is a sign out front advertising Bible studies for kids on Saturdays. Sunday worship begins at eleven o'clock in the morning. The board has a clever quote on it about God and being lost without Him.

Seems legit.

I turn back to see the SUV parked at the curb, but Byron is not in it. He's around the corner at the side entrance. He'd given me specific instructions for how to handle various scenarios before we left the vehicle. As I walk through the unlocked front door, I pray I remember them all.

And that no one kills me.

I pass through what would have been the lobby of the office building. There is no one here. I call out a hello to someone (anyone?), but I'm met with silence. Not unusual for late afternoon on a Wednesday, I reassure myself.

I walk through the lobby to an expansive room used for church service. A handmade altar is ahead of me, at the back of the building. A large white cross looms over an oak lectern. There are some battered wooden pews in several rows on either side of me. I stand in the aisle with my feet frozen to the ugly gray linoleum tiles.

I'm about to run to the altar and land on my knees in prayer when my phone rings in my pocket.

It's Byron.

"What?"

"Is anyone in there with you?"

"No."

"A black car just pulled up, but it went around to the back. Watch the back entrance."

"I will."

"Remember what I told you," he says.

"I got it."

"Did you call the number?"

"Not yet," I say in frustration. "I'm talking to you."

"Hang up and call it."

I do as hc asks, using the unknown number I'd programmed into my phone. This time the call goes through. A male voice answers after three rings.

"Are you at the address?"

"Yes. Who is this?"

My question is met with a dial tone.

I text Byron with trembling hands, telling him I made the call and a man answered before disconnecting. He calls me back immediately.

"I'm watching the back and side entrance from the corner of Seventh and Market. No one has left the vehicle that pulled in. Sit tight, I'm going to try the number."

Byron writes me back in seconds to tell me the phone number is no longer working.

Fuck.

My knees are trembling as much as my hands now. I grip the carved wood of the pew to my right and sit, staying close to the center aisle.

The front door of the church opens and slams closed behind me. I whip around to see who is coming through the door.

I've never met him in person, but I know exactly who he is.

John Ireland strides towards me with purpose. My eyes follow him as he moves from the back of the room and takes a seat across the aisle from me.

To describe him as intimidating is an understatement.

In the flesh – and within spitting distance of my personal space – the air of nefariousness surrounding him is almost tangible.

At least there's an aisle between us.

"Ms. Greene." His voice is low and raspy, like a smoker with a two-pack-a-day habit. He's staring ahead at the cross several feet away.

"Yes." I stop gawking at him and face the front of the room, matching his posture.

"You're alone in here?"

"Yes. What do you want?"

"That depends on you."

"You've got my attention." I shift in my seat, then cross my legs and pull my shoulders back. "You could have just called my office for an appointment."

"I wasn't sure you'd see me," he says. "And I'd prefer not to have the press know I'm spending any time in this armpit of a city. Discretion was necessary."

"Oh," my voice drips sarcasm before I can control it. "You won't be buying a vacation home in Stanton? I thought you were enthusiastic about Lake County real estate."

"Sometimes the most vile places are where the most money can be made. Isn't that why your father practiced law here?"

This fucking bastard.

"You nearly killed my dog," I seethe as I turn to glare at him. "I'm not inclined to sit here and have a conversation with you. Not about your opinion of Stanton and especially not about my father."

"That was unfortunate." He doesn't hide his smugness. "About the dog, I mean." He's still staring straight ahead.

And is that a grin on his fucking face?

"It was not intentional," he continues. "My associate was concerned for his safety when your dog came at him."

"Well maybe your *associates* should stop breaking and entering," I throw at him. "The next person that shows up at my home uninvited will suffer reciprocal damage to their body. And trust me, it will be no accident."

He turns to look at me, his large arm resting on the pew ahead of him. He's wearing a dark suit and an ivory shirt. He has no tie on. He is every bad character I could imagine rolled into one hefty frame of hatred.

"Just tell me what the fuck you want."

He's taking me in, regarding me with an emotion I can't pinpoint. At his lack of response, I go on.

"Did you find what you were looking for at my house, Mr. Ireland? Because I have nothing to hide. It's my understanding that might not be the case for you."

I have no doubt Mark Whitmore's death was a direct result of this man's whims. Ireland and his daughter were trying to puppeteer Aidan, and the bastard blatantly confirmed some henchman he hired had been the one to hurt my dog.

As all of this slams down on me with the weight of a brick building, he turns to me, shaking his head as his face reddens. I can't tell whether he's crimson from alcohol abuse or anger (or both), but my own fury is full throttle when he finally answers me.

"You've got some fire in you. Pretty girl, too. It's unfortunate we have to be on opposite sides here," he says. "Been a long time since I had someone on my team with that fiesty New York attitude."

Less than three minutes and I fucking loathe this human being.

"Get to the point, Mr. Ireland."

"You need to convince Mr. Pierce to abandon his project in Stanton and sell your client's land to me. Or," he adds, "in the alternative, he can acquire Gianni Rossi's parcel and convey that to me."

Okay, the first part I get – even though I'll be dead before I let him own Myers' land – and I know Aidan feels the same way.

The second part I'm clueless about.

But I refuse to reveal that.

"I'm sure you're well aware that Aidan will not abandon his plans here for anyone."

Even me.

"I'm not so sure about that. From what I understand his motivations are very much driven by you."

"Your sources are wrong," I assert. There is no point in denying we'd been together. Ireland has video proof of that.

But I can downplay it.

"We're sleeping together. That's all, Mr. Ireland. I assure you I'm just as much a business colleague to Mr. Pierce as you are."

He looks at me intently, trying to discern if I'm telling the truth. My most steadfast posture is in place, my game-on expression governing my eyes.

"Whether or not that's true, it's clear to me you have some influence over him. This is something you'd be wise to keep out of the media, if you get my meaning. Someone might leak information that neither of you would want as public knowledge. I understand your marriage was a unique arrangement, shall we say?"

This heartless bastard.

I'm stunned – and livid – that he's bringing up Ben.

"And more importantly," he asserts as he rises, "you do not want my daughter made aware of you. She tends to be possessive of Aidan."

"Your daughter is in a treatment program for a drug problem," I spit back. "I doubt she concerns herself with what's going on here in Central New York."

"She's been released early." He takes a step into the aisle. "I helped her with those arrangements this morning."

What the fuck?

I can't hide my shock.

"I believe she just landed at JFK. It's my understanding she's meeting with Aidan this evening. I'm sure that doesn't bother you, given you're just colleagues. But it's likely he won't be back here for some time. They have a lot to catch up on after her time away."

Oh, hell no.

His daughter might be throwing herself in front of Aidan to manipulate him, but Aidan could handle her.

"You convince him to let go of one of those parcels and convey it to me," Ireland insists as he moves closer. "I'd hate for any more unfortunate accidents to happen to you or your associates, Ms. Greene." He stands over me, trying to intimidate me with his stature.

I'm feeling meek on the inside, but my rage toughens my words.

"I'll do no such thing, Mr. Ireland." I raise my chin in indignation as he stands between the pews, towering above me. "I'm fairly certain you're too late. I'd suggest you forget about acquiring either parcel in New York."

I can't read his expression. Either he's trying to determine if I'm being honest or he's genuinely amused.

"You won't walk away with what you want," I go on. "If Aidan finds out you're now threatening me, I'm not sure you'll walk away at all."

He leans down into my personal space. I can smell alcohol on his breath and a scent of masculinity that turns my stomach. He is foreboding to a degree I've never experienced.

Involuntarily I'm cowering, leaning away from him. I can't look in his dark eyes.

"You're not wrong," he says. "Pierce is a formidable threat. But both of you should think twice about who you're threatening."

"I think Pierce is the one defending himself," I mumble.

His smile widens as if he knows something I don't.

"You think Pierce is a saint? That he's some wounded soul to save? A philanthropist with a heart of gold? Trust me, sweetie. If you knew what he really was, you would be running in the opposite direction."

"Considering the nature of my relationship with Pierce is more business than personal," I assert, "your warnings are irrelevant. I'm able to differentiate a working relationship with occasional physical benefits from a serious romance, Mr. Ireland. Though I know your daughter doesn't have the same capability."

He glares back at me.

That dig must've hit a nerve.

I keep going while I've got ammunition left.

"I'm far more interested in staying away from someone who's been an accessory to the murder of one of my colleagues."

A snarky laugh erupts from him, sending shivers up my spine.

"That's quite an accusation," he says through his laughter. "And ironic given what you don't know about your Mr. Pierce."

I don't respond as his laughter recedes.

"You'll deliver my message to Pierce, and hopefully we won't need to be in further contact." He pauses, a look of malice coming over him. "Unless you decide you want to know the truth about the dashing billionaire you're just fucking. I'd be happy to recite you a bedtime story if you're ever interested."

He rests a swelled knuckle under my chin and forces me to look at him. I cringe as a mix of fear and disgust spread a wave of heat over me.

"And I have no objection to you telling him we've met. In fact," he snarls, "I'm counting on it."

I slide backwards slowly until he stands straight, removing himself from my personal space. I escape to the far end of the bench and leave without looking back. By the time I reach the lobby doors I'm on a dead run, intending to bolt for the SUV.

As I exit the front of the building, I barrel into Byron. His muscled chest catches me with all the softness of an offensive lineman, but I'm overcome with gratitude that he's here. His arms circle me in a protective bear hug.

"Go," I manage. I have to force myself to breathe normally. "*Let's go.*"

Adrenaline rules me, my eyes burning with tears that well to the surface but refuse to fall. I break free of Byron's arms and run across the street, retreating behind his vehicle to wait for him. The doors are locked.

I look through the windows, watching as Byron remotes the SUV unlocked.

He doesn't cross the street to join me.

Instead he nods his head, gesturing for me to get in.

What the hell is he doing?

I climb in and he remotes the vehicle locked again, then heads into the church.

34

Aidan

June 13, 2016
Monday Evening

I tire Alexis out after our elevator ride and we spend a quiet evening at the loft. By ten o'clock, she's in my bed fast asleep and I leave her to spend the next hour in my home office. I go over next steps for the Center, including how I might get Hope Kennedy and her probation department to assist me.

I moved past the phase of getting the local municipalities to approve my strategies last week. I finally met with the planners for the structure on Myers' land and laid them out for everyone concerned, which I'd been attempting to do since pushing everything back to go to California.

Thankfully, the meetings had gone well and I was met with resounding support.

The plans still have to be stamped for approval officially, but that meeting is scheduled to occur just before the gala. Everyone involved is finally operating with the common goal of alleviating the problems in Lake County one phase at a time.

More importantly, they've all acknowledged I'm the only one capable of organizing this effort while also having the financial means to pull it off.

All that remains is to get the individuals in the trenches on board too, the people that already worked in this vein.

People like Hope Kennedy.

I've given up that train of thought to go over the surveillance footage of the hooded perpetrator smashing my storefront window one last time, hoping to catch something I hadn't before.

I'm taken off guard when Lionel calls me at midnight, as Monday is becoming Tuesday.

"Yeah, Lionel. What's going on?"

"I received an email from Renewable Energy."

"And?"

For once in my employ he doesn't hesitate, even though he's uncertain.

"They'd like to move up your Wednesday meeting to ten a.m. tomorrow, if that's agreeable with you."

"Where?"

"The location is the same. At their Manhattan office. The meeting will be with the assistant to Ken Johnson, rather than one of the low men on the totem pole they'd previously scheduled you with."

Ken Johnson is the C.E.O. This is good news. I'm getting to my intended audience sooner than predicted.

"Great, except that's in less than twelve hours. I'd have to leave now."

"I've reserved your suite. They're ready for you. Drive time should be approximately four hours."

"Tell them I'll be there. What do you think their motive is for the push?" I have my own opinion, but I want Lionel's take.

"The underling I'd previously been in touch with passed the information up the ladder. I'm told Mr. Johnson got wind of it and passed you off to his assistant, but insisted she see you as soon as possible. I think he knows you've got something worth hearing about. Or presumes you do."

"I'll leave now. Check in with Curtis and make sure Stella is handled."

"Yes, sir."

"Report back to me by the morning."

"Will that be all?"

"I need to get in touch with Nate Edwards." An idea comes to me out of the clear blue, and I search for scrap paper to jot down notes.

"I'm not sure how I can help with that, sir."

"You can't. I'm just thinking out loud. Let me know when you have confirmation about Stella. Thanks, Lionel."

"Good night, sir."

We disconnect, and I go to the master closet to quietly pack a bag. I text Byron to let him know what's going on, then text Nate, hoping he's awake and near his phone. He'd only been back in Florida since last night.

It's not likely he's knee deep in his next project yet. I need to talk to him before tomorrow.

I dial Ivan next.

"Yes, sir."

"I need you at the loft immediately. I'm headed to Manhattan and I need you to stay with Alexis until tomorrow morning."

"Of course."

"Byron will relieve you in the morning so you can fly down. I'm meeting with R.E.E. at ten."

"Do you need me there for the meeting?"

"Not necessary. It's with the assistant to the C.E.O. It will be short. I'll put forth a few details, but I'm sure I'll be waiting for a call back until Mr. Johnson will see me."

His office will no doubt stall while Johnson investigates whether I can deliver what he covets.

"If you're in town when he decides he's ready," I add, "that will be fine."

"Yes, sir. I'll be at the loft in ten minutes."

As I'm driving to Manhattan in the Lincoln, I recall the way I had to leave Alexis without telling her. She was sleeping soundly when I kissed her goodbye. Leaving her without a conversation was unsettling, but I left her a note. Granted it was vague, but I felt it better to leave her out of this.

Nate returns my call before I make it to Pennsylvania, coming through just as I'd hoped. He was exactly the resource I needed, an insurance policy when I negotiate the sale to R.E.E. Now I can be assured no drilling occurs as Gianni Rossi insisted.

I drive in silence, contemplative but confident I'm holding all the cards.

I'm in my suite at The Soho Grand at nine a.m., back from a short run and workout in the hotel's fitness room when Lionel calls my cell.

"Go ahead."

"Curtis says Ms. Ireland is still inpatient at The Meadows."

"As of when?"

"Last night. Midnight Pacific time. I advised him to return there by nine this morning."

"Any other news?"

"No, sir. Everything here is handled. I've sold off the last of the commercial properties here. That contract should be emailed to you and Bill Hoffman by the afternoon. We'll need to address your home in Santa Barbara but, beyond that, your business assets are nearly all liquidated here."

"Fantastic. Great work, Lionel. I'll be in touch."

I disconnect and head for the shower. I want to call Alexis (she did send a text asking me to), but she'd be full of questions I can't answer. I don't want to put myself in a position of being dishonest with her. Ivan has left Stanton by air and advised that she's s in Byron's capable hands.

For now, I need to press on.

The personal assistant to Ken Johnson is Lynn Henley.

She is nearly as tall as I am with a slender frame. Ms. Henley is wearing a conservative black dress. She reminds me of an American version of Samira, though Ms. Henley is much older. Her brown hair is tied up in a ponytail, and she has the same all-business demeanor as my assistant.

In her office, there is not a piece of paper in sight. Filing cabinets stretch out along the wall behind her. A standing workstation is positioned in front of a bank of large windows that overlook the street twenty-three floors down. Photographs of various landscapes decorate the stark white walls, their frames hung in a rigid straight line.

Nothing in the office is out of place, but there are no personal touches in here. The room is as serious as the woman occupying it.

"Mr. Pierce," she says. After our introduction, her secretary departs for the reception desk. "I'm glad you could be here on such short notice."

"It's not a problem. I had other business here."

"I understand you have a proposal for the company."

"I do."

"And it's my understanding it has to do with Gianni Rossi's parcel of land just outside the city?"

"That's correct."

"I was under the impression that land was already being acquired by someone else."

Her tone is clipped and high-handed. She may resemble Samira, but her attitude is far colder.

And she is certainly not as smart.

"You were wrong."

"I see. And what evidence might you have to demonstrate that?"

"I will own the Rossi parcel before the week is out," I say. "Originally, I did not intend to hang onto it for long."

She regards me with continued skepticism.

"What are your intentions with three hundred acres of vacant land? I understood your interests were in Lake County for a philanthropic endeavor."

"That is accurate. However, I've recently considered expanding my pursuits here on the East Coast."

"May I ask in what field?"

"Green energy alternatives," I say. "Not unlike what your company claims to be a leader in."

Her expression is telling. She's unable to hide the fact that she thinks I'm full of shit, though her response is polite.

"Even with your varied and successful background, I'm not confident you would be successful in that endeavor, Mr. Pierce."

"You're entitled to your opinion. But it would be irresponsible of you not to find out for certain, wouldn't it? I doubt your employer would be happy knowing you passed up the opportunity for this parcel. But if you're not interested, I'm fully prepared to move forward with my own plans and more to the point," I add, "likely put you out of business."

She smirks at my confidence, again mistaking it for naivety. Her response is one word.

"Doubtful."

"Are you confident about that? Because I'm fully aware your green energy alternatives are nothing but a guise of the original ambitions of Waterman Oil. Given that, I'm doubtful your solar practices could ever rival the enhanced methods I've got in mind."

Her expression screams surprise, but she's quiet. She recovers from her fading surety as best she can.

"I have evidence of what your company has been covering up since its inception," I continue. "I can assure you it's me who is doubtful. I doubt your company would ever recover if this information is brought to light."

"Even if you were right, Mr. Pierce – which I must assert that you are one hundred percent incorrect – how would we know you're not intimidating us with your threats simply to keep us from acquiring either parcel?"

"Quite honestly, you don't." I can't help a sarcastic grin from coming over me. "But you should trust that my agenda is for the greater good." I throw my business card on her empty desk. "The company you're loyal to will never be able to make that claim, Ms. Henley."

Her expression is dismissive as I rise out of my chair.

"Thanks for coming by, Mr. Pierce."

"My pleasure. Tell Mr. Johnson he's got twenty-four hours." I move for the door. "After that, the offer is off the table."

I leave the Renewable Energy suite and exit the elevator back on ground level. Ivan greets me in the lobby of the building.

"Sir," he says, "how did it go?"

"We'll know soon." We exit under the beautiful morning, which is opposite the clouded uncertainty I feel.

Ms. Henley may be a bigger hurdle than I'd predicted, especially if pride kept her from presenting my offer to the C.E.O. If she indicated to him I wasn't a viable threat to their business, Johnson would dismiss me and I'd be locked into Plan B.

"Where to now?"

"Bill Hoffman's office."

On the short ride, I dial Byron. He's stationed outside Alexis' office and tells me everything is status quo. I ask him not to divulge that we've spoken. We disconnect, and I call Gianni Rossi.

"Mr. Pierce," he says in friendly greeting, "I understand we have a deal."

"Yes. I'm just heading to Bill's office to confirm the details. Can we close Friday?"

"I don't see a problem with that, as long as you can get me proof about what R.E.E. is going to do with the land."

"I'm not sure I'm going to sell to them after all," I say. "But I should know by tonight."

"What are you embarking on with my three hundred acres now? Your own version of Disneyland?"

"No," I muster a laugh. "Solar farms and other green energy alternatives. The most advanced technology available."

"You brought Nate Edwards on board."

"I might have."

"You're a smart man, Pierce. Let me know how it plays out. I'm available through Friday. If not, it will have to be after July first. I'm headed to Europe for a few weeks this Saturday."

"We'll have the matter wrapped up by Friday," I insist. "Tell your attorney to count on it."

Bill Hoffman is leaning across his desk towards me.

"What the fuck are you doing, Pierce? Have you lost your mind?"

"No. Can we be ready to close by Friday?"

He responds with a question that comes out as a statement as he sits back in his chair. "You want me to be ready to close on a multi-million dollar deal for Rossi's land in four days."

"Yes, Bill." I'm getting frustrated with his redundant assertions. "Can you do it or not?"

"I suppose," he says. "You're sure you can fund by then?"

"Lionel has secured funds," I say. "It's not a problem."

"Get the money into my escrow account by Thursday," he says. "I'll get it done. And who are we turning around and selling to?"

The very second the question is out of his mouth, my phone rings. The call is coming in from an unknown number with a Manhattan exchange.

"I need to take this, Bill. I think we're about to find out."

By one in the afternoon, I'm back at R.E.E.'s suite of offices. This time I wait outside the doors of the C.E.O., one floor higher than Ms. Henley's office. Ivan is stationed like a guard at Buckingham Palace a few feet away, unmoving when Ken Johnson's secretary comes out from his office. The demure blonde gives Ivan a once over, then looks to me.

"Mr. Johnson will see you now," she says. "Go on in."

I nod to Ivan, and he stays put as I make my way in.

The office is larger than Ms. Henley's but decorated in a similar modern and understated style. Furnishings are few but expensive. There are photographs along the walls similar to the ones displayed downstairs.

The C.E.O. of Renewable Energy is seated behind his desk in front of a laptop. There are family photos gracing the bookshelves behind him.

He's dressed impeccably in a black suit. He's likely in his fifties, if I go by the sandy colored hair receding from his forehead. In contrast, his fit build and neatly trimmed beard make him appear younger. He stands to greet me as I approach his desk.

"Mr. Pierce," he says, "please have a seat. I understand you are acquiring some land that might be of interest to us."

I sit down across from him. "That's correct."

"I don't know as we're looking to expand in New York right now." He's ignoring me, letting me know I'm as insignificant to him as an eager intern. He jots down some notes on a legal pad, looks at his screen, writes some more. "We had a site in mind," he adds, "but it was recently taken out of play by you."

"That's true," I say, "and I'm not interested in giving that up."

"Well," he says. He finally stops writing. "I'd be willing to listen if you'd like to enlighten me about this new parcel."

Who does this guy think he's kidding?

I know I'm holding the key to their expansion in my hands.

"I'm not certain I'm willing to sell it after all."

"Lynn said that might be the case. You're looking to get into our field?"

"Into clean renewable energy, yes. But hydro-fracking and drilling?" I shake my head. "No."

His reply is robotic, as though he's rehearsed the line repeatedly.

"Drilling is not of any interest to R.E.E."

"Do you still have an interest in Gianni Rossi's parcel?"

"We might," he finally admits. "It would be a great solar site."

"That's all it would ever be," I insist. "If we can agree on that, I'm willing to negotiate the sale to you." Direct is the best approach with this guy. Otherwise he'll dance around this topic all day long. He is more evasive than I'd predicted.

He takes a breath and releases it, looking contemplative.

"Mr. Johnson, I'm sure you're aware that one of your attorneys recently turned up dead."

His posture changes when I mention Mark Whitmore.

"If I have anything to say about it, Mr. Whitmore's death will not be in vain. He uncovered some information that I believe led to his untimely demise. I fully intend to make that information public if you choose to fight me on this."

He says nothing. He fiddles with the mouse next to his laptop, then closes the lid of the machine and slides it away. He clasps his hands on the desk.

"I'm not sure what you're talking about."

"I'd expect you to deny it. Regardless, I'm in possession of this evidence revealing your company's true intentions about the Myers' parcel. I'm going to venture a guess that what I do with that evidence may be important to you."

Ken Johnson is suddenly rattled.

His eyes dart around the room, to his notepad, back to me.

I have his attention.

I've also gotten under his skin.

"A respected journalist is snooping around your company. He was investigating Mark's disappearance and subsequently his death. I'm certain I could make his investigation easier, if I'm left with no other choice."

Johnson's complexion pales. He adjusts himself in his leather chair.

"Would you like me to go on, or shall we end this now?"

If he doesn't crack soon, I'm walking out of here.

I'd take Nate up on his ideas for the land if I had to, just to keep this company out of the picture. If this guy is not swayed by this, if he refuses to acknowledge the control I have in this situation…

Johnson leans back in his chair and closes his eyes.

"What do you want for the Rossi parcel?"

Check mate.

"No more than I pay for it, including enough to cover the costs to acquire it. But I have other conditions."

He raises his eyebrows in a gesture of curiosity.

"John Ireland is about to be investigated in California."

Okay, a lie – but it was for a good cause.

His eyes go wide. It's obvious he wasn't expecting that name to come up.

"I would implore you to remove yourself from any business dealings with him," I go on. "Aligning with him is only going to mean trouble for you, as Mark Whitmore might attest to if he were still alive."

He nods. He believes me, as much as he may not want to. I continue while I've got his full attention.

"Neither R.E.E. or any affiliates will pursue land in Lake County. That will be put in writing. And further, I have the right of first refusal if R.E.E. ever sells the Rossi parcel."

"If you're concerned about drilling, you needn't be. The State has put a moratorium on it, anyway."

I can't help scoff at his assertion.

"Of course I'm aware of that. I'm also aware that there are continuous efforts being made to reverse that decision. But if you're insistent the moratorium will hold, you should have no reason to reject my condition that Lake County is off limits."

"I'll have to run both conditions by the Board."

"Do what you need to, but it's non-negotiable."

"Understood."

"If you buy the land and move forward with the solar farm, I'll sell.

There will be no drilling on that site," I assert. "Ever."

"Again, I understand. Are there further conditions? I'd like to get this moving."

"John Ireland will be precluded from becoming an owner of the Rossi land. That includes any shell company he may form, or any company he is peripherally involved with."

He resolves more quickly than I'd anticipated.

"Fine. Name your price, Pierce."

"Three million plus costs. And we complete the sale on Monday."

He hesitates a moment, but his answer is firm.

"Done. Let's get down to the details." He flips his laptop open again. "I'll clear my day and call the board together now. Can we meet back here this evening? I believe I can get our attorney here by then."

"I'll be available. My attorney will wait for your call. I'll send your assistant his information. There is one last item, though."

"Jesus, you're a pushy bastard. What else?"

You've seen nothing yet, asshole.

"Outside the purchase price, you will establish a sizable account for Mark Whitmore's widow and her family for their pain and suffering," I say, "also by Monday."

"I can't accommodate that request in such a short amount of time," he bristles. "Just accomplishing this purchase is going to be a task. The only way I can pull this off is because we were ready to pull the trigger on the land in Lake County. This transaction would simply replace that."

"I don't care if you have to pull it from your personal bank account. In fact, I may insist on that. A million to Laura Whitmore, five hundred thousand to each of her children in the trust account I have set up, which will match the funds I've provided."

He shakes his head and, though I know he's pissed about it, I can see he's going to cave on this, too. The risk for the company is too great.

After a long pause, he finally speaks.

"I'll have proof of funds for you by the weekend."

"Thank you, Mr. Johnson. I'll see you this evening. It has certainly been a pleasure."

I call Byron Tuesday evening, finally confident that I can talk to him and Alexis and assure them that everything is okay.

I'd been back and forth with Johnson and his staff all day. Bill and I left his office at five o'clock to meet with R.E.E. at theirs. For the last hour and a half, we've been hashing out all the details in the company's boardroom.

Bill and I are on a brief dinner break in a Greek restaurant next door to R.E.E.'s offices.

Alexis is none too thrilled that I've gone M.I.A., but I don't let her deflate my excitement. I've gone after what I wanted and gotten it, to the benefit of the Center, my uncle and Mark Whitmore's family. The only concessions I've had to make with R.E.E. to secure the deal are irrelevant to me.

Alexis is safe at home, surrounded by her friends and protected by Byron.

Things are finally improving.

Bill gestures that he's got an incoming call. We're being asked back to R.E.E.'s suite upstairs.

I tell Alexis I love her and disconnect, anxious to get this deal done and get back to her as soon as humanly possible.

Tuesday night I collapse into bed at the hotel, utterly spent. I've been running on three hours of sleep since Monday night and I'm beyond drained.

But my ducks are in the neatest fucking row possible.

The deal with Rossi is set to close Friday morning and the sale to R.E.E. will follow on Monday. Rossi approved my contract with R.E.E. when I'd taken it to his home at ten o'clock this evening. I'd be back at R.E.E. first thing in the morning to finalize contracts with them now that I had Rossi's approval.

Stella is still at the Meadows with updates from Curtis coming in every six hours throughout the day. I relieved him of his duties tonight and asked him to head back there in the morning. I confirmed with Jasmine Hernandez yesterday that Stella was not due to be released until next week as planned.

By then, Ireland would be out of the picture, at least with regard to any of the New York land he'd been after.

I could move on with the Center in Stanton now and, by this time tomorrow, be back with Alexis where I belong.

By Wednesday afternoon, I'm beyond satisfied that things have fallen into place so well.

I spent most of the day with R.E.E., finalizing the sale details.

Both the purchase and sale of the Rossi parcel are all but done, save exchange of funds. I won't need to be here for that. I can leave as early as tonight, once I know Lionel has secured funds to Bill Hoffman.

Ken Johnson privately assured me that Mark Whitmore's family will be taken care of, with proof to be presented to me by Friday. He admitted two of his board members had to provide assistance in coming up with such a large sum so quickly, but those colleagues were aware of the stakes and contributed willingly.

I've just finished a rigorous workout in the hotel gym. I'm sweaty and in need of a shower when my cell rings.

"Lionel. How is the patient?"

"She's gone, sir."

"Excuse me?"

"She was there when Curtis checked at six a.m.," he says. "When he went back..."

I cut him off. "That would have been nine a.m. here. It's now four in the afternoon. Where the hell is she?"

"Curtis is outside The Meadows now, sir. She was signed out right after he left. Six-thirty a.m. Pacific time."

"By whom?"

"Her designated agent," he says. "Her father."

Fuck my life.

"Do you have any idea where she is?"

"Unfortunately, I believe they are both headed to New York, sir. They may be there already."

"Relieve Curtis," I say. "He's no longer needed."

Twenty minutes later, I'm showered and waiting for Dimitri to call me back. I'm impatient and try him again, thankful when he answers.

"Yeah, man," he says. "What's up?"

"I need you to track down John and Stella," I say. "Now."

"I thought she was inpatient?"

"He had her released early this morning. Can you find out where they went? I'm told they were headed here to New York."

"I'll call you right back. I'm at the dealership. I just need to get my laptop from next door so I'm secure."

"Fine. Hurry up."

I disconnect, seething with anger.

What the fuck is Ireland up to?

I pace the room for the minutes it takes for Dimitri to get back to me.

"Dude," he says when I answer. "You're not going to like this."

"Just fucking tell me."

"You're right, they both went to New York. Are you in Stanton?"

"No."

"Oh, good."

"But Alexis is. She's with Byron. Why?"

"Oh, shit bro. Where are you?"

"Manhattan."

"Oh, fuck," he says. "That's really bad."

I'm getting flat out pissed at my friend. "Explain, Dimitri."

"They took separate flights. Stella flew commercial. She landed at JFK a half hour ago."

"And Ireland?"

"It looks like he flew privately into LaGuardia three hours ago," he says. "And then he chartered a connecting flight."

"To where?"

"Stanton," Dimitri says. "He's in the same city as your girl right now."

"Can you track Stella's phone?"

"I can sure as fuck try."

I pull up her number and share it with him, and he works his magic some three thousand miles west.

"I got her," he says. "She's in Manhattan. I can't be certain, but it looks like she's close to the Rossi building. It's hard to pin it down with the software I'm using."

Goddammit.

"I'm sure that's where she is. Track down Ireland," I say. "I can't get to Stanton in time. I don't know what the fuck he's up to. I'm at least an hour and a half out by air."

"Will do," he says. "I'll let you know as soon as I have something."

I try Byron's cell to no avail. Alexis is not answering either. Her phone immediately goes to voicemail.

This is highly unusual.

Not knowing what's going on in Stanton puts me over the edge. I feel like my whole world is caving in.

If Ireland is in Stanton, in close proximity to her – I can't bring myself to play out the scenario in my head.

My phone rings in my hand.

"Alanna, thank God. Is Stella with you?"

"She just left."

"What the hell does she want?"

"You," she says. I hear her exhale a drag from her cigarette. "She's looking for you."

"How did she know I was down here?"

"She didn't. She wanted me to tell her where to find you in Stanton. I told her I had no idea, that we hadn't talked in some time."

I swear under my breath. "I'm sorry you're being dragged into this, Alanna."

"Don't apologize," she says. "It isn't your fault. Where is John?"

"I understand he's in Stanton, probably looking for me."

"Are you sure he doesn't know about Alexis?"

"I don't know how he could," I say. "Only my family and our close friends know. There's been nothing reported in the media."

"You need to get back up there, Aidan. And get out of the city before Stella tracks you down."

I'm standing in Bill Hoffman's office, giving him explicit instructions so he can wrap up the deals without me. Ivan is waiting outside, ready to fly us back to Stanton when we're done here. It's four-thirty, and I'm in agony that I can't be in two places at once.

Dimitri is unable to locate John Ireland.

My attorney is carrying on about the realty company's lawsuit and their acceptance of my half million dollar proposal, ignoring my insistence that getting the fuck out of here is a matter of urgency.

"Bill, I've got to get back to Stanton. We can cover this later."

We're interrupted by the intercom buzzing on his desk phone. He pushes the button to answer.

"Yes, Betty."

The voice of his elderly assistant comes through the phone from her office a few rooms away. "Is Mr. Pierce still here?"

"Yes. Why?"

"Tina from Reception downstairs says you have a client asking to see you, Mr. Hoffman. Prior to that she inquired whether Mr. Pierce is due in the office to see you this week."

Bill is impatient. "What did Tina tell her?"

"Nothing, sir. She's still waiting downstairs."

"Who is it, Betty?" I raise my voice so she can hear me. I'm standing at the window across the room, staring down at the city street.

But I know the answer before Betty confirms.

I can tell by the distinct sense of dread that's come over me.

"It's Stella," she says. "Stella Ireland."

Music Playlist for

Sway

The Amped Series: BOOK TWO

"Big Shot" – Billy Joel
"I Won't Give Up" – Jason Mraz
"Born To Run" – Bruce Springsteen

Alexis' Playlist for Aidan
"Pillowtalk" – ZAYNE
"Hard to Say I'm Sorry" – Az Yet ft. Peter Cetera
"Trust In Me" – Etta James
"Baby Can I Hold You" – Tracy Chapman
"Close" – Nick Jonas ft. Tove Lo
"Suspended" – Matt Nathanson (Live Acoustic)

"Survival of the Fittest" – Mobb Deep
"My Love" – Boog Brown, Apollo Brown ft. Poodie the Byz
"Scarborough Fair" – Simon and Garfunkel
"Nick of Time" – Bonnie Raitt
"Walk This Way" – Run DMC and Aerosmith
"Made Up Mind" – Tedeschi Trucks Band
"You're So Vain" – Carly Simon
"Remember the Name" – Fort Minor ft. Styles of Beyond
"Come See About Me" – Tedeschi Trucks Band
"Crash Into Me" – Dave Matthews Band
"Can't Hold Us" – Macklemore and Ryan Lewis
"All I Do Is Win" – DJ Khaled ft. T-Pain, Ludacris, Snoop Dogg & Rick Ross
"One Flight Down" – Norah Jones
"Nightingale" – Norah Jones
"At Long Last Love" – Frank Sinatra
"High On You" – Survivor
"Do I Have to Say the Words?" – Bryan Adams

Author Biography

M.J. Woods lives in Central New York with her family and her Bernese Mountain Dog. She has worked in the legal field of a small town for over twenty years and dreamed of becoming an author since the dawn of the home computer.

She is a member of the Central New York Romance Writers and the Romance Writers of America.

To find out more about the author including upcoming releases, giveaways and the latest Amped Series news, visit
www.mjwoodsbooks.com

"Balance" (The Amped Series: Book One)
is now available in paperback, hardcover and digital format.

Alexis and Aidan's story continues in
The Amped Series: Book Three
COMING SOON

CPSIA information can be obtained
at www.ICGtesting.com
Printed in the USA
BVOW08s0354220118
505498BV00002B/300/P

9 781457 555978